Valkyries
on the
Rise

A Colliding Realms Novel

TRL Boyd

Note: This novel is a work of fiction. Names, characters, places, and incidents are either products of the author's imagination or used fictionally. All characters are fictional, and any similarity to people living or dead is purely coincidental.

Copyright © 2024 TRL Boyd

All rights reserved.

ISBN: 978-0-6452892-4-4

DEDICATION

This book is dedicated to my beautiful grandmother,
Dorothy Boyd, and my adorable nanny, Patricia Furlong.
Thank you for believing in my dreams and inspiring my love
of writing. I miss and love you both.

CHAPTER ONE

Crouched behind a wooden bench on Pier 51, Tora Thurgood tightens the hair elastic around her long black ponytail and motions to her partner Bo Drabble to stay hidden. He ducks down as far as he can, the tips of his dark black hair just visible above the metal trash can.

Murky water sprays the pier, staining the concrete path with burnt debris and ash. Auburn leaves whip manically in circles around the swings and play equipment, like children dancing in the night.

It's only a matter of time before her target shows its ugly face. They always return a second night, testing the boundaries and defenses of the Realm of Man. And tonight — her squad is prepared.

Tora suppresses a grin. This is what she lives for. This is what she was born for. The hunt. It's like a religion, and she is completely and utterly devout.

The roundabout carousel creaks and turns in a slow circle. Silver moonlight bounces off the metal handrails and casts a rotating glow on the slide and swings.

These are the best nights to hunt. The nights unburdened by heavy equipment, infrared goggles, and lights; when the moon is bright enough to light the streets. They only need black army pants and shirts to blend into the shadows.

"Row row row your boat, gently down the stream. Merrily merrily merrily merrily life is but a dream," a childlike voice hums melodically on the winds; the words slow and drawn out.

Tora tenses and peeks around the bench, her hand poised over the cold steel blade strapped to her hip. The air ripples around the roundabout carousel, swirling with vibrant colors of blue, green, pink, and purple. Clear glass snowflake crystals form a straight line, floating in midair. It's beautiful; like a glowing aurora borealis gate of color, and like most things of beauty — it's deadly.

The crystals crack. A high-pitched screech pierces the night. Tora winces and grits her teeth, the sound stabbing through her ears like an ice pick. Water pushes through the growing cracks. First one, then two, then five, then nine; splitting until the crystals explode, shattering into tiny pieces of crystal sand. Water gushes out over the carousel, leaving only rippling lights floating in midair.

Tora stretches her jaw, trying to ease the ringing in her ears. Fucking portals. At this rate, she'll be deaf by the time she's twenty-five.

A small pale child claws out of the portal rip, her innocent blue eyes slightly too large for her angelic face and cherub cheeks; her spiraling curls and frilly pink babydoll dress like something out of the 1930s.

The child spins once around the roundabout carousel and steps off, her feet bare and covered in sludge. Louder she sings as she walks to the pier's edge overlooking the Hudson River. "Row row row your boat, gently down the stream. Merrily merrily merrily merrily, life is but a dream."

Tora widens her eyes. Her stomach drops. This is the creepiest goddamned thing she has ever seen, and she's seen some pretty fucked up shit over the past year.

Creepy singing children were not in the brochure when she moved to Greenwich Village. The civilian report was right. It was a child that came through the portal last night.

Rippling waves splash against the pier. A motor roars in the distance. Forcing her feet still, Tora keeps her eyes trained on the child and gestures to Bo to get ready.

The child climbs onto the railing and sings louder until her voice distorts and laps, sounding as though multiple voices are singing in a round format, starting from the beginning at different points throughout the song, each tone lower than the next.

Tora swallows hard, ignoring the voice in the back of her head telling her to run. Creepy bloody kid. She can feel her ovaries shriveling up and dying.

The child claps gleefully and giggles as a boat speeds into view. The people onboard laugh and holler like idiots, drawing too much attention to themselves.

A smile pulls at the corner of Tora's lips. The plan is working. They either attack now, or they run, and the Odd Squad never runs.

Tora springs up from her hiding place and sprints towards the small child. Bo closes in on the other side, the sound of the boat camouflaging their pounding footsteps.

They're so close — only a few steps away, but Bo kicks a stray soda can and sends it clattering along the pier, the sound like a shotgun in the night.

The child whips its head around and snarls, revealing razor-sharp piranha teeth.

"Fuck!" Tora pushes her legs harder, leaping over the sandpit and sliding under the monkey bars. So much for the plan. It took her squad hours to find enough fuel to power that boat and the plan goes to shit thanks to some tosser.

The glamor falls away. The child's eyes narrow to slits. It screeches and flexes its long black taloned fingers as Bo nears and pulls a blade from the back of his belt.

"Fuck fuck fuck!" Tora pants. Bo's about to get shredded. He hasn't got a hope in hell against a full-frontal attack from this demon. He's human, and so are his reflexes.

Using an old lamp post, Tora swings herself up onto the climbing equipment roof and launches herself at the demon as it leaps off the railing. She slams into the demon's side and hits the pavement hard, tangled in a ball of claws, knives, and teeth.

Warmth spreads from her knee to her shin as blood oozes through the new hole in her favorite black cargo pants.

"Fuck!" Tora kicks the demon hard in the stomach with the base of her boot, pushing it away from her. It took her a month to find a decent pair of hunting pants that fit. She had to scour through countless abandoned shop racks and draws. It was lucky she found a pair on a child mannequin.

Jumping to its feet, the demon child licks its ink-black lips and stares longingly at her bleeding leg, the smell of blood inciting its hunger.

Hell no! Tora scrambles to her feet and pulls a long blade from the holder strapped to her thigh. She's no one's snack!

The demon snarls and lunges, its tiny body blurring with the motion.

"Ah!" Tora sucks air back through her teeth as red-hot pain slices through her bicep.

Oblivious to Bo sneaking up behind it with his blade drawn, the gleeful demon laughs and licks blood from the tips of its talons, excitement dilating its pupils. The boat speeds passed the pier, directed towards the shore.

"Idiots!" Tora grunts. She doesn't need backup. The demon will run if it thinks it can't win.

Aiming for the head, Bo lunges, throwing his full body weight behind the blade but the demon bounces to the side at the last second, dancing in a state of bloodlust, and the blade embeds in its shoulder. The demon screeches like a bat and whips around, backhanding Bo hard across the face, sending him careening back into the railing.

Tora roars and charges, her vision blurring with red-hot anger. No one hurts her partner. She drops to the ground like she's sliding into fourth and kicks the demon hard on the kneecap with the base of her boot.

The demon screams and wails like a child as it crumbles to the pavement cradling its knee, the bone sticking out of the side. Before it can move, Tora dives on top of it and pins it to the ground.

"Fucking bitch cockwaffle assmunch whore!" The demon bucks and spits in her face.

Tora laughs. She can't help it. It's the first time she's been called a cockwaffle, and she's kind of impressed that the demon knows English, even if it is only profanity.

Using the railing, Bo pulls himself up and wipes the blood from his nose as the color slowly returns to his cheeks, his pupils almost completely drowned out by his deep brown eyes. "Fuck that was close. I owe you one."

"One?" Tora raises her eyebrows and grins. At least once a week she saves him from spider demons and psychotic malevolent fae. He's just lucky he's got a cute butt worth saving.

It's not that Bo's not a great fighter and hunter. He is. But Bo is human and hasn't been training to fight and kill his entire life, not like she has. Like the rest of the Realm of Man, Bo learned about the nine realms the hard way.

Roughly a year ago, the lives of all humans changed forever when the War of the Gods spilled into the Realm of Man. Tora was twenty years old, standing in a foreign realm with her mother and best friend Astra.

At first, they thought it was rain. Water fell from the sky in large drops. Auburn leaves spiraled along the ground in beautiful weaving patterns, climbing the trees of Washington Square Park.

She remembers the water, the smell of sulfur, and the smoke and fire that followed. Then from the heavens came hell, raining unspeakable wrath on all below.

Night after night Tora hunts, reliving the horror of the demons who rained down from the sky, falling through layered portals of light, water, and crystal; remembering the rising oceans, burning landscapes, and raging demons mindlessly killing and destroying everything in their path. It's what drives her.

The portal gates connecting the nine realms ripped open in the war between the gods, angels, and demons. Hades wanted war. He wanted revenge on the gods for forsaking him to Hell so he seduced and murdered the moon goddess Luna to gain entry to the Gates of the Gods and brought an army of ugly ass demons through the portal, causing the rift.

The gods aren't the Roman, Egyptian, Norse, or even Greek gods known throughout human history. They are a long line of descendants, taking on the names of their ancestors and mentors they admired.

Humans worshiped the same elemental gods in one way or another, just known by different names. One may have worshiped a mentor while others worshiped the apprentice.

Both sides suffered heavy losses, but none more than the Realm of Man caught in the crossfire. The War not only killed billions of humans and destroyed most of the landscape, it left the Realm of Man vulnerable.

The portal gates that once protected them from even the knowledge of malevolent fae and demons now posed the greatest threat. The gates were faulty and irreparable as the gods took their sweet ass time recuperating from the war.

"Don't hurt me," the demon pleads as its face reverts to that of an innocent child. Black tears trickle down its cheeks. "I'm... I'm scared. Will you be my mummy?"

Tora snorts. That's a first. Most of the demons they find in Greenwich Village are hideous spider-looking things that howl and growl like dogs. They don't beg for their lives. Then again, this is the first time they've come across a demon with a human face.

Unfortunately for the demon, Tora doesn't have a maternal bone in her body. "You know, I've never liked kids."

Screeching angrily, the demon opens its mouth wide. Saliva drips from its serpent-like tongue. Without a second thought, Tora drives the blade into the back of its throat, splattering black oozing blood over her face, arms, and black tank top.

Tora slumps to the ground, her tired muscles aching. The demon is dead. They did it; even if she did get covered in demon juice in the process. Her standard black uniform hides the stains but does nothing to disguise the rancid egg, chunky milk, and dog shit smell.

The child demon convulses. Its head drops lifelessly to the side.

Fucking demons. They're just as disgusting on the inside as they are on the outside. At least she doesn't have to dispose of the body. Dead demons disintegrate when the sun hits them, and the sun should be rising any minute now. Only the malevolent fae leave a corpse.

"You enjoyed that way too much." Bo pulls her to her feet.

Grinning, Tora wipes her blade on the demon's dress and then secures it to her hip. Nothing makes her feel more alive than the hunt; the adrenaline coursing through her veins, heart pumping in her chest. It's what she trained for. It's what she was bred for.

Both fae and demons underestimate her abilities based on her five-foot stature but she's the daughter of a Valkyrie, trained to use her strengths and weaknesses to her advantage.

"Sun's nearly up. That means it's someone's birthday." Bo pulls her tight against him and grins, careful to avoid the iron-tipped spear strapped to her back. "Want to celebrate?"

"Oh, you like this smell, do you?" Tora tilts her head back. "I could bottle and sell it at the markets. Call it something fancy like Demon Breath? Or Essence of Demon?"

"You smell fine to me." Bo chuckles and licks his lips, his eyes roaming to her cleavage as he tucks a loose strand of her dark black hair behind her ear. His hand lingers on the back of her neck.

Tora blushes. Silence settles in her ears as Bo's lips move closer, his warm honey and coconut scent dancing on her tongue. If her heart beats any faster, she's going to have a coronary. But as much as she wants to kiss him; she can't.

"Bo, we can't." Tora pulls away and glances out at the water where the small boat was moments ago. "Not here. Not where people can see."

Groaning, Bo drops his arms, his eyes drowning in disappointment. "Oh, come on Tora! Not this again."

"You don't understand," Tora argues. "I'm dead if she finds out. It's her one rule."

"Yeah, yeah, yeah. I've heard it before. But you know what Tora? Your mother may not discriminate based on the dark color of my skin, but she's still a racist against humans." Bo spits. "What? We're good enough to fight with but not date? You live in the human realm! Are you meant to be celibate for the rest of your life? It's fucking ridiculous!"

"Bo…" Tora reaches for his hand.

"Whatever." Bo pulls his arm away and storms off, clearly wanting to put some distance between them. "I'm going to find the others. We're done for the night."

Tora sighs. Bo doesn't understand. One of the first things her mother Freya said when she realized they were stuck in the Realm of Man was: Keep your mouth shut and your legs closed.

At first, her mother didn't want the humans to know about Valkyries, the realms, and the Creator, but that was an impossible secret to keep. She needed her wings to find supplies and fight the demons and fae coming through the portal. But interspecies relationships... she won't condone that, not when it could have catastrophic results.

To create the Nephilim witches and warlocks, the gods bred with humans. They created the Valkyrie bloodline by breeding with angels. Who knows what would happen if a human and a Valkyrie had a child, and her mother won't let them play God.

Golden rays of sunshine peek over the horizon. Tora lifts her face to the sky and briefly closes her aching eyes. Daybreak – time for hunters and demons to rest, and time for dead demons to disintegrate.

Nudging the small demon body with her boot, she waits for the flesh and oozing blood to burn and disintegrate, for the cleansing sun to erase all traces of the demon.

Black vacant eyes stare back, void of any life. Its fork-like tongue hangs loosely out of its mouth, sitting on the pavement.

Tora frowns. It doesn't make any sense. She's sure it's dead. It should disintegrate like all the other demons. There's no way the child is fae. Sharp piranha teeth are a fae pixie characteristic, but the talons are definitely demonic.

Groaning, she grabs the demon under the armpits and drags it over to the still glowing portal. The last thing she wants to do is touch the smelly thing, but if it doesn't disintegrate, it goes back through the portal before it shuts.

"Fucking kids!" She shoves the damn thing through the rift and the portal closes with a sharp snap and a burst of water and light.

Exhaustion weighs heavily on her limbs as she climbs onto the roof of the children's play equipment and watches the sun rise over the fallen city of New York, the landscape black and broken.

The once high-rise buildings still crumble in the distance, the foundations unsteady and disturbed by sporadically opening and closing portals.

Flashes of crystals and stunning lights surround the perimeter of Greenwich Village as demons and fae cross through the portals.

Tora yawns and rubs her temples. And to think this is the life and adventure she craved when she lived in the Realm of Angels. She still loves the hunt, but things are changing. She can feel it in her bones. The portals that once opened and closed reasonably fast, linger. Demons are more curious; the malevolent fae are hungrier; and the demon they fought tonight, that was entirely new. It's the first time she's seen a demon with a human face.

When a resident flagged her and her squad down last night and told them that a child was attacking someone down at the pier, she thought they were batshit crazy. If it wasn't for Bo insisting they investigate, they wouldn't have witnessed the demon spawn stepping back into the portal.

Something is coming. Something big, and for the sake of the Realm of Man, she hopes they're prepared.

CHAPTER TWO

"Tora Thurgood!"

Ripped from her sleep, Tora springs up from her mattress on the floor and smacks her head hard on a fallen beam propped up against the wall.

"Fuck!" She screams and grips her head as throbbing pain explodes in her skull.

"Get down here now! You're late for training," her mother scolds.

"I'm awake!" Tora throws off the blankets and storms across the broken floorboards to the bathroom, careful to avoid the gaping holes and rotting wood. She would kill for a decent night's sleep without being woken by a screaming banshee every morning. It's like living with a drill sergeant. The woman's voice could double as a fog horn, and she's not even in the room.

After hunting all night, into the early hours of the morning, you'd think the woman would give her a break. But no. Not Freya Thurgood. A few hours of sleep are plenty, she says. Be grateful you get to sleep at all, she says. Back in my day, Valkyries slept once a week and still fought in the forgotten wars, she says.

It's enough to make her want to smack her mother in the face. It's her birthday. Her twenty-first. The only birthday in a Valkyrie's life that means something and is celebrated. The day of the three cycles of seven. The day she would have gotten her wings and angelic power.

It's too bad her mother really doesn't give a shit. She shunned the ritual and basically gave the finger to the Valkyrie bloodline; to Arora, the great-grandmother of all Valkyries; to Estrid, grandmother of all Valkyries, and to Freyja, mother of all Valkyries.

It started eons ago with a little interspecies romance when an angel named Arora and a god named Odin hooked up, popped out a kid, and named it Estrid.

The poor kid was the first of the angels to be born without wings, and she didn't get any powers from her father.

Estrid followed in her mother's footsteps and had a little affair of her own with Ares, the God of War. Nine months later, Estrid gave birth to a beautiful daughter named Freyja and raised her in secret from the gods. But on her twenty-first birthday, Ares found out about his daughter and drove his flaming sword into the middle of her forehead, calling her an abomination. Happy Birthday, Freyja!

Long story short; Estrid begged her father Odin to restore her daughter's soul. He ignored her cries, however, the Goddess Nyx did not. She agreed, but there was a catch. A big one. The daughters of Freyja would fight in servitude to the gods for eternity, restoring the souls of the chosen few for battle.

If found worthy of battle, on the three cycles of seven of each daughter's life, they would undergo a ritual and be reborn a fully-fledged Valkyrie.

In an act of desperation, Estrid agreed, not realizing the full extent of her promise. Every single descendant of Freyja, every single generation to come would be born into servitude to the gods and would have to bear at least one child each to any chosen god to carry on the bloodline.

Freyja rose from the dead with huge white swan wings and two markings on her body in the shape of a sword and swan wings; one on her forehead where the blade had pierced her pineal gland and one on her wrist that extended to a glowing purple soul sword. Her eyes burned royal purple as all in her bloodline would. Her strength, agility, healing abilities, and senses were unlike anything the angels had ever seen.

The Valkyrie bloodline was born.

No one but a fully-fledged Valkyrie knows what the ritual entails, and none have ever spoken of it. Not that it matters. Her mother already made it perfectly clear that she won't be performing the ritual, no matter how many times Tora begs, which means she'll never get her wings; she'll never feel the air circling her body; she'll never know the excitement of swooping down on the enemy in battle or collecting a soul for resurrection.

It's the only reason her best friend Astra wanted to undergo the ritual at all. She's been dreaming of getting her wings since they were kids. But now they'll never be fully-fledged Valkyries; never be whole.

"Tora! Now!" her mother screams.

"I'm coming!" Tora snaps.

Her mother refuses to enslave them to a life of battle in the name of gods who care nothing for them. It's the reason she fled the Realm of Angels in the first place.

On the day the War of the Gods spilled into the Realm of Man, the gods were desperate and demanded that fledging Valkyries undergo the ritual early to replenish their army. The gods didn't care that Valkyries were the offspring of god and angel. They didn't care that the fledglings would age and die within three years if the Valkyrie ritual was performed before the three cycles of seven.

Tora was twenty, and so was Astra; only one year away from the final ritual, but the gods didn't care. They wanted to win the war, no matter the cost.

Hundreds of fledglings died in the War; thousands even. Her mother Freya, leader of the Valkyries, stole her and Astra away to protect them, but she couldn't save them all.

Freya meant to return to the war once Tora and Astra were safe, but when the rift in the portal gate opened in the Realm of Man, she stayed to fight. She could never return home after that, not after deserting her post. Her mother was the first and only Valkyrie to break the pact between Nyx and Freyja.

Some of the gods descended with an army of angel warriors to protect the humans, but the rifts were too many and the warriors too few. The War lasted a month, and in the end, when the fires burned out and the water receded, the Realm of Man never recovered.

Tora, Astra, and her mother were lucky. They were in Greenwich Village when hell rained down on the Realm of Man; one of the few places that survived. A lot of the buildings were destroyed or torn up, but some are still livable.

As long as they keep the perimeter crystals active, cast their protection salt circles, and grow their own food, they survive day by day. The same can't be said for Tora if she takes much longer to get ready, but she needs to get the demon stink off her skin and brush her teeth. One shower is not enough.

All in all, last night wasn't too bad. She got a couple of new bruises on her arms, a scratch to the bicep, and a scraped knee. Not bad at all for a night on the hunt.

Even without the ritual, Tora and Astra are stronger, more agile, and have quicker reflexes than angels or humans, but they're still vulnerable to injury, they can't heal themselves, and their speed isn't much faster than a human. It's probably why her mother is always yelling at her for being late. The woman's running at double speed.

Jogging down the rickety stairs, Tora finds her mother, Freya, staring out of the broken kitchen window, the sun streaming down on her face. She looks like a battle goddess dressed ready to fight in her white vest and skirt, golden breast, thigh, and upper arm plates. Her winged helmet wraps around the back of her golden mane of hair.

The ancient traditional Valkyrie uniform. Striking to look at; ridiculously impractical. For starters, wearing a white skirt in a fight is stupid. Not only does it flash your panties to the world, the white fabric shows up every single splat of blood.

That was the point back in the old days. The Valkyries wore the blood with pride, but after centuries of soaking their clothes after every battle, you'd think they would have changed the uniform to a more practical color.

"Where's Star?" Tora rests her foot on a dining table chair and laces her shin-high army boots.

"Astra is outside training. Where you should be." Her mother glares at her over her shoulder, her royal purple eyes flashing with shards of white. The black swan wings and sword symbol adorning her forehead mark her for what she is. A Valkyrie.

"Okay, I get it alright." Tora drops her foot on the ground. "Give me a break. I had a late night, and it's my birthday."

"I'm aware of that," Freya says, her tone dry and irritated. "And before you ask, the answer is no. I won't be performing the ritual on you today."

Tora rolls her eyes. After pestering her for nearly a year straight, she knows better than to beg. Nothing will change her mother's mind. She'll never be a fully-fledged Valkyrie. Never. "I wasn't even going to ask."

Ignoring the bitterness in her voice, Freya stares back out the window, her hands locked firmly behind her back. "Anything to report from last night's hunt?"

"Yeah actually." Tora leans on the counter. "I took the squad to Pier 51 to scope out an unusual demon sighting. The demon; I've never seen anything like it before. It wore the face of a human child with talons and piranha teeth. The creepy little fucker was singing a kid's nursery rhyme."

"What?" Freya whips her head around, her eyes wide. "What happened?"

Tora takes a fresh blueberry muffin off the kitchen table. It looks like Astra fixed the solar power and has been baking again. It sure as hell wasn't her mother. The woman hasn't cooked anything in over a year, not since leaving the Realm of Angels.

"The squad and I bated her onto the pier and took care of it. She didn't disintegrate though so I had to throw her back through the portal like we do the malevolent fae." Tora shoves half the muffin in her mouth and chases it down with a glass of water.

"A crossroad demon in Greenwich?" Her mother frowns. "The wards are weakening quicker than I thought."

"A crossroad demon?" Tora screws up her face. That's news. As far as she knows, demons only hang out in the Demon Realm, Hell, and quick trips to the Realm of Man for snacks. "What the hell is that?"

"A crossroad demon is exactly what it sounds like." Her mother turns back to stare out the window again. "A demon from the Realm of the Crossroads, where all portals connect."

"That's helpful." Tora rolls her eyes. She was hoping for a little more description than that. Like what's the difference between the demons of the crossroads and the nasty fuckers they usually get in Greenwich? "And what do you mean the wards are weak? The portal opened at the pier, not outside the perimeter."

"So it did." Her mother says, refusing to elaborate.

Tora watches her mother through narrowed eyes. The woman is being even more cryptic than usual, and it's seriously starting to piss her off. How is she meant to do her job and protect the village if she doesn't have all the information?

There's something her mother's not telling her. Freya drove spelled clear quartz crystal boulders lined in silver into the ground on each corner of Greenwich Village to create a protective barrier around the survivors. She's never told anyone where she got them, or what witch or warlock spelled them, but whoever did it, had some serious mojo.

The wards don't stop portals from opening, but they do stop demons and fae from walking into the village from other areas of the Realm of Man. So why does her mother suddenly think they should repel portals?

"And, you're okay?" Freya glances at her. "Unhurt?"

Tora chokes on the last of her muffin. "What do you mean?"

"I mean are you hurt?" Her mother snaps. "Did it bite you?"

Tora jerks. That's it. Something's definitely up. Freya Thurgood is actually worried about her. That hasn't happened since she was a child. The ice queen rarely shows any concern or affection for anyone.

"I'm fine Mom. Just a bit bruised." Tora approaches her mother like she would a cornered animal and decides to do something she hasn't done since she was a child. She wraps her arms around her and hugs her tight, knowing she won't return the gesture, but not caring either. Her mother actually cares. She sees her as more than just a soldier. It's one of the best birthday presents she could have asked for.

Freya tenses and straightens her spine. "Good. Then you won't object to a perimeter run. Check the crystal wards."

"Seriously?" Tora drops her arms and steps back. One minute of affection is all she wanted, and the woman can't even do that. And from the look on her face, she's not kidding. Birthday or not, it looks like she's going on a perimeter run.

Groaning, Tora takes her blades off the kitchen counter and straps them to her leg, the frost in her mother's eyes enough to freeze the nose off her face. She should know better than to show the ice queen affection. It only leads to punishment. It was kind of worth it though to see the strained look on her face. "You know; Dr Arnold on 8th Avenue is a psychiatrist. I'm sure he'd love to analyze you."

Freya raises her eyebrows. Her nostrils flare.

"Love you too Mom." Tora winks playfully and blows her a kiss as she walks out the door, leaving before she can think up some other torturous task.

Dr Arnold would have a field day with her mother and not just because she's an ancient Valkyrie or uneasy around affection. The woman is a walking relic, over a century old.

Tora passed on what information she had on the nine realms, gods, angels, demons, and the Creator to Dr Arnold for his book, but no doubt her mother would be a more thorough source.

Before the war, humans had no idea what lay beyond death, nor did they completely grasp the concept of gods, angels, and demons. It wasn't until the malevolent fae and demons started snatching humans and animals that people believed the stories of the nine realms. Humans are stubborn though with many believing their god is the Creator of all realms.

As Tora understands it, the Creator rules over nine realms; the Demon Realm, Malevolent Fae Realm, The Realm of Man, Benevolent Fae Realm, The Realm of Angels, The Realm of Gods, The Realm of Abundance, Heaven, and Hell.

Each realm is a mirror of the next, layered on top of each other; the land mass and resources similar. It is the inhabitants who influence the evolution of the realm, or its destruction, with portal gates only accessible to those who know how to use them.

There are also two smaller realms known as the Spirit Realm where ghosts who refuse to move on linger, and the Crossroads, where all realm roads meet and judgment is passed.

Each universal soul undergoes several tests over various lifetimes before being able to rest. Death marks the end of each trial where the soul returns to the crossroads for resurrection and begins the next journey.

Souls begin as infants in the Demon Realm, then follow onto the Malevolent Fae Realm, Realm of Man, Benevolent Fae Realm, Angel Realm, and then the Realm of Gods as they learn and progress through the tests. Gods can choose to live for hundreds of years, although they risk corrupting their souls the longer they live.

Once they die, gods either retire to the Realm of Abundance to live without responsibility for Man before beginning the trials once again, or simply progress to Heaven and dissolve into eternal bliss.

Souls can descend into Hell at any stage of the trials, including the gods if the soul is deemed unworthy and needs to be cleansed with brimstone, smoke, and fire.

Tora doubts the asshole gods will be progressing onto anything other than a fiery vacation in Hell when they die. There's no way their souls are worthy, not after the war, and not after sentencing so many Valkyries to death.

"Star?" Tora steps out into their ground-floor garden.

Warm rays of sunshine beam down on the abundant vegetable gardens and fruit trees. A beautiful blue and black butterfly darts in front of her face as a brown chicken races under her feet, chasing a grasshopper, its loud clucking echoing through her ears.

"Over here!" Astra calls out from behind a cluster of fruit trees.

Tora follows the sound of her voice. Astra never used to be self-conscious about training, not until they moved to the Realm of Man. It was like one-on-one training with Freya brought out her insecurities. "Are you hiding again?"

Astra throws a jab at the wooden dummy and pinches her soft purple eyes closed on impact. "I don't want your mom to see."

Tora doesn't have the heart to tell her Freya can see her from the upstairs window. If anyone can relate to Freya's judgment, it's Tora. Astra lost her mother in the War of the Gods and has looked to Freya for approval ever since, but no matter how hard she tries, Freya won't allow her on the hunt.

It's not personal. It's not that there's anything wrong with Astra. She just isn't meant for battle. Anyone can see that. Her strength lies in healing, not combat. Back in the Realm of Angels, she would have undergone a completely different ritual and been inducted into the medical team, but since Freya was the leader of the Valkyries, Astra has somehow gotten it into her head that she needs to be a fighter to make her proud.

Tora can't make her understand. Freya is proud of her whether she can fight or not. Her mother just sucks at emotion.

"Want to come for a run?" Tora asks, hoping to take her mind off it.

Astra snorts and continues sparring. Pieces of her curly strawberry blonde hair fall loose from her bun and frame her delicate face. "What did you do this time?"

"I hugged her." Tora throws her hands up in mock outrage like she doesn't constantly tease reactions from her mother. "The woman froze up like a popsicle."

Chuckling, Astra wipes her hands on her green khaki pants and reaches for her water bottle. The chicken screeches and pecks at her boot.

"Hey, you..." Astra picks up the chicken and gently carries it a few steps away before placing it on the ground again.

A loud crash echoes in the yard.

Astra gasps and whips her head around.

"Woah!" Tora gapes.

A chunk of stone from their dilapidated three-story complex lies on the ground, exactly where Astra was standing a second ago.

"Oh my god!" Astra looks up at the half-missing wall on the second floor and wipes the dust off her bright yellow t-shirt. "Seriously Tora! You can't continue sleeping up there. It's dangerous."

"The chickens live on what's left of the third floor," Tora argues. "And it's fine. I sleep better up there. The floor's boobytrapped. If anyone tries to break in, they'll fall through the holes and land on you guys."

"Nice." Astra snorts and takes a swig of water. "So how was last night? Did Bo banish your woo-woo demons again?

"Uh! I would never!" Tora fans her face. "And a lady never tells."

Astra scoffs. "Since when are you a lady?"

"Shut up." Tora laughs and dodges the crazy chicken trying to peck a hole in her boot. "So, are you up for a run?"

"That's a hard pass." Astra picks up the feathered beast and coos gently, calming the chicken almost instantly. "I don't want to make your mother angry. She wants me down at the trading markets after I tend to the chickens."

"Oh god..." Tora groans. "Not the markets."

She forgot the stupid markets were on today. Every week it's the same shit. Sitting behind a makeshift table, trading an egg for an orange, an orange for an onion. It's mind-numbingly boring, and her mother makes them go every week.

In the first month after the War, Freya helped the survivors by flying outside of the perimeter, known as the Deadlands, scavenging everything she could find, from food to medicine. She left the resources in the middle of the village for people to take as they needed.

That was a huge mistake. Fear made the idiot humans stockpile whatever they could and add to the chaos by fighting each other. Unbelievably, the toilet paper was the first thing to go. The humans' first priority wasn't water, it wasn't food or shelter, it was wiping their own asses.

After that, the community had to vote in human leaders to govern the village so the rest would behave. The leaders set up a weekly Trading Market to force everyone to work as a community. A few shaky weeks later, the people started to work together.

Freya made countless trips out into the Deadlands, stripping the surrounding hardware and garden shops bare; collecting soil, seeds, pots, and planters. It was hilarious watching her mother, the most revered Valkyrie in history, flying into the village with livestock in her arms.

Now the once gray city buildings, fire escapes, rooftops, and balconies are littered with fruit and vegetable beds, both horizontal and vertical, growing up the walls.

Entire buildings work together to produce enough food for the residents. Some of the more knowledgeable residents were even able to introduce solar electricity and running water with what little materials the village had.

Age-old methods of preserving meat were taught by the elderly in the village in a large seminar in Washington Square Park, including salting, spicing, smoking, pickling, and drying.

Livestock is held and managed by the leaders in a corner of Washington Square Park, one of the few places portals never open and is heavily policed by armed guards.

Each week at the market, the leaders supply everyone with a small portion of meat, butter, cheese, and milk treated at ultra-high temperatures so it lasts for up to three months while the villagers trade their homegrown fruits and vegetables. Even wheat is grown on the tops of some of the buildings and milled down to flour.

Once most of the cities were destroyed, the water that flowed underground was reclaimed by the Minetta Brook. Freshwater rises into many basements and pipes around the village and is sterilized for drinking. They also have thousands of water tanks that catch the rain used for plumbing, showers, and cooking.

As payment for her assistance, Freya was "allowed" to keep a flock of chickens she found on one of her searches; not that the humans could have stopped her from taking the chickens. Freya said she was keeping the chickens, and no one had the balls to argue.

Tora opens the large front double wooden doors as Astra heads back inside. "I'll meet you at the markets in a few hours."

"Okay. Oh Tora?" Astra swings around the doorframe and smiles, the chicken still in her arms. "Happy Birthday. Be sure to thank Bo when he gives you his present."

Tora rolls her eyes as Astra lifts her eyebrows up and down suggestively. Subtly is not Astra's strong suit, neither is moving her eyebrows around. All she manages to do is open her eyes really wide.

"You're an idiot." Tora snorts and heads out.

CHAPTER THREE

Twenty-One. She can't believe it. A year ago, she was counting down the days, excited to undergo the ritual and become a fully-fledged Valkyrie, but then Hades decided to break into the Realm of the Gods and fuck everything up.

Birthdays aren't celebrated in the Realm of Angels like in the Realm of Man. They mark your age and the age of ritual. That's it. She's essentially been looking forward to her twenty-first birthday for twenty-one years because of the ritual, and now it's just another day of training, hunting, and surviving thanks to that selfish prick.

If it wasn't for him, she would be undergoing the ritual right now instead of cautiously eyeing off the street as she stretches.

Demons and fae aren't the only things that lurk in the shadows. Humans can be just as sadistic and cruel as the malevolent fae.

If she had her way, she wouldn't just beat the crap out of the troublemakers and gangs, she would capture the assholes and leave them as an offering for the demons and fae, or at least kick them out of the village. There are a thousand or more people in Greenwich. They can afford to lose a couple more.

The human leaders don't see it that way though. They believe their God saved all the people in the village for a reason; that their God limited the number of portals that opened to save them.

Some say the potter's field under Washington Square Park stops the portals while others say it was a spell cast by the witches and warlocks of Greenwich Village.

It all sounds like superstitious bullshit to Tora. She's been in Greenwich for a year, and she hasn't met any witches, not that she knows of. Demons and the malevolent fae feed on fear, blood, pain, and anarchy. It's what draws them through the rifts. The village survived much of the destruction of the war, so of course there are going to be fewer demons and fae. Less to feed on.

There could be millions of survivors outside the perimeter. Who knows? But keeping the thugs around just to increase the human population is stupid. It's only a matter of time before they seriously injure or kill someone.

Tora's not scared of a couple of humans, but the thugs are in the back of her mind as she begins her run on West 14th Street.

Villagers hurry down the street, pushing old shopping trolleys, rolling suitcases, bikes, and dragging carts filled with produce to trade at the Washington Square Park Market.

Some wave, some nod, and some pretend they don't see her at all. She doesn't take it personally though. Day in and day out it's the same faces over and over. Some days it just makes you want to scream.

Once proud high-rise buildings and shops line the streets and form a perimeter around the village; the smashed windows, missing floors, and crumbling facades a constant reminder of the war.

Large glittering silver gargoyles peer out over the rooftops, facing the Deadlands, a symbol of hope and survival against the demons and fae.

Tora stops on the corner of Broadway and drops down to check the large boulder-sized clear quartz crystal embedded in the road. The silver casing has a bit of wear and tear, but there's nothing wrong with it. The wards should be holding. She doesn't know what her mother is talking about.

No one would tamper with the crystals. Everyone understands the danger. Salt circles keep households safe when demons or fae attack autonomously, but they wouldn't protect them against a barrage of attacks from the thousands of portals outside of the perimeter like the crystals do.

"Tora?" A familiar voice calls from across the street.

Tora glances back over her shoulder and smiles when she sees her friend, Dr Charlie Arnold, and his heavily pregnant wife Michelle Arnold rolling a new baby stroller out of a rundown store.

"Hey! Dr A. Mrs A." Tora jogs across the street, all concerns over her mother disappearing. "What's up? You headed to the market?"

Holding her large bulging stomach, Mrs Arnold shakes her head. "I think this is it for us today."

The poor woman looks like she's about to fall over. Sweat drips down the side of her neck. Her white blonde hair is twirled into a knot on the back of her head, and her shoes look like they're made from some sort of loose fabric.

Tora pinches her lips in sympathy. Being pregnant looks seriously painful. Mrs Arnold looks like she's about to burst out of her pastel pink coat. Her ankles and feet are visibly swollen, and her usually porcelain skin is covered in blemishes and red splotches.

Dr Arnold doesn't look much better. Since the last time she saw him, his dark black hairline has receded, and his eyes are drawn and sunken in. Even his dark tanned skin looks kind of pale.

"You okay Dr A?" Tora asks. She swears, every day he wears the same pair of blue denim jeans and black collared shirt. It's like he's in uniform. Not that she can judge. Her wardrobe pretty much consists of black, black, and more black. What else do people expect? She fights demons and fae every night. She's always covered in some kind of disgusting crap. The black just hides it better.

"Call me Charlie, Tora." Dr Arnold smiles, his voice deep and full of bass. "I'm fine. But when the wife doesn't sleep, the husband doesn't sleep. I'll tell you, for a petite woman, her snore sounds like a growling bear, and she kicks like a mule."

Mrs Arnold gasps and smacks his arm. Laughter bubbles from her lips. "I do not."

"Don't worry. I still love you." Dr Arnold grins and kisses her shoulder before turning back to Tora. "So, how are you? Are you being careful? You're not putting yourself in unnecessary danger, are you?"

"I'm good Dr A." Tora smiles to herself. She's never had someone like Dr Arnold in her life before; someone who constantly worries about her. God knows who her paternal father is, but she imagines a good father would act the same.

"Don't baby the girl Charlie." Mrs Arnold shakes her head. "Tora is the most capable person we know."

"I know that," Dr Arnold retorts. "But she's so young. She shouldn't be out there fighting."

"She's a Valkyrie honey." Mrs Arnold rolls her eyes. "She doesn't need the big bad Psychiatrist saving her."

Tora chuckles. "Do you need me to trade anything for you at the markets? Have you made any blankets?"

"Oh no honey." Mrs Arnold pats her hand. "That's very sweet, but we're fine. I'm still working on a few of the blankets."

"Our neighbors have been kind enough to trade away from the markets so Shell and I can stay home," Dr Arnold explains.

It's not unusual for blocks of units and streets of neighbors to trade amongst themselves. It's not encouraged on a regular basis as the leaders want everyone to be involved and come together as a community, but they understand that side trading happens. They just want to make sure everyone in the community has a chance to trade for things they want or need.

"How's the book going?" Tora asks.

When the War of the Gods crashed into the Realm of Man, it not only destroyed human lives and cities, it shook the very fabric of their existence. Everything they thought to be true was challenged, so Dr Arnold decided to write a book to help people understand and share the knowledge with future generations.

"It's getting there. It just needs a bit of reworking." Dr Arnold laughs at himself. "A lot of reworking."

"The book was fine two edits ago." Mrs Arnold rolls her eyes. "He won't stop obsessing over it. You don't need to impress agents or publishers anymore honey."

"It has to be perfect Shell." Dr Arnold argues, his light brown eyes wide. "It basically re-writes everything we know about the universe."

"Ah huh." Mrs Arnold grins. "But editing the text a thousand times on that rickety old typewriter isn't going to change the context. It's not going to make it easier for people to swallow."

"Well, that's my sign to go." Tora chuckles awkwardly and starts back across the street. It's not her fault the human race lost the knowledge of the nine realms and the Creator eons ago, but she feels responsible for shaking their beliefs. Dr Arnold wouldn't have all the information if it wasn't for her. "See you later Dr A; Mrs A."

"Charlie!" Dr Arnold calls out, his tone light. He knows she won't call him Charlie, and it has nothing to do with respect. She just likes the name Dr A.

Jogging down Broadway, Tora veers off onto Houston Street and finishes her perimeter run, checking the crystals on the way. As she reaches the piers, her pace slows. Sweat trickles down the side of her face. Salt air gently caresses her flushed cheeks.

Five small children climb over the play equipment and roundabout carousel, laughing and singing while their parents sit on a nearby bench with mugs in their hands, oblivious to the demon blood staining the concrete.

The children see her and stare. One little blonde-haired boy spins in circles on the roundabout carousel, singing in unison with the others.

"Ring around a rosie..."

Tora shivers and backs away, continuing her perimeter run. After last night, a child singing will never sound the same. It makes her want to stab out her eardrums.

She doesn't understand the human race; demons and fae are running around outside and inside the perimeter, yet doing mundane things from their pre-war lives, like sitting on a bench drinking coffee makes them feel safe.

Everyone goes about their business, trying to survive in this broken world and find some kind of normality, blissfully ignorant of what hunts them at night. The residents of Greenwich Village know that demons and malevolent fae exist; they know to stay indoors and cast their protection salt circles before sundown, but they rarely come face to face with the demons and malevolent fae that plague the area thanks to the hunters who patrol the streets, and her mother in the air.

It's crazy. A coffee isn't going to save you from a demon attack. Learning to fight and protect yourself will.

Humans are particularly susceptible to the charms of the malevolent fae. The fae are both beautiful and deadly, indulging in their every urge and taking pleasure in the suffering of others.

Their large two-toned tattered and torn gothic-style wings mark the dark faeries for what they are while the pixies and dark elves find it easier to blend in. None of them can hide their need for destruction, pain, and misery as they feed their desires. They are nothing like the benevolent fae, who thankfully stay mostly in their realm.

In the earlier days, after the War, the malevolent fae often lured or kidnapped humans from Greenwich Village, dragging them back through the portal gates. After the first few times, the humans actually listened and stayed locked inside at night.

The few humans who have returned through the portals claim to have been lured under false pretenses and glamours, yet after only a few hours, they beg to go back to the Malevolent Fae Realm.

The fae call them the Unlucky. They don't last long once they escape. They are the ones who either commit suicide or leave the village in a depressive trance, never to return.

As bad as the malevolent fae are, the demons are much worse, more feral, and barbaric, their minds like hungry animals.

The demons who rained down from the sky a year ago were large, fearsome, and humanoid; built with muscle, horns, tusks, and burned skin, but what the humans didn't see were the other types of demons that crawled out from the bowels of their realm; skeleton-like demons with elongated limbs and jaws, hulking crab like demons, mutated bear looking demons, huge wolf-like demons, short fat scabby demons, and pus spitting demons. The list goes on. It would take hundreds of years and some very brave explorers willing to travel to the Demon Realm to catalog them all.

That's what humans find difficult to understand. The Demon Realm is not Hell. It's the same as any other realm, a replica of Earth, filled with different types of creatures. It's just where Hades collects his warriors and workers from, the same as the gods do from the Realm of Angels.

Day and night her mother flies out of the village, looking for survivors, or anything remotely useful. Lately though, she's become even more distant. Their conversations are shorter, and their training hours are longer. Her mother is nervous about something, and Tora bets it has something to do with the child demon she fought last night.

Something is changing, something is coming, and she needs to be prepared, even if her mother won't tell her what it is.

CHAPTER FOUR

Men, women, and children flood under the large arch of Washington Square Park, searching through the stalls lining the pavement, trading for what they need.

Large beautiful trees, flowers, plants, and shrubs line the walkways, brimming with life. Butterflies, beetles, and bees hop from flower to flower, buzzing and dancing amongst the pollen. It's a stark contrast to the outside world, where everything is dead, collapsing, and burnt.

Fighting the crowds, Tora circles the stalls and searches for Astra, the smell of herbs, spices, fresh fruit, and vegetables filling her nose. Survivors mingle together around the fountain, desperate for any sense of normality in their isolated village, ignoring the destruction and chaos that lies just beyond the perimeter.

It never takes long to spot Astra in a crowd, and it's not just because she's angelically beautiful. The girl towers over most of the humans and has the most beautiful highlights in her long strawberry blonde hair. It's like she's the daughter of Aphrodite.

It's not fair. Tora is the only short-ass Valkyrie in history. She still doesn't know what the hell happened. Neither gods nor Valkyries are short, so regardless of who her father was, she should have had some sort of height advantage in her genetic makeup, just like every other Valkyrie since the beginning of time.

Making her way over to the egg stall, Tora eyes the long line of customers lingering by the front and suppresses a groan. She doesn't mind the crowds, she doesn't mind that the stall is busy, but she does mind the tall lanky suck-up standing next to Astra, helping her serve. Ethan. Her boyfriend.

They've been dating since the day of the war after Astra saved him from falling debris. She claims it was his sea glass eyes, spikey blonde hair, and traditionally handsome looks she was attracted to, but Tora thinks it was like some weird rescuer syndrome in reverse. Either that or it's because he's the tallest guy in the area at six foot six.

The love-struck idiot fell for the obnoxious jerk the moment she saved him and claims he's her twin flame. There's no way Astra's soul mate is a human who wears tight khaki shorts, tight shirts, and brown shoes.

It's not that he's done anything wrong. That's not the problem. The problem is he's too nice. Everything is textbook with him from his neatly styled hair, clean pressed clothes, and polite old-fashioned attitude.

Who goes on romantic walks and picnics by the pier or in the park in the afternoon when the surrounding city has been demolished and you're under constant threat from demons and malevolent fae?

Who kisses someone's hand, walks to the roadside of the pavement even though there are no cars, and opens doors for someone when death surrounds you?

And where the hell does he get all the gifts from; jewelry, chocolate, musical instruments, and nick-nacks? Most of the shops have been stripped of anything of traditional value. The only things left are practical items like the baby stroller Dr Arnold and his wife found.

No one is that nice when the world has gone to shit and you have to live day to day, hoping you'll survive. Ethan is so available, so nice, so thoughtful. It's like he watched a whole bunch of old movies to learn how to woo a woman.

Tora doesn't trust him, not that she can tell Astra that. She loves him; loves the idea of marriage, children, and building a home. She doesn't see his condescending stare and contempt for most of the villagers. The guy doesn't have one single friend besides Astra, and for good reason. He is a douche.

Biting her tongue, Tora joins them behind the makeshift table and pinches her lips into a smile, hiding her disdain. "Hey, sorry it took me so long. Mom had me running hand-to-hand knife and sword drills forever. The bitch even cut me."

Tora holds up her right arm. Caked blood coats her elbow and forearm. That's what she gets for her birthday. A slice across the forearm. Happy Birthday, Tora; Love Mom.

It's not the cut she's pissed off about. She's covered in scars from sparring with her mother. It was the ferocity and aggression behind the training that Tora has a problem with. There was a real desperation in her mother's movements like she needed Tora to beat her.

It's her birthday for fucks sake. The ice queen could have at least gone easy on her, maybe said Happy Birthday instead of slicing into her forearm and headbutting her multiple times. That would have been nice.

"Oh my god." Astra grabs her bicep. "Did she do this too?"

Tora frowns and looks at her arm. White puss bubbles from the scratch on her bicep, the surrounding area red and angry. The demon scratch; she completely forgot about it. It looks pretty gross, but weirdly enough, it doesn't hurt. "Umm, no. That was from the child demon last night."

Ethan looks over Astra's shoulder and recoils. "Ah, Tora! That's disgusting! You should get that looked at."

"Demon child?" Astra drops her arm. "Did you just say demon child?"

"I'll tell you about it later," Tora promises, but she isn't sure she should. Astra has always wanted a family, and the demons freak her out enough as it is. It might mess with her head knowing there are demons out there that look like children, especially creepy singing children.

"Let me clean that up. Ethan can handle the store for a minute." Astra pulls her to the back of the stall and rummages through her pink messenger bag until she finds some disinfectant and wipes. She pours a clear liquid substance over the wound and dabs it with a wipe, cleaning away the puss.

"Fuck Star!" Tora hisses and pulls her arm away. The scrape sizzles and burns, bubbling under the skin. "What the hell is that stuff?"

"Vodka." Astra grins and secures a bandage on her arm. "The best defense against demon germs. I'm surprised you don't recognize it. You drink enough of it. Now stop being a baby and get back to work."

"Waa." Tora mocks and pokes out her tongue.

What a waste of good vodka. She'll have to be more careful in the future if she wants to ration the good stuff for drinking. Come to think of it, maybe Astra wouldn't mind if she dipped into her sanitizing stash to get through the markets. It is her birthday after-all.

"Don't even think about it!" Astra glances back over her shoulder as she joins Ethan at the front of the stall and gives her a pointed look. "Not. For. You."

Tora pokes out her tongue. "Buzzkill."

Even without the vodka, the day goes by in a blur of noise, the voices of the villagers mingling together. They trade for hours; an egg for an apple, a potato for an egg, an egg for some soap.

By mid-afternoon, their stock dwindles, and they're left with only a few eggs to trade and an abundance of fresh fruit, nuts, and vegetables.

And bonus... Astra already collected their weekly portion of meat, cheese, milk, and butter, so they can sneak away earlier than expected.

It's a Happy Birthday after-all. They can have an early dinner, then she can meet Bo for a bit of night hunting and some recreational activities of their own. He can't stay mad at her forever. They're not in a relationship; they're not even in love. It's a bit of fun between two friends; a way to bring a bit of excitement and joy into their miserable lives.

"Tora..." Astra jabs her with her bony elbow.

"Ow!" Tora rubs her muscle, the scratch from the demon throbbing like a bruise. "What'd you do that for?"

Discreetly nodding towards the crowd, Astra pinches her lips into a smile for the last of the customers leaving their stall and shoots her a concerned look.

Tora follows her line of sight, the jovial atmosphere of the markets quieting to a hum. The crowd splits. Five people step into view, dressed simply in black jeans and jackets, their faces hidden by hoods.

Based on the shapes under the fabric, Tora guesses it's two women and three men. It happens every time there's a market. The local thugs too lazy or stupid to grow their own food intimidate the other survivors, stealing and threatening families.

The human leaders employ a few guards to police the market but they aren't trained in law enforcement. They're just regular people and scare easily. Those who do have any type of law enforcement or army experience are stationed with the livestock.

The thugs scope out the produce and steal a piece of fruit or a vegetable here and there, but it's the families they threaten that's the biggest problem. The thugs find the stalls with the produce they want and target the homes of the owners later, away from the markets. No one knows who it will be next, and there are no phones and no technology, so it's not like the families can call for help.

Smirking, Tora backs away from the stall, out of view. The thugs haven't targeted them yet thanks to both hers and her mother's reputation, but it looks like today is the day, the day Tora has been waiting for since the markets opened. The day she is justified in teaching these fuckers a little lesson. The human leaders can stick their passive policing up their asses. This means war.

Circling the back of the stalls, Tora eyes the five as they approach the egg stall and lean on the makeshift table. Ethan automatically pushes Astra behind him, putting a protective barrier between her and the thugs.

Tora hates the guy but she has to give him props for protecting Astra. He would take a bullet for the girl without blinking.

One of the male thugs snatches an egg off the table and smashes it on Ethan's forehead without warning. One of the females slams her fist down on the last two eggs on the table.

Tora clenches her jaw, anger hot and fierce flooding her veins. Her face burns. Her heart races in her chest. She doesn't care about the egg on Ethan's face; she doesn't even care about the eggs. No more eggs mean no more stall. What she does care about is the fact that Astra looks like she's about to pee herself.

Charging through the crowd, Tora leaps onto the ring leader's back and wraps her arm around his throat, pulling back hard with her dead weight. She's sick of these thugs and their intimidating bullshit. No one fucks with her friend.

Remaining in front of Astra, Ethan flips the table and scatters the other thugs away. The crowd quietens and turns to watch the spectacle, too afraid to do anything to help. This is the problem. Even though the rest of the survivors outnumber the thugs, they're too scared to do anything about it. It's ridiculous. And the leaders are just as cowardly.

Tora has no such problem. She locks the thug in a tight choke hold and forces him to his knees. She was born to fight; born for violence, and she isn't afraid to take down assholes who deserve it.

"Do we have a problem here?" Tora narrows her eyes at the remaining four and tightens her hold, her heart singing in her chest. She never feels more alive than when she's fighting for a cause. That's one thing training her whole life didn't do; it couldn't do. It didn't prepare her for how good it feels to kick the crap out of someone who deserves it.

"Let him go!" A shrill voice yells. Brown eyes glare at her from under a hoodie.

Tora wrinkles her nose and pretends to think about it. Under the hoodie, she can make out a scar that lines the side of the girl's face traveling from her ear down to her lips.

"Umm, no." Tora laughs. "What the fuck do you think this is? Like I would just let him go. Back off and get the fuck out of the markets, then I might let him go."

The four thugs step forward with snarls on their faces. Tora tightens her grip causing the thug to choke and gasp for air. The hood of his jacket falls off, revealing a head of thick pale gray hair and pale gray eyes rimmed in deep blue.

"Flenn?" Ethan frowns.

Tora whips her head around. "You know this thug?"

"What? Me? No." Ethan shakes his head. "I mean yes. But no. I know who he is, but I don't know him know him."

Liar, Tora wants to scream. Ethan's way too nervous and jittery to be telling the truth. It takes all her strength not to kick him in the nuts and send him flying across the markets. The only thing that stops her is Astra. She would never forgive her.

"I wouldn't." Astra warns and takes up position beside her as the thugs inch forward, the shake of her hands and wobble in her voice noticeable to Tora and Ethan alone. "She will snap his neck if she has to."

Reluctantly, Ethan takes up position on the other side of her. A crowd gathers, watching them with both fear and curiosity. It's not often they get to see someone fight back, especially since the hunters work at night.

"Back off guys." The thug chokes out in barely a whisper. "We'll leave."

One set of brown eyes and three sets of blue glare blades of hatred at her from under the hoodies as they back away, their lips curled like feral animals.

"Okay. We backed off," the female says. "Just let him go and we'll leave."

"Yeah, yeah." Tora releases the thug and pushes him onto the ground. Hopefully, the fuckers get the message. Not everyone in the village can be intimidated. "And stay the hell away from the market."

The thug grins a slimy lopsided grin and pulls up his hood. "See you around Tora."

Tora rolls her eyes as he and his friends merge back into the crowd. Some creep knowing her name doesn't scare her. Everybody in Greenwich Village knows the names of the Valkyries. It's not like a different species shows up on your doorstep every day.

It just pisses her off that the thugs continue to get away with terrorizing the neighborhood. It's been going on for months and the leaders do nothing. They think they're just scared harmless kids, but that guy was not a kid, and they are not harmless.

They carry weapons, wear facial coverings or hoods, and that guy was at least the same age as her, maybe a few years older.

"At least we can go home now, right?" Tora spins around. "No more eggs, no more stall."

Astra forces herself to smile as she cleans up the mess, fear and shame rolling off her in waves. A deep sadness shadows her light pastel purple eyes.

Tora slumps her shoulders. The last thing she wanted to do was upset Astra. She tries so hard, but the girl hates violence and struggles to contain her own fear. It's one of the reasons the Valkyries never would have performed the ritual on her. A Valkyrie needs to embrace fear and violence like an old friend, not avoid it.

"Maybe you should take off," Ethan whispers to Tora. "I'll make sure she gets home safe."

Tora hates to admit it, but the creep is right. Hanging around isn't going to make Astra feel any better about herself.

"Fine." Tora concedes. "I'll make up an excuse."

Ethan smiles like the Cheshire cat yet his eyes remain blank.

Tora snarls and suppresses the urge to throw him outside the protective barrier. The fucker knew that thug's name and now he's trying to get rid of her. Asshole. It wouldn't surprise her if he hung out with the thugs all the time.

"Hey, Star!" Tora yells in Ethan's face. "I need some supplies for tonight. I'll see you at home for dinner."

Struggling to keep his face neutral, Ethan flinches but remains where he is as she basically spits in his face.

"Okay. I've got it covered here." Oblivious, Astra loads the groceries into an old shopping trolley. "But don't be late. I have a surprise for your birthday."

"Really?" Tora perks up and moves away from Ethan.

A surprise; for her? She's never had a surprise on her birthday. The closest she came was when Astra picked her a white and pink lily when they were seven. She only had it for a few minutes before her mother told them off for picking something they weren't going to eat.

"It's your birthday?" Ethan frowns. "How old?"

Tora ignores him. She loves surprises and gifts. No one ever gives gifts in the Realm of Angels. That's a human custom. "What kind of surprise?"

"I told you, Ethan. She's 21." Astra chuckles, the sadness shadowing her eyes lifting with Tora's excitement. "And I'm not telling you. That's the point of a surprise."

"Fine. Have it your way." Tora pouts and waves as she makes her way out of the park. Who knows? With the way this afternoon is going, her mother might just change her mind about the ritual and make her a fully-fledged Valkyrie. Miracles happen, right?

CHAPTER FIVE

Climbing fire escapes, flipping from balcony to balcony, and jumping from roof to roof, Tora challenges her short legs, training her strength to accommodate for her lack of height. She could do this all day and not get tired. It keeps her mind off the ritual her mother refuses to perform and helps her get used to the different landscape.

When they first came to the Realm of Man, it took Astra and Tora a few weeks to adjust to their new surroundings, especially Tora when she was on the hunt. She had to test out the buildings and structures to make sure they were strong enough to hold her weight and that she could leap easily from the fire escapes, balconies, and surrounding structures. It was something new and exciting, so of course she had to master it.

There are no tall buildings in the Realm of Angels nor are there any roads or machinery. They have houses, meeting halls, and places of warmth built into and around the caves and trees, but angels don't like to alter the environment around them.

They use woven fabric for the roofs, floors, and walls, using the wool of their sheep, but unlike the sheep's wool in the Realm of Man, the wool hardens once woven, wet, and dried. It's just as strong as cement and lighter and more flexible than wood, making it easier to shape. Their clothes are all woven using the large soft white ferns of their palm trees, much the same as silk in the Realm of Man.

If there's one thing Tora misses about the Realm of Angels, it's training in the wide-open spaces. Being confined to Greenwich Village is like being a lab rat in a maze, chasing a bit of demon cheese. She misses leaping from rocky cliffs, climbing gigantic trees in the never-ending forests, trekking up mountains, flipping from tree to tree, and sparring with the other Valkyries. It didn't take her long to get the hang of the urban landscape, but it's not the same as untamed terrain.

After an hour or two of training, Tora wipes the sweat from her face and heads home, excited for her surprise. Maybe it's a birthday cake. Maybe it's a present. Maybe it's nothing at all except a birthday dinner or a piece of paper that says Happy Birthday. She doesn't care either way. The fact that Astra knew her well enough to make her twenty-first birthday special in any way is gift enough. It's something she never knew she always wanted. A birthday surprise.

"I'm home!" Tora calls out as she bounds into the kitchen, excited about her birthday for the first time in months. She doesn't have time to shower so she hopes Astra doesn't mind her sweaty hunting gear stinking up the room. She should be used to it by now.

Nothing but silence greets her.

Confused, she peeks out the window overlooking the ground-floor garden, but no one's there either. She searches the living room and bedrooms on the first floor and finds no one. No one at all.

Tora frowns. "Star?"

"I'm up with the chickens!" Astra yells from the third floor, laughter in her voice.

Oh god… she hopes the surprise isn't an egg. She's had enough eggs to last a lifetime, maybe two. There's nothing much up on the third floor. It's where they keep the chickens. The left half of the roof and the walls caved in during the war, but with some creative structural improvements, her mother was able to prevent the rest of the floor from completely collapsing.

The second floor isn't that great either, but it's where Tora feels most comfortable sleeping. It's private and boobytrapped with broken floors and falling beams. Thieves and thugs can get in, but they can't get out, not in one piece anyway.

"Surprise!" The floor erupts in a chorus of noise.

Tora jerks and throws a right-handed punch, unsure of what is happening or where the danger is.

"Surprise child." Her mother Freya catches her fist before impact, her voice resonating like a hymn. "Happy Birthday."

Tora blinks. The chickens are gone, replaced by a table filled with all different types of food from roast chicken to potatoes, salads, and fruits. Solar fairy lights hang around the room, strung over the crumbling walls, beams, structure supports, and old doorways. The sun lowers in the distance, casting a warm orange glow on the wooden chairs and floorboards.

In the corner, there's a table full of wrapped gifts in colorful paper and cloth. Bo stands with Dr Arnold and his heavily pregnant wife Michelle. The other squad members, Shannon, Maree, Cheryl, Mandy, Teresa, Victor, and Phil hover over the food, waiting until they're allowed to dig in, all dressed in black army pants and black shirts, ready for the hunt. Her people, her family, her squad, and her friends, all together in her home to celebrate her birthday.

"Happy Birthday!" Astra hugs her tightly. "I know it's not the Valkyrie ritual but how about a party instead?"

"I can't believe you did this." Tora chokes back tears. No one has ever done anything like this for her before. A day to celebrate her life, her birth. It doesn't even bother her that the butthole Ethan is there skulking by the staircase. Nothing could ruin this perfect night. "I thought you were going to give me an egg."

"An egg?" Astra bursts out laughing. "God, I wish I'd given you an egg."

Tora chuckles. An egg would have been a weird ass gift but it's been a weird ass year.

"Hey T?" Victor Zhào yells, his light leafy green eyes alive with mischief. "Where's the Vodka? I'm ready to get fucked up!"

Tora rolls her eyes. Trust Victor to go straight for the alcohol. He would drink the distillery dry if he could. "No drinking jughead. The hunt starts at sundown. Drink on your own time."

Victor's the one who introduced her to vodka after their first hunt as a squad. Before that, she'd only ever tasted the amber ale of the Valkyries.

"Told ya dumbass." Phil Bans, the eldest of the Odd Squad smacks him over the back of the head then shakes out his hand. "What the hell is on your head? Concrete?"

Victor's dark black hair is gelled into spikes, making him look even more like a porcupine than normal. There must be an entire tube of gel in his hair. You could dead set use his head as a sword.

"Your hair stabbed me!" Phil laughs and holds up his hand to show the small indents.

It took Tora a few weeks to get Phil to trust her when they started working together. She didn't even know he had a wife and two little twin girls for an entire month. The guy has seen more death than all the squad put together and not just in the War of the Gods.

Phil was in the Marines for twenty years and took Victor under his wing when he joined three years ago. Scars line the right side of his face and cheek, netting across his shaved head. He doesn't talk about it much but Tora can see the loss on his face, the hollow dimming of his light blue eyes.

"Can we at least eat now?" Teresa Sanchez hovers over the roast chicken and bread rolls like she's waiting for the starting gun in a race. Her black hair is braided on either side of her head, much like the Vikings of old, her brown eyes filled only with hunger. An image of something Bo calls "Pac-man eating a burger" is stamped on her cheeks and forehead in blue ink.

"Yeah T. You took your sweet ass time getting here." Shannon Dates grins at Teresa, her gray-blue eyes soft and warm. "Teresa's been drooling for half an hour."

Without warning, Teresa jumps onto Cheryl Liu's back and hugs her like a koala. Cheryl tries to shake her off but Teresa licks the side of her face and grins. "Tastes like chicken."

Tora laughs. Teresa is like a tsunami wrapped inside a hurricane. You always walk away from her frazzled, bruised, or wet.

Before the war, she was a doctor at the children's hospital. Needless to say, her skills have come in handy more than once. The human leaders wanted Teresa off the hunt in case they needed another Doctor but she refuses to be away from Shannon.

"Get off crazy!" Cheryl manages to shake her off and peels her dark black hair off her saliva-covered cheek.

Cheryl is the Queen of Resting Bitchface. Before the war, she was a high-flying Lawyer in New York City on her way to becoming a partner in one of the most sought-after firms. The hours were killer and kept her away from her husband and kids, but she always thought it would be worth it in the end, that she would be able to spend more time with them once she became a partner.

But her plan got shot to shit when the war crossed over into the Realm of Man and killed her entire family, including her husband, her young six-year-old son, her parents, in-laws, grandparents, uncles, aunties, and cousins.

It was her son's sixth birthday party, and as always, she was running late. She was with a client in Greenwich Village. Her family was celebrating at a local park on the other side of the city. Greenwich survived; the rest of the city did not.

Working was the only thing that saved her life but Cheryl doesn't see it that way. She would rather have died with her family than survive without them.

"Oh, you loved it." Teresa bounces up behind Cheryl and licks the other side of her face.

"Ugh!" Cheryl jerks and wipes at her face, outrage darkening her features further. She kicks back her chair and chases Teresa around the room, screaming obscenities and grabbing small bits of glitter and decorations off the tables to throw at her.

"That's my girl." Shannon chuckles, her eyes following Teresa around the room.

It looks like Shannon's being a little festive tonight and dyed her short bleached blonde hair in a rainbow of pastel colors. Shannon and Teresa met about six months before the war hit at a local bar in Greenwich where Shannon worked as a bartender, but it wasn't until after the war that they got together. Neither were shy but the timing wasn't right.

Shannon is the calmest, most amazing human Tora has ever met. There's not a whole lot that can rattle the girl. Her life before the war was anything but mundane. She traveled everywhere across the globe, checked out museums, artifacts, art, went to concerts any chance she got, and took advantage of everything the human world had to offer. The girl knew how to live.

"Idiots." Maree Ball rolls her sea-blue eyes and ties her brown shoulder-length hair into a bun, making sure any wispy bits are secured. Her black hunting gear is pristine and wrinkle-free; her black boots shine with fresh polish.

Maree was the last to join the Odd Squad, only stepping forward when shy Mandy Henders joined. No one really knows Maree's story except that she stumbled into Greenwich Village hours after the city was destroyed, covered in cuts, blood, and bruises with Mandy by her side.

No one has been able to find out what happened to her, nor do they know anything about her life before the war, but she is fiercely protective of Mandy. She treats her like a daughter and constantly tries to shelter her from fighting the demons and fae, even though Mandy is more than capable.

Mandy is the youngest and sweetest of the squad. Her golden blonde hair is neat and trimmed to her shoulder in waves. Her eyes are large, baby blue, and lined with long black eyelashes. It's her shy, polite attitude that confuses most people. She's the last person you would expect to find hunting demons and fae, but the girl has a natural talent.

By the time the war spilled over into the Realm of Man, Mandy had already lost her parents and younger brother in a horrific car crash weeks before, leaving her with severe burns to her chest and left arm. The foster family who cared for her after the crash perished in the War of the Gods, but she had only known them for a few hours at the time. That's when she met Maree.

The girl surprised them all on one of the first hunts when she saved Phil's life. She wasn't even part of the squad at the time. She just sort of appeared out of the darkness and drove a long rusty knife into the heart of one of the fae who had gotten the jump on Phil. Hours later, she and Maree officially joined the squad.

Tora grins. The Odd Squad. Her highly untrained, undisciplined team of alcoholic misfits. Useless at a dinner party; deadly on the hunt.

"Actually…" Freya interrupts, the authority in her voice freezing everyone in the room. "I changed the schedule. The Odd Squad won't be hunting tonight. I've replaced you with the Ninja Squad."

"The Ninja Squad?" Tora screws up her face. "Who the hell are the Ninja Squad?"

Bo laughs and joins them. "It's the Stealth Squad. They changed their name again."

Tora rolls her eyes. Four squads of nine hunters patrol the village, including the Odd Squad, the Saint Squad, the Dog Squad, and the Ninja Squad, previously known as the Stealth Squad, previously known as the Demon Squad, previously known as the Awesome Squad. There are plenty more name changes but she lost count months ago.

Every night, three squads patrol the village and the perimeter on a rotating roster while her mother Freya patrols the sky inside and outside the village.

"Drinks are up!" Astra rolls in a trolley full of alcohol bottles, her face flushed. Ethan hovers not far behind her.

The Odd Squad cheer and rush to the trolley, grabbing glasses and bottles in a blur of hands.

"You didn't need to do that Mom," Tora says, surprised her mother thought to give her the night off. It's not like her at all. For the last year, the hunt has always come first. If her mother had it her way, the four squads would constantly be on patrol. The only reason she gives them two days off is because the humans complained. Valkyries don't do weekends. "I like the hunt. You know that."

"You're not hunting tonight. That's final." Freya snaps and joins Dr and Mrs Arnold in the corner.

Tora flinches like she was slapped.

"That was weird." Bo frowns.

"I know, right?" Tora throws up her hands. At least she's not crazy. It's not just her imagination. Her mother is acting strange. Even more bitchy than usual. "She's been weird for a while now."

Why wouldn't she want her on the hunt tonight? After the child demon attack last night, she thought she'd want her out there day and night. It's not like Freya to give her a night off. It's not like Freya to say yes to a party, even

65

if Astra did all the organizing. Something else is going on. She just doesn't know what.

"I'll check the pier on my way home; make sure no more creepy kids come out to play," Bo says. "The Ninja Squad are guaranteed to skip it after last night."

Tora smiles. Bo — beautiful, reliable Bo. Before the War of the Gods, he volunteered at a homeless shelter and worked at one of the local high schools as a coach. When the War of the Gods hit, he was on a bus on his way into Greenwich Village with one of his classes. There was nothing he could do. It happened so fast. An angel and a demon were locked in battle and slammed into the bus at lightning speed.

The bus was torn in two. The front slid into Greenwich Village at one hundred miles an hour and slammed into a building. It was a miracle that Bo survived. He broke his leg, both his arms, and was covered in deep lacerations, littering his body with scars. The bus driver died instantly. The rest of the bus and the thirty-eight sixteen-year-old students on board died in the Deadlands. It wasn't the crash that killed them. It wasn't the impact. It was a hoard of fire-breathing lizard demons that torched the bus.

Bo blames himself for their deaths. It was his idea to go on a field trip to the Whitney Museum of American Art, and even though it had nothing to do with gym class, the school allowed it. He also blames himself for the death of his parents and seventeen-year-old sister who arrived at his apartment on the other side of town that morning for a surprise week-long visit. He couldn't save his students, he couldn't save his parents, and he couldn't save his young sister. He couldn't save anyone. No one could.

"Hey T!" Victor downs his third vodka shot. "Get your munchkin butt over here and drink with us."

Teresa sits on Shannon's lap with her arm draped around her shoulder and steals her shot. "Yeah, you're the birthday girl!"

"Want to get wasted?" Bo nudges her with his elbow and winks, all traces of anger from their argument gone.

Grinning, Tora locks arms with Bo and drags him over to the squad. How can she say no to that? Good friends, family, food, and vodka? That's all a birthday girl needs. She'll deal with her mother tomorrow. "Not too wasted. You owe me a private celebration later."

Putting all thoughts of her mother's motives out of her mind, Tora relaxes and settles into her birthday celebrations, drinking shots with the squad, mingling with the Arnolds, Astra, and even her mother. The only one she ignores is Ethan, not that he or Astra notice. He sits by Astra's side, listening in on their conversations with a look of superiority on his stupid face.

For hours the squad drinks, recanting stories of the hunt while Dr Arnold listens intently, taking notes in his pocketbook. Astra and Tora reminisce about their lives back home in the Realm of Angels, capturing everyone's attention.

Even her mother seems to be enjoying herself. She shares a rare smile, listening to the stories of their home. For the first time in her life, the woman looks relaxed, although she's more than likely relieved the day is nearly over, and Tora can never ask her to perform the ritual again.

"Oh my god." Tora jumps to her feet as Astra carries a birthday cake into the room with twenty-one lit candles on top. A birthday cake — for her. Her very first birthday cake. She didn't even see her leave the room.

"Happy Birthday to you," Astra sings the traditional human birthday song. Freya joins in.

Tora can't help but laugh. Both her mother and Astra sound like mating cats, but it means the world to her that they learned the words. Everyone but Ethan sings along, tightening Tora's throat with gratitude.

Only Astra would think to give her the one thing she's wanted since she first saw a birthday party in the park. A celebration, a cake; a ritual, even if it is only blowing out the candles.

"Make a wish." Astra grins. "Anything at all"

Closing her eyes, Tora makes a wish and blows out the candles, knowing it won't come true; a wish to be a fully-fledged Valkyrie, for her mother to magically change her mind. It will never happen, but she never thought she'd have a birthday party either.

"Who wants cake?" Astra laughs as Mrs Arnold practically shoulder barges the Odd Squad to get the first piece.

"Never get in the way of a pregnant woman and a piece of cake." Dr Arnold winks at her mother.

"Don't I know it?" Her mother laughs.

Tora gapes. It's like her mother is a person — like a normal person. It's creepier than seeing a demon with ringlets.

"How about a tour?" Bo whispers close to Tora's ear.

Blushing, Tora glances around the room to make sure no one is paying them any attention then starts towards the stairs. She knows she shouldn't. The chances of getting caught are high, but she can't help herself. It's her birthday and she wants to celebrate.

"I'll show you where the restroom is," Tora says loud enough for her mother's observant ears and stumbles down the stairs.

No one pays them any attention, too caught up in the festivities and prospect of cake. Chocolate cake is somewhat of a commodity in their world, and no one wants to miss out. They won't even notice they're gone, and her mother's talking to Dr Arnold about his book and the nine realms so she'll be stuck there for ages. They're safe.

Giggling, Tora grabs Bo's warm hand and drags him toward her room on the second floor, her mind a blanket of intoxicating fog and excitement.

No one but Tora ever goes on the second floor, and the broken and creaky boards should tell them if anyone decides to go for a wander.

Heart pounding in her ears, Tora pulls Bo into her bathroom and pushes him up against the wall. Fire burns through her stomach and into her chest, her skin alive with electricity as a sense of urgency floods her veins.

In the back of her mind, she knows it's too risky. They could be caught at any second, but the thought only excites her further. She hasn't felt like this since they first made out after taking down a spider demon months ago.

Bo's hot breath caresses her neck. He licks his lips and lifts her onto the basin, his moan filled with lust as his tongue desperately searches her mouth. An explosion of heat scorches her body, spreading across her skin like wildfire. Her breathing deepens into a light moan as she reaches for the buckle on his belt and struggles with the latch.

"Get off my daughter." Her mother's low menacing voice growls like an angry dog.

Bo jerks back. "Freya…"

"Mom!" Tora gasps and jumps off the sink, the thunderous look on her mother's face stabbing at her stomach.

Fuck!

"Party's over." Her mother tightens her jaw and storms out of the room, her footsteps echoing like a bass drum.

Tora stares at the broken floor tiles, unable to move, unable to breathe. This is so bad. She is so dead; like buried in the ground being eaten by worms dead.

"Fuck!" She grips the sink. She can hear her mother upstairs kicking everyone out, instructing Phil to escort Ethan home and Shannon and Teresa to escort the Arnolds.

"Fuck fuck fuck fuck!" Tora panics and thumps the sink. Her flushed face, raw lips, and wide pastel purple eyes stare back through the cracked mirror. This can't be happening. Freya will never forgive her. She'll never trust her again.

Fuck!

Footsteps pound down the stairs as the party disperses, her squad and friends mumbling amongst themselves as to the reason for the sudden end to the festivities and Tora and Bo's whereabouts.

"It'll be okay Tora." Bo rests his hands on her shoulders and tries to calm her. "She was going to find out eventually. Once she gets used to the idea, she'll come around."

"No Bo." Tora scoffs and jerks her shoulders out of his grasp; mad at him; mad at herself, at her mother; the world. "She won't. You don't know my mother."

"Tora…" Bo sighs, the same argument ready on his lips.

"Just go, Bo. I'll talk to you later." Tora drops her forehead on the mirror. How could she be so stupid? Her mother will never understand. The woman has never had a relationship in her life. Valkyries rarely do. She'll be lucky if she doesn't stitch up her vagina with barbed wire.

Steeling his jaw, Bo shakes his head and leaves. He doesn't understand. He's human. How could he? The existence of angels, demons, gods, and Valkyries is new to him. He doesn't understand the consequences.

Daughter or not, Freya is going to tear her apart. She disobeyed a direct order from her mother, from her Commander. The punishment within the Valkyries' ranks would be death. She doubts her mother will execute her, but the punishment won't be light, nor will it be quick. It will be long, tedious, and drawn out, just like the remainder of Tora's celibate life will be.

Resigned to her fate, Tora waits until she hears the front door close and drags herself up the stairs, ready for whatever punishment or argument her mother has waiting for her. It's not going to be pretty. Somehow, she doubts she'll ever forget her twenty-first birthday now. First a party, then a hanging. She is so dead.

Silent tears fall down Astra's cheeks as she sweeps the room to keep herself busy. She locks eyes with Tora and drops her shoulders in defeat. She doesn't have to say a word. Astra knows exactly what happened and is frightened her mother will realize she's with Ethan; frightened she'll find out they both disobeyed the rules.

With her large pristine white swan-like wings spread out behind her, Freya stands on the edge of the floor, looking out at the city below, her shoulders and muscles tensed; the wall mostly destroyed in the War of the Gods.

"Mom…" Tora braces herself. "I…"

"One rule Tora!" Freya flexes her wings and glances back over her shoulder, her eyes murderous and rimmed in red. "Keep your legs shut!"

"I know, but…" Tora automatically tries to defend herself but has nothing to say. It's true. She broke the rules. She has no excuse, except that she doesn't want to be celibate and alone, confined to live in the Realm of Man without any type of affection for the rest of her life. But her mother would never understand that. She never understands anything but the battle.

"I don't want to hear it! You will not leave this house until I return. Both of you!" Freya snaps, her purple eyes flashing with shards of white. "Pack your things. We leave after midnight."

"Leave?" Astra drops the broom. "What do you mean leave? Where are we going?"

Tora screws up her face. What the hell is her mother on about? There's nowhere to go. They can't go back home to the Realm of the Angels, and the surrounding city is a demon death trap, even for fledgling Valkyries.

"Montauk. The town survived and is protected. They're able to block the demon portals completely. I was going to go myself to find out their secret, but since you two can't be trusted, you will come with me and stay there. We can make it there in a few days, less if we don't sleep."

Raising her chin, Freya flaps her large white wings and takes off into the night without another word, her silhouette cloaked by the building storm.

"No!" Astra sobs and rushes to the edge.

Tora stares at the floor. Montauk. So that's her mother's plan. Stuff them away in a protected town where the dangerous humans can't impregnate them. No hunting, no fighting, no love, and no sex. That's her punishment. Sentenced to a life of boredom.

"Fuck!" Tora kicks a chair and smashes the wood against the wall before pegging an empty vodka bottle off the third floor. "Why does she always have to be such a bitch? She won't perform the ritual, she won't let us go home, and she expects us to remain celibate and subdued forever!"

Covering her face with her hands, Astra crumbles to the floor, her entire body convulsing as she struggles to breathe through the tears.

"Oh Star." Tora drops down beside her. God, she can be so stupid and insensitive. This affects them both. Astra will never be able to see Ethan again, and as much as she hates the guy, Astra is in love with him.

This is all her fault. If she had just waited until her mother left, or waited until the next night on the hunt, none of this would have happened. But no. She had to get drunk and fondle the guests. "I'm so sorry. This is all my fault."

"She... she... she... can't. I can't." Astra hiccups and curls into the fetal position with her head resting on Tora's knees. Tears stream down her face. "We can't."

"We'll think of something." Tora lies and strokes Astra's hair, making a promise she knows she can't keep. Once her mother has decided on something, there is no convincing her otherwise. As far as her mother is concerned, they are soldiers in a war and don't get to have lives of their own. "Before she comes home, we'll think of something to change her mind. We have to."

CHAPTER SIX

Staring at the kitchen table, Astra and Tora contemplate their futures. They both know there's nothing they can do. Freya can't be reasoned with. She is as unyielding in life as she is in battle. She does not compromise, especially when she's angry and feels betrayed.

"I'm going to find Bo." Tora wobbles to her feet, the vodka strong in her veins. If her mother is going to make them move, she's at least going to say goodbye to Bo and the squad. Fuck the consequences. "I'll be back in an hour."

"Your mother will kill you if she finds out." Astra rubs her face, her shoulders rounded in defeat.

Tora shrugs. Her mother's already shattered their lives by making them move. She's not about to leave without saying goodbye to Bo and the squad. They're family, and they won't understand. They'll think she abandoned them. "What more can she do to us? She's already making us move."

"You're right." Astra lifts her head. Tears stain her cheeks. "I'm going to go see Ethan."

"I'll walk you." Tora forces her lips into a smile and helps Astra to her feet, trying to hide her hatred for the turd of a man. "It's on the way."

The only good thing to come from moving is that she'll never have to see Astra's douchebag boyfriend again.

Setting out into the dark street, Tora and Astra promise to return in an hour. Tora drops Astra off at Ethan's on the next street over and continues in a jog down to the pier, watching carefully for any portals, demons, or fae.

The streets are quiet, barely lit by the moon as it peeks out from behind the clouds. Thunder rumbles in the distance as storm clouds gather in the sky. Tora taps the leg of her cargo pants, making sure her torch is still safely tucked away in her pocket as she passes the piers, relieved there are no child demons tonight.

Demons and fae aren't her concern right now. It's her mother and the Ninja Squad she needs to avoid. If her mother finds out what she's doing, she'll make them leave immediately and she'll never get to say goodbye.

If the Ninja Squad finds her, they'll escort her home or tell her mother when she checks in, just to show her up. She can imagine their smug faces as Freya tears strips off her. They would love it.

"Tora?" Bo emerges from the shadows.

Tora skids to a stop, a pang of sadness weighing heavily on her chest as Bo walks towards her, his black hoodie held tight around his body, molding around his large muscles.

Her throat tightens. She knew she would miss him but she didn't realize how much until now. She'll miss the stubble on his face, the roughness of his hands, the honey in his voice, and the warmth of his skin. Who will keep an eye on him when she's gone? Who will take her place in his bed?

Wasting no time on awkward apologies, Tora runs and jumps up into his arms. There's no point in hiding anymore. Her mother knows everything and the worst is happening. "What are you still doing out here?"

Chuckling, Bo gently puts her on the ground. "Vic sent me out to find more booze, not that they need it. They'll probably pass out by the time I get back."

Tora smiles and looks away as her eyes fill with hot tears. She's going to miss the Odd Squad; Teresa's free spirit, Victor's humor, Mandy's shyness, Maree's stoic mothering, Phil's gruff exterior, Shannon's loyalty, and most of all, she's going to miss Bo. Beautiful, brave, reliable Bo. The glue that holds them all together.

It's going to be hard to say goodbye, to explain why she has to leave, especially since they're drunk, but she has no other choice. It's the last chance she'll get.

"What are you doing out here?" Bo scans the street. "Is everything okay? Did your mother calm down?"

Shaking her head, Tora tells him everything; how her mother freaked out and is making them move.

"This is all my fault." Bo sighs. His shoulders slump. "If I had listened to you, this wouldn't have happened?"

"It's not your fault," Tora argues as a thousand tiny cuts slice her heart, her arteries stinging with loss. She and Bo aren't soul mates. They both know that, but over the past year, they've become comrades, friends, family, then lovers, a tiny bit of passion and beauty in this broken world. They heal each other, and after tonight, that's over.

"God, the village is going to freak when they find out you guys left." Bo rubs the back of his neck. "Fuck! They're going to kill me. Are you sure we can't convince her to stay?"

"Freya Thurgood will not go back on an order." Tora shakes her head, her heart heavy as she thinks about her future; a future without Bo, without the squad, without Dr Arnold and the other survivors. "Just tell the village it's a recon mission to stop the portals. It's not a total lie."

Maybe once her mother understood love and friendship. Tucked away in Tora's childhood memories, she remembers her mother sharing an ale on their deck with other Valkyries, but those days are long gone. Her mother doesn't like to get close to anyone, not even her own daughter anymore.

"Will I ever see you again?" Bo looks away.

"I — I don't think so." A sob escapes Tora's lips as she wipes a stray tear. After tonight, it will just be her, Astra, and her mother; strangers from a foreign realm in a town that will more than likely fear them. It took forever to get the people of Greenwich to accept them. They'll be outcast, hated, and maybe even blamed. Moving is going to be horrible for so many reasons. "I just came to say goodbye."

Wrapping his large arm around her shoulders, Bo hugs her tight to his body and walks her back to the squad's place at the Whitney Art Museum, the smell of coconut, vodka, and fire smoke lingering on his skin. It's one of the things she'll miss most about him. His warm scent and the heat from his skin has always had a way of comforting her.

She will never feel his touch again, hear his deep voice, taste his lips, or smell his warm scent. Her mother can always fly back to Greenwich, but without the ritual, Tora will never get her wings, and it's a few days' trek through the Deadlands without them.

This is it. This is goodbye; forever.

"Come with me," Bo whispers and takes her hand as he unlocks the door and guides her into one of the exhibition rooms.

A large open room greets her, the surrounding walls covered in magnificent paintings from before the war. Marble stands with sculptures are placed strategically around the room. In the middle of the floor, a large tent glows brilliantly against the darkness, surrounded by a glowing lake of aqua pebbles, lighting the entire room.

"I found some phosphorescent powder and paint a few days ago. I thought I'd try it out, and if it worked, I'd paint some things around town; you know, so it's easier to see at night. This was meant to be your birthday present. A romantic night at the lake." Bo glances back at the display and grins.

Tora widens her eyes. It's stunning, like something out of a fairytale. She can't believe how lucky she is to have two amazing people in her life like Astra and Bo. They both gave her something beautiful for her birthday while her mother gave her something devastating.

"It's beautiful." Tora chokes, fighting back tears. To find any moment of beauty in their broken world is a miracle. It makes her wonder how many moments of beauty she will have without Bo.

"Not as beautiful as you." Bo rests his hands on her hips and walks his fingers around to her back.

Chuckling, Tora pulls him close. "Just kiss me, you idiot."

Bo doesn't need to be told twice. His tongue dances elegantly in her mouth as he presses his muscular body up against hers and lifts her into the air, wrapping her legs around his waist.

Pins and needles break out across her skin. Fire burns her throat, scorching her insides, her clothes suddenly too restrictive and suffocating as she pulls off her jacket. Bo moves his lips from her mouth and kisses her neck as she gasps for air, her face flushing red, her body alive with currents of desire cascading like a waterfall from her head down to her toes.

It doesn't matter where she lives now. Her mother will watch her like a hawk. She'll never get to feel the excitement of a first kiss again, the warmth of another body against her skin. This is it. No more love, no more lust, no more hunting, just a long boring life.

But right now, there's Bo. This night will have to last her a lifetime.

Tora pulls off her shirt and takes Bo's from his back, the heat of his body burning through her black cotton bra and sinking deep into her chest. Every fiber of her body wants to let go, to give in and forget about the outside world, but a creaking sound pricks at her ears. As much as she wants to ignore it, she can't.

"Bo, stop." Tora breathes in a moan. "I heard something."

"Don't worry. It's probably one of the squad." Bo continues licking, kissing, and nibbling on her neck.

Tora inhales sharply as he bites her weak spot, right where the shoulder and the neck connect. She tries to resist, but her body betrays her, melting like warm water across frozen skin. "I don't want them to see me half naked."

"So, take it all off." Bo grins and continues to make her squirm, nuzzling her neck.

Giggling, Tora smacks his shoulder. She's hardly shy, but exposing herself to the entire squad isn't exactly the way she wants to be remembered.

"Yeah. Take it all off." An unfamiliar male voice echoes off the museum walls.

Bo spins around and shoves her behind him, using his large bulking body to protect her. Tora gasps.

Shit! They forgot to lock the door.

"The museum is closed." Bo squints into the darkness. "Find someplace else."

Holding her arm across her chest, Tora fumbles on the ground for her shirt, her cheeks flushed with embarrassment. Busted twice in one night. Just her luck. At least it's not her mother again. It's not one of the Odd Squad either. It must be one of the stupider residents, venturing out at night. It would serve them right if they got eaten by a demon or kidnapped by the fae.

Out of the darkness, a hooded figure steps into the glow of the pebbles and tent, a slimy lop-sided grin the only thing they can see from under the dark hood.

"Oh, we don't want your home." The man practically sings and removes his hood, revealing a head of light gray hair and pale gray eyes rimmed in deep blue. A thick band has been shaved into his eyebrow where a row of three circular piercings hang.

"Mother Fucker." Tora groans as she realizes who the intruder guy is.

Tonight of all nights, her last night in Greenwich Village, the stupid ass thugs from the market target her.

Fuck! She can't catch a break tonight.

CHAPTER SEVEN

Idiots! The thugs finally target them for their eggs and they get the location wrong. All they're going to get is a bunch of art and the drunken Odd Squad.

The main guy is the thug from the market, the one Ethan called Flenn. Eight other people of varying sizes and sex step out of the shadows, all with dark blue hoods drawn over their heads.

"We just want her." Flenn nods at Tora.

Tora smirks. This is hilarious. The thugs aren't trying to steal from them. They're looking for a fight. How goddamned stupid can they be? She's a Valkyrie who hunts demons every night. Eight humans aren't a threat. She's going to kick this guy's ass. That's if she can find her damn shirt.

"Get out." Bo snaps, his voice low and menacing.

Flenn grins. "Make me."

Giving up on finding her shirt, Tora stands by Bo's side, her arms loose and ready to fight as the thugs spread out in a semicircle, blocking off their exits.

After everything that's happened in the last year, she knew the thugs were stupid, but she didn't know they were this stupid. No civilian in their right mind would attack a military squad, so why would they think hunters and a Valkyrie were easy targets?

One of the thug's inches around to her side and charges without warning. Tora whips her head over her shoulder, squats low, and sweeps her leg, causing the thug to trip. She stands and punches them in the face, the satisfying crunch of breaking bones vibrating against her knuckles. The thug slides along the polished concrete floor into the shadows.

Another lunges at Bo. He jabs the thug in the throat, forcing them back. The thug grabs at his neck and falls back into a pillar.

Hearing the commotion, the rest of the squad stumble down the stairs in a drunken mess, tripping over each other; all except Phil who must have been smart enough to go home to his wife and two little girls. The squad sees the thugs and laugh.

"Wrong home fuckers!" Teresa launches onto the back of one of the thugs' and jams two fingers into their eye. The thug screams, the sound like a high-pitched two-toned bat.

Flailing, the thug manages to throw Teresa off and doubles over, cradling its face.

Tora widens her eyes and looks at Bo's paling face. A stab of fear juts into the back of her throat. Bo knows as well as she does that humans don't scream like that; they don't have two-toned voices, and they don't sound like bats

The other thugs begin to move in around them but Flenn holds out his arm, motioning for them to stop.

Rolling on the ground in fits of laughter, Teresa holds up the thug's eye like a trophy, too drunk to understand what's happening. The rest of the squad eye each other warily, no doubt thinking the same as Bo and Tora.

The thug lifts his head and smiles as blood drips down his cheek onto his lips, staining his sharp piranha teeth black.

"Pixie." Mandy gasps and takes a step back.

Blood-red blotches bleed across the pixie's skin as his glamor falls away. Black vine-like tattoo markings snake across his face and neck. The other thugs remove their hoods, revealing six other red-skinned pixies with black vine-like markings covering their bodies and dark hair, and two humans, including Flenn.

Tora frowns. The malevolent fae don't work with humans. They kidnap them, use them, maim them, and eat them. They don't hang out with them, and they definitely don't take orders from them.

"God humans are stupid." Flenn takes off his black hoodie, throws it at the pixie closest to Tora, and pulls the collar up of his crisp white shirt. "Salt circles only work on unevolved demons and the stupid-stitious fae."

"Shit!" Tora mutters under her breath and scans the room, looking for the exits. They are so fucked. Flenn's not human either.

"It's superstitious dumbass." Shannon snarls, completely missing his joke.

"Not too bright, are you?" Flenn curls his lip and fixes the sleeves of his black Armani suit, disdain dripping from his tongue. "Let me break this down for you rainbow bright. Salt circles work on lower-level demons. It's like bug repellant. It doesn't work on the fae, and it doesn't work on the rest of demon kind. Only the stupidest of fae think it's bad luck to cross a salt circle, like an old wives' tale. You've been killing bugs. That's it. You're just pest control."

Tora stares at the floor as Flenn's dark laughter echoes in her ears. Bugs? The demons were just bugs? They've been killing bugs all this time?

"Fuck!" Tora swears under her breath. Her mother told her there were different types of demons but she didn't fully understand. For every butterfly in the Realm of Man, there is a demon equivalent in the Demon Realm.

For every dog, cat, lion, monkey, fly, and human, there is an equivalent in the Demon Realm, the same as any other realm. And if salt circles don't work on them, what hope do they have if they come through the portals? Why haven't they come through the portals?

"Ah. The short one understands." Flenn leans on the wall and crosses his arms over his chest.

Tora's head snaps up. She glares into Flenn's smug pale gray eyes rimmed in deep blue.

"Then you might understand this." Flenn tilts his head. "Come with us now and I'll think about sparing one or two of your friends. You can even choose which ones."

"Bullshit!" The now one-eyed pixie snarls and bares his teeth, the gaping hole where his eye used to be bleeding dark oozing blood. "Bitch took my eye. Law says eye for an eye."

"Over my dead body!" Shannon lunges forward but Maree holds her back.

Grinning, Teresa dangles the pixie's eye in the air and blows him a kiss. The pixie growls and starts towards her.

"Enough!" Flenn glares daggers at the pixie, causing him to shrink back then turns his attention to Tora. "Now... What do you say shorty?"

"Fuck you asshole." Tora spits at his feet, her pores seething with hatred. She's not sacrificing anyone.

"Time to die fuckers!" Victor grabs a horned statue off a display pillar and charges one of the pixies.

That's all it takes for the rest of the squad to jump in, creating pure chaos. Mandy slams a vase over one of the human's heads and follows through with a hard kick to the chest. Teresa scrambles to her feet, all humor gone from her face as the one-eyed pixie charges at her, dark blood staining its red skin. Shannon sprints towards them. Cheryl skids across the ground and kicks a male pixie in the crotch, dropping him hard to the ground, holding his groin.

"Tora!" Bo pulls his blade from his boot and holds it out to his side.

Tearing her eyes away from her squad, Tora turns to find the female pixie she knocked down earlier advancing at her side, the male pixie Bo throat punched advancing on the other side. She can't get distracted. She has to trust the squad to fight for themselves. They've hunted together every night for nearly a year. They can take down a few fae.

Retrieving the knife strapped to her leg, Tora keeps close to Bo, protecting his back as he protects hers. The female pixie sneers, baring razor-sharp teeth coated in black oozing blood from her newly broken nose. An old scar travels from her ear to her lips.

Tora narrows her eyes. It's the thug from the market. The one with the scar. The pixies were there. Out in the open in the middle of the day. Malevolent fae were moving unnoticed in Greenwich Village. She knew something was different about the demons and fae lately but she had no way of knowing this.

Their information was wrong. Her mother's information on salt circles was wrong. Greenwich Village isn't safe or protected at all. Demons and fae can do whatever the fuck they want, whenever the fuck they want. No one and nowhere is safe.

The female pixie lunges, her razor-sharp clawed nails ready to strike.

"I said enough!" Flenn throws out his arms, his voice booming throughout the museum. Red energy releases from his body, the blast rippling like an atomic bomb, the rings targeting everyone in the room.

The female pixie freezes mid-lunge. The glass walls shatter.

"I can't move,' Bo yells over a crack of thunder.

A string of incoherent swear words mingle together as the Odd Squad struggle against their invisible restraints. Tora tries to move but she's frozen, every muscle in her body flexed and aching.

They are so fucked. Flenn's a warlock. A Nephilim. A byproduct of god and human. If her mother had performed the ritual, she would be able to defeat him, but not as a fledgling. She doesn't have the power.

Chuckling, Flenn taps his lips with his finger and slowly paces around the room. "You know, all this could have been avoided if you, Bo, is it? If you just gave up the girl when I asked."

"Never!" Bo growls.

"Okay!" Tora forces the word out of her mouth. "If you want me, take me. Just leave my squad alone."

It's not a surrender. Valkyries never surrender, but it will buy some time for the Odd Squad to get a message to her mother to come save her ass.

Flenn smirks, the blue border around his gray-colored eyes glowing. He approaches Victor struggling against the restraint and holds out his hand. A long sharp silver blade manifests in his palm as he grabs Victor's hair and pulls back his head.

Tora widens her eyes, panic tightening her throat. "Just take me and leave. I'm giving you what you wanted!"

"Too late short stuff." Without taking his eyes off Tora, Flenn drives the blade through Victor's chest.

"No!" Tora screams. Her insides shake like an earthquake as tears well in her eyes and a deep ache leaches out of her bones.

Victor's eyes widen. He coughs, splattering blood all over Flenn's black suit and white shirt. A gurgled sound bubbles from his chest as his head lolls to the side and his light brown eyes dim with death.

"Asshole!" Teresa cries, tears streaming down her face.

Flenn whips his head over his shoulder and grins like a giddy schoolgirl. "What was that? You call next?"

"No!" Shannon screams as Flenn skips over to Teresa like a child, her face burning red. Veins protrude out of her neck as she tries to break the restraints. "Leave her alone!"

"Flenn! Stop!" Tora yells and blinks back tears, her stomach souring with desperation. Her muscles burn as she tries to free herself. This is all her fault. She should have just gone with him. The squad would have left, found her mother and she would have saved her by now. Her friends are dying because of her stupid pride. "Please. Leave them alone. Just take me instead."

"No Flenn. Stop. Please. Leave them alone." Flenn mocks and rolls his eyes. "Boo fucking hoo."

In one quick move, he slices Teresa's throat. Blood gushes down her shirt onto the floor as a gurgled sound bubbles from her lips. Her eyes roll back in her head.

"No!" A heartbreaking scream rips free from Shannon's throat as tears stream down her face. She convulses and throws up on her shirt, still unable to move.

"Oh god. Will you all shut up! You had to know that was coming." Flinching away from Shannon in disgust, Flenn wipes his blade on Teresa's shirt and paces the room. He shakes his head and makes jazz fingers with his hands. "Ooh, big surprise. The asshole warlock is going to kill you all."

Tora stares at the lifeless shells of her two squad members, her two friends, their bodies still standing as the spell keeps them locked in place. Her chest aches. Her eyes burn with loss and hatred; her stomach curdles in disbelief.

They can't be dead. Only hours ago, they sat together, eating, drinking, and celebrating. They weren't even on the hunt. It was their night off.

Training didn't prepare her for a sadistic warlock. It didn't prepare her to watch her friends die. Training was supposed to prevent her from feeling helpless and weak, but right now, that's exactly how she feels. She just wants her mom.

There's nothing she can do. There's nothing anyone can do. They're all going to die, and it's her fault. If she hadn't humiliated the warlock at the markets, this never would have happened.

"Who's next?" Flenn asks, his voice gleeful and melodic. He looks at each of the Odd Squad then claps his hands. "I know. The quiet one always gets a big reaction."

"Stop! Just take me." Tora shouts, desperate to convince him to leave the squad alone. "I'll do whatever you want."

Flenn arches his left eyebrow and grins that stupid lopsided grin. "Oh, I know you will little bird. I want you to die, and you will soon enough. Just as soon as I'm done here with your little friends."

Mandy whimpers as Flenn approaches. Lightning zigzags across the sky, dancing along the museum floor. Thunder rumbles, deep and foreboding. Rain taps on the glass ceiling and walls, filling the halls with white noise.

"No!" Maree screams. "You fucking bastard. She's a child!"

"Watch out!" the scarred female pixie yells suddenly.

A bolt of lightning splits the sky as large pristine white wings smash through the ceiling, raining glass down on their heads.

"What the?" Flenn erects a protective barrier around himself and squints upwards, keeping the shards of glass from penetrating his skin.

Tora gasps. Her chest expands with hope.

"Fuck!" Flenn stumbles as a dagger lodges in his shoulder. He drops his blade.

"Mom!" Tora stumbles out of the immobilization spell. She never thought she'd be happy to see her mother. She came. She found them. They're okay. Everything is going to be okay.

The immobilization spell breaks. Victor and Teresa's bodies fall to the ground, dead. Crying, Shannon scrambles over to Teresa's blood-soaked corpse and pulls her into her arms.

Tora blinks rapidly through the chaos as the pixies and humans make a run for it, no doubt trying to escape through a portal while her mother, Maree, Cheryl, and Mandy give chase.

Gripping her blade, Tora charges at Flenn as Bo does the same. Her heart hammers in her chest. She's never killed a warlock before, but there's a first time for everything. The fucker is going to die screaming.

Reaching him first, Bo stabs blindly at Flenn in rage, but the warlock manages to twist his wrist and stab a blade through his shoulder. Crying out in pain, Bo falls to his knees and drops the knife as Tora flings her blade at Flenn's head. But it's no use. He's too fast. He catches the blade and ducks as Tora lunges at his neck with another knife.

Laughing, Flenn punches Tora hard in the face and slides across the ground like liquid, slicing through her heels on his way passed. He slams the blade into the back of her thigh.

Hot pain mirrors her screams as it climbs her leg and collapses her to her knees. Refusing to give up, she reaches for another blade, her target reflected through the last remaining glass wall, but she's too late. Flenn stands behind her, his hand gripping the hilt of a knife, ready to strike.

Tora drops her shoulders in defeat, any energy she has left leaking out of her veins. Even as Bo scrambles on the ground for his knife, she knows he won't be able to save her in time. This is it. This is the end. The warlock is too strong, too fast. Her legend will be how the fledgling Valkyrie died on her twenty-first birthday instead of undergoing the ritual.

"Happy Birthday Tora." Flenn grins his slimy lopsided grin.

"Get away from my daughter!" Her mother's voice booms off the museum walls. She appears out of the darkness like an avenging angel, her white and gold uniform glowing in the darkness.

Grabbing Flenn around the back of the neck, she snatches him up into the air, her purple eyes blazing like fire. With one sharp thrust, she propels Flenn through the remaining glass window, out into the chaotic storm.

Collapsing to the ground, Tora stares up in awe of her mother surrounded by raindrops and shattering glass. The woman is like a nuclear bomb. Never has she seen her so angry and full of rage. No wonder she was the Commander of the Valkyries.

"Tora!" Bo drops to her side. "Oh god! You're bleeding bad."

The world swims in colors as blood gushes from her wounds, the blade in her leg pulsating against her ligaments. She shivers violently, freezing despite the moderate temperature. The knife must have been spelled. She hasn't bled this much throughout her entire life.

Beautiful white wings descend from the ceiling as the golden battle goddess glides down to her side.

"The warlock is gone. He disappeared," Freya says.

"Mom?" Tora croaks.

"Oh Tora." Freya leans down and chokes back a sob. "What…"

Her mother suddenly stops mid-sentence. Her mouth opens in shock as tears fall down her cheeks.

"Mom?" Tora frowns through the fog of pain, confused her mother is crying at all.

Coughing, her mother looks down at her chest. Then Tora sees it. A glowing purple sword lodged through her mother's heart, straight through her golden armor. Blood blooms through her white Valkyrie uniform and puddles on the floor.

"Mom!" Tora screams as her mother sways on her feet.

"Freya Thurgood. For abandoning your post, you are sentenced to death." A female voice echoes over the storm. "The will of the gods, so mote it be."

Smiling softly, Freya Thurgood looks down warmly at Tora, her eyes filled with nothing but love. She drops to the ground dead and disintegrates into golden dust.

Tora screams as pain explodes in her chest, imploding deep into her soul. Her stomach clenches as waves of nausea rocket through her body. Her mother is dead. Someone stabbed her. Someone killed her. Killed a fully-fledged Valkyrie. It's not possible. She can't be dead. Valkyries are near immortal. Only a demon blade can kill a Valkyrie.

"For fucks sake! Shut her up!" Someone yells as Bo is knocked out and dragged away.

Two people come out of nowhere and pin Tora's arms to the ground as another two pin her legs. She desperately bucks and kicks but it's no use; they're too strong.

Four perfectly sculpted female faces stare down at her with royal purple eyes; all of them tall, stunningly beautiful with tight braiding in their hair and huge pristine white wings spread out on their backs.

Each wear distinctive double-breasted razorback vests with intricate metal weaving, tight black pants with pockets, chains, large belts, and knife holders strapped to their waists, hips, and legs. A tattoo of a sword and spread-out swan wings adorn their foreheads, stretching to the bridge of their noses, the same as her mother had.

"Tora Thurgood?" A woman with lily-white hair and skin as black as night kneels by her head, holding her right arm.

Valkyries. Valkyries killed her mother. But why? And how? She was one of them; fought with them for centuries; was their Commander. There shouldn't even be anymore Valkyries. They supposedly died out in the War of the Gods.

"You killed her!" Tora sobs and bucks, trying to free herself, her heart aching with unbearable loss. The bitches killed her mother; her fierce beautiful mother. "You killed my mom! She was one of you, and you killed her!"

"Sounds like confirmation to me." A woman with cinnamon skin and white and black braids shrugs and flips a medallion in her hand as she comes back into the room, the same Valkyrie marking on her forehead. "Two minutes to go and only one way to find out."

Tora narrows her eyes. She's the one who took Bo, the one who knocked him out and dragged him away. If she survives this, the woman is dead, Valkyrie or not.

"Do it." The woman with white hair nods and holds out her right hand. A white tattoo on her wrist, the same as on her forehead burns with purple light, extending down past her hand until she holds the hilt of a glowing sword.

The woman with cinnamon skin and white and black braids takes over holding Tora's right arm down as the woman with white hair takes her place behind Tora's head.

Tora gasps and struggles against the Valkyries'. They're going to stab her through the head. The white-haired Valkyrie is going to kill her, and there's nothing anyone can do about it. Her mother saved her from death, only to die herself, and now she's about to die anyway. It was all for nothing. And Astra — what will this mean for Astra? Will they go after her next?

The Valkyries close their eyes and whisper around her. "We are the Choosers of the Slain, the Shield Maidens of Myth. Join us now sister, come forthwith."

The woman with cinnamon skin and black and white hair pushes the medallion against Tora's wrist. Tora jerks and screams as scolding pain burns down her hand, the smell of charred flesh filling her nose. She never knew Valkyries to be so cruel, to take any pleasure in death or torture of their own kind. The Valkyries she knew were valiant and proud.

"What do you want!" Tora screams, fear cursing through her veins. Searing pain travels up her arm.

"I want you to die." The woman with white hair and skin dark as night drives the glowing sword into the middle of Tora's forehead.

CHAPTER EIGHT

"You!" Someone kicks Tora hard in the side, jarring her awake, every inch of her body burning with pain. "Get up!"

Tora groans and forces her eyes open as a wave of vertigo whitewashes her vision. She struggles to sit up, her head throbbing like a jackhammer. The glow from the tent and pebbles burns her eyes. The storm outside rages, flashing with shards of lighting and deep rumbling thunder.

"Wh… what happened?" Tora rubs her head. The world seems brighter, louder, and full of chaos. Her stomach aches with anxiety as foggy memories mix together like a flip book, moving quickly before her eyes.

"I killed you." A female voice says simply.

Tora jolts as a flood of memories slam into her like a hurricane; memories of her and Bo making out in the exhibition room, the thugs breaking in; the warlock, the pixies, her squad... Oh god her squad.

"Oh god; Victor; Teresa." Tora pinches her eyes closed and sits up. She heaves, nausea attacking her in waves. Teresa and Victor are dead. Two members of her squad are dead. They're never coming back. Flenn that asshole warlock killed them. He killed them right in front of her, in front of the whole squad, and he enjoyed himself while he did it.

"Woah, take it easy." A woman with blonde hair and pale white skin helps her sit up. "Just breathe. Your senses are heightened now. It can take a bit of getting used to."

Tora's eyes burn as hot tears threaten to spill down her cheeks. A deep ache vibrates in her bones. That sadistic fuck. Flenn didn't have to kill Teresa or Victor. They were immobilized. They weren't a threat. He did it purely for enjoyment, for the power it gave him and the devastation it caused.

Five women stand around her, all with royal purple eyes and the Valkyrie marking in the middle of their foreheads. Valkyries. Strange considering she thought they were all dead.

"Where are the rest of my squad?" Tora rubs her forehead, her skin aching deep into her skull.

"They're in the building." A woman with black and white braided hair and cinnamon skin smirks and picks her claw-like nails with a small throwing knife.

Tora frowns. "What does that me…"

"I'm Liv." A woman with blonde braided hair and pale white skin cuts her off and squats down in front of her, her eyes purple like the others, but somehow lighter in spirit. She points to a woman with black braids and lily-white skin inspecting the art of the museum. "That's Tove."

"Liv? Seriously?" A woman with lily-white braids and skin as dark as night throws her arm up in annoyance, her long fingernails painted in liquid black lacquer.

"What?" Liv pouts and plays with one of her braids. "She'll have to learn our names eventually."

The lily-white haired woman shakes her head. "Not five seconds after I killed the girl. Give her a minute."

Tora flinches. Dead? What the hell is the woman talking about? If it's supposed to be some sort of joke, it's really not funny, not funny at all.

"That's Revna." Liv rolls her eyes. "She's like our leader."

"I'm Mist." A woman with light cinnamon skin and black and white braided hair sits on the ground with her knees pulled to her chest. "The bitch picking her nails with the knife, that's Inga."

Inga blows her a kiss.

Forcing her muscles to comply, Tora struggles to her feet, her head spinning in a kaleidoscope of colors. She doesn't have time to deal with Valkyries right now. They can wait. The sooner she finds the scumbag warlock, the sooner she can get revenge for her friends.

"She's so little and cute." Liv claps her hands and bounces on her feet. "I've never seen a short Valkyrie before."

"No one has." Inga scoffs. "Someone fucked up there."

"And her eyes, they aren't the same as ours. They're lighter," Liv continues. "I mean, look at her little legs." Liv giggles and runs her finger up the side of Tora's thigh.

"Hands off!" Tora snaps and slaps her hand away, trying to figure out what the hell is going on.

Outside, the storm rages, raining and flooding the floor of the museum through the broken glass ceiling and walls.

"Here." Revna holds out her black shirt and quickly looks away, a deep blush reddening her cheeks. "I think this is yours."

Inga straightens her spine and glares daggers at Tora, her face contorted in rage.

Gasping, Tora snatches the shirt out of her hand and pulls it over her head. For a minute she forgot she was half-naked, fighting in just her bra and cargo pants. "Look, I'm a bit foggy on the details. What happened exactly? Who are you guys?"

"We are Harbingers of Death. We mark the end," Inga says, her voice vibrating around the walls.

"We are the Choosers of the Slain, the Daughters of War," Mist says. "We are the Valkyries."

"Really." Tora rolls her eyes. How many times have they rehearsed that little speech? She knows they're Valkyries. The tattoos on the foreheads and huge ass wings hanging off their backs are a dead giveaway. She just doesn't know what the hell they're doing in the Realm of Man. As far as she knew, all the Valkyries died in the War of the Gods. "I know all that. What are you doing here? Does my mother know you're here? Does she know you're alive?"

The Valkyries glance at each other and squirm uncomfortably.

"What?" Tora looks around the room in confusion. "Does she or not?"

"I'm sure she figured it out." Inga smirks.

A wave of dizziness blurs Tora's vision. She grabs the wall for support and pinches her eyes closed, her forehead throbbing. It's like having an out-of-body experience; like she inhaled a bucket of cocaine and chased it down with a bottle of absinth.

"Okay, whatever." Tora shakes her head to clear it. "I don't have time for this shit. I need to talk to my friends, Bo, and my mother. Talk to her about your Daughters of War crap. I'm sure she'd love it. She needs to know that the fae and demons can cross at any time, and I need to find that fucker Flenn."

"Forget about that!" Inga snaps. "A few extra demons and fae is nothing. Get it through your ditzy head. You're dead. Literally. We killed you when we performed the ritual. You're a fully-fledged Valkyrie now. You have bigger things to worry about, like the coming war. And just so you know, Valkyries can't have human boyfriends so dump the guy already before the gods find out. It's nothing but a death sentence."

"What?" Tora screws up her face. "What are you on about?"

"Look for yourself." Inga points at a large mirrored piece of art stuck to the wall of the stairs, ironically in the shape of two huge swan wings.

Tentatively, Tora approaches the mirrored art, not knowing what to expect. The glowing aqua pebbles reflect off the glass, lighting her reflection. Tora gapes. Her heart sings in her ears like a heavy metal band as her hands tremble with a mix of excitement and awe. They completed the ritual. She's a fully-fledged Valkyrie, just like she's always wanted. The Valkyries completed the ritual. She'll get her wings.

Two black wings and a sword mark her forehead, the same marking that is now burned into the soft side of her right wrist.

After pestering her mother for an entire year, she'd almost given up hope of becoming a fully-fledged Valkyrie; on fulfilling her destiny. But Bo... The bitchy Valkyrie is right. She can't date Bo anymore, and it has nothing to do with interspecies breeding. The gods would kill Bo just to teach her a lesson for breaking their rules, especially now she is technically enrolled in their army.

"The secret Valkyrie ritual you've heard about all your life? It's death. The blade has to penetrate the pineal gland in the middle of the forehead on the day of three cycles of seven, forging the mark to your skin," Liv explains. "The weapon marking on your wrist is made before death so you don't have to carry your soul sword with you all the time."

"The Days of Judgment are coming," Revna says, her face suddenly drawn. "We need you with us to form and replenish an army."

Tora's head spins. She can barely wrap her head around the fact that she's technically dead, let alone the Days of Judgement. "So, I'm dead? That's the ritual. Murder?"

"Well, yeah." Revna shrugs. "As long as you're of Valkyrie blood, you come back as a spirit maiden. A Valkyrie. And thankfully, we were right. You are Tora Thurgood, daughter of Freya."

They're acting like it's no big deal; like literally killing her is no big deal. No wonder her mother didn't want to perform the ritual.

"Tora. War is brewing between all the realms. You must have felt a shift; a change?" Tove says. "The war will open the gates for judgment. It is prophesized."

Tora pinches her lips together. She has felt a change, but a prophecy? Why does there always have to be a goddamned prophecy? It's like the Creator gets bored and throws in a bit of mayhem to fuck everything up.

"The seventh daughter of the seventh daughter with heavenly blood in her veins will rain down destruction on the earth below. The heavens will fall, realms will clash, and the underworld will ignite in icy flames. Beware she who bears the white mark," Mist says as though in a trance.

"The prophecy will play out no matter what we do. The prophesized Witch Goddess cannot be killed," Revna says, anticipating any questions. "We need every Valkyrie to help form an army. We are all that is left."

"Not every Valkyrie." Inga smirks.

Tora blinks at the floor. That's a lot for one newly inducted Valkyrie to take in. She's a Valkyrie now. A fully-fledged Valkyrie about to fight in some war. Against her mother's wishes. "My mother is going to kill me."

"Then it's a good thing we already killed her." Inga sheathes her small throwing knife and looks Tora dead in the eye.

"Inga!" Mist scolds.

Burning heat flushes Tora's face. Her heart slams into her ribcage as the rest of her memories come rushing back. Her mother saved her from the warlock then she... she was stabbed through the chest with a glowing sword, the sword that was driven into her very own forehead. Revna's sword.

"No... You... you can't kill a fully-fledged Valkyrie. Not without a hell blade. It's impossible." Tora says, her voice wavering. Her hands shake. Only Hades and his generals carry hell blades, and they can't leave hell, not since the portals were sealed off to their realm.

"A Valkyrie blade and a hell blade are the only weapons that will kill a Valkyrie. Both weapons trap the soul so the body won't heal," Inga says. "Your mother was judged and found unworthy of the Valkyrie legacy for being a deserter in the War of the Gods."

A deserter? A deserter! Freya Thurgood fought and led the Valkyrie army for centuries. Her only crime was saving her daughter and her daughter's friend. That's the only reason she fled to the Realm of Man. Performing the ritual early is sentencing a Valkyrie to an early death. It was an unreasonable order.

Hands trembling, Tora tightens her jaw and glares at Revna. It can't be true. Her mother can't be dead. She's not supposed to die. A Valkyrie is not meant to die, not like this. "You killed my mother?"

Revna opens her mouth to answer, but Inga interrupts. "No, she didn't. It was me. I had my orders from the gods and I followed them."

Adrenaline hot and fierce spreads like wildfire through Tora's veins. Her muscles tighten and flex as memories of her mother fill her eyes and fall down her cheeks. She was never the warmest mother, but she was a good mother.

In the Realm of Angels, they lived in the house her mother built with her own two hands, positioned in and around a large oak tree with views of Mirage Lake and the surrounding forest. They trained day and night, both with other Valkyrie fledglings and on their own time. Her mother spent hours with her, teaching her to treat injuries, hunt, make their own alcohol, how to cook, how to read, and how to speak and write in different languages.

Even while on the hunt in the Realm of Man, her mother found ways to look out for her. Sometimes it was a flyover, other times she intervened. No matter what, she always managed to keep Tora and Astra safe. And now she's gone.

"You'll see her again." Liv offers in a tiny voice. "In the War, those chosen will fight, including your mother."

Tearing her bloodshot eyes away from Revna, Tora transfers her glare to Inga. She killed her mother. Stabbed her in the back like a coward. Her mother; leader of the Valkyries. Her mother... her mom.

Sharp pain flares in her forearm. The image of swan wings and a sword glows purple on her wrist, stretching down to her hand as tears sting her eyes.

"Holy shit!" Tove widens her eyes.

"She's going to pull her sword!" Liv bounces on her feet. "Already!"

"Bullshit!" Inga snaps.

The burn in her hand intensifies as an internal fire vibrates through her bones. Tora curls her lip and focuses on Inga, on the woman who killed her mother, trying to figure out how to kill the bitch before the others react.

Needles of pain shoot through her arm. Cold metal glides down her hand until she grips the hilt of a sword glowing purple and silver.

"Bravo little Valkyrie." Revna raises her eyebrows. "No one has ever pulled their soul sword that fast."

Gripping the hilt, Tora levels the sword at Inga as tears slip free from her eyes and her stomach fills with bile. She finally gets a soul sword and her mother isn't around to see it. Her mother is dead. The only blood relative she has ever known. Dead. And it's all Inga's fault.

Smirking, Inga slowly holds up her hands in surrender. Revna darts to Inga's side as the others inch around her.

"Ah!" Tora flicks the sword towards Inga's neck. "Don't even think about it."

"What are you going to do?" Inga laughs. "Kill me? Kill all of us? We need all the Valkyries we can get for the war."

Tora smirks through her tears. "Not every Valkyrie."

Inga's face drops. A flash of irritation sparks in her eyes.

Under different circumstances, Tora would feel some sort of satisfaction in catching the bad guy, even though it's usually a demon, but this Valkyrie killed her mother. Nothing is going to bring her back, not even ridding the world of this evil bitch.

"Tora, don't do this," Revna pleads. "It's not going to end well. No one wanted your mother to die, but the gods made the order. What else could we do?"

"You could have told them to fuck off!" Tora snaps and whips her head towards Revna. "Why do the gods have so much power over the angels? What have they done for us? What? They sentenced thousands of Valkyries to death when the elders were forced to perform the ritual on the fledglings before the three cycles of seven. The only thing my mother did wrong was protect me! And now you kill her and perform the ritual anyway. How fucking ironic. Are all angels stupid? Or just Valkyries?"

The Valkyries look at one another in confusion. Only Revna and Inga appear to understand what she's saying.

"You didn't know?" Tora scoffs at their ignorance. The other Valkyries clearly had no idea that performing the ritual early would result in an early death. "Did they at least wait until you were twenty-one to perform the ritual?"

"The girls are of age." Revna lowers her head. "Their mothers were of the same mind as yours, hiding the girls in the Realm of Angels, all except Inga. Inga was hidden in the Realm of Man, although not as lucky as you. She was isolated and survived on her own until I found her."

"Well, that explains her social skills," Tora snipes.

"You little bitch!" Inga lunges but Mist holds her back.

"So what? You killed their mothers too?" Tora narrows her eyes at Revna.

Liv, Tove, and Mist glance at each other, uncertainty etched into their faces.

Revna shakes her head, a deep sadness in her purple eyes. "They were orphaned in the War of the Gods. I was the last remaining Valkyrie. I just turned twenty."

"I... I didn't know the gods wanted to perform the ritual early." Liv whimpers.

"Revna stalled the gods at the risk of her own life." Inga crosses her arms over her chest. "She lied to the gods and insisted that your mothers hid you in the Realm of Man, knowing full well you were in the Realm of Angels. That's how she found me, and she hid me until I was of age."

"Wait" Mist looks at Revna. "You're only twenty? That means..."

"I was one of the Fledglings." Revna meets the eyes of each of the Valkyries, lastly Tora's. "The last surviving Valkyrie from the War of the Gods. My mother performed the ritual with a blood circle as she was dying. There had to be one Valkyrie left to find the hidden fledglings, to perform the ritual or the Valkyrie line would be broken. Until recently, it was assumed that Freya died. The others hid their children but returned to fight."

"You don't look twenty," Tove says. "No offense Rev, but you look like you're in your thirties; forties even."

Revna pinches her lips into a small smile. "When the ritual is performed early, aging is accelerated. Most Valkyries live until they're at least a few hundred years old? My years will progress over three years. The first year isn't so bad. I've aged maybe fifteen to twenty years over twelve months. This year, my second year will be faster. The third, my last year, I will age almost daily."

Tove, Mist, and Liv gasp. Inga looks away, pain etched deep into her eyes.

"Well, that sucks for you, but that doesn't change the fact that this bitch deserves to die." Tora strengthens her hold on the blade. None of this excuses their actions. Inga has to pay for what she's done. Her mother is gone; dead, because Inga was just following orders. "Any last words?

Inga looks up through her long eyelashes and grins. "Not exactly. More like a reminder."

"Yeah? What's that?" Tora shifts her weight impatiently. Nothing the Valkyrie says will make her change her mind. What did they think would happen? That they could kill her mother and she wouldn't care? That she would forgive and forget?

"I have your friends." Inga sneers. "Kill me and the others will kill them too."

Tora swears under her breath. The Valkyries of old would never kill innocent people, not like these desperate stand-ins.

"Where are they?" Tora demands, her blood boiling in her veins. Her sword disappears as her anger splits into rage and concern. There will be plenty of time to kill Inga. She will find her no matter where the bitch goes, but right now, she can't lose anyone else. "Where are my friends?"

"They're upstairs." Liv releases a large breath and slumps her shoulders in relief. "Don't worry, they're safe."

Valkyries apparently take hostages now too. Self-righteous assholes. The Valkyries she knew would never take hostages, would never kill one of their own. The Valkyries she knew were honorable and fought for the safety of the realms, not to save their own necks. She glares at Revna. "Let them go."

"We will." Revna relaxes her shoulders and shoots Inga a quick glare. "But first, I need you to promise that you will join the Valkyries. Help us fight."

"You expect me to work with you? Seriously?" Tora balks at their nerve. They come into her village, kill her mother, and expect her to just shrug it off? The Valkyries have not only changed their values, they're dumb as fuck. "You know, I would have joined if she hadn't killed my mother."

"It was unavoidable. If we didn't take your mother's soul, the gods would have done much worse. And you don't have a choice. War is coming Tora. If you do nothing, the realms will be destroyed, including the Realm of Man and the Realm of Angels. You don't have to like us, but to save all our worlds, you need to work with us," Revna reasons.

Tora bites her tongue. If it's true, then she really does have no choice. How can she condemn the realms to destruction because of one life; her mother's life? As much as she hates it, she will have to work with the other Valkyries, for a while at least. She'll get her revenge; eventually.

"Fine. I'll fight with you, but this isn't over." Tora glares at Inga, her murderous intent clear.

Inga chuckles and stalks away. "Whatever."

"There's one more thing," Revna says as Tora starts towards the stairs.

Tora grips the railing and clenches her jaw. What more could they possibly want? They killed her mother; technically killed her too. What? Do they want her blood? Her firstborn?

"What?" Tora spits.

Revna sighs. "Your friend Astra. She will be the last to come of age. The day of her birth, she will undergo the ritual."

"What?" Tora spins on her heel, shock radiating through her bones. "No way. Leave her out of this. If she were in the Realm of Angels, no way would she have been made into a warrior Valkyrie. Astra is a healer."

"We are all warriors, Tora." Mist lowers her eyes solemnly. "Medics or fighters. That's what we were bred for."

"No. Nah ah. No way." Tora shakes her head and backs away. They can't have Astra. They can't perform the ritual on her. Astra wouldn't survive being a fully-fledged Valkyrie. It will kill her; turn her into a crumbling ball of mess. She couldn't take the souls of the slain, she couldn't lead and fight in an army. Not Astra. It would change her. It would break her. The girl apologizes to the chickens every time she takes an egg for fucks sake. She does not belong on a battlefield.

"We will come for her in two days. It is better that you prepare her," Mist says, her voice soft. "As you can see, the process is somewhat shocking.

From what we have observed of your friend Astra, she would shut down. History shows that passive Valkyries who resist the change become catatonic."

Tora widens her eyes. "And you still want to perform the ritual on her?"

"We don't have a choice." Revna hardens her royal purple eyes, showing no kindness or warmth. "We need her."

Tora gapes. It doesn't matter what she says. The Valkyries have made up their minds. They aren't going to listen to reason. They don't care that the ritual will render her best friend catatonic. They think only of the coming war; of their duty to the gods and realms. Astra is nothing more than another soldier to them. Another pawn on a chessboard. They're just as fucked up as the gods.

Shaking her head, Tora storms up the stairs, disgusted by her own kind. "You guys suck!"

Once she makes sure her squad is safe, she's getting Astra the hell out of Greenwich Village. Her mother seemed to think that Montauk was safe, so that's where they're going. The plan isn't changing. Astra's birthday is in two days. That gives them two days leverage, and if they're lucky, they'll survive this shit show.

CHAPTER NINE

Moving in a daze, Tora finds the squad on the top floor of the Whitney Museum and cuts the ropes tying them together, their clothes and hair drenched from the rain. Shannon curls into the fetal position and silently cries.

Tora's ears ring as loss and guilt weigh heavily on her shoulders. Teresa was Shannon's everything. Her love, her lifeline, her twin flame, her sanity. Tora has no idea what to say to her. It's her fault Teresa, Victor, and her mother died. She was the one who humiliated the warlock at the markets. She was the reason he wanted revenge. She was the reason her mother was distracted and stabbed through the heart. No one would have died if it weren't for her. And over what? Three smashed eggs?

Things would have been very different if she'd just stayed at home like her mother told her to. They would be on their way to Montauk by now, and Teresa, Victor, and her mother would still be alive.

It makes her wonder whether her mother knew about the Valkyries. She had been acting strange for months, and forcing them to move over a forbidden romance was definitely an overreaction, even for her mother. It might be the real reason she wanted to leave Greenwich; to keep her and Astra safe, like she always has… had.

All she knows for sure is that her mother thought Montauk was safe, so that's where she's taking Astra, as soon as possible.

"What do you mean you're leaving?" Cheryl demands. "Victor and Teresa die and you're just leaving!"

"I have to Cheryl; to protect Astra." Tora drops to the ground and props herself up against a pillar, her limbs heavy.

"Fuck Astra!" Cheryl snaps. "She's exactly like you. She can protect herself!"

Tora bristles but stops herself from saying anything. Cheryl doesn't understand. It would be like forcing a pacifist to fight, to go against their very nature.

"You can't leave." Maree wraps a comforting arm around Mandy's shoulders. "We need you. What if that guy comes back?"

"He's not coming back." Sighing, Tora drops her head in her hands, her body aching with exhaustion. All she wants to do is drown her sorrows and grieve, but there's no time for that, no time if she wants to keep Astra safe. That will have to wait. One day she will avenge her mother and friends and then she will grieve.

"The warlock was after me because I humiliated him at the market. It was my fault. This is all my fault. Victor and Teresa died because of me." Tora lifts her head then drops it back against the pillar.

"No. They didn't." Shannon pushes herself up into a sitting position, tears staining her pale freckled face. "They died because the leaders of this town are idiots. Those thugs have been threatening villagers for months, and the village leaders haven't done a thing about it. We would have known they were malevolent fae if they bothered to do an investigation, if they had let us do an investigation at least. It's a post-apocalyptic world for fucks sake, and the leaders are worried about sweeping the streets clean and keeping dust off the furniture."

Shannon's not wrong. The leaders are in denial. Yes, they should try to give the villagers some sense of normalcy for comfort, but it shouldn't come at the cost of their safety.

"I'm sorry I have to leave, but I don't have a choice." Tora looks at each of the squad, pleading with them to understand. Most of the squad lost everything in the War of the Gods. They have to understand. She can't let Astra die. She has to save her. "I lost my mother. I can't lose Astra too."

Mandy looks at Maree and pinches her lips into a sad smile, her face splattered with drops of blood. "We can't expect her to sacrifice the only family she has left. We know what it's like to lose everyone. She has to try. Wouldn't you do the same if it were your daughter?"

Tora raises her eyebrows and glances at Bo. That's the first time they've heard anything about Maree's life before the war. They had no idea she even had a daughter.

Maree swallows hard and nods. They all know how close Tora and Astra are. They're like sisters; always have been, and if they don't leave before Astra's birthday, what happened to Tora, will happen to her, and that can't happen. Astra won't survive it.

Pinching his lips together in resolve, Bo pulls Tora to her feet. "You should leave now. The storm will give you a bit of cover. It won't be easy for the Valkyries to track you in this weather. It's the best you can hope for. I'll help you get out of the city."

Tora smiles as warmth spreads through her chest. Reliable Bo. Beautiful, brave, reliable Bo. She doesn't know what she's going to do without him.

"Just be careful." Maree chokes back tears as both she and Mandy hug her at the same time.

"I will." Tora smiles into Maree's hair and stifles her own tears. She's going to miss the Odd Squad. It's like the War of the Gods all over again, when she had to leave her home. "I'll miss you all, but we'll see each other again. I promise."

Shannon hugs her next and whispers in her ear. "We'll get our revenge for Teresa and Vic. They're not going to get away with this. Even warlocks and pixies bleed."

"Don't be reckless Shan." Tora pulls away and touches their foreheads together. "Make a plan. Follow the plan. Don't just wing it. A war is coming to all the realms and the rest of the village needs to be ready. You guys need to convince the others. Get the rest of the squads on board, even the Ninja Squad."

Crossing her arms over her chest, Cheryl glares daggers at Tora with misplaced anger and hatred.

"Cheryl…" Tora sighs and starts towards her.

Refusing to hear her out, Cheryl holds up her hand and tightens her jaw as she storms off. "Fuck off Tora. Fuck off and save your little friend. We'll take care of everyone else."

Bowing her head, Tora accepts the judgment without argument. Cheryl might regret it later, she might not. Either way, her words are true. She is choosing to save Astra over Greenwich Village, over the human race. No matter the consequences, she will always choose Astra; the last of her family.

"Ready?" Bo straps his remaining blades and sword to his body.

"Wait." Tora stops, unable to believe she didn't think of it before. She has no idea how to get to Montauk. Before tonight, she hadn't even heard of the place. "Crap! How the hell do I get to Montauk?"

"That's easy. Follow 6th Avenue until you reach West 36 Street..." Bo begins.

"6th Avenue?" Tora cocks her head. She knows that street. It's her least favorite street in the entire village. "That's where Ethan lives. I can pick up Star on the way."

"That makes it easy. So, then turn right after the Fairway Market in Chelsea." Bo pauses. "I'm just trying to think what shops and buildings are around so you know you're in the right place."

"Umm, Bo?" Tora raises her eyebrows. "I was thinking more of a map, not play-by-play directions. It's the Deadlands, remember? There probably aren't any street signs or shops left; just bits and pieces of streets."

"Crap." Bo gives her an apologetic look. "Sorry. I don't have a map."

Tora bites her lip in thought. Most humans used phones or GPS to navigate the roads before the War of the Gods, so road maps are scarce, but if anyone has one, it would be Dr Arnold. "Dr A; he might have one. If not, one of the libraries?"

"We can check." Bo shrugs and starts down the stairs with Tora close behind. He stops by the glowing display and hands her a couple of A5-sized canvases painted in white phosphorescent paint. "But I think most of the road and street maps were burned over winter."

Praying Dr Arnold has what she needs, Tora tucks the canvases into one of her large leg pockets and follows Bo out onto the dark street.

~

Rain pelts down on the pavement, singing like bells in Tora's ears. Thunder and lightning rip apart the sky. It's the perfect weather for hiding on the open street, and not just for her and Bo.

Hunters hate storms. Not only is their vision compromised by the lack of light and constant rainfall, judgment is altered by flashing lightning, hearing is hampered by rain and thunder, touch and movement are numbed by the cold. The smell of sulfur and smoke is washed away and overwhelmed by moisture, and the taste of the air is different. Everything changes under the conditions of a storm.

Sprinting down the street, Bo and Tora scan the shadows for bursts of light and reflected crystals. They don't have much time. Tora and Astra need to make a start for Montauk as soon as possible to reach safety by Astra's birthday.

They jog down Gansevoort Street and turn onto Greenwich Street, the rain like mildew on her tongue. The Valkyries said her senses would heighten, and they weren't wrong. Each individual raindrop echoes in her ears, scurrying rodents and insects scratch inside her skull like nails on a chalkboard. It's seriously giving her a headache. There's too much noise. It's like having a wicked hangover.

Her other senses aren't much easier to deal with. Different sized raindrops fall with clarity in front of her eyes, stealing her focus. Dirt, soil, lingering sulfur, and smoke burn her nose. Even in the darkness, she can see better than if she was wearing infrared glasses, the fabric of the realms highlighted in water.

"You okay?" Bo glances back at her, noticing her discomfort.

"Yeah fine." Tora shakes her head as they turn onto 8th Street. It might take a while, but before the war comes, she really needs to get a handle on her new senses, and figure out a way to isolate the important things. It could mean life or death. "Dr A's is just a few blocks down. Head towards my place on West 12th."

Reaching Dr Arnold's place in record time, Tora bangs on the door and calls out his name as Bo keeps watch behind her, making sure they weren't followed.

"Tora? What's wrong?" Dr Arnold yawns and puts on his glasses as he opens the door, his eyes crusted with sleep. He takes in Tora and Bo's soaking wet clothes and balks. "My god, you're drenched! What's happening? Is that a tattoo on your head?"

"I'm sorry to wake you Dr A, but it's an emergency." Tora apologizes and wipes the water from her eyes, feeling like an asshole for interrupting his already limited sleep. She probably woke up poor Mrs Arnold too, a risky move considering Dr Arnold says she's like a pregnant bear when she gets woken up. "I really need your help."

"Of course. Anything. Come in, come in." Dr Arnold steps away from the door and motions for them to come inside, his flannel pajamas disheveled and wrinkled.

Grateful, Bo and Tora hurry inside. It's not just that they're in a hurry, the streets are dangerous for anyone during a storm, including hunters. The squads won't be splitting up into teams tonight. They'll keep together and scope out the city from within many of the surrounding buildings. Although now she knows that demons and fae can cross the salt circles, nowhere is safe.

The apartment greets them with an old vintage style warmth of deep brown couches, mahogany bookshelves, and maroon red rugs. Cream knitted blankets lay draped over the backs of the couches and piled on the dining table.

Mrs Arnold's been busy. There are at least twenty blankets ready for trade at the markets.

"I need a map," Tora blurts out, wasting no time.

"A map?" Dr Arnold locks the front door and screws up his face. "What, of Greenwich?"

Tora shakes her head. "No. I need to know how to get to Montauk."

"What? Why?" Dr Arnold frowns and shows them down the hall to his office.

Lanterns hang from hooks lining the hall. Old glow in the dark stars and solar systems decorate the walls and ceilings in an attempt to light the apartment. The office is darker but Tora can easily see with her new Valkyrie vision abilities and the lanterns on Dr Arnold's antique mahogany desk. He gestures to a small section at the bottom of his bookcase and sits on the cream leather chaise. "All the maps I was able to save are on the bottom shelf. Take what you need."

"Thanks Dr A." Tora drops down on the floor and pulls out the maps, scattering them on the wooden floorboards.

"Ah, Tora?" Bo joins her with one of the lanterns. "Do you even know what you're looking at? Have you seen a map before?"

Tora blushes. God, she's an idiot. Angels don't use maps in the Realm of Angels. They just fly around until they find what they're looking for. It's like a built-in radar. Those who can't fly, like the fledgling Valkyries don't have any need to travel until they're twenty-one anyway. "No, but how hard can it be?"

Opening one of the books, Tora tries to figure out what the hell she's looking at without looking stupid. There are hundreds of maps of different areas with strange numbers and markings. She turns the book sideways, then upside down, then back upright but it doesn't help. The map makes no sense.

"Fine. You look." Tora slaps the book into Bo's stomach and sits on the edge of Dr Arnold's desk, annoyed by his arrogance.

"You wouldn't have gotten far with a map of London anyway." Bo chuckles and searches through the pile.

"Tora?" Dr Arnold sits forward on the chaise, a deep crease denting his forehead. "What's happening? Why do you need a map?"

Tora opens her mouth to answer then shuts it again. So much has happened in the last fourteen hours, and she doesn't know where to start. The warlock at the markets, the attack, her mother, the demons and fae, Teresa and Victor, the Valkyries... it's just so overwhelming. She's struggling to keep it together, to not break down and cry. This must be how Dr Arnold's patients used to feel.

With nothing to lose, Tora starts from the beginning, telling Dr Arnold about the warlock Flenn and his gang at the markets, that they're malevolent fae. She continues, telling him that her mother wanted to leave, that they were attacked at Bo's place, what the warlock Flenn said about the demon portal gates and salt circles.

Dr Arnold's eyes widen. A flash of pure fear distorts his face as his eyes naturally turn to his bedroom down the hall where his heavily pregnant wife sleeps. He fears for his wife and unborn child's safety, yet he listens intently, never interrupting as she talks.

Tears fill her eyes as she talks about the deaths of Teresa and Victor, killed by the asshole Flenn. Her cheeks burn bright red as she relives the death of her mother, killed by that Valkyrie bitch, Inga, less than an hour ago. And finally, she tells him about the ritual performed on her and intended for Astra.

Dr Arnold swallows hard and covers his mouth with his trembling hands. Sweat drips down his neck. "Tora, I, I'm so sorry about you and your mother; about Victor and Theresa."

Pinching her eyes closed, Tora nods her gratitude. It feels good to talk about it, even though it hurts like hell. Dr Arnold must have been a great psychiatrist before the War of the Gods.

Floorboards creak outside the room. Tora and Bo whip their heads towards the noise, on full alert now they know the salt circles do nothing. A faint sobbing sound echoes in the hall.

"Shell?" Dr Arnold hurries to the door to find his wife crying, her hands held tightly over her mouth. "Oh Shell."

He wraps his arms around her and guides her back down the hall, promising to keep her and the baby safe; a promise he probably knows he can't keep. There is nowhere to go, and nowhere to hide. Nowhere is safe. No one is safe.

Tora sighs and slumps her shoulders. It looks like she's ruining everyone's night tonight. It feels like she's abandoning a sinking ship, abandoning her friends, but if she and Astra stay in Greenwich Village, the Valkyries will find them and Astra won't survive. They don't have a choice.

"Found it!" Bo holds up a folded map triumphantly as Dr Arnold returns, a black backpack held in his hand.

"Here, we want you to have this." Dr Arnold holds out the bag. "It's just some water, protein and chocolate bars, and a couple of emergency space blankets."

Overwhelmed, Tora slowly gets to her feet and pushes his hand back. In this day and age, a bag like this is worth more than gold. She can't believe he's giving it to her. "I can't take your food. You guys need it."

"Please take it," Dr Arnold insists. "We have plenty. We were saving them, but if another war is coming, we may as well enjoy them while we can. Live each day like it's the last."

The instant defeat in his voice brings tears to Tora's eyes. No matter what happens, after Astra's birthday, she will return to Greenwich, even if it kills her. She can't leave her friends unprotected. They just need to hold on for two days without her. The hunting squads have been trained well by her mother; they can hold down the fort for a couple of days. They have to.

"I'll be back Charlie." Tora pulls him into a bear hug. "I promise I'll be back."

Dr Arnold widens his eyes in surprise. His mouth hangs open like he swallowed a ball. "You used my name."

"Yeah, I did Charlie, so I know you hear me. Once Astra's birthday passes, I'll come straight back," Tora promises and pulls away. "Just lay low for a few days. Keep the curtains drawn. Don't leave the apartment unless you have to. Don't answer the door. The more abandoned you can make this apartment block look, the better. Bo will collect the eggs from the chickens and bring them to you. And whatever you two do, do not have the baby until I get back."

"Just look after you and Astra first, okay?" Dr Arnold puts the bag in her hand and fights back his own tears. "Do not be reckless."

Tora can't help but smile. The guy is scared half to death and he still thinks of her safety first. In her twenty years of living in the Realm of Angels, she never once questioned who her father was. She understood the rules and accepted them like the good little fledgling Valkyrie she was. None of the other Valkyries knew who their fathers were, so it was normal to only have a mother in her life. That was until she met Dr Arnold and experienced fatherly love.

Now she finds herself wondering who her father was. Whether he loved her mother at all; whether he was even attracted to her, or whether her conception was a strategic arrangement to grow the Valkyrie army, like every other Valkyrie child in history.

"Ready?" Bo hovers by the door, anxious to get on the road.

"Keep the windows covered as much as possible." Tora backs away and takes the map from Bo, tucking it into her boot for safekeeping. "Keep the noise to a minimum, and try not to use any lights."

"I'll keep checking the crystals while you're gone," Bo promises. "I'll see what other crystals I can find. They might help protect the homes."

Tora nods and bites her tongue, annoyed at herself for not thinking of the crystals herself. "Ask around; see whether you can find a witch. There has to be a few here somewhere. My mom couldn't have set those crystals herself."

Dr Arnold walks them to the door, his head hung low, already defeated before the next war begins. "Do you think he's right? That demons and fae can cross at will?"

Tora thinks of the child demon they fought the other night and knows without a doubt, it's true. God knows what's coming through the portal next. She doesn't want to say it, but they're all fucked. "I don't know what stopped them before, but yes, I believe him. War is coming to the Realms. I think it's already started."

As if on cue, a shrieking howl echoes through the night.

CHAPTER TEN

Promising to return in a few days, Tora and Bo take to the streets, out into the storm. Rain pounds down on their heads, soaking through their clothes. A cold wind tunnels through the empty streets, whipping debris and rubbish into a frenzy.

Tora jogs alongside Bo, glancing at him every few steps. Her stomach aches at the thought of leaving her friends but what is she meant to do? Sacrifice Astra to save the others? On paper it makes sense. One life for countless others, but it's Astra; her best friend; practically her sister. She can't lose her. She's the last of her family; her last link to home. She has to believe that the hunters can handle whatever comes through the portals. Freya trained them and trained them well. They should be able to cover her for a couple of days.

Tears well in her eyes at the thought of her mother and the squad without Teresa and Victor. Grief bites at her limbs as she pushes her legs faster than they've gone before, like she can sweat the pain and loss out of her pores. But even overexerting herself does nothing.

A bright flash of light sparks like a firecracker in Tora's peripheral vision. Grabbing Bo's arm, she skids to a stop and drags him back through a puddle, holding her other hand over his mouth to silence his protest. There's something in the alley. Even with rain in her eyes, she's sure of it.

Holding her finger to her lips, she pokes her head around the side of the building. Bright aurora borealis lights shine in the dark stormy night, glowing aqua, green, blue, pink, and purple.

Thunder roars. Lightning zigzags across the sky, highlighting the portal as it rips the fabric of the realm. Crystals form in a broken line as the portal rips open, and water gushes onto the road.

Pressing up against the building, Bo peeks around the corner and widens his eyes. Slowly, a large oversized head pokes through the opening. Light and dark gray fur cover most of the snout and face, marred with sections of only blood and bone; no skin or flesh. Two black bat-like ears fold back, listening intently for its prey. Golden yellow eyes search the alleyway, standing out in the dark like two glowing almond-shaped spotlights.

Goosebumps spread across Tora's skin as a huge wolf-like creature the size of a dumpster stalks out of the portal, its body covered in the same fur, blood, and bone as the face. Scars slash in all directions on the demon wolf, crisscrossing in barbed wire cuts.

Bo swallows hard. The creature cautiously paces in a circle.

Flenn wasn't kidding when he said they had no idea what they were up against. The beast is the most frightening thing Tora has ever seen, and it's not just because of its size and appearance. The wolf demonstrates intelligence, much more advanced than any normal animal; cautious and calculating in its movements. It's waiting for something.

The huge wolf rears up onto its hind legs and howls; an eerie two-toned sound mixed between the howl of a wolf, and the shriek of a bat. Tora gasps as shrieking howls echo back, coming from all corners of Greenwich Village and the inner streets, the sound vibrating deep into her bones.

"Bo? Did you..." Tora blinks, not trusting her new hearing abilities. It sounds like there are more of the beasts in the village. At least five or more.

"We have to get inside. Now!" Bo hurries from door to door, trying to find one that's unlocked while Tora keeps watch on the demon wolf. There's no way they can fight the huge beast. Not without studying it first, finding out its weaknesses.

Dropping back down on all fours, the demon wolf remains by the portal, scanning the streets. Shards of portal crystals stick to the tips of its fur like dry ice, glowing in the dark night. The ground shakes under its weight.

A smaller wolf pokes its head through the portal and sniffs the air; this one a pup, maybe the height and size of an office desk. It steps through the gate and stands beside the demon wolf, a smaller mirror image of the large one.

Tora leans into the wall, trying to get a better look. It's a she-wolf demon. A mother wolf demon. If she was alone, she'd pull her soul sword and charge the beasts, but she can't fight and keep Bo safe at the same time. He would back her up, even if it meant his death.

"Ethan's place is on this block," Tora whispers as Bo rushes back in a panic when none of the doors unlock. "Star gave me a key to the apartment block door in case I ever needed to get off the street."

Another child wolf jumps through the portal, followed by another, and another, and another. Five baby wolf demons and the mother nuzzle each other before spinning to face the end of the alley, exactly where Tora and Bo are hiding.

"Let's go!" Tora grabs Bo's arm and takes off in a sprint down the street, a giddy euphoria sharpening her senses, allowing her to push her body to its physical limits and keep up with Bo's long legs, reaching Ethan's apartment doors in mere seconds.

Unlocking the large wooden apartment block door, Tora pulls Bo inside and locks it closed behind them. The six wolf demons howl into the storm.

Across the village, howls echo their call. The ground shakes as the wolves run, their heavy footsteps vibrating through the buildings and roads.

"Are you hearing this?" Bo widens his eyes even further.

Sprinting up the stairs, they reach Ethan's apartment on the third floor and bang on the door. After a few seconds, Ethan appears bare-chested in just a pair of blue flannel pajama pants. Astra stands behind him in an oversized white male dressing gown.

"What are you guys..." Ethan starts but Tora pushes him into the apartment and pulls Bo inside with her. She shuts the door and puts her fingers to her lips.

Catching on quickly, Ethan reinforces the door lock with a metal locking lever and wraps a comforting arm around Astra's shoulders, her eyes like large saucers.

Tora and Bo look through the window down at the streets below, lit only by flashes of lightning. At first, they see nothing. The streets are completely quiet, but then they see it; glowing crystals stuck to the demon wolves' fur, stalking by the apartment block door.

"Is that a... a demon wolf?" Ethan peers over their shoulder, his voice shaking.

Trembling, Astra grips Tora's hand. "Tor? What's going on?"

The wolves suddenly lift their heads and sniff the air as something grabs their attention.

Tora holds her breath and puts her finger to her lips, her heart thudding hard against her ribcage. If the wolves find them, they're dead. Sure, she could probably take out one or two of them, but six? Even Tora isn't arrogant enough to think she could defeat six huge ass wolf demons hours after being made into a fully-fledged Valkyrie.

Howling, the six wolves stalk down the road, their large paws pounding on the ground, shaking the surrounding buildings.

Tora releases her breath and drops her shoulders in relief as she drags Astra to the couch, away from the window. "A fucking she-wolf demon and five pups just came through a portal gate. From the sound of it, I'd say there are a few packs out there."

They need to get out of the city, and fast if they want to survive the demon wolves and the Valkyries. She's not sure what's worse; the demons, the Valkyries, or the fact that she and Bo obviously interrupted an intimate goodbye between Astra and Ethan.

It's the first time she's been in Ethan's apartment and hopefully it will be the last. The place screams toxic asshole from his velvety blue couch, ugly cream shag rugs, bookcases filled with old books and movies, to the stupid metal nick-nacks positioned evenly throughout the room, and six-seater gothic dining table.

The guy has one friend. Why the hell does he need an antique dining table?

Two mugs sit on coasters on the clear glass coffee table. Solar energy powers the decorative lamps. Everything in the room has been picked and placed perfectly, like the War of the Gods never happened. There's not even one speck of dust on the floor.

"God. We are so fucked." Bo slumps on the window sill and wipes the sweat from his face. "How are we going to get out of the city with the packs out there hunting?"

"Wait. What?" Ethan screws up his face. "You're going with them?"

Bo glances at Tora but says nothing.

"Star," Tora lowers her head, fighting back her grief. "I need to tell you something; something about Mom."

"Your forehead; the symbol." Astra widens her eyes. "Your mother did the ritual. You're a fully-fledged Valkyrie! You convinced her to do the ritual? Did you get her to change her mind about Montauk too?"

"I... no. I..." Tora stutters, the hope in Astra's voice stabbing at her heart.

"You weren't able to change her mind?" Astra deflates as tears form in her eyes; her trembling lips bruised from kissing. She looks like a child wrapped in a father's robe, tied hastily around her waist. "We're leaving. Aren't we?"

Tora pinches her lips tight. This is the hardest conversation she has ever had to have and not only because it's going to be hard for Astra to hear. Saying the words, saying her mother died out loud makes it sound so final. She can't take them back. It's real. Her mother is really dead.

"No. I didn't get the chance to talk to her. Mom is… she's… umm…" Tora takes a deep breath and closes her eyes, hating the words on her tongue. "She's dead. Freya was killed by a Valkyrie blade."

Astra reels back. Her purple eyes widen and fill with instant tears. Just like Tora, Astra thought of Freya as invincible. They never worried about her, confident she could handle anything and everything, and come back with stories, not scars, and never death.

Ethan gasps.

"What do you mean? How? I… I don't understand?" Astra stutters. Tears stream down her face. "I thought a demon blade was the only weapon that could kill a Valkyrie? And since when are there other Valkyries?"

Fighting back her own tears, Tora tells Astra everything; about the warlock and pixies from the market, about Teresa and Victor, about the Valkyries, about her mother, about the coming war and prophecy, and lastly, the Valkyrie ritual.

Astra cries hard, sobbing heavily until she heaves. Freya may not have been her mother, but she was the only motherly figure Astra had left, the only hope for the Valkyries, their only hope of returning to the Realm of Angels one day.

"So, the big secret ritual is murder? They killed your mom, pretty much killed you, and they want to kill Star too?" Ethan scoffs and sits as close to Astra as possible, practically putting his butt cheeks on her leg. "Great legacy."

Tora glares at him as he uses her nickname for Astra. No one but Tora uses that name, and he damn well knows it. The asshole is just trying to piss her off.

Even Astra seems confused by his use of the nickname. She frowns and tilts her head, studying his face, but shakes it off quickly and takes a steadying breath. "Shouldn't we stay so the Valkyries can perform the ritual on me?"

"What?" Tora and Ethan whip their heads around like a couple of meerkats. They may not agree on many things and secretly hate each other's guts, but they agree on one thing; Astra stays safe.

Tora can barely believe her ears. Being a warrior Valkyrie was never Astra's goal in the Realm of Angels, now she changes her mind when they finally find out what the ritual entails? It's insane.

"You can't." Ethan panics, looking to Bo and Tora for help. "What about..."

"Didn't you hear anything I said? Even the Valkyries think you're likely to be left catatonic from the ritual." Tora snaps, cutting him off. "It's too dangerous. You're not meant to be a warrior Valkyrie."

"We've had the same training. Tora. I'm just as prepared as you." Astra glares at her, her voice low and full of hurt. "Stop babying me."

"I'm not babying you. Yes, you're trained, but it's not what you're built for. If you saw half the shit I've seen in the last year, you would never leave the apartment!" Tora paces. "I mean, Bo and I just barely escaped the six demon wolves hunting down on the street. There was a reason my mother never sent you out on patrols, and that's because she knew you couldn't handle it. Don't get yourself killed trying to prove you're something you're not."

Fresh tears spring to Astra's eyes. She looks away quickly and excuses herself to Ethan's bedroom. Ethan of course follows.

"Ugh!" Tora kicks the crappy couch in frustration. She can't understand why Astra would voluntarily undergo the ritual when she's never wanted to be a warrior before. Why is it suddenly so important? Even the Valkyries think she'll be catatonic if she's not prepared, and despite what Astra thinks, she is not at all prepared.

"Don't you think you were a bit harsh?" Bo glances out the window and scans the street below through the zig-zagging lightning.

"No." Tora scoffs. "Not if it stops her getting killed or being catatonic."

The world has gone mad. In what universe does she agree with Ethan and argue with Bo? It's wrong on so many levels. Astra can barely take the eggs from the chickens. She thinks it's like stealing their babies. It's the one thing Freya made her do to toughen her up a little, and she still apologizes to the chickens and cries every now and then when she does it.

"I know T, but you could have been a bit softer on her." Bo reasons.

"If she can't handle a bit of aggressive truth, how is she going to get through the ritual in one piece?" Tora argues. "I barely raised my v..."

"Shh!" Bo suddenly sits up and pushes his face against the window, not game enough to open it when there are demons and malevolent fae about. "The she-wolf is back, but I can't see the pups."

"You know what Tora!" Astra storms into the room, Ethan close on her heels. "I may not be as good as you, but I am smarter than you and would...."

"Shh! Shut up." Bo snaps and drops to the ground.

Ethan frowns. "What are you doing?"

"The she-wolf looked up. She heard us," Bo whispers. "It can fucking hear us."

"Fuck." Tora immediately looks for every exit out of the apartment and ties her black leather jacket around her waist, freeing her arms for flexibility.

If the she-wolf wants in, the wooden door downstairs isn't going to do shit, and neither is Ethan's apartment door.

"Well, what do we do?" Astra whispers, trying to hide the shake in her voice. "How do we fight it?"

"I don't know!" Tora whisper shouts. They've never fought a she-wolf demon before. It's always been large long-limbed spider and cockroach-like demons that look like they've been through a meat grinder and put back together. Or the insect-like demons that buzz in your ears and bite chunks of flesh from your body. "That asshole Flenn said things were going to change. The salt circles don't work. I don't even know if the crystals work."

Astra pales and drops down on the couch, her breathing hard and fast. Ethan sits behind her, trying to calm her down.

Tora pinches her eyebrows together in sympathy. This is exactly what she was talking about. Astra is not a warrior. She is not prepared to fight. Anytime something unpredictable happens, she panics or breaks down. What would she do out on the battlefield?

The she-wolf demon howls. Tora whips her head towards the door as a loud crash shatters the night and heavy footsteps pound up the stairs, the sound of taloned nails scraping the ground, slamming through them like a hammer drill.

Stifling a scream, Astra jumps to her feet and stares wide eyed at the door. "It's inside."

146

"It's okay Star." Tora darts to her side and scans the apartment, their argument forgotten. There's not one goddamned thing she can use as a weapon in this stupid house. It's like he babyproofed the apartment. Who does that when demons and fae are roaming the streets? There's not even a fire poking stick or a pointy ornament. Nothing.

"What do we do now?" Ethan's voice breaks as fear squeezes his voice box.

Bo quickly opens the windows leading onto the fire escape and climbs out, half his body still in the apartment. "Now, we run."

CHAPTER ELEVEN

Bo, Tora, Astra, and Ethan climb out onto the fire escape, the pounding of the beast loud in their ears. The beast slams its way into the lower floor apartments, the roaring howl causing the hairs on Tora's arms to stand.

Thank god Ethan is the only person who lives in the apartment block. There's no way they could save everyone from these beasts. They'll be lucky to save themselves.

Tora's stomach clenches as the beast moves swiftly, rummaging and tearing apart the lower floors. She guessed they were intelligent from their movements in the alley and on the street, but this is ridiculous. No wolf or untrained animal in the Realm of Man, or the Realm of Angels would purposely look for them floor by floor, apartment by apartment.

"Up or down?" Bo squints up the fire escape as heavy rain pounds on his head.

Astra shivers and looks down at the street below. "If we go up, we're sitting ducks."

It doesn't matter whether they go up or down. It's already too late. Tora can hear the beast outside the apartment door, her Valkyrie hearing pricking at the sound of its angry breathing. She thought they had more time.

"Get down!" Tora yells and braces for attack as the beast slams into the door.

Everyone drops to the metal landing, expecting the beast to shatter the door and come at them through the glass, but the door holds, the hinges rattling and screeching like bending steel.

Tora frowns. It doesn't make any sense. The beast was able to smash through twelve apartment doors in less than a few minutes. Why not Ethan's?

"It's reinforced with steel." Ethan answers her unspoken question and pulls Astra to her feet. "It won't hold for long though. There's not much steel in it."

Tora narrows her eyes and gets to her feet. The more Ethan talks, the less she trusts him. He knew the warlock's name, and now his door magically holds against a hulking demon? Something's not right. The creep is lying. She can feel it in her bones like tooth decay rotting her gums.

"We go down." Ethan drags Astra to the end of the fire escape as the beast slams into the door again, rattling the frame. "Now, we go now."

Tora whips her head towards the door then peers down at the street. As much as she wants to throw him over the railing, she can't. They don't have time and Astra would kill her. Ethan's right. The door won't hold much longer, no matter what he did to it.

"Hey!" Tora shouts over the storm.

"Tor, we have to go now." Astra pleads, her voice shaking as she and Ethan skid to a stop.

"Not that way." Tora points down at the road. Specs of glowing green and blue light weave up and down the street. Even under the cover of night and the chaotic storm, with her new Valkyrie vision, she sees them; three demon wolf pups pacing up and down the road, hovering just below them, shards of portal crystals frosting the tips of their fur. "We go up."

"I don't see anything." Ethan screws up his face.

"Just go." Tora rolls her eyes and pushes Astra up the fire escape, Ethan a few steps behind. Even when they're running for their lives, the guy is a pain in the ass.

Bo shakes his head and climbs the fire escape behind her. If anyone knows how much she hates Ethan, it's Bo. He's listened to her complain night after night for nearly a year.

The apartment door rattles as the demon wolf charges and howls. Wolves throughout the city echo its call. Puddles of water ripple with the vibrations of heavy footsteps on the roads below.

Tora's stomach rolls as guilt gnaws at her conscience. They aren't the only ones running for their lives tonight. Three squads are on patrol, roaming the open streets of Greenwich. She just hopes they were smart enough to get inside and up high. The residents would be absolutely shitting themselves right now, cowering under their beds which is probably the safest place for them.

They're going to hate her when they find out she left. They're going to think she abandoned them. Even worse, they'll probably think she's a coward. Nothing will be the same after tonight, after the villagers find out her mother is dead, and the salt circles do nothing, it's going to be utter chaos.

A few days. That's all she needs to get Astra to safety. The Squads just need to keep the residents safe until she gets back.

Reaching the roof, Tora scans the area, looking for a way out of this mess. They can't go down the stairs. The wolves would intercept them. Their only way out is to jump across. The buildings are close enough. If they can get up enough speed, they should make it.

A loud crash rocks the building. Shattering glass rains down on the street below.

"Fuck! Go go go! Jump!" Tora shouts and points to the next building, her heart pounding in her chest. The beast made it through the door and window. Ready or not, here it comes.

Bending steel screeches as the beast climbs the fire escape, its taloned claws hammering the metal like a fully automatic gun.

Astra and Ethan hesitate and look down over the ledge; fear pushing them closer together. Demonstrating, Bo runs and leaps across the buildings like a pro and lands effortlessly on the other side. He holds out his arms and beckons them forward.

Tora grits her teeth in annoyance. If they take any longer, they're going to end up dog food. "Now!"

Staying together, Ethan and Astra back up a couple of steps and take a running leap across the buildings, their hands clasped tightly together.

"Behind you!" Bo shouts.

Tora spins as a low growl sounds behind her. Two demon wolf pups stalk towards her, the hairs on their necks and backs standing on edge. Their golden eyes spiral like glowing orbs of glitter.

Fuck! Where's animal control when you need them? Why couldn't one of the human rangers have survived and joined the squad? She can't jump now. The pups will follow and put the others in more danger.

"Keep going!" Tora yells, hoping the pups aren't as intelligent as their mother.

"Like hell!" Bo leaps back onto the building and lands by her side. The pups growl louder and howl in excitement.

"We're not leaving you!" Astra shouts back, her eyes welling with tears.

"She'll be fine." Ethan drags her to the other side of the roof, trying to get her to leave. "She does this all the time."

Tora scoffs. What a scheming weasel. The fuck-knuckle would love it if she was out of the picture. He'd have Astra all to himself and wouldn't have to pretend to like her anymore.

A shrieking howl echoes like thunder as the mother she-wolf demon claws over the side of the building onto the roof. She stalks around the edges and eyes them like a chew toy, her head low.

Bo and Tora whip out their blades and stand back-to-back, inching away from the beast, careful to keep their distance from the pups as well. Normal wolves are intelligent enough. They're able to trap and circle their prey. She's not about to underestimate demon wolves.

Bo looks back and forth between the pups and the mother, his blade held ready in his hand. "What's the plan?"

Tora raises her eyebrows and glances back at Bo. What's the plan? There is no fucking plan. They'll be lucky if their blades even puncture the demon's skin.

"Stab stab stab." Tora winks at him, feigning more confidence than she feels. "Don't get killed. That's the plan."

The pup closest to her licks its lips and impatiently shifts its weight from paw to paw. Tora tenses, waiting for the attack, but it's a trick. The pup closest to Bo lunges first.

Tora gasps. A roaring fire ignites in her veins as irritation bubbles in her stomach. Goddamned demons. If demon wolves are smarter than normal wolves, it's safe to assume that humanoid demons are smarter than humans. They are so fucked. All the realms are so fucked.

Linking their arms, Tora swings Bo out of the way and uses the motion to slice swiftly across the pup's nose. The pup whimpers like a screeching bird and cowers.

Tora grins, Their blades work! The demon's skin isn't as tough as she thought.

The mother she-wolf demon roars. The call is echoed throughout the city, even closer than before. The other wolf packs on the streets are closing in. It won't be long before they reach them.

"Shit." Bo widens his eyes. "We are so fucked."

The she-wolf lunges, aiming for Bo, her golden eyes burning. Lightning sizzles in the sky, zig-zagging through large black thunderhead clouds. The wolf's taloned paws slice across the cemented roof as it nears, its teeth bared in a snarl.

Anger hot and fierce flushes Tora's face. Fucking demons! They keep targeting Bo, seeing him as the lesser threat. It just pisses her off even more.

Charging forward, Tora shoulder barges Bo out of the way, her Valkyrie blood singing with joy as adrenaline pumps viciously through her veins. The Valkyrie marking on her inner wrist burns, glowing an otherworldly purple. It extends down her hand until she grips the hilt of a sword; her Valkyrie sword; her soul sword.

Tora grins, every atom of her body exploding in ecstasy as intoxicating power curses through her veins. Sex is nothing compared to a good battle, especially now she's a fully-fledged Valkyrie. Now she understands how her mother went without a boyfriend or sex for all those years. To a Valkyrie, a battle is foreplay and a war is practically an orgy.

"Holy shit!" Bo gapes at her in awe and wipes the rain from his eyes. "I want one."

Spinning, Tora dodges the demon wolf and plunges her sword forward, stabbing the beast in the leg, the satisfying halt of her blade making her smile as it snags in the demon's flesh.

Screeching, the demon drops to its stomach and howls. Her pups echo her pain and anger both on the roof and below the building.

Shivers run up and down her spine. There is something seriously wrong with her. She's always loved the fight, but it's like she no longer feels fear, only excitement when faced with battle.

Keeping Bo behind her despite his protests, she holds her sword out in front of her. Together, the two pups bare their teeth and lunge, snarling angrily. Tora knocks Bo out of the way and jumps high into the air, using her dead weight to plunge the sword into one of the demon pups' heads, killing it instantly.

Pulling the sword free, she quickly stabs forward, slamming the blade through the mouth and skull of the other pups. Their eyes roll back into their head. She pulls out the blade, black blood dripping from the tip.

The mother she-wolf shrieks like a bat, a vibrating two-toned growl rumbling like an avalanche through the building. It gets to its feet and snarls, baring its large sabretooth-like teeth.

"Oh fuck." Bo stammers and stumbles back, his blade gripped tight in his hand.

The demon's eyes focus on Tora and Tora alone, the one who killed her pups. Steeling herself, Tora instinctively runs in an attempt to lead the demon away, giddy excitement bubbling in her stomach as the beast bares down behind her.

As she reaches the edge, she spins and uses the force of the demon's wrath to drive the sword through its heart as it slams them both off the roof.

"Tora!" Bo screams.

"No!" Astra screams. "No!"

Fire scorches Tora's shoulder blades, digging deep into her bones. She screams, thinking this is it, this is truly death. Maybe the others were wrong. Maybe a demon can kill a Valkyrie without a demon blade. But suddenly, she finds herself floating in midair as the demon wolf continues to fall to the ground dead beside her.

Slowly Tora looks over her shoulder, fearing the worst, that the Valkyries found her, but it's not them. Pristine white swan wings flap behind her, keeping her airborne, attached to her own back, sticking out of either side of her razorback shirt.

Her wings. Her Valkyrie wings. She finally got her wings.

The pups below howl and cry; their call answered all over the city as the ground shakes like an earthquake.

Tora shoots up into the sky and grabs a stunned Bo by the armpits, carrying him over to Astra and Ethan. The demon packs are coming. Valkyrie or not, she can't fight them all by herself.

Bo gapes. Tears fill Astra's eyes. Ethan curls his lip.

"You got your wings." Astra smiles through her tears.

Tora flushes, her chest and throat filled with guilt. Wings are the only reason Astra wanted to become a Valkyrie. Like Tora, she wanted to fly through the skies on a clear night and feel the wind flowing through her hair; just like the Angels they were meant to be. It's what they've both dreamed of since they were little.

"Star... I..." Tora lands in front of Astra, finally understanding that it's her choice whether she becomes a fully-fledged Valkyrie or not. She's not her mother, and she doesn't get to decide for her. "I'm so sorry. You were right. It's your choice. If you want to undergo the ritual, I won't stand in your way."

Astra wipes her tears and shakes her head. "No, you were right. I'm not built for this, not for battle. It's time I finally admit that to myself and stop trying to be something I'm not."

"Err, guys?" Ethan peeks over the edge of the building. "We have a problem."

Tora doesn't need to look to know what he's talking about, but she does anyway. At least twenty wolves stalk the streets below, their golden glitter eyes narrowed to slits.

Dumb luck saved them so far. There's no way she'll be able to take out all the demons and keep her friends safe by herself. To make things worse, black figures move in the shadows, scrambling across the roads and up the sides of the street.

Tora sighs. Idiots! The Ninja Squad are going to get themselves killed. They're all dressed in matching black pajamas like they're playing a game. Even the Odd Squad would avoid this pack if they were on patrol, or at least join ranks with the other two squads for a better chance. They rely too heavily on her mother to save them, and they don't know she's dead.

The wolves ignore the Ninja Squad, clearly not seeing them as a threat, and rear back onto their hind legs. One by one, they climb the fire escape, their golden eyes trained on Tora.

Tora widens her eyes. The wolves are coming after her. They aren't interested in the Ninja Squad or killing for food. These wolves want revenge for the mother she-wolf and her pups.

"Ah, Tora? We have another problem." Bo looks to the sky as the moon peeks around the clouds. "Can demons fly?"

Tora's head snaps up. That's the last thing they need; flying demons, but for every bird in the Realm of Man, the Demon Realm has an equivalent. There are guaranteed to be flying demons.

Five winged creatures hover high in the clouds, circling the chaos below. Lightning splits apart the sky, flashing behind the winged beings.

Tora gasps. "Not demons. Valkyries."

With a battle cry that sends chills down Tora's spine, the five Valkyries descend at lightning speed, their glowing swords held out in front of them.

They attack the demon wolves head-on, slashing and stabbing their way through the packs, working in tandem to keep the Ninja Squad safe.

"Now's our chance!" Bo shouts.

Tora drags her eyes away, fighting the urge to join the battle. He's right. The Valkyries are distracted. It's their best chance of escaping the city unnoticed and their only chance of saving Greenwich Village.

Two days. Two days is all she needs to keep Astra safe from the ritual and return with whatever magic keeps Montauk protected from portals. Without it, Greenwich will be overrun with demons and fae in no time.

Until then, she has to believe the Valkyries will help fight the demons and fae. They're not going anywhere until Astra's birthday, they said so themselves, and no Valkyrie can resist a fight. As long as they think Astra is in Greenwich, the village will be safe.

"Let's go." Tora nods at Astra. "We'll have to go on foot. I can fly us, but it's risky. The Valkyries will see us. We'll have to walk part of the way at least."

Jumping across four rooftops, Tora, Bo, Ethan, and Astra climb down a fire escape and take the back alley, away from the fight. Keeping to the shadows, they hurry down the street, glancing back as they go until they reach the edge of the Greenwich Village perimeter.

"I'll be back in a few days," Tora promises Bo and rolls her eyes at Astra and Ethan a few steps away, locked in a tearful hug goodbye. "Montauk has some kind of protection over the town. If I can bring it back, Greenwich has a chance of surviving. As long as the Valkyries think Astra is here, they will help whether they want to or not. They won't be able to stop themselves."

Relief softens Bo's face. He wouldn't say it, but the thought of her leaving probably freaked him out as much as it did Cheryl.

"Do not remove these crystals." Tora points to one of the large boulder sized crystals. "The village can't afford demons coming in from the outside."

"Yes mam." Bo grins and pulls her towards him. "So, does you coming back have anything to do with me at all?"

Tora pinches her lips into a smile, dreading this conversation more than anything. With everything happening so fast, she hasn't had a chance to talk to him about their relationship. The Valkyries made it very clear. The gods will kill Bo if they continue to date.

She's only had to break up with one person before. Laton, an angel she fooled around with in the Realm of Angels. The jerk wanted to keep their relationship a secret because she was a Valkyrie; an angel without wings. Asshole. As soon as she realized, she broke it off with him and broke his nose too.

"Bo… listen, I… we…" Tora lowers her head and gently pushes his hands off her hips. "We need…"

"Before you start…" Bo interrupts and lifts her chin so her eyes meet his. "I heard what the Valkyries said. You can't date a human."

"But how?" Tora frowns. "You were bound upstairs."

"Museum walls." Bo grins. "They don't give you much privacy."

"Oh." Tora flushes, thinking of what she and Bo almost did in the exhibition room. The entire squad would have heard them, maybe even the entire street.

Bo laughs, guessing her thoughts. "The squad are loud as hell. They wouldn't have heard us. Don't worry. I wouldn't do that to you."

Relieved, Tora smiles. "So, you're okay with us just being friends then?"

"Of course." Bo leans over and kisses her forehead. "Friends are better than nothing. It's not like we were getting married or anything, right?"

"Exactly." Tora agrees, relieved he's not upset. She's always known she and Bo wouldn't end up together, but it was fun while it lasted.

Astra and Ethan on the other hand; that's a different matter. They grip each other tightly, tears falling down their cheeks as they kiss and whisper in each other's ears. It makes Tora want to puke. The sooner she gets Astra away from him, the better.

"Keep an eye on him." Tora lowers her voice and nods towards Ethan. "I don't know how, but he knew the warlock's name, and there's no way steel kept out that demon wolf. There's something seriously off about him."

Bo raises his eyebrows. "You're kidding?"

"I'm not." Tora flares her nostrils. "Don't trust him."

Bo nods and eyes Ethan from a distance, suspicion tightening his jaw.

"Star? You ready?" Tora interrupts. If they keep going, she's going to need a pair of pliers to tear them apart. "We've got to go now."

Locked in a passionate embrace, Astra and Ethan ignore her and continue their goodbye. Tora rolls her eyes. She can't understand what Astra sees in the guy. He gives off so many red flags, and Astra either ignores them on purpose, or she really is that oblivious and naive.

Astra was there when Ethan called the warlock by name. She was there when the door held. She was there when he tried to get her to leave Tora behind with the wolf demons. Astra is not stupid. She has to know something is wrong with Ethan, yet she still clings to him and promises to find a way back. It makes Tora want to shake her. They say love is blind, but she didn't realize it made people stupid.

"Okay, that's enough." Tora grabs Astra's arm and pulls her across the street, over the perimeter line. It's a horribly bitchy thing to do, but she doesn't care. If she has to watch them suck face any longer, she's going to puke.

For the first time in a long time, Tora and Astra stand outside the village perimeter, looking in at the place they called home for a year. Bo and Ethan wave and disappear from the street, swallowed by the dark city of Greenwich Village.

Bright lights flash in the distance where the Valkyries and the squads battle the wolf demons. Thunderhead clouds roll across the sky, flashing with strikes of lightning and rumbling thunder.

A deep sense of dread curdles Tora's stomach. It feels like she's abandoning Bo, the squad, and her friends when they need her the most, but it's not just about protecting Astra; not anymore. If they don't find Montauk's secret to keeping out the demons, Greenwich Village won't survive, no one will.

CHAPTER TWELVE

Jogging through the dark streets, Astra and Tora get as far from Greenwich Village as they can, cautiously dodging fallen debris and scanning what's left of the streets for demons, fae, and opportunistic humans. Who knows what lurks in the Deadlands?

Sulfur and smoke clog their lungs, soaking into their hair and clothes. Overgrown weeds, algae, and mold climb over cars and buses, abandoned during the War of the Gods. Tora gives Astra one of the bright glowing canvases Bo made and carries one herself. They aren't bright enough to use as torches but at least they won't lose each other in the darkness. With her Valkyrie vision, she can steer them in the right direction.

Her mother Freya often talked about the abilities of the Valkyries, but neither she nor Astra ever truly understood. It's more than just an increased

165

sense of smell, taste, touch, sight, and sound, it's being able to feel the senses in a new intense way. She can taste the moisture in the air, hear the cockroaches scurrying in the debris, see the particles of the realm barriers, smell the sulfur and smoke of demons' past, and feel the gravity of the earth pressing against her skin.

It makes her wish for her mother, to be able to talk to her, see her, hug her even though she would have squirmed and tried to get away. There are so many things she would have said had she known they were her last moments.

For starters, she wouldn't have argued with her about a guy. It wasn't that her mother wanted her to remain celibate, she was simply protecting both her and Bo should the gods find out.

Lactic acid burns through her muscles as the events of the past twenty-four hours slows her pace. Victor is gone. Teresa is gone. Her mother... gone. A few hours ago, they were all drinking and eating, enjoying a night off for her birthday, and now they're all gone. Everything has changed. Just when they thought they were getting a handle on the demons and fae, the game completely changed.

"Are you okay?" Astra whispers and slows her step. "Are you tired?"

Swallowing her tears, Tora nods and pushes the grief and guilt back down into the pit of her stomach. "I'm fine. Remember what Mom used to say? Valkyries don't need sleep. Don't condition your body to need it."

Astra rolls her eyes. "Honey. I loved your mother, but she also questioned the need to bathe regularly."

Chuckling, Tora remembers their first month in the Realm of Man when her mother refused to shower. The woman could have slayed demons with her smell alone. They were all used to bathing in fresh creeks and lakes back in the Realm of Angels, and Freya didn't trust the showers. She thought it was unnatural, so instead, she washed off in the Hudson River. It took a month of insults to get her to shower.

"We'll need to sleep eventually." Astra stifles a yawn. Her eyes droop despite her fear.

Tora continuously scans the area. It looks like they're having a lucky night. The Deadlands are crawling with demons and fae, but so far, they haven't seen a single threat.

"When we find somewhere safer," Tora says as they approach the midtown tunnel. She may not be able to feel fear like she used to, but she sure as hell knows she should fear the tunnel. "Let's just get through the tunnel first."

The tunnel is probably crawling with demons and fae. It's the perfect place for demons to hunt. They just need to get through as quickly and quietly as possible.

"What?" Astra pales and stops walking, her eyes wide and frightened. "We're going in there?"

"We have to," Tora squeezes Astra's hand and eyes the dark tunnel. If there was any other way to cross the water, she would take it in a second, but she can't risk flying, not with the Valkyries close by.

Swallowing hard, Astra nods and follows Tora into the tunnel, the glowing canvas held tight in her hand.

Water drips from the ceiling and trickles through the cracks of the aging structure, the presence of magic thick in the air, scented in light lavender and cedarwood, keeping the water from overtaking the tunnel. Cars sit abandoned and rusting in the middle of the road, covered in green sludge, grime, and mold.

Tora has no idea why the Nephilim witches and warlocks want this tunnel accessible, but she doesn't particularly care, just as long as it gets them to Montauk and back.

"Ugh gross." Tora gags as she spots a huge sewer rat gnawing on an elf's ear and continues to trudge through the ankle-deep water filled with slime and debris.

"What? What is it?" Astra freezes and points the glowing canvas at her feet. "Did I step in something?"

Tora swallows the bile rising in her throat. It's a good thing the glowing canvas isn't bright enough to be a torch. If Astra knew what was beneath their feet, she'd run in the opposite direction. "You really don't want to know."

Body parts and rotting corpses litter the ground; a human arm, a pixie toe, a dead crawler demon, a spider demon's leg. If Astra can't see it, she doesn't need to know about it.

Dripping water echoes in Tora's ears like a gunshot, heightening her anxiety, her hearing sensitive to any and all sounds. The smell of rotting corpses, mold, and rust assault her nose, suppressing any hunger pains she might have felt.

Being a fully-fledged Valkyrie has its perks, but even some of those perks can be a curse. She could do without being able to smell the feces-like odor of rotting corpses, and the constant assault of sulfur.

"This is disgusting." Astra gags. "I can barely see, but god, I can smell everything. How long will we be in the tunnel?"

Pulling out the map, Tora tries to find the tunnel and shrugs, still not entirely sure what she's looking at. Her only measure is her mother's time estimate of a few days and Bo's route marking on the map. "I don't know. Half an hour, an hour maybe. Maybe three? I have no idea"

"The quicker the better." Astra links their arms and picks up her pace, wanting out of the tunnel even more than Tora.

Climbing over god knows what, and stepping in fuck knows who, Tora and Astra quickly make their way through the tunnel. Tora has seen a lot of death and disgusting shit in her time, but the midtown tunnel has to be one of the worst so far.

It's like all the crap, urine, blood, and rot has washed off the surrounding cities and settled in the tunnel. All she needs now is a child demon to pop out of the shadows singing the Baby Shark song Bo used to irritate her with.

"I see it!" Astra claps her hands. "I see the light at the end of the tunnel!"

Tora snorts. "I can't believe you just said that. That was so human."

The tunnel must be shorter than she thought if they're already near the end. They haven't been walking that long, not that she's complaining. Getting the hell out of the death tunnel sounds like heaven.

"I know right!" Astra chuckles. "Who says a Valkyrie can't pass for human?"

"Barely." Tora starts to laugh but stops as pressure builds in her skull.

Frowning, she shoves the map in her boot and pulls Astra back to her side. They can't be near the end of the tunnel. Astra said, 'light at the end of the tunnel.' Light, as in electricity or sunshine. It's the middle of the night, and there are no lights or electricity out in the Deadlands.

"Oh shit!" Tora pushes Astra to the ground as a portal gate explodes up ahead. Shards of purple crystal fly about the tunnel and embed into the walls. Water pours out of the portal gate, gushing along the ground. Bright lights glow like a beacon in the darkened tunnel.

Astra shivers on her knees, her blue jeans soaked through. "What was that?"

"Pressure gate. Some of the rifts burst open instead of ripping," Tora whispers, her heart pounding in her ears. "I had a few crystals embed in my leg a few months back; remember?"

A fast-tapping sound, like fingernails on a keyboard, echoes through the tunnel. Astra and Tora freeze. They lock eyes silently.

They're not alone in the tunnel. Not anymore.

Astra's lip trembles.

The sound gets louder and faster, rumbling through the tunnel like an avalanche. Cautiously, Tora puts her finger to her lips and peeks over an abandoned car. Black-tipped claws clap against the ground as huge blood covered demon crabs scramble out of the portal.

Tora widens her eyes. There are at least ten of them, maybe more, all the size of Great Danes, their teeth like vampires, each with eight claws that look perfectly capable of cutting a man's leg in half.

"Fuck." Tora grunts. They need to get out of the tunnel fast. These demons are only lower-level demons, but who knows what else will come through the portal behind them?

If they can sneak passed without being noticed, they might make it out of the tunnel alive. She's fought crab demons before, but never this many at once, and she doesn't want to draw the attention of anything else that may be lurking in the shadows out in the Deadlands.

Pointing to the side of the tunnel, Tora remains silent and directs Astra away from the demons. They duck and weave around abandoned cars, trucks, and buses, avoiding debris and bodies, trying not to slosh around in the water.

They don't get far before Astra gasps and stops. She pales and points one shaking finger into the distance, wisps of her strawberry blonde hair blowing around her face.

Tora frowns, every cell in her body suddenly alert.

They're in a tunnel. There shouldn't be a breeze.

Not even twenty feet away, another portal shimmers brilliantly against the dark tunnel walls. Next to it, another portal rips open, then another, then another, then another. One of the portals snaps shut and disappears.

Astra whimpers. "Is that normal?"

Her mother warned her the portals were unpredictable, opening and closing constantly outside of the village perimeter, away from the crystals. She's never seen anything like it. Thousands of demons and fae could just walk through the portals, and there's nothing she could do about it. Her senses and reflexes are more powerful, but it doesn't mean she can take on thousands of demons and fae by herself.

"I don't know," Tora whispers. The last thing she wants to do is scare Astra, but she doesn't know what else to say. Lying isn't going to help.

A female with black and fuchsia hair sticks her head through one of the portal gates, her irises burning bright fuchsia, rimmed in a thick black outline. Another female with white hair streaked in multicolored blue, red, purple, and black peeks through one of the other portals, her hazel eyes wide and curious.

"Boo!" The black and fuchsia-haired female juts her head out like a chicken.

The other female flinches but recovers quickly and rolls her eyes. "You're an idiot Tia."

Chuckling, the female with black and fuchsia hair steps out of the portal, her large gothic tattered and torn fuchsia and black ombre wings flexing at her back. "Fuck off Britney. This is no place for children."

"Fuck you Tia." The one named Britney spits and curls her lip as she pulls her head back through the portal gate.

Stuck between the crab demons and the faery, Tora puts her finger to her lips and pushes Astra down as far as she can so they're hidden. She doesn't know which is worse, the fae or the demons. She's never been in this situation before. The portals in the village never open this close together and never at the same time.

The faery paces slowly, her thigh-high eight-inch heeled boots crunching on bones and debris. Skin-tight black leather pants and a black lace bodice hug her body, pushing up her large breasts.

"I can taste your fear shit monkeys." The faery sings and licks her deep red lips, tasting the fear in the air. "Well, one of you anyway."

"Move." Tora pushes Astra forward. They scramble on all fours and duck down behind a truck, hoping the size and old fumes will hide them from the faery and crabs.

Tora peeks around one side, checking on the faery while Astra peeks around the other side to check on the crabs. They need to get the hell out of the tunnel. If they wait, they're dead. They're like a snack in a tube... like cookie dough.

"We're fucking cookie dough," Tora mutters and shakes her head.

Astra suddenly lets out a blood-curdling scream, her voice bouncing off the walls and piercing through her ears. Tora whips her head around and pulls Astra back behind her, the Valkyrie mark on her wrist burning as her soul sword shoots down her arm. She grips the hilt and holds the glowing purple sword in front of her.

Three blood covered demon crabs stand in formation, their antennae rubbing together, smelling their surroundings.

The faery can go fuck herself. There's no fucking way they're going to be taken out by a goddamned crab, even if it is a demon crab.

The crabs rear up onto two of their massive clawed legs and roar like an angry pack of bears, shocking Tora into silence. She doesn't think. She just swings, slicing one of the crabs in two, then pulls back her sword and stabs one of the creepy bastards through the stomach and flicks the large body away from her. The third crab runs away, scurrying back towards the portal.

Chaos reigns as the crabs' roar like bears and begin screeching in high-pitched tones, bumping into each other and stabbing at the air with their claws.

Astra gasps and grips Tora's arm as the crabs drive their taloned claws through each other, lashing out at anything that gets near them. "What are they doing?"

"I have no idea." Tora shakes her head, her eyes weeping from the crab's blood, the fumes like paint stripper. It's the first time she's ever seen demons attack each other. It's also the first time she's heard a crab demon make a sound, but from what the warlock said, nothing she knows about the demons is correct.

"Crab demons are blind and deaf you idiots." The faery Tia mocks behind them. "They respond to vibration."

Spinning Astra behind her, Tora levels her sword at the malevolent faery, her arm itching to thrust and strike. The bitch came out of nowhere and Tora didn't hear a thing, even with her new Valkyrie hearing.

Grinning, the malevolent faery taps her dark black nails on the side of the truck, her vibrant fuchsia eyes sparkling. The crabs respond to the vibrations and rear up on their back claws.

"Better move quickly ladies." Flexing her large gothic wings, the faery shoots up into the air and lands on top of the truck as the crab demons dash toward them. "Crab demons may be blind, but the fuckers are fast, and they eat anything. Better get moving."

Tora and Astra widen their eyes and scramble up onto the roof of the truck, taking their chances with the faery instead of the demon crabs. They watch in horror as the demon crabs grab entire skulls in their claws and smash them to pieces like twigs.

"Nasty little fuckers, aren't they?" Tia crouches down and peers over the edge.

"What do you want?" Tora snaps, refusing to play the faery's game. "If you're not here to eat or kill us, why the hell are you here?"

Tia shrugs. "Think of me as a tourist; an interested observer."

"Interested in what?" Tora frowns. What could the faery possibly gain from setting the crabs on them again and watching the fight? She might get a little bit of fear and anger to feed on, but that's it. It's a lot of trouble for nothing more than a snack when she could torture them for a feast.

"Tor... Tora." Astra trembles and pulls on her arm, her eyes as wide as saucers.

"This, I believe, is what they call the main attraction." Tia nods towards an open portal.

A humanoid demon at least eight feet tall stands at the entrance, large rhino tusks jutting out of either side of its chin. Its teeth are dog-like, with sharp canines; its skin like burned charcoal alligator husk with thick black boned dreadlocks instead of hair.

It has the snout of a dog, but the eyes and ears are humanlike. Copper armor scorches its already burned charcoal skin as it flakes and bleeds. In its hand, the demon holds a battle ax, its eyes ginger red.

Tora's throat tightens. The demons from her nightmares. The ones who rained down from the sky during the War of the Gods. "What the fuck is that?"

"That, is a Baleful Demon, bred for the army of Hades. This Realm's equivalent of a caveman." Tia sits on the roof of the truck with her legs crossed beneath her.

"Caveman?" Tora frowns. "They died out long ago."

"In this realm." Tia smirks. "They live side by side with the human equivalent in the Demon Realm."

"What's the human equivalent?" Astra asks in almost a whisper.

"You'll find out sweetpea." Tia winks and gestures at the demon. "Well, go on then. Fight."

"You want me to fight that thing?" Tora widens her eyes.

"I don't want you to do anything." Tia scoffs. "I just came for the entertainment. Besides, isn't that what you're trained for; Valkyrie?"

The demon is like something out of a human horror movie; like a mix between the Orcs and the Predator movies. She was there when the War of the Gods spilled into the Realm of Man. She was there when the humanoid demons rained down from the sky. She dreams about them often, but she never saw them up close. No wonder the realm was torn to shreds.

The demon stomps towards them, its large boots crunching on skulls, bones, and crab demons; its eyes trained on Astra and Tora. It sneers.

"What do we do?" Astra squeaks and takes an involuntary step back.

"You fight or you die, dumbass." Tia rolls her eyes and leans her elbow on her knee, staring at the large foreheaded demon.

"Fine!" Tora hands Astra the backpack.

The sadistic bitch wants a show? She'll give her a show.

The demon roars. Tora grips the hilt of her sword, her pastel purple eyes burning with anger. Her large white swan-like wings spring free from her back as she jumps down off the truck.

Fucking fae. The bitch could at least help if she's not going to eat them.

"Fight it is." Tora holds her sword ready as the demon advances. The demon looks twice as large and twice as ugly down on the ground, but the bigger the enemy, the harder they fall.

Tia claps her hands gleefully as the demon charges and raises its axe.

Years of training and centuries of Valkyrie blood spur her movements as she swings her sword, adrenaline coursing hard through her veins, her sword burning purple.

Tora can't stop the grin from spreading across her face as butterflies take flight in her stomach. This is what she trained for. This is what the life of a Valkyrie should be. Battle. It's ingrained into her DNA. There is no flight, there is only the fight.

The demon deflects with the handle of his axe and swings it at her head. Tora ducks and slides out of the way, coughing and gagging on the putrid sulfur smell of demon breath.

"Oh gods. Don't they have toothbrushes in the Demon Realm?" Tora chokes.

"Oi! Dumbass!" Tia laughs as the demon swings his axe again and again. "Baleful Demons don't speak English. Try grunting or jumping around like a gorilla; he might understand that."

Rolling her eyes, Tora ducks and weaves, dodging the demon's frenzied attack. Just perfect. Not only does she have an audience, the malevolent bitch thinks she's a comedian.

Ignoring the faery, Tora spots an opening and thrusts her sword at the demon's stomach, but the demon is too quick, too agile for a beast its size.

Pivoting sideways, the demon latches onto her blade and smiles like a psycho through a mess of teeth and tusks as the soul sword burns into the flesh of his hand before punching Tora hard in the face with the flat side of his axe.

"Fuck!" Tora stumbles and lets go of her sword as blood pisses out of her nose. Tears cascade like a waterfall from her eyes, the sting of defeat burning through her sinuses.

Laughing, the demon flings her sword up into the air and catches the hilt as she regains her footing.

"Huh! And she loses her sword already!" Tia cheers and throws her arms up in the air.

Tora grits her teeth through the pain and wipes her weeping eyes as sweat pours down her neck. Panic ripples through her entire body, turning her stomach to acid. She can't believe she lost her sword. She's had it for like what… Five minutes? How pathetic. Her mother would kill her for being so weak.

Without her Valkyrie sword, how the fuck is she meant to kill this thing? Her knives and blades might injure it, but no way would they puncture deep enough to kill it. It's got alligator skin for fucks sake. It doesn't even need armor.

The demon charges at her with her own sword.

Tora reaches for her knife but hisses as a sharp pain pulsates from the Valkyrie marking on her wrist. She frowns as the marking burns bright purple and spreads down into each of her fingers.

The demon growls low in his throat and stops his advance as the sword disintegrates from his hand and appears in hers.

Tora grins down at her soul sword, relief spreading through her veins like a cool balm. The sword won't leave her. It's a part of her; unable to be separated. It technically is her.

"Boo! No fair!" Tia cups her mouth to amplify her voice. "That's cheating! Ref!"

"Shut up!" Astra snaps and paces back and forth, squeezing her hands together tightly.

The demon roars and charges once again, the sound of its voice like thunder in the damp tunnel. Tora tightens her grip and holds her sword ready but the ugly ass demon jumps over her head at the last second and lands on the bonnet of the truck.

Tora gasps and looks up. Standing on the edge of the truck's roof, Astra pales and backs away. She's not staring at the malevolent faery. She's not even staring at the Baleful Demon. Astra is watching the horde of demon crabs scamper across the ground and climb up the large wheels of the truck, responding to the vibrations.

"Mother fucker!" Tora shoots up into the air, her large white feathered wings beating at her back, and lands on the roof in front of Astra.

The demon is smarter than she thought. Not only is he going after Astra to bait her, he's using the demon crabs to help him. Dirty fucking bastard! None of the other demons have been this smart. She shouldn't have underestimated him. She shouldn't have taken her eyes off Astra at all.

Tia smirks and spins around on her bum to watch, studying Tora with renewed interest. The demon ignores the malevolent faery and jumps onto the roof, the metal bending and warping under its weight. Its eyes burn ginger red. It huffs like a bull and stalks towards them.

"Agh!" Tora yells and charges the demon, her rage like rocket fuel in her veins, pushing her harder and faster. She needs the demon away from Astra. She needs the demon to die. And she needs to get Astra the fuck away from the demon crabs and the malevolent faery.

The demon deflects her attack with his battle axe, pushing her back, the metal harder than steel and black as night.

Astra gasps.

Tora curls her lip. The metal. It's the same metal used in the demon blades, one of the only weapons that can kill a Valkyrie. That's why this demon's skin is burning and flaking. Just like a Valkyrie sword, it burns demon flesh.

But why would Hades suddenly risk his warriors by burning their flesh? He never has before. Only Generals carry demon blades as it doesn't affect them.

It feels like Hades is getting desperate. It also feels like Hades is targeting the Valkyries. But why?

"Fucker!" Tora yells and pulls back her sword. The demon pulls back his battle axe, reacting exactly as Tora had hoped. Instead of striking, she pulls her trusty blade from her hip in one quick movement and flings it at the demon, taking it off guard.

Satisfaction bubbles in her blood as the blade plunges deep into the demon's neck, penetrating its alligator-like skin. The demon screeches and thrashes his head from side to side, white foam bubbling from his mouth and dripping off his chin.

"Huh!" Tora cheers and casts a smug look over her shoulder at the malevolent faery.

"Watch out!" Astra screams.

The demon launches itself at Tora and slams down his axe as she whips her head back around. She raises her sword in defense and is forced down on one knee, the full weight of the demon and axe held above her.

Astra screams. Two crab demons clamper over the side of the truck, covered in blood and puss.

Desperately, Tora tries to push the heavy ass demon back to get to Astra; to save her from the crab demons but it's no use. The demon is too heavy; too strong, and his weapon weighs a ton.

Lactic acid burns deep in her arms, abs, and legs; her chest aching with the need to keep Astra safe as the demon's rancid breath and rotting skin coats her lungs.

Fucking Baleful Demons! Why couldn't they have just died out like the caveman did?

"No!" Astra screams and shoves one of the crab demons in the demon's face, its claws crunching down on bone as it attaches to the Baleful Demon's face.

The demon roars and drops his axe as the demon crab mutilates his burned face. Hundreds of crabs scamper out of the portal and climb up the truck, attacking the demon in packs.

Careful to remain quiet, Tora drops her arms and watches the dying humanoid demon as he screams and is torn apart while being dragged off the roof, back through the portal by the demon crabs, clicking animatedly as the portal snaps shut behind them.

Tora can't believe it. Astra saved her. The girl who is afraid of fighting, literally picked up a disgusting Great Dane sized demon crab and shoved it in another disgusting demon's face. Maybe Astra would have made a great Valkyrie after-all.

"Bravo! Great show. I did not expect that." Laughing, Tia claps her hands and jumps down off the truck as she starts towards the flickering portal. "I like the twist at the end. I might come and see it again sometime."

Tora narrows her eyes and grits her teeth. She should chase after the bitch of a faery and drive her sword through her big fat mouth, but she doesn't have the energy, not right now.

"Come on." Astra pulls Tora to her feet and keeps an eye on the faery. "Let's get out of here before something else comes through the portal."

Glaring at the back of the faery's head, Tora jumps down off the truck and keeps stride with Astra along the tunnel. Bitch is the only word to describe the faery. Most fae that come through the portal are there for one thing; food and pleasure. They feed off the blood, pain, anger, and hate of every single species in the realms, but this one; this one was more interested in watching the outcome of the fight, and Tora has a sneaking suspicion it has something to do with the coming war the Valkyries spoke of.

Something tells her this isn't the last she's seen of the malevolent bitch of a faery.

CHAPTER THIRTEEN

Tora inhales deeply as they emerge on the other side of the Midtown Tunnel. Endless darkness expands around them, no longer contained by the tunnel walls. There could be hundreds of demons hiding out in the wide-open spaces but Tora doesn't care. It's like she can breathe again. Like the clamp crushing her chest has been released. She wants to drop to the ground and kiss the dirt, tongue and all. She doesn't care if they get rained on. Hell, she doesn't care if they get struck by lightning. Anything is better than the tunnel of death; anything.

The ritual appears to have changed her sense of fear but not her sense of urgency and anxiety. Her stomach feels like she swallowed a pack of razor blades.

That Baleful Demon was even more hideous than she imagined, than she dreamed of. The training dummies they used in the Realm of Angels are like cute stuffed teddy bears compared to that ugly beast, and the malevolent faery said they were like the human cavemen. So, what the hell is the human equivalent going to be like?

The warlock knew something was happening with the portals, the malevolent faery knew something was happening with the portals. The war is starting, and they're stuck in the middle of it.

Following what little road she can see under the overgrown weeds and dirt, Tora continually scans their dark surroundings, flinching at every spark of light. Debris, moss, vines, mold, and flowers litter the streets, buildings, street lights, and signs. Countless buildings and structures are all but demolished and crumbling.

No one and nothing could have survived the war out in the Deadlands, or after. It's the place where hope goes to die. They walk for hours without seeing a single human, animal, or building that isn't almost completely demolished which might explain why they haven't run across another mob of demons.

Drenched, yawning, and covered in crap, Astra leans on a fence separating the forest and the road and grips her stomach, her face pale and drawn. "We've got to stop Tora. Please? We've been walking for hours, and it's been more than twenty-four hours since either of us slept."

Pulling the map out of her boot, Tora shuts her eyes tight then opens them wide, trying to ease her fatigue. Leaves rustle in the breeze, joining in the sound of musical raindrops tapping on the ground as the storm dissipates. Thousands of trees line either side of the road, separated by short metal fences. Some are charcoal, split and fallen, but the forest rejuvenates itself, growing from the ashes.

Despite what her mother used to say, even a newly fully-fledged Valkyrie needs to rest, and Astra is right. It feels like forever since she slept. Thank god there are no mirrors out in the Deadlands. She's pretty sure she looks like the walking dead.

"Alright. If I'm reading the map right, we're at Forest Park in Queens." Tora cracks her tight neck muscles and tucks the map back into her boot. "We sleep under the trees. It's too dangerous near the buildings."

Jumping the fence, Tora and Astra find a cluster of large trees reasonably close to the road and set up camp. Lingering close to buildings in previously built-up areas is one of the stupidest things anyone can do, even if they are mostly demolished. It's the first place demons and malevolent fae look for their prey, knowing that humans prefer the comforts they were used to. Using the roads isn't much safer but they have no other way of knowing the way to Montauk, not with Tora's limited map-reading ability.

"So, what did you pack?" Astra opens the backpack and peers inside.

"I have no idea. Dr A made me take it. He said there's some protein bars and water I think." Tora scans the dark forest. They're alone for now, but who knows how long that will last. A few hours of rest are all they can afford, and they can scarcely afford that. If the Valkyries have discovered they're gone, it doesn't matter how far away they are. They will find them.

Digging through the backpack, Astra finds a couple of thermal space blankets and bottles of water. She holds one of each out to Tora. "Here, take these."

Laying her blanket on the ground to keep them dry, Tora uncaps the water bottle and props herself up against the large tree, the trunk hard against the back of her head but no less inviting. She drinks greedily as the cool liquid slides down her throat into her stomach. Her muscles untangle, thankful for the fluid and rest. If she'd known they were going to be running for their lives tonight, she would have avoided the vodka.

In the last twenty-four hours, she fought a child demon, trained with her mother, fought at the markets, inhaled half a bottle of vodka, nearly died twice at the hands of the warlock, actually died once only to be resurrected, and fought wolf demons, crab demons, and an ugly ass Baleful Demon. Fully-fledged Valkyrie or not, she deserves a rest, at least for a little while.

It feels like she hasn't had time to grieve. Everything has happened so fast; too fast. She stares up at the trees, her body crying out for sleep, her mind refusing to give it as one question plagues her mind, like one line of a song stuck on repeat. Was her mother reaped for War like the Valkyries said? Or did her soul progress or recycle?

It's not something Valkyries talk about, but given their prime responsibilities are killing and resurrecting, she always assumed their souls were recycled, cleansed with fire, smoke, and brimstone before beginning the trials once again. It is their sacrifice for the nine realms.

Tora sighs as a deep ache hollows out her chest. Her mother will never get to see the beautiful waterfalls, diamond mountains, and amethyst lakes of the Realm of Angels again. Neither will Astra; neither will she.

If Hades hadn't been such a selfish prick, none of this would have happened. Her mother would still be alive, and the nine realms would be intact. She would be home; she would be happy, arguing with her mother about wanting to hang out with Astra and the rest of the fledglings down at the stream, partying with the male angels from their community.

Life was simpler in the Realm of Angels. There were no schools, not like human ones anyway. Each day, her mother would tell her stories, teach her life skills, and train her in the art of battle.

When families wanted to share knowledge with the rest of the community, it was shared at great gatherings in the fields. Angles have always enjoyed telling stories of themselves and their ancestors, sharing their knowledge and history.

There were no jobs like in the Realm of Man. Everyone simply did what they enjoyed, what they needed to do, and what they were good at. For Valkyries, that was fighting.

"You asleep?" Astra whispers.

Tora shakes her head and tenses as flashes of light spark in the distance; her bones weary with fatigue. "Not yet."

They can't linger for long, not out in the open like this, but they need sleep. Astra more so than Tora. A couple of hours should be okay as long as neither she nor Astra have any nightmares. If the fae catch their fear scent, they're dead.

Rolling on her side, Astra props herself up on her elbow and plays with a blade of grass, her eyes lowered to the ground. "Do you think this is happening everywhere? In all the realms."

Tora pinches her lips into a small smile. She knows exactly what Astra's thinking. She's thinking about the Realm of Angels, about their home and whether demons and malevolent fae are wreaking havoc back there, the same thing Tora has been thinking about for nearly a year.

"I don't know for sure, but I've been out there almost every night for a year, and the only things coming through those portals are demons and malevolent fae," Tora says. "No angels, no gods, no benevolent fae, and no ghosts. I think it's only the three lower realms affected. The Demon Realm, the Malevolent Fae Realm, and the Realm of Man."

Astra glances up from the blade of grass, her eyes softening with relief.

A lot of the Angels may have been prejudiced against the Valkyries because they were different, because they were born without wings, but the Realm of Angels was still their home. Neither of them would want anything to happen to their beautiful home.

"Do you think there's anyone left?" Astra asks. "Any of the adult angels?"

"Not all the Angels would have fought in the war." Tora drops her head to the side. "The gods would have used every single Valkyrie resource first."

Bitterness drips from her lips like poison. The Valkyrie bloodline is long and proud, but the war cost them more than any other species in all the realms. Fledgling Valkyries as young as six were forced to undergo the ritual because their abilities outweigh any angel, and thanks to the selfish gods, the Valkyries are nearly extinct. All that remains are Tora, Astra, and the bitches who killed her mother. What a legacy.

"Do you think we'll ever go back?" Astra lays her head down beside her.

Tora scoffs. "After everything the Gods put us through, why would we want to? Do you want to go home?"

"No. There's nothing for me there." Astra shakes her head. "At least here I have you and Ethan."

Tora rolls her eyes and tries not to gag. Fucking Ethan. It might be worth moving back to the Realm of Angels just to get Astra away from that creep. The guy is full of shit. He knew the warlock's name and was more than happy for Tora to die on the roof fighting the wolf demons. There's something not right with that guy, and one day, she's going to prove it; even if it kills her.

"Do you miss Bo?" Astra asks.

Tora snorts. With everything else going on, missing Bo is the least of her problems. "Yes and no. We broke up just before we left."

"What?" Astra sits up like it's the worst thing in the world. "Why? Are you okay?"

"Valkyries aren't allowed to date humans." Tora shrugs. "It wasn't just my mother's rule. It was a Valkyrie rule, a rule passed down by the gods. The punishment is death. I love Bo, but not in the way I should to risk either of our lives."

"Oh." Astra lowers her eyes, no doubt thinking about herself and Ethan. They'd always assumed her mother made up the rule. They never once thought it would end in death.

"I wouldn't worry Star," Tora says in an effort to ease her worries. "They're not going to make you into a fully-fledged Valkyrie. Not if I can help it. The rule won't apply to you, but it wouldn't be a bad idea to stay away from Ethan for a while."

Astra frowns and rests her back against the tree, refusing to acknowledge the suggestion. "I guess your mother was right after-all."

"Freya was right about a lot of things." Tora chokes as a deep ache spreads through her bones, missing her mother more than she thought possible. Never once did she think losing her mother was an option. The woman was an Amazon; a Valkyrie; a Warrior. Unflappable in every way, except for affection. A little bit of affection always threw her off. Now that she's gone, Tora wishes she had shown her more.

"Do you want to talk about it?" Astra leans forward and tries to catch her eye, her voice soft.

"Not really." Tora rolls on her side, hoping to end the conversation and hide the tears building in her eyes. They're out in the middle of the Deadlands. She can't afford to give in to her grief out here. Not now; not yet.

"Tor?" Astra rests her hand on her shoulder. "You can't keep it in. You need to talk about it."

"Which part?" Tora snorts and wipes her cheek discreetly as a stray tear escapes her eye, the weight of the world suddenly heavy on her shoulders. "The part where my mother died, the part where I died, or the part where we're absolutely fucked?"

Sighing, Astra lays back down beside her. "We'll get through this Tor. As long as we stick together, we'll get through this."

Tears break free from Tora's eyes as Astra wraps her arm around her, and holds her tightly from behind, whispering promises of better times.

Without her mother, she feels lost. She's been preparing for this war her entire life, but without Freya, she feels like a child learning to walk again, alone. She needs her mother. She wants her mom. The woman who could stand up to anything. But she's gone; disintegrated into dust. She can't even give her a proper ceremony, burning her body on a long boat like the Vikings of old. The Valkyrie blade demolished her body, and the bitch Inga just gets away with it.

They're on the run in the middle of the Deadlands because of the Valkyries. Her mother is dead because of the Valkyries. This whole mess is because of the Valkyries and the gods.

Suddenly the ritual she begged for every day over the past year seems more like a curse than a privilege.

Tears stream steadily down Tora's face as she closes her eyes and tries to get a grip on herself. Her mother would want her to fight, to get Astra to safety, and to do that, she needs a few hours of sleep, just enough to regain her strength.

In the quiet of the surrounding forest, without the immediate threat of demons and fae, Tora steadies her breathing until sleep takes her, tears still silently streaming down her face. She doesn't dream. She doesn't move. She just sleeps.

CHAPTER FOURTEEN

A mere two hours later, Tora wakes feeling alive and rested, like she slept for a good twelve hours. Nothing hurts. Nothing stings. It's strange considering she's usually in some sort of pain from her injuries and bruises, not to mention severely sleep-deprived.

Shivering, Astra buries herself deeper under the thermal blanket, rousing but refusing to wake, the foil cocooning her like a burrito.

Frowning, Tora sits up and inspects her injuries, new and old. The scrape and scar from the demon child is gone from her bicep. The slice on her forearm from sparring with her mother is gone. The bone-deep scar from when she jumped off the Emerald Cliffs when she was eight is gone. There's not so much as a bruise left on her body, or a goosebump for that matter.

Come to think of it, her mother was scar-free, never complained of the cold, and rarely slept for more than an hour or two at a time, if she slept at all.

The Valkyrie ritual... it has to be. She knew Valkyries healed faster than fledglings, but not this quick. It's unbelievable. But then... why do Valkyries have healers like Astra?

That's a question for another time. Right now, they need to get moving. They can't afford to linger any longer. They shouldn't have lingered at all. They need to get far from Greenwich Village and quickly.

"Star? Time to wake up." Tora shakes Astra's arm. "Come on. We have to go. The sun will be up soon."

Grumbling, Astra pulls her blanket over her head, her strawberry blonde hair plastered to the side of her face. "Five more minutes."

"Nope. No. Nuh ah." Tora pulls the blanket off. "Get up sleeping beauty. We're lucky the seven dwarfs haven't eaten us yet."

"Ugh! Fine." Astra groans and stomps off to relieve herself behind a tree. "And that's not how the story goes."

"Yes, it is. The seven dwarves stole Sleeping Beauty's glass shoe and hid at Grandma's house. When she came looking for it, they pretended to be grandma and ate her. Wait... no. That's not it." Tora sneaks off to pee behind another tree and tries to remember how the children's story goes.

Teresa told her many stories over the past year while on the hunt. Fiction she called it. It's one of the strangest human customs Tora has ever heard of. Why would anyone make up stories that weren't true, and why would anyone want to read them for fun?

"Oh wait! I remember." Tora meets Astra back at the tree. "They waited until she went to sleep then the prince ate her, or kissed her, then the dwarfs ate the shoe?"

"You should just stop." Astra screws up her face and puts away the thermal blankets. "Like really. You just massacred three kids' stories in a matter of seconds. Never read to any children; ever. Okay? Promise?"

Tora snorts. That's the last thing she was planning on doing, especially after fighting that child demon. "Done."

Digging through the backpack, Astra pulls out a couple of protein bars and a bag of almonds. "Breakfast?"

Tora rips open a protein bar and shoves the entire thing in her mouth. They wasted enough time resting. They can't stop for breakfast too.

"Eat on the way," Tora mumbles around a mouth full. "Let's go."

Shaking her head, Astra shoulders the backpack and eats her protein bar like a normal person as she follows Tora out of the trees. They need to get a move on if they want to reach Montauk by Astra's birthday.

By Tora's estimate, they have roughly another thirty-six hours to go. Things would be so much faster if she could just fly them there.

Tora glances back over her shoulder at Astra and smirks. Why can't she fly them there? They're far enough away from Greenwich that the Valkyries wouldn't see them. It would be a hell of a lot safer than walking.

"What?" Astra says around a mouthful of protein bar and slows her step. "What are you doing?"

"Nothing." Tora bats her eyelashes innocently and drops back to Astra's side, a huge grin on her face.

"Don't nothing me." Astra leans away and narrows her eyes. "I know that look. That's the look that made me jump off the Emerald Cliffs into the ocean when we were kids. The one that broke my leg? What are you up to?"

"That wasn't my fault!" Tora balks, remembering it like yesterday. "We were like eight, and you're the one who wanted to know what it was like to fly."

"Yeah, but you're the one who grabbed my hand and pulled me over the cliff with you!" Astra scoffs. "I'm not doing it. Whatever it is. I'm not doing it."

Astra continues forward as Tora falls behind. Jumping from the cliffs is still one of the most amazing feelings she has ever had, even though she tore up her shin really bad. The freedom of freefalling, the wind in her hair. Astra wouldn't admit it, but she was grateful Tora made her jump. Even with a broken leg, she couldn't stop smiling.

Tying her jacket around her waist, Tora grins and releases her huge white wings. What are friends for if it's not to push you to try new things and experience life?

Running forward a few steps, Tora lifts off the ground and scoops Astra up by her armpits, her large wings beating steadily behind her. She laughs as Astra screams and squirms. "Stop fidgeting or I'm going to drop you. You're heavy enough as it is."

Astra gasps. "Are you calling me fat!"

Tora rolls her eyes. "Shut up and let me fly. Just enjoy it. This isn't as easy as it looks."

It's only been since they arrived in the Realm of Man that Astra cares about her weight. No one cared back home. The only prejudices were against the Valkyries for being born without wings. No one cared if you were heavy or what color your skin was.

"You're really hurting my arms Tor." Astra squirms, her legs dangling beneath her. "This isn't going to work."

Tora sighs. It couldn't be easy, could it? Flying would take no time at all, but if it hurts and Astra is going to complain the whole way, it's not going to work. Physics wasn't something they learned back in the Realm of Angels, but common sense was fundamental. If she can fly faster, the force should push Astra's legs back and ease the burden on her back and Astra's arms.

"Just let me try something first, okay?" Tora strengthens her grip. "If it doesn't work, I'll put you down."

"What?" Astra widens her eyes. Her face pales even further. "What are you going to do?"

Tora just grins.

"Tor?" Astra asks louder, an edge of panic in her voice. "Tora!

Beating her huge white wings as fast as they'll go, Tora picks up speed and pulls her wings back behind her like a torpedoing missile, pushing both their bodies back until they're flying through the air like the Superman comic Bo loves.

A cold wind burns her cheeks as the world screams by around them. Her long black hair streams behind her, knotting and matting as it whips around in circles. Her heart, mind, and soul sing in perfect harmony, finally complete; finally whole. And she thought jumping from the cliffs was fun. This is what she was meant to be. This is the true Valkyrie legacy.

"Err!" Tora flinches out of her euphoria as something wet splashes her in the face, souring her stomach. God, she hopes it wasn't a bug or a bird.

That would be just her luck. Her first time flying out in the open and she gets covered in bird shit.

"Tora!" Astra's muffled voice drifts on the wind.

Frowning, Tora uses her shoulder to wipe the sludge off her face and catches a glimpse of Astra's flushed cheeks. Her stomach drops. Streams of vomit spray out of Astra's mouth and sweep under them.

Fuck! It must be what hit her in the face. There's no way she can keep flying if it makes her sick. Astra's going to kill her. She's not going to forget this anytime soon.

Quickly descending and slowing her pace, Tora touches the ground gently and lets go of Astra. "Fuck Star. Are you okay?"

Tora's large wings disappear as Astra runs forward a few steps and continues to throw up on the road. Tora holds her hair back and suppresses the nausea eating away at her stomach.

"Ugh; you threw up in my face!" Tora uses her free hand to wipe at her face again in case any specs remain.

"You suck." Astra manages to say between convulsions.

Tora bites her lip. "Maybe there's a reason you never see Valkyries carrying passengers. The speed is probably too much for the body."

"Ya think?" Astra spits on the ground and sits back in the dirt, breathing heavily. "How fast were we going?"

Searching the road for any signs, Tora instead finds a handwritten sign stuck in the ground. "This sign says Northern State Pkwy, Westbury?"

"It's handwritten!" Astra complains.

"So?" Tora shrugs and looks at her map. "The world's gone to shit. What else do you expect? Looks like 200 miles an hour or so, I think?"

"Fuck Tora." Astra struggles to her feet. "No wonder I was sick."

Tora cringes. She didn't realize she was going so fast. Next time she won't try so hard when she has a passenger. "Sorry. I'll go slower next time."

"Next time?" Astra gapes. "Are you kidding me? No! No next time!"

"But we covered like 16-17 miles in minutes," Tora argues.

"I said no." Astra gets to her feet and stomps off.

Tora rolls her eyes. "Wrong way."

"Wrong way," Astra mocks and stomps back the other way.

Stifling her laughter, Tora follows. At least they were able to cut a few hours off their trip. Astra will come around, especially if they find themselves surrounded by portals again like in the tunnel.

The clock is ticking, and not in their favor. The sooner they're in Montauk, the better. Just because the city is safe from demon and fae portals, it won't keep the Valkyries out, but they are safer having one enemy to deal with at a time.

As soon as they reach Montauk and find out what the secret is to keeping out the portals, she can fly back to Greenwich Village and save the town.

CHAPTER FIFTEEN

Destruction surrounds them as Tora and Astra follow the dirt and leaf-laden road. Burned branches creak in the breeze. Bones litter the ground. Hundreds of rusted cars sit abandoned, covered in dirt and grime. Some are completely totaled, unrecognizable as vehicles except for the odd tire or two; others have crushed roofs, windows, and bonnets.

"Heads up." Tora bobs her head towards the forming crystal lines shimmering in the distance and kicks a faded scrap of food packaging off her ankle. "Portals ahead."

Astra looks up but the portals are gone, disappearing as quickly as they came. "What do you think would have happened if a portal opened right in front of you, or where you were standing? Could one open to Montauk?"

"I'm not sure. I haven't seen any that connect to other places in this realm. The rips originated in the Demon Realm, so I guess you'd end up there or in the Malevolent Fae Realm." Tora shrugs.

The portals in Greenwich Village are nothing compared to the ones in the Deadlands. The village portals open one at a time, stay open for longer, and usually at night, although that will all change if that asshole warlock is right. Who knows? Maybe the portals will open in different areas of the Realm of Man. It would make traveling a lot easier, but it would also make life a lot more dangerous. The crystals protecting the village would be useless if demons and fae could cross through portals from anywhere in the Realm of Man.

Readjusting her hold on the bag, Astra keeps her eyes on the road ahead, briefly glancing to the sides as she walks, clearly looking for portals. "Do you think everyone is okay back in the village? Do you think more portals have opened like the warlock said?"

Regret darkens Tora's path. There might not be a village to go back to if the Valkyries realized they were gone and left the village unprotected. But the Valkyries would have found them by now if that had happened. For now, the village should be safe, and when she returns with the secrets of Montauk, it will stay safe. "The Valkyries won't ignore the demons and malevolent fae. They'll help fight. We saw that for ourselves. As long as they don't know we left, it'll be okay until we get back."

"So, you're going to fly back once we know what the secret is?" Astra glances at Tora and quickly lowers her head like she's embarrassed or concerned about something.

"Well yeah. The quicker the better." Tora frowns. "Don't worry; I won't leave until after your birthday."

"It's not that." Astra looks away and tries to hide the fear sparking in her eyes. "It's just… you'll come back for me, right?"

"Of course!" Tora whips her head up, surprised she even had to ask. She would never leave her. Okay, she thought about it for a split second to keep her away from that doucheface Ethan, but she never would have done it. They've been through so much together. Astra's like a sister. She's not about to abandon her now, or ever. "I won't leave you Astra; not for long."

Closing her eyes, Astra smiles and nods in relief.

Why the hell would she think she'd leave her? Astra should know better. She is the only family she has left. It can't be because of the stupid fight about flying. It's one of the dumbest fights they've had, and that's including the time she cut Astra's hair when they were seven.

Tora cocks her head. "Why would you think I'd leave you?"

Astra sighs heavily. "Because you hate Ethan."

"What?" Tora pauses and widens her eyes. "What do you mean?"

Crap! How the hell did Astra figure it out? She's always been civil to the dickface when Astra's around. The crybaby probably sold her out. She knows how this works. The best friend dates an asshole, and she's the one who gets shafted.

Astra rolls her eyes. "Come on Tor. It's obvious you hate him. You can barely look at him, let alone speak to him. And that's okay. Not everyone gets along. I was just scared you'd leave me in Montauk to separate us."

Huh. That is so not the reaction she expected Astra to have. She expected tears, screaming, and maybe a little violence, but she underestimated Astra. She is more mature and reasonable than she'll ever be.

"Astra; I can't force you to do anything, and I wouldn't force you apart," Tora says. As much as she hates Ethan, it's not her choice who Astra dates. Leaving Astra in Montauk wouldn't just keep her away from Ethan, it would keep Tora away from the only family she has left, and she can't do that. "Your love life is your decision, not mine."

Astra pinches her lips into a smile and kicks a pebble along the road, her shoulders lowering as the tension eases. Still, she keeps her head down, refusing to look Tora in the eye.

"Why don't you like Ethan?" Astra glances up at her quickly and looks back down at her feet.

"Ugh! Star; you don't want to hear this." Tora groans. She knows better than to slag off a friend's boyfriend, no matter how much she hates him.

"Please? Just help me understand." Astra begs. "It's not like there's anything else to do out here."

Silence rings heavy in the air. A smoky breeze scratches at her nose. For the last year, Astra has been completely oblivious to any of the warning signs, blind to Mr Perfect's act, but maybe she'll change her mind if she sees him the way Tora does.

Now her mother's gone, nothing is stopping Ethan and Astra from dating out in the open. They could live together, get married, have kids. It would be an utter nightmare. Tora would never get her away from him. This might be her only chance.

"Fine." Tora concedes. "But don't say I didn't warn you. What do you want to know?"

"When did you start hating him?" Astra asks. "And why?"

Tora sighs, not liking where this conversation is headed. "I don't know. The first couple of times I met him, I guess. He's just so perfect all the time. It's like he's trying too hard. He says everything right. Does everything right. It's like he stepped out of one of those old human movies."

Astra frowns and screws up her nose. "Wait… you hate him because he's perfect? Seriously? What? Do you have a crush on him?"

"Ugh! No!" Tora gags and heaves, the thought of her and Ethan dating making her want to dive headfirst into a demon pit. "God no."

"Then I don't understand." Astra shakes her head. "What's wrong with being perfect?"

"It's not real Star. No one's like that," Tora tries to explain.

It's not that easy to list the things you hate about someone and sound justified. Even she can hear how weak her argument is. Ooh, he holds the door open for you. He's old-fashioned. What an asshole. But it's more than that. It's a feeling deep in her gut. Everything he says and does feels choreographed. He's a big fat faker. She just doesn't know why.

"And how did he know the warlock's name at the market?" Tora asks. "The one that attacked me at Bo's?"

Astra tilts her head and looks her hard in the eyes, all warmth disappearing from her face, like a black hole sucking all the joy from the world. "What?"

Tora immediately regrets her words.

"What are you saying?" Astra narrows her eyes. "Are you saying he set you up?"

"I…" Tora searches her brain for an answer but gets nothing. This is what she wanted to avoid. A fight with Astra about Ethan. There's a big difference between disliking your friend's boyfriend and outright accusing him of being a traitor. She knows that and still she had to say something; couldn't keep her mouth shut.

Tightening her jaw, Astra spins and flounces down the road, her long blonde ponytail whipping back and forth behind her.

"Star! Come on! Don't be like this." Tora curses herself and chases after her. No good ever comes from telling a friend the truth about their boyfriend. "I told you I didn't want to talk about it."

"So that makes it okay?" Astra whips her head over her shoulder. "I just thought you were jealous because it's always been the two of us. But no! You actually hate him and think he's a traitor!"

"I didn't say that!" Tora yells back, although that's kind of exactly what she implied "I asked a question. A reasonable question. How did he know the warlock's name Star? Can you explain it?"

"No!" Astra throws her hands in the air, her face bright crimson. "I can't. But maybe the warlock befriended him? Maybe he didn't know he was a warlock? Did you think of that? You didn't know at the markets either. It's an easy mistake to make Tora. It's not like he was wearing a fucking sign. But I wouldn't instantly think he was a traitor!"

Tora shrinks back. This is what she was scared of. Ethan would have left her to die on that roof, but nothing she says will sink in. She's in love with him. He can do no wrong. Anything Tora says, Astra will simply dismiss and make up some kind of excuse for his behavior.

"Astra! Come on. Wait up!" Tora chases her down the road. If they were anywhere else but the Deadlands, she would give her a little space to cool off, but they don't have that kind of luxury right now. They need to stay together, even if she has to lie to make that happen. Their lives depend on it. "I'm sorry okay? I take it back."

Astra lengthens her stride, refusing to acknowledge her, let alone speak to her.

"Please Star. I'm sorry." Tora catches up. "You're right. I shouldn't have judged him."

The lie burns like acid on her tongue. Ethan's a creep. She has every right to judge him, especially since he wanted to leave her to die on the roof, but she needs Astra to forgive her. She needs her to be safe.

"No, you shouldn't have," Astra snaps and crosses her arms over her chest.

"I said I was sorry." Tora softens her voice, her stomach aching as it twists itself into a pretzel. She can't handle Astra being mad at her; not now. She's the only family she has left. "Please don't be mad at me. You're all I have."

Groaning, Astra drops her shoulders and spins around. "Ugh! Fine."

"Really?" Tora skids to a stop. Astra never forgives her that fast. She likes to draw out her punishment, like some sort of sadistic psychological torture. "You mean you're not mad at me anymore?"

Astra scoffs and wipes the beads of sweat trickling down her face. "Oh no, I'm still mad."

"But you forgive me?" Tora frowns in confusion. She doesn't know what she'd do if Astra didn't forgive her. There's not much else she can say or do to make it up to her.

"Not yet." Astra's hard angry eyes soften. "But I will; eventually."

The knot twisting Tora's stomach eases. The thought of losing Astra because of Ethan just makes her feel sick. It's what he's wanted all along. Astra all to himself, but she is all the family Tora has left, and she's not letting her go without a fight.

No matter what, she will always keep her safe, always protect her, even against a creep like Ethan. She just has to hope that Astra will see Ethan for who he really is on her own and be there for her when she does.

Tora grins and bumps her shoulder, trying to lighten the mood. "How about now?"

Astra rolls her eyes. Sweat leeches out of her skin and soaks through her clothes, streaming down her neck like a faucet. She wrinkles her nose and sniffs the air. "Umm, Tor? Do you smell that?"

Frowning, Tora sniffs the air and scans the area, the smell of sulfur, smoke, pine, and burning flesh assaulting her nose. She widens her eyes. It's the unmistakable smell of the Demon Realm. There has to be a portal somewhere close; maybe more than one. Nothing on earth smells as bad as the Demon Realm.

"I don't see a portal," Astra whispers and inches closer to Tora, her voice trembling.

"Stay close." Tora holds out her arm, the Valkyrie mark on her wrist burning purple as her soul sword glides down into her hand. Burned leaves spiral around their feet, twirling into the air in the humid breeze. Bits of ash stick to their hair.

"God; why is it so hot?" Astra pulls at her shirt, her face, hair, and body covered in sweat, pouring off her like a water rapid. "It's like a thousand degrees out here."

Screwing up her face, Tora looks down at the road beneath them. She doesn't feel anything, but Astra is practically melting in front of her.

Leaves, dirt, and debris bubble in the melting tar, sticking to the side of their shoes. A discarded cola can bobs up and down, fighting as the quickly liquifying road folds over the top of it and swallows it whole.

Tora gasps and pulls Astra off the road, frantically looking for the portal as the sound of ripping realm fabric screeches through their ears. It's hot. Too hot for just one portal. There should be thousands of them to produce this kind of heat, yet she can't see one.

Astra jerks and screams as a cracking sound shakes their bones, like lightning striking a tree, but there's nothing on the horizon. No storms, no portals, only the landscape, the entire area shimmering under the hot sun.

"Oh fuck." Tora swallows hard. Her stomach drops.

The landscape – it shouldn't be shimmering. It's early morning, and the sun is weak.

"What?" Astra whips her head back and forth, panic tightening her voice. "I know that look! Oh god, what? What's happening?"

Taking a deep steadying breath, Tora points her sword towards the horizon and walks in a slow circle, red dust settling on her clothes and sword. "See the shimmering landscape?"

"Yeah? So?" Astra shakes her head, her soft purple eyes large with fear. "The sun's coming up. Shouldn't we be running or hiding right now?"

"It's Fall Star. The sun just came up." Tora forces her body to relax, knowing panicking will only make things worse. "Running won't do anything. There's nowhere to go."

Astra's hands tremble violently, spreading to her legs and body. Her face turns ghost white as her eyes well with tears. A line of crystals form a ring around them, the size of an athletic field. "Oh god. We're... we're surrounded by portals; aren't we?"

Tora winces as intense pressure pushes against the now rippling barrier, the pain in her ears sharp and bone deep. Next to her, Astra screams and holds her hands over her ears as tears freely flow down her cheeks.

The crystals explode, flying in all different directions and embed in the trees. A torrent of water gushes out of the sky like Niagara Falls, leaving only glowing fluorescent lights.

"Oh god. Oh shit. Oh fuck." Astra crumbles to the ground and grips her knees as water washes in and around them.

"Get up!" Tora snaps as a rush of adrenaline obliterates her patience. Her large white wings spring free from her back, tearing apart her jacket. She pulls Astra to her feet and gives her a shake, trying to knock the fear out of her, or at least some sense into her.

Now is not the time to fall apart. Astra will be dead in seconds if she stays on the ground, and if the demons have hell blades, she will be dead too.

"Astra!" Tora grabs the two blades strapped to Astra's legs and puts the handles in her hands. "I need you to fight. Do you understand me? You need to fight to survive. I can't do this on my own."

Tears stream down Astra's face, her purple eyes large and unfocused as she stares at the shimmering portals surrounding them.

"You can do this Star." Tora squeezes her hand around the hilt of a blade and turns back to the portals, hoping like hell she's right. Even with her new Valkyrie abilities, there's no way she can take on whatever is coming through the portals. There's too many of them. She's never seen so many portals merged together. They're fucked... completely and absolutely fucked.

CHAPTER SIXTEEN

A long thin brown boned leg covered in thousands of razor-sharp spikes pierces the portal gate, standing as tall as a small car; the spikes glittering like diamonds.

Tora readies her sword, her blood singing with anticipation. Spider demons. These she is familiar with. They've plagued the streets of Greenwich Village for the last year like an infestation.

The spider demon charges out of the portal, its entire brown body covered in spiky diamond thorns. The beast growls like an angry dog and stalks towards them, eight human-shaped orange eyes trained on Tora's sword.

"Oh my god." Astra whimpers.

"It'll be okay. I've fought them..." Tora glances back over her shoulder and shuts her mouth. Astra faces in the opposite direction, gaping as hundreds of creatures the size of toddlers jump out of a portal.

Their bright yellow skin oozes with pockets of green puss, dripping down onto their bent legs. Their heads are large and oval with a long bloody slit for a mouth, filled with pin-like teeth.

"T... Tor?" Astra stammers as yellow eyes stare at them from a distance, sizing them up as prey.

"It's okay. We'll be okay," Tora lies, having never seen these things before.

One of the nasty little fuckers snatches a rabbit from the ground with its long-forked tongue and dislodges its jaw, driving its sharp pin teeth into its flesh. It crouches on the ground, its three taloned legs digging into the dirt, the rabbit still sitting whole in its closed mouth.

"Great." Tora shudders against her souring stomach and swallows the bile rising in her throat. "I think they're demon frogs. That's all we need. That's seriously disgusting."

The demon swallows and burps before leaping forward to join the growing group of demon frogs, each one equally as disgusting as the next. A huge bubble balloons at their throats. They open their mouths and release a deafening sound, like a mix between a V8 engine and a cat on heat.

Astra yelps as the spider demon growls louder behind them and advances.

Whipping around, Tora charges the beast with her sword held tight in her hand, her heart beating like a double kick bass drum, thumping in chorus with her heavy boots and large powerful wings, her mother's training ringing clear in her mind: *Do not hesitate. Strike down the enemy as it charges, not when it reaches you.*

Lifting off the ground, Tora flies in circles around the beast, picking up speed with each lap, trying to disorientate its eight hideous orange eyes. Without Bo or the Odd Squad to distract it, she needs another tactic, and this is the best she can do under the circumstances. She's not about to use Astra as bait, not when she's barely able to stand.

The trees blur around her, the green and black coloring mixing in with the bright yellow frog demons and the rising sun, creating a rainbow of color. She can almost hear music in her ears, like a pool of sound surrounding them, harmonizing with the earth.

No wonder her mother loved being a Valkyrie. When she was a fledgling, she had to scramble down on the ground and try to get up high enough to drive a spear through the spider demon's head. Every single time, she came home covered in demon guts, cuts, and bruises, but not anymore. The wings she always dreamed of complete her. Finally, she's whole; who she was always meant to be.

The tactic works. The ugly-ass spider demon spins around and swipes at the air as it sways on its feet.

Grinning, Tora darts forward and slices easily through one of the beast's legs then takes a chunk out of its hideous face. The demon roars and swipes at the air over and over, but it's too slow and can't focus its eyes.

"Dance fucker dance!" Tora mocks and holds up her sword as she shoots back out of its reach, a mix of excitement and adrenaline bubbling under her skin.

If only the Odd Squad could see her now. It would bring them hope against the dark days ahead. Dr A would study her wings for hours and take notes in his little pocketbook. Victor and Teresa would have tried to ride her like a horse into battle; if only they were alive.

A jolt of rage pushes her forward. She darts in and slices off another of the demon's legs before darting out again, taking out her anger on the beast, imagining it's Flenn, the warlock who stole the lives of her friends.

The beast howls and flails as Tora flies in to finish the job, slashing at its remaining legs until it collapses to the ground in a pool of blood.

"Hurry up!" Astra screams.

Tora whips her head around to find Astra plunging her long blade into the mouth of one of the frog demons. She squeals and flicks the blade around trying to get the thing off and backs up closer to Tora.

"Star!" Tora drives her sword into the demon's head, killing it quickly before returning to Astra's side and slicing through a frog demon as it leaps at her. Bright orange and black blood drips from her blade and sizzles in the dirt.

"So, do you forgive me now?" Tora jokes and coughs as the smell of rotten eggs fouls up the air.

"Are you serious?" Astra balks and winces away from the smell of the dying frog. "You're asking me now?"

"Never mind." Tora rolls her eyes and studies the demon frogs in front of her. She forgot who she was talking to. Astra hasn't been out on the hunt before. It might be a bit too soon for jokes.

One of the demon frogs breaks away from the others and spits a ball of phlegm high into the air. Tora watches in horror as it lands on the dead frog and begins sizzling, burning through the tough skin to the flesh below.

"They have acid spit?" Astra shrieks as the other demon frogs scramble towards their dead friend and tear chunks off its flesh, licking green and orange puss from its corpse.

"Ugh! Gross!" Tora gags and turns away. "And they're cannibals."

They need to get the hell out of there, and quick. If one of the demon frogs decides to spit on them, they're dead.

Grabbing Astra's arm, Tora starts to drag her away to put some distance between them and the demon frogs, but Astra suddenly screams and drops to the ground as a high-pitched sound rips through their ears.

Tora gasps and covers her head as another portal rips open above them and hundreds of crystals rain down on their heads. Large rocks of hail fall through the open portal, coupled with torrents of rain and howling winds. Lightning lights up the sky and hits the ground inches from their feet.

Tora raises her wings and cocoons Astra underneath, trying her best to protect her. The surrounding portals flash from glowing lights to dark red and black swirling patterns. Chaotic winds blow ash, red dust, and burned debris around in circles.

"What's happening?" Astra yells over the storm.

"I don't know!" Tora whips her head from side to side, her heart pushing the adrenaline hard and fast through her veins. The circular portals around them split as new portals open inside of them, and the portal above continues to rain down on their heads.

They are so fucked. She's never seen anything like this before. It's like being in the middle of a hurricane of portals. Even the ugly ass demon frogs look scared as they huddle together in a mass gathering.

"Ring around a rosie, a pocket full of posies. Ashes, Ashes, we all fall down." A little girl's voice sings through the chaos.

Tora freezes and widens her eyes, her throat suddenly dry. The Valkyrie transformation may have numbed her emotions and supposedly changed her body's reaction to fear, but that sound – that sound would scare the crap out of the oldest and strongest Valkyrie.

A child with porcelain skin skips through the portal wearing a sweet old-fashioned white baby doll dress. Ringlets frame her delicate little face, pink cheeks, and button nose. The child's voice distorts and laps, sounding as though multiple voices are singing in a round format, starting from the beginning at different points throughout the song, each voice lower than the next, just the same as the last creepy kid. It blinks its large baby blue eyes and grins, baring razor-sharp piranha teeth.

Tora swallows hard. It's exactly the same as last time, except the child's lips are not moving. The goddamned thing isn't singing at all. Another identical demon child steps through the portal, followed by another, then another, then another, each singing in a round format, the song losing all sense of rhyme or rhythm.

"Oh my god." Astra whimpers.

Tora pulls Astra to her feet and blinks back tears as Sulfur and lavender burn her eyes. On their right, six large oversized heads poke through one of the portals, their glowing golden-yellow eyes trained on Tora. They stalk through the gate, their fur black and dark gray. Blood drips down their cheeks, the exposed bones chipped and void of any flesh or skin, their snouts and faces covered in deep wounds and scars.

"Tora?" Astra trembles violently.

"Demon wolves." Tora clenches her jaw and tightens her grip on her sword as the wolves bare their teeth in a snarl. The wolves look pissed. She wouldn't be surprised if they knew she killed that she-wolf and the pups.

Tora jerks and turns as another spider demon charges through a portal on their left, barking and snarling. She turns again to the sound of heavy footsteps as five Baleful Demons march through the portal behind them, squashing some of the frog demons as they trek through dirt and debris.

They each stand between seven and eight feet tall with thick black-boned dreadlocks instead of hair. Large rhino tusks jut out of either side of their chins below their dog-like snouts and to the side of their sharp bright orange dog-like teeth.

Rain sizzles on their burned charcoal alligator husk skin, their copper armor scorching deep into their flesh. Their ginger-red eyes stare forward, filled with nothing but blood and rage

Tora struggles to control her breathing as a wave of vertigo threatens to knock her on her ass. The adrenaline pumping through her veins doubles, then triples, causing her heart to beat erratically in her chest. If she's not careful, she's going to overdose on her own adrenaline. She needs to calm down.

The storm rages inside the portals, leaking into the Realm of Man. They're going to die. It's that simple. No Valkyrie or warrior could take on this many demons alone and live to tell the tale. She can't even fly them out of there. The portals are above and surrounding them. There's no hope. This is it. This is the end. This is how they die, and when they die, Greenwich Village will die too without the secrets of Montauk.

There's no hope for the human race. Her mother told her there were pockets of survivors out there somewhere, but there's no way anyone could survive out in the Deadlands, not with the unpredictable portals and millions of demons waiting on the other side. Not even a Valkyrie could survive this.

"Tor?" Astra latches onto her bicep as a red-skinned pixie with short black spiky hair pointing in all directions, and black spiraling tattoo-like markings covering her body, stumbles through the layered portal, holding a bottle of brown liquor in her hand. Her arm is draped around a male elf with red hair and a crooked smile, and a female faery with orange and dark gray tattered and torn two-toned gothic-style wings. Her bright fire-red hair cascades in curls down her back and dances in the wind as she inhales a full bottle of whisky. All are dressed in matching red plaid outfits, like they've just been to a private school.

Another red-skinned pixie with a shaved head and black spiraling tattoo-like markings covering his body falls out of the portal behind them and face plants in the mud, completely blind drunk.

Tora widens her eyes. "You're fucking kidding me!"

The three fae glance around in confusion and look down at their drunken pixie friend on the ground. They start laughing and throw themselves on the ground, rolling around in fits of laughter.

"Can this morning get any worse?" Tora sighs.

They should have stayed in Greenwich Village and taken their chances with the Valkyries. At least there they could have hidden in the city and kept moving every few hours to avoid detection. Anything would be better than this. This is just death.

"What do we do?" Astra whimpers and holds her stomach. Tears stream down her face.

"We fight" Tora flares up her sword, the blade glowing bright purple. If she's going to go down, she's going down fighting. "And if all goes well, we die."

CHAPTER SEVENTEEN

A torrent of rain slams into the dirt as thunder and lightning rip apart the portal overhead. Chaotic winds lash at their faces, covering them in red dust and ash.

Keeping Astra close to her back, Tora turns in a circle, sizing up the enemy and looking for any escape. There's no flying out of this fight... they're fucked; completely and utterly fucked.

Tora can fight, so can Astra if it comes down to it, but they're still just one Valkyrie and one fledgling against hundreds of demon frogs, five child demons, six full-sized wolf demons, one spider demon, five Baleful Demons, and four malevolent fae. They're surrounded, and nothing short of a miracle can save them now.

Still being a fledgling, Astra probably won't suffer for long before she dies, but Tora... Tora can't die, except by the blade of a Valkyrie sword or a Hell Blade. The demons could tear her apart and she would still be glued back into existence somehow just to be tortured again, and again, and again, and again; like a never-ending snack pack.

"Tor... I have to tell you something before we die." Astra trembles and adjusts her stance, resting her hand and blade close to her stomach.

"Star – whatever it is..." Tora starts.

"I'm pregnant." Astra cuts her off.

Tora whips her head over her shoulder and gapes, her ears ringing with thunder and cracking lightning. Her lungs gasp for air as an invisible force sucker punches her in the guts. Pregnant? Astra's pregnant – to Ethan? A fledgling Valkyrie pregnant to a human?

"Get out of the way you idiots!" A male voice booms from above.

Tora whips her head up as two creatures fall from the portal above.

"Move!" Another voice yells.

Moving quickly, Tora tackles Astra out of the way, protecting her with her wings as the two creatures land just behind them. Squinting, she scrambles to her feet with her sword ready, struggling to see through the rain and tornado winds whipping through the portal.

"Star? You okay?" Tora quickly glances at Astra on the ground behind her, her veins pulsating in her neck. "Is the baby okay?"

A large smile spreads across Astra's face. Tears spring to her eyes as she gets to her feet. "We're fine Aunty Tora."

Tora blinks as Astra's words sink in. Warmth spreads through her chest. She's never wanted to get married or have children, but the thought of being Aunty Tora – it's just too amazing to think about.

If it's the last thing she does, she's going to get Astra and the baby out of this mess alive, even if she has to take them through one of the portals to escape. Their best chance is the Malevolent Fae Realm. The Demon Realm is just suicide.

Grinning at Astra, Tora spins to face their immediate threat; the two creatures who fell from the portal above. Two elves stand with their backs to them, surveying the surroundings, their ears pointed at the tips; one male and one female.

The female's pink floral summer dress and bare feet are a stark contrast to the destruction and demons surrounding them. The male is her opposite in black cargo pants, black shirt, and black boots.

As they turn, Tora levels her sword at the female's throat and narrows her eyes. They both jerk backward and hold their arms up high, their ice-blue eyes widening.

A shimmering liquid silver circles around the female's neck in a weaving pattern, crawling higher up to her chin, protecting her from the blade. The male clenches his jaw, his ice-blue eyes burning with hatred.

"Am I too late kiddies?" A familiar voice chuckles.

A malevolent faery lands beside them, beating her large black and fuchsia gothic wings.

"You!" Tora curls her lip. It's the malevolent faery from the tunnel; the one named Tia.

"Introductions later." Tia winks and lashes out at a frog demon sneaking towards Astra's feet, her liquid silver-like blades slicing effortlessly through their bodies. Her tattered and torn fuchsia pink and black ombre gothic-style wings flex at her back. Blood sprays over her legs and the remaining frogs, making the psycho grin.

The faery is helping them. The fucking malevolent faery is helping them!

The child demons assess the battlefield and grin at Tia as they skip back through the portal, disappearing from the fight.

"Chicken shits!" Tia yells after them.

"Tor? Tora!" Astra grabs Tora's arm and forces her to turn. "You've got to see this."

The tall yet petite-framed female elf in the floral dress blinks her innocent ice-blue eyes through dark eyelashes and sighs sadly as the huge six demon wolves surround her. The wolves close in, screeching loudly like bats.

"Nia!" The male elf pulls a large medieval sword and a long Scimitar sword from the holders strapped to his back, the blades swirling with liquid silver. He starts towards the female elf, his blue eyes burning like ice as liquid silver crawls around his biceps and neck, swirling in spirals and patterns up to his brown-tinged hair shaved close to his scalp, then under his shirt and muscular chest.

Tora quickly turns away, her face burning bright red. Heat burns her neck and chest as her stomach flops around like a dying fish. She must have hit her head. Yesterday, she broke up with Bo, and now she's checking out the enemy, one of the fae… an elf?

"I'm fine Brae." The female elf Nia tucks her long silky white blonde hair over her shoulder, her voice melodic, like angelic flutes. Liquid silver dances in waves and spirals over her entire body, reaching down to her fingertips.

As one of the wolves' lunge, Nia flicks her fingers towards the beast, releasing a splatter of liquid metal from her fingernails. The metal spins into a large disc with serrated blades surrounding it and tears through the beast, splitting it in half before returning to Nia's fingers.

Blood, fur, charred flesh, and guts splatter over the other wolves, inciting their anger. Tora watches in horror as the wolves howl in unison and charge the petite elf.

Lowering her head, the elf Nia flicks both her hands outwards, sending ten forming discs spinning towards the wolves. Tears fall down her cheeks as the blades slice easily through the remaining beasts, the force like an explosion of blood and flesh, spraying everywhere around them.

Tora gapes in awe. Imagine all the time she could save fighting demons and malevolent fae with that type of weapon. She would be unstoppable. Like her soul sword, she wouldn't even need to carry it. It would just be constantly circling her body.

The male elf Brae battles with the Baleful Demons, slicing through them with his swords, the liquid silver working purely as armor, moving to block each strike from the demon cavemen. Dark blood coats his arms and sprays over his face and head, but he barely blinks, focused only on killing the demons.

Distracted, he doesn't notice the spider demon inching towards him. The demon drools and lifts one of its long diamond-spiked legs, ready to stab him in the back.

"Watch out!" Tora shoots up into the air, her sword flaring bright purple, her wings propelling her forward at lightning speed. She can't let the elf die saving their lives. The fae aren't her favorite race based on experience, but she's not an asshole.

Whipping around, the beast roars and rears up onto its back legs, watching her through eight cunning human-shaped orange eyes, using its spike-covered legs to swipe at her through the air.

Ducking and driving her sword forward, Tora stabs at the beast as lightning tears apart the sky, her blood singing with the thrill of the fight and the call of her ancestors.

Blood glides down the demon's arms and legs, but the damage is nothing more than a flesh wound. There's no time to try and distract the demon first. She needs to finish this as quickly as possible and get Astra away from the fae and remaining demons.

The demon opens its ugly black mouth and reveals two huge diamond-tipped fangs extending down through its gums. From underneath its body, a long tail unfolds, the end razor-tipped like a scorpion.

Tora gasps. This is not the spider demon she knows. It's a mutation. Spider demons do not have razor-tipped scorpion tails. She darts backward, trying to get out of the demon's reach but she's not quick enough.

A scream rips free from her throat as one of the spider legs punctures straight through her shoulder and red-hot pain shoots down her arm and back.

"Tora!" Astra screams, fear lacing her voice as the beast uses its two front legs like a pair of chopsticks and draws Tora back toward its mouth.

Trying not to panic, Tora kicks out her legs and flaps her large powerful wings, trying to free herself. She grits her teeth against the deep throbbing pain and pulls back with all her strength, refusing to be the only Valkyrie in history eaten and shat out by a spider demon.

"Hey!" Astra yells and throws a rock at the demon. "Ugly!"

The beast howls and rears back as the rock hits it in the face.

Ignoring the fresh pain shooting through her body, Tora arches back at the same time and dislodges the demon's leg from her shoulder. Warmth spreads down her arm and chest as blood leaks from the serrated wound.

"Leave her alone!" Astra screams.

"Astra?" Tora searches for Astra in the chaos below and widens her eyes. Directly below her, Astra stands toe to toe with the spider demon, hacking through the beast's lower legs, swinging her sword over and over again as she screams a battle cry over the storm.

Pride swells in her chest. A smile pulls at her lips. Astra might make a good warrior after-all. Despite the rain, her grip is tight. Despite her fear, her aim is true. And so is Tora's.

Releasing a roar that would rival any beast, Tora charges and plunges her sword into the side of the demon's head. It howls as she twists her sword, tearing through the beast's skull.

"Watch out!" Astra yells, but it's too late.

Tora screams as the beast stabs her through the back with its spiked tail, releasing its venom and shredding her flesh. Red hot pain seeps into her back and spreads quickly through her muscles.

Tora widens her eyes. Her sword dissolves as she falls to the ground, her wings disappearing behind her. Darkness threatens to take her as fiery pain spreads down her arm and side, her fast-beating heart pushing the poison deeper into her body.

Some Valkyrie she turned out to be. Stabbed twice by the same demon. Her legacy will be nothing. Absolutely nothing. She didn't save anyone; not Astra, not her squad; not Greenwich Village; not even herself.

Through the fog of pain and venom, Tora barely flinches as the intoxicated female pixie with red skin and black spiraling patterns covering her body leaps on top of her and laughs, her piranha teeth stained in blood.

"I got one!" the pixie shouts and takes a swig of bourbon from her bottle, her spiky black hair shooting in all directions. The pixie throws away the empty bottle and pins her arms to the ground, her bright green eyes shaking from side to side.

Using the last of her strength, Tora bucks and squirms, trying to free herself, but her strength wanes as the demon venom throbs in her veins. This can't be the way she dies, not as a snack pack for a drunken pixie. It's too humiliating. She would rather have been eaten by the hideous spider demon.

Drooling, the pixie leans down and licks the trickling blood off her wound.

"Get off her!" Astra runs up behind the pixie and plunges her blade straight through the back of her head.

Blood splatters on Tora's face. The pixie falls to the side, dead.

Through the numbing venom, Tora can only watch as the malevolent faery, Tia, spins into the air and drives a sword through the spider demon's skull, finishing the job she started. The elven male Brae slices effortlessly through the last of the Baleful Demons and struts towards her.

"I've got you. It's okay," Astra coos as she starts to lose consciousness.

The venom floods Tora's veins and organs, slowly shutting down her body. The world spins in and out of darkness. Out of the corner of her eye, she sees a group of drunken malevolent fae hurtling toward Astra; an elf, a faery, and a pixie, but there's nothing she can do about it. She can't move. She can't speak. She can only stare and drool, her rapid heartbeat the only response to indicate anything is wrong.

"Oi! You; you ugly little fuckers!" Tia yells at the remaining fae and spins her sword. She lifts her eyebrows up and down and grins. "It's home time."

The fae stop and stare, nothing but fear on their dirty faces.

Effortlessly, Tia moves at a ridiculous speed and knocks out the remaining faery, elf, and pixie with the hilt of her sword, hurling them back through the portal to the Malevolent Fae Realm.

Tora blinks. That's it. All the demons are gone. All the fae are gone, except for the three that helped them. Astra is safe... for now.

Shadows seep into her vision. Her eyes grow heavy. The world goes black.

CHAPTER EIGHTEEN

Waking alone in a foreign room, Tora springs out of the silver-lined wooden bed and pulls her soul sword, gripping the hilt tightly, her eyes trying to focus through the fog of sleep.

Elegant spiraling architecture weaves around the room, complementing the elaborately knotted bed frame, mirror, vanity, closet, and window, all lined in glittering white silver. The bedspread is a soft satin baby blue with matching pillowcases and sheets.

Wide eyed, Tora scans the room, her heart beating hard against her ribcage. Either she's dead or in some alternate universe. This can't be the Realm of Man. Nothing stays this clean and picture-perfect in their demolished realm. So, where the hell is she? And where the fuck is Astra?

Jerking, she stares at the wooden door as the glittering white silver door knob slowly turns. Her stomach sinks. Someone's coming.

Quickly ducking behind the door, she waits, her sword drawn and ready. This place may not look like your typical demon or malevolent fae den, but that doesn't mean the thing on the other side of the door isn't a threat.

Slowly, the door creaks open. A wooden tray lined with silver peeks through the door first followed by an arm.

Springing forward, Tora grabs the arm and pulls whoever it is into the room, and slams the door shut behind them, every muscle in her body tensed ready for a fight.

The tray flies across the room and lands on the polished floors.

"Tora!" Astra scrambles onto her hands and knees and grabs the tray. "You nearly broke it. God! What are you doing?"

"Star?" Tora releases her sword and frowns in confusion. Astra remains on the floor, fussing over the tray, wearing a soft purple floral summer dress, not a speck of dust or dirt on her, like they weren't just in a fight for their lives.

"Are you okay?" Tora starts towards her, her head a mess of questions. "What's going on? Are you hurt? Are you a slave? What are you wearing?"

Rolling her eyes, Astra picks up the tray and sits on the bed. "Breakfast is going on. Cream cheese bagels and tea. And I'm wearing a dress!"

Tora frowns, her Valkyrie marks throbbing in irritation. A second ago, she was trying to avoid being eaten by a spider demon and now Astra is bringing her cream cheese bagels and a decorative pot of tea?

"Okay, what the fuck?" Tora snatches half a bagel off the tray and stomps over to the window to figure out what the fuck they've gotten into now. They must have fallen through a portal. It's the only explanation. "Where the fuck are we?"

Pulling back the curtain, she takes a bite of the bagel and instantly chokes on the sight below. Her eyes water as silence rings in her ears. It's like a picture or one of those postcards. The streets below are clean and shiny. Tall old-fashioned lanterns line the roads.

Across the street, a luscious blue lagoon sits nestled in a beautiful park filled with age-old trees of oaks, willows, and witch hazels. Children skip down the street with their parents. Adults rush in and out of coffee shops dressed in suits and human work attire. Cars zoom up and down the road, stopping at working traffic lights and pedestrian crossings.

Tora blinks, not believing her eyes. None of the cute cookie-cutter homes and shop fronts look even remotely touched by the War of the Gods, and they have cars… actual working cars!

"Seriously Astra; where the fuck are we?" Tora stares wide eyed at Astra, unable to close her mouth.

Astra chuckles. "Montauk. Or Olivia as they now call it."

It's too much. Too unbelievable. Tora sits on the ground with her knees close to her chest and stares at the floor, trying desperately to understand what's going on. They're in Montauk? The last thing she remembers was blacking out on the road after being stung by the spider demon, and that was at least another thirty hours away from Montauk. "How long have I been out?"

"An hour maybe," Astra answers. "You're completely healed though. Lucky you're a fully-fledged Valkyrie, otherwise you'd be dead."

"And we got here how?" Tora lifts her eyebrows in question, unsure if she wants to know the answer.

"The benevolent elves brought us through a portal." Astra smiles and holds the hem of her floral dress. "And Nia leant me this dress."

Tora bites into the bagel to give her brain time to catch up. The elves brought them to Montauk. The two elves from the fight. The ones that helped them. Brae and Nia. They're benevolent fae.

Rubbing her face, Tora tries to wrap her head around it all. The benevolent fae are meant to stay in their realm and avoid every other realm and race out there, not that she's complaining. Without their help, they'd be dead right now. Well, Astra would be dead. Tora would be in all kinds of hell and torture since she technically can't die.

"Okay then. So, what's the deal with this place? Montauk or Olivia, whatever they call it?" Tora asks.

"Yeah, that's the weird bit," Astra says. "Montauk didn't survive the War of the Gods like we thought, not exactly anyway. The benevolent fae created this town eighteen years ago because of the prophecy. It was situated on the east coast, protected by an invisible bubble-like shield, but they moved it to Montauk after the War of the Gods spilled into the Realm of Man and the waters rose too high."

Taking another bite of her bagel, Tora nods like she understands and tries to wrap her head around this fairytale crap. "Go on."

"Olivia is a simulation realm created by the benevolent fae to try and stop some prophecy from coming true. The people in it are real, both humans and fae, and they have no idea about the War of the Gods or the world outside of Olivia. As far as they know, everything is normal. People go to school, work, watch television, listen to music, use cell phones, and shop; everything normal before the war. Us being here is dangerous for them but the fae also understand that we, especially you, are Valkyries and they value our purpose in the coming war, so we can stay for now as long as we play along."

"Do they know why we're here?" Tora frowns.

Astra sighs. "Yes, they know. They were disappointed that I'm not going to undergo the ritual, but they also think it's my choice, and I shouldn't be made to do something that may render me catatonic."

"Do they know that your…" Tora nods at Astra's stomach, indicating her pregnancy.

"No!" Astra cuts in and puts her finger to her lips.

Tora frowns and bites the inside of her bottom lip. If the benevolent fae are so wonderful, what the hell are they doing listening to their conversation? Benevolent fae her ass!

"What about this prophecy? I assume it's the seventh of the seventh one the Valkyries were talking about?" Tora asks. "I thought it couldn't be stopped?"

"The second verse of the prophecy gave them hope. Strength returns to its rightful heir, power building within; the witchling hides in shadow, hunted by her kin. Breaking down the barriers, scorned by anger and hate; empowered by pure vengeance, beware she who holds our fate," Astra answers.

"So, they thought this cookie-cutter world would stop this all-powerful Witch Goddess from throwing a vengeful tantrum?" Tora shakes her head. That's just stupid. A perfect world isn't going to stop an all-powerful witch from losing her shit. It could even make things worse. "Good luck to them I guess."

"They've kept her identity a secret for eighteen years," Astra says. "She has no idea what she is. The humans don't know either, and they know nothing about the fae or the outside world, not for the last year. Before the war, the humans could travel outside the town, but had no idea the town was cloaked or different in any way."

"How do they prevent people from leaving and finding out the truth for themselves?" Tora frowns.

"A pandemic virus. No travel allowed, and no outsiders allowed in. It's not perfect. People try to call their family and friends outside of the town, but they either get a busy signal or the phone goes dead. They're worried, but the fae handle it." Astra shrugs.

"They handle it? That doesn't sound dodgy at all." Tora rolls her eyes and downs a cup of tea, relishing the rare taste of both as they go down. "Wait… does this hurt our plan? Do they have some secret that protects them from portals opening, or is it because it's a realm of its own?"

"No idea. I haven't had a chance to ask them yet." Astra picks up the tray and wrinkles her nose. "Umm… There's a bathroom through the door over there. The showers are a-maz-ing." She nods to an arched wooden door on the other side of the room.

"Hey! What are you saying?" Tora says in mock outrage.

"You stink Tora. Like really bad." Astra grins and takes the tray with her on her way out. "Clean clothes are on the sink."

"It's not a floral dress, is it?" Tora yells as Astra closes the door behind her, her laughter echoing down the hall. She would rather walk around naked than be caught dead in a floral summer dress.

Relieved to at least be away from the Valkyries and the hordes of demons out in the Deadlands, Tora checks out the bathroom where she finds a pair of tight black pants and a razor-back bodice top.

In truth, she's looking forward to a shower. Even she can smell the rotten-egg dead spider frog wolf crab demon on her skin, and the bathtub is huge. At least three people could fit into it and the shower head looks like a moon disc. It beats the hell out of her trickling lukewarm shower back in Greenwich. Even the toilet is fancy with its silver trim and a button that literally washes your ass.

Showering under the powerful shower head, Tora moans as extra bursts of steam push through silver nozzles in the wall, relaxing her tight muscles. The hot water and cherry blossom soap glide over her hair and skin, washing away the mud, dirt, puss, and blood until finally, the water runs clear. It's better than food; better than vodka, even better than sex.

The clothes that the elves left her are a perfect fit, molding to her body like a second skin, similar if not the same uniform the Valkyries were wearing; a distinctive black double-breasted razor back vest with intricate metal weaving, black cargo pants with pockets, chains, a large belt, and leather holders strapped to her thighs.

After she brushes her teeth and pulls her wet black hair into a messy bun, she ventures down the long corridor, the weaving wooden patterns from the room carrying on throughout the large house.

There's no use putting it off. She may as well get it over with and meet the fae herself. Astra's met them and she seems to think they're okay, so maybe they are. Maybe it will be easier than she thought to save Greenwich. The fae might just help them.

Arched doors line the corridor. The wooden walls are littered with portraits and photographs of elven warriors, women, and children, each like a moving hologram or projection.

Soft voices hang in the air as Astra's laughter beckons her down the stairs to a large sitting room at the front of the house with rich mahogany bookshelves embedded into the walls. Huge arched framed windows overlook beautiful overhanging trees with deep green leaves, winding vines, and a stunning swimming pond.

The female and male elf that helped them with the demons sit regally on deep blue armchairs, the female dressed in a clean white sundress, and the male in black bottom pants and a loose cotton shirt. They talking animatedly with an older female elf seated on what looks to be more of a throne than a chair.

Long dark black hair falls in waves passed the elven woman's shoulders, sitting just above her off the shoulder white silk gown. Her voice drips with authority as she speaks with the two young elves, her facial features as sharp as her unwelcoming ice-blue eyes.

A faery with green silk wings and vibrant green eyes sits with them and shakes her head, sending her long blonde cascading curls dancing around her elbows. She pinches her delicate pink lips in sympathy as the elven woman scolds the younger elves for venturing out into the Deadlands. Her long sleeve crocheted white top has obviously been made for a faery, hanging softly across and behind the neck, leaving the upper portion of her back bare, coupled with a pair of blue denim jeans.

Astra and the malevolent faery, Tia, chat by a glossy wooden table in the background, laughing and snacking on sweets.

Since no one seems to notice her, Tora clears her throat and immediately regrets it as everyone in the room turns to stare. She suddenly feels very self-conscious, like she walked into battle naked.

"Tora!" Astra bounces over to her side and sniffs her shoulder. "Not so stinky anymore."

Tora chuckles, grateful for her friend's ability to make her feel comfortable anywhere, even when it's not her house. "Yeah, thanks for that."

"Please, sit." The older female elf gestures at the soft blue fabric couch and arches her thinly shaped eyebrows. "Would you like some tea or coffee?"

"Coffee?" Tora sinks into the cushiony couch. "I would kill for a coffee."

"Hmm. Indeed." The elven woman purses her lips like she sucked on a lemon, and rings a small crystal bell. A second later, an unusual-looking man enters the room.

The man stands at least six foot tall with dark brown dreadlocks down to his shoulders. His forest green eyes scan the room, cautious like an animal, his broad shoulders and muscular body covered by a simple black collared shirt and black shorts. The thump of his large hooves echoes off the sitting room walls as he walks towards them.

Tora freezes and widens her eyes, trying to minimize her reaction. The top half of his body is human like any man aged in his twenties but he has the lower body of a goat.

"Braxen. Bring a pot of coffee for our visitors." The elf waves her hand dismissively.

Tora tries not to openly gape. It's a satyr! After everything she's seen, a half man half goat shouldn't surprise her but as far as the angels, Valkyries, and the gods knew, satyrs died out long ago. They're supposed to be extinct.

Folding her hands on her lap, the elven woman turns her steely eyes back to Tora. "Do you want to tell me why you were searching for our town, and why I shouldn't have you killed?"

"Mother!" Nia gasps.

Tora pinches her lips into a tight smile as Astra sits down beside her and grips her hand, her jovial demeanor crumbling into fear.

There's the fae she knows. Cruel and sadistic. The benevolent fae are meant to be more progressive and accepting than humans, malevolent fae, or demons, but Tora's always suspected that it's bullshit. They're just as bad as each other; angels and gods included.

"Okay kids... this is boring." Tia drops a half-eaten strawberry covered in chocolate on the floor and walks towards the arched doorway, her spiked heels scraping against the wooden floorboards. "Call me when the fun starts."

"How dare..." the elven woman starts but Tia's already gone.

Tora sneaks a quick look at Astra's frightened face and squeezes her hand in reassurance. The malevolent faery had the right idea. Tora wishes she could join her and take Astra with her, but they need to play nice and figure out the secret to keeping Greenwich safe.

"Mother." Brae frowns. "There's no need to threaten anyone."

"You will speak when spoken to!" The elven woman snaps, her voice bouncing off the walls. "Children should be seen and not heard. I may be your mother but I am your queen first!"

Brae steels his jaw, his ice-blue eyes full of anger and humiliation. It makes Tora want to punch the old bitch in the face. Her mother wasn't cruel like this old hag, but she can understand the utter betrayal of being chided by your mother in front of others.

"Raina..." the faery woman starts but is silenced by a glare from the elven woman. She sighs and bows her head. "My apologies your majesty. Queen Raina." She glances at Tora and softens her vibrant green eyes. "You know the Valkyries are no threat to Olivia."

"So say you." Queen Raina lifts her chin and looks down her nose at Astra and Tora. "But the Valkyrie and the fledgling cannot remain here."

"They shouldn't be able to force Astra to become a Valkyrie," Nia says, her voice tight. "It could kill her."

"That is not for you to decide, daughter." Queen Raina sharpens her glare as the satyr returns with a pot of coffee and mugs. He juggles the armload and puts them down on the coffee table.

"Next time use a tray!" Queen Raina snaps and pours the coffee. "And pick up the strawberry that beast left behind!"

Grunting, the satyr stomps over to pick up the strawberry and retreats from the room, but not before sharing a lingering look with Nia.

Tora looks away quickly, not wanting to intrude on their moment. That's heartbreak about to happen there. She can't imagine the Queen of all Bitches allowing her daughter to date anyone let alone a man that's half goat.

"Let's start again." The faery woman stands and flexes a pair of large majestic green silk wings lined in a gray silver dust. She holds out her hand and offers a smile. "My name is Kiara."

Tora shakes her hand and smiles, immediately taking a liking to the faery. She projects nothing but warmth and kindness and smells faintly of chamomile tea and rocket fuel; a strange mix, but somehow it works on her. "I'm Tora. You've met Astra already."

The faery's smile broadens, her natural warmth including Astra as she takes her seat once again. "I have."

"What is it you want from us exactly Valkyrie?" Queen Raina taps her long silver-painted nails on the arm of the chair, her aggression unwavering.

Tora picks up the mug of coffee and takes a sip to give herself time to think. The faery and the younger elves might be open to sharing their knowledge, but she doubts the bitchy elven woman would. Maybe if she got them alone, they'd help her.

"We only need to stay another day," Astra blurts out. "And we were hoping you'd tell us how you keep the demon portals out of our home."

"I knew it!" Queen Raina bellows, causing everyone in the room to flinch. "You are after our secrets."

"Mother; that's hardly what she said," Nia argues. "Besides, we've created plenty of pocket realms in the Realm of Man to save the humans."

"That's different." Queen Raina snaps. "It was our choice, and the humans know nothing of our methods."

Tora sighs. They're not going to get an answer now, not from Queen Raina, and not from the others. She can see it on the horrid woman's face. "We don't want your secrets. We want to protect our village."

"That's admirable, but you won't be doing it at the expense of mine." Queen Raina glances at her daughter and stands, prompting Kiara, Nia, and Brae to do the same. "As for hiding here, you may stay no more than forty hours."

Frowning, Tora stands, trying to figure out how many hours it is until Astra's Birthday. Their little demon battle and the fact she was passed out does very little to help. "Forty hours? That's…"

"Exactly one minute past midnight on your friend's birthday." Queen Raina lifts her chin. "Although, be warned; if you put my town in any danger, I will not hesitate to throw you out or hand you over. Do you understand?"

Gritting her teeth, Tora concedes and nods. What else can she do? She just has to hope the Valkyries don't come after them and that she can figure out the town's secret before they leave. Astra will be safe from the Valkyries, but the survivors in Greenwich will die without that secret. They all will.

"While in Olivia, you will not mention the outside world to any of the residents. Do not speak to them unless spoken to, and keep your answers short. You are from Greenwich Village. The city is thriving as it always has. You are both employees of the human government, assessing the town's safety practices and stay-at-home orders during the pandemic. That should provide you with a cover to get by." Queen Raina starts towards the door. "Keep your distance from Selene. The girl is cunning and may see through your lies. And cover that forehead tattoo! It will draw unwanted attention."

Tora and Astra glance at each other, guessing that Selene is the prophesized Witch Goddess everyone is talking about.

"Anything else?" Tora curls her lip. The woman lets this Selene, the prophesized Witch Goddess destined to destroy the realms, roam around freely but she and Tora are the threat? She just wants to shake the bitch. They're so stupid. Why don't they just kill the witch to stop the prophecy?

"Yes. One more thing." Queen Raina whips her head over her shoulder and grins. "If you disrupt my town in any way, I will kill the fledgling and torture you until the end of time. Do you understand?"

Tora nods and suppresses the urge to punch the woman in the face. Nothing would make the sour bitch happier than torturing her and killing Astra. She can hear it in her voice. It's the first time she's ever met any of the benevolent fae and as far as she can tell, there's not much difference between them and the assholes who stumble through the portals. The sooner they get out of Olivia, the better.

CHAPTER NINETEEN

The room hums in blissful silence, the missing presence of the Queen Bitch calming the tension. An old antique wooden grandfather clock ticks steadily against the wall. Warm rays of sunshine beam through the large arch-shaped windows and dance on the wooden floorboards.

"I'm so sorry about my mother." Nia shakes her head and covers her face in embarrassment as her brother Brae sits next to her, his back rigid and on guard.

"Raina means well." The faery Kiara sits back down. "She only has the town's safety in mind."

Astra pinches her lips into a smile. "We understand. That's exactly what we want for Greenwich Village. Isn't it Tora?"

Everyone looks at Tora as though expecting an answer, but she can't remain polite and silent any longer. Ever since she heard about the prophecy, the same question has been burning a hole in her stomach. Why hasn't anyone killed the prophesized Witch Goddess? The one destined to destroy the realms. One single life would save countless souls in every single one of the realms. It doesn't make any sense.

"Why doesn't anyone take out the prophesized Witch Goddess?" Tora looks directly at the faery Kiara, feeling she would know better than the others.

Kiara flinches and offers her a sad smile. "Selene cannot die."

"What do you mean she can't die?" Tora frowns. Everything can die. Only the Creator is truly eternal. "Even gods can die. Everyone has a weakness; Valkyries, gods, and souls included."

Brae shakes his head. "Not this one. She is the first of her kind. And she doesn't deserve to die. She hasn't done anything wrong."

"Yet." Tora scoffs. For an elven prince and warrior, he's not that smart. Hot as hell, but bloody stupid. A true warrior would see the advantage of taking out the threat before it becomes a problem. It's logic.

"You would judge and execute someone based on what they might do, not what they've done?" Nia's eyes sadden. "Selene is my best friend. Brae's too. I can tell you now that she doesn't deserve to die."

"She's your friend?" Astra widens her eyes.

Nia smiles warmly and nods. "She's moody, but she's a good person."

"What about you?" Tora looks to the older faery, assuming she at least has some common sense. It's not personal. It's logic. One person to save the realms. It's simple math.

"Selene is my daughter." Kiara's eyes soften. "And she has done nothing wrong."

"Daughter?" Tora gapes as her face reddens, her tongue suddenly thick and dry. If she'd known she was her daughter, she wouldn't have said anything at all. Forget sneaking around to find out the town's secret. She'll be lucky if they don't kick them out now. "I... I don't understand. I thought she was a god."

"I adopted Selene the day she was born. Her birth parents, Gaia and Uranus found a white birthmark around her belly button: a full moon with a crescent on either side and knew she was the marked god in the prophecy," Kiara says. "The other gods would have tried to kill or contain her on sight."

"Selene is the seventh daughter of the Goddess Gaia, who is the seventh daughter of the Goddess Artaelia. That makes her a god and a witch." Brae elaborates. "Ever since the prophecy, gods have been forbidden from having more than six children, a law enforced to prevent a god with witch-like powers. Gaia and Uranus broke that law when they conceived Selene.

They believed Gaia was one of six, not seven, but Gaia's mother bore another child who died during childbirth."

"So, she lives to destroy the realms because she's your friend and your daughter?" Tora eyes the group. They would literally sacrifice the nine realms to save one life. It doesn't make sense.

"Would you kill Astra?" Kiara lifts her eyebrows.

Tora opens her mouth then shuts it again. It's true. She wouldn't sacrifice Astra for anything. Just like Brae, Nia, and Kiara, she would condemn the realms to death before sacrificing her friend.

"None of us would ever hurt Selene. We love her," Nia says. "But you still misunderstand. It's not only that we won't kill her, she literally cannot be killed. Selene is more than a god. She is immortal; eternal. She will never die. Ever. She cannot choose to die like the other gods. She cannot be killed like other gods or Nephilim witches. She is untouchable."

Tora's head spins. She was led to believe the only being that was truly immortal was the Creator. He, or she, or it, cannot die. It will always be as it always has.

That means that this Selene is a Creator, or based on the prophecy, a Destroyer. Everything in life has an opposite. Everyone believes that in one way or another, but never did she think there would be an opposite to the Creator.

This is bigger than she thought. The realms are going to collapse, and there is nothing she or anyone else can do about it. Their only hope is this stupid simulated town, Olivia.

"So, no matter what…" Astra trembles. "The world will end."

Tora flinches and stares at the floor, her eyes unfocused and blurry. That's what the Valkyries said. The prophecy will come true no matter what they do. They can only prepare for the coming war.

A knock at the front door makes everyone jump, Tora included.

"Nia!" A female voice calls from the front door.

"No no no. I'm late!" Nia widens her eyes and quickly runs around the room stuffing her laptop and other things into a tope bag.

Brae rolls his eyes. "Nia goes to school with Selene. She loves it even though it's fake."

"Shut up Brae." Nia glances back over her shoulder. "The knowledge isn't fake. Learning is learning, and this is the only way mother will let me learn about the Realm of Man."

"Here." Nia hands Tora a circular object and hurries to the door. "The concealer will hide your mark. I'll be home later this afternoon."

"Selene?" Kiara makes her way to the door, her wings disappearing into a glamor behind her.

"Ma?" The voice calls back.

"Did your father drop your brother off at school yet?" Kiara calls out.

"Yeah, Malcolm dropped me off here after," Selene says. "He said he'd pick us up this afternoon."

"Thanks honey," Kiara says as she collects her things. "Have a great day."

"Yeah yeah," Selene groans.

Tora and Astra glance at each other. The Witch Goddess is right outside. If it wasn't for Brae and Kiara, they would both rush the window to get a glimpse of this all powerful being, but judging from Brae's rigid posture, it wouldn't be a smart idea.

"Bye!" Nia sings as she closes the front door behind her. Muted voices drift further away as Nia and Selene walk to the school.

"I have to go too." Kiara waves and hurries out the door. "Have fun!"

Cracking his neck, Brae stands and hovers by the doorframe. "I have to train my warriors and keep an eye on Nia and Selene. You two can stay here or go for a walk around town. I've left you a bunch of human money in a bowl by the door. Buy yourself some lunch or coffee or whatever; buy a souvenir, but do not mention anything about the outside world or Selene to anyone. Even Selene doesn't know what she is. Got it?"

Tora blushes under the full attention of Brae's gaze and nods as he leaves, leaving her and Astra alone in the middle of the elven home. Well, almost alone. The satyr is still around somewhere.

"Well, that was a bust." Astra sinks deep into the couch, mercifully misreading Tora's crush for annoyance.

"Not entirely." Tora rests her boots on the decorative wooden coffee table and opens the makeup compact. There's nothing they can do about the Witch Goddess, but with the town's secret, they can give Greenwich Village a chance. There's no way she's putting this crap on her face though. Who cares if people stare. "You and the baby are safe for now, and we have forty hours to figure out how the town is kept safe."

"You included the baby." Tears spring to Astra's eyes.

"Of course I did." Tora screws up her face. "What did you think I'd do? I love you, and your little fetus too."

"Eww! That sounds gross when you say it like that." Astra laughs, exactly what Tora was hoping for. They need to focus on what they can do, not what they can't do. It's the only way to get through this.

"Does Ethan know?" Tora asks even though she's pretty sure she knows the answer.

"He knows. It's the only reason he agreed to let me come here." Astra smiles. "He knows you'll keep me safer than anyone in the world."

Tora frowns. He let her come? She doesn't like the sound of that. It's like he has some sort of control over her, not that she can bring it up after their fight in the Deadlands. "Then why did you fight me on the Valkyrie ritual?"

"I... I don't know. Valkyries have children, and I didn't think it would change anything," Astra says.

Tora shakes her head. "Honey, you get stabbed in the head during the ritual. You would die, the same as I did. Okay, I'm alive, kind of, but who knows what that would do to the baby."

"But other Valkyries must have undergone the ritual while pregnant," Astra argues.

"Maybe. I don't know, but if they were pregnant, they were pregnant with the child of a god, not a human. Big difference." Tora gets to her feet and leaves the compact on the coffee table, determined to save their village. "Come on. Let's check out the town."

They don't have that much time. If they're going to figure out the secrets of Olivia, they need to get a move on.

"Aren't you going to cover your mark?" Astra follows.

"Not in this lifetime." Tora scoffs and takes a stash of money from the bowl near the front door on her way out. The mark is part of who she is. She's waited her entire life to become a fully-fledged Valkyrie. She's not about to dishonor that by covering her markings, especially not because the Queen Bitch told her to.

Following the signs towards the town center, Tora smiles politely at the people that glance in their direction and links arms with Astra, ignoring the shocked and sometimes fearful looks of the people that pass.

The streets are full of a mix of commuters dressed in suits, work uniforms, jeans, and casual clothes as the residents of Olivia continue with their daily lives, going to work, school, and running errands, oblivious to the outside world. The large high school at the end of the street overflows with laughter, shouting, and a mess of noise.

It's fucking ridiculous. What happens if the veil ever comes down? Every single person in Olivia would be dead in seconds. They're scared of a mark that looks like a tattoo? How are they going to react to a demon or a pixie? They would shit themselves.

It's nice to be safe and all but the fae should really prepare the people of Olivia just in case. If the Witch Goddess is as powerful as they make out, she should be able to handle a few demons and fae herself. It's such a wasted opportunity.

Turning down main street, Tora and Astra widen their eyes, amazed by the normalcy of the area. The streets are pristine and washed clean. Cute colorful shop fronts housing grocery stores, specialty stores, boutique clothing outlets, bars, cafes, restaurants, and an old heritage movie theater line the street, the architecture tipped with glittery silver, looking a lot like snow.

They stop at a bustling café filled with patrons and a takeaway window built on the side. A vintage sign reads, *All the Usual Things Café.*

Tora peeks through the window and instantly thinks of Mrs Arnold and the squad back in Greenwich. They would die if they saw the assortment of cakes, pastries, candy, and hand-crafted chocolates inside the glass cabinet at the counter.

Quirky mismatched tables, chairs, and old-fashioned booths sit haphazardly around the room. A mix of strange inventions are sealed behind glass cabinets; some ancient; some new; some resembling the steel used in the town's architecture and the armor worn by Brae and Nia.

"Let's just grab a coffee to go and check out the streets for any clues," Tora says and orders a large cappuccino for herself and a hot chocolate for Astra.

A few minutes later, the male barista with deep blue eyes and dreadlocks winks at her as he hands her the drinks. "Cool tat. Drinks are on me."

Blushing, Tora thanks the barista and walks off down the street. They scour the entire town, down the main street filled with shops, past the school, the University, hundreds of houses, and the surrounding forest but there's nothing to indicate what the fae use to keep the area safe. There are no crystals, no wards; nothing obvious at all.

Hours later with aching feet, Astra and Tora find themselves back on the main street of Olivia, casually browsing the merchandise of a shop named Goo Goo Gah Gah's. Astra gushes over the tiny baby shoes, socks, and jumpsuits while Tora secretly buys a beautiful glittering silver rattle and a matching necklace with a pacifier pendant. She tucks it into her pocket before Astra can see.

Greenwich has a baby store with clothes and essential items, but nothing as pretty or as valuable as the rattle, and Astra's child deserves something beautiful, even if he or she is half Ethan's.

The benevolent fae might not care that Astra carries the child of a human and a Valkyrie, but then again, they might. They can't chance it. No one can know about Astra, not in Olivia.

"I don't get it." Tora frowns as they leave the store, more than a little irritated by the ringing door chime. "They don't have any wards or crystals at all. What the hell could they be using to keep the demon portals out?"

"Oh, hey, there's Nia." Astra waves her arm around. "Hey Nia! Over here!"

Tora turns around to see Nia walking down the street, a tall slim girl with defined muscles and a mix of golden highlights in her long hair by her side. Brae trails behind; his thunderous expression sinking her stomach.

Crap. He told them to keep away from the Selene girl and from the look of the chick by Nia's side, that's exactly who's walking down the street with them. Her hair is down to her waist, streaked naturally with browns, blondes, and reds. Her forest green eyes catch the light and shimmer with flecks of gold and silver. Her sun-kissed skin is blemish-free with perfect muscle tone.

Oblivious, Astra runs up to Nia and gushes about the cute little shops around the town. Tora slowly approaches, wanting to avoid the awkward exchange. The Witch Goddess is tall; not as tall as Astra, but she's at least five foot ten or more.

"Umm... that's great. I'm glad you guys like the town." Nia glances around and bites her lip. "Hopefully all our practices are up to code?"

Astra tilts her head in confusion, completely missing their cover story.

"Everything appears to be in order." Tora cuts in, keeping her answer vague and to the point.

The girl Selene narrows her green eyes, flecks of golden sunlight burning in her irises, her black jeans, hooded black shirt and knee-high boots in complete contrast to Nia's white summer dress. Tora can feel herself shrinking under the goddess's gaze but is powerless to do anything to stop it, her intimidating presence like a weighted boulder.

"And who the hell are you two?" Selene curls her lip, disdain dripping from her tongue.

"Selene!" Nia chides. "Don't be rude. Astra and Tora are visiting on behalf of the government to check our health and safety protocols because of the pandemic."

Selene looks them over from head to toe, clearly not buying the excuse. Anger and hate drip from her skin, like a gray fog thickening the air.

"They don't look like government workers." Selene arches her left eyebrow and glares at Tora. "This one looks like a hobbit crossed over into the matrix. Seriously? What type of government worker gets a tattoo in the middle of the forehead?"

Brae stifles his laughter. "They're from Greenwich Village Selene. It's not so unusual there."

Having no idea what a hobbit or the matrix is, Tora keeps her mouth shut, knowing full well she's being insulted somehow. It feels like she's walking on eggshells. Like the ground opened and is threatening to pull her into Hell.

And this is the "nice" girl who carries the fate of the realms in her hands. They are so fucked. They are so fucking fucked.

Astra blinks her wide soft purple eyes, not understanding that they're being insulted. "Oh... umm. It's nice to meet you, Selene."

Rolling her eyes, Selene looks to Nia and points at All the Usual Things Café. "Whatever. I'm going over there. I'm meeting Nik and Jess. I'll catch you later."

Brae stiffens. "Those two again?"

"Don't be an ass, Brae." Selene starts across the street, her stride long and irritated.

"They're trouble Selene!" Brae yells.

Without looking back, Selene flips him off and continues across the street. "Go home Brae!"

Frowning, Tora looks between Selene and the two elves. It's strange. Selene seems to be protective and annoyed by them at the same time. She joins up with a girl with pale skin and black spiky hair, and another with a brown ponytail. Brae and Nia watch them, their eyes portraying their concern.

"What's that all about?" Tora watches as Selene throws back two shots of black coffee and takes a takeaway mug with her as she and her friends get into a yellow Camry.

"I thought I told you to stay away from Selene?" Brae glares at them, making Tora feel the size of an ant. She doesn't know why, but she hates that he's mad at her, and she hates herself for hating that he's mad at her. He's an elf. She shouldn't be attracted to him.

Astra sighs and finally catches on. "I'm so sorry. That was my fault. I didn't think. I just saw you guys walking down the street and was happy to see a familiar face."

"Don't worry about it." Nia smiles, warmth radiating from her skin. "No harm done."

"Ah, really?" Tora points to where Selene was standing moments ago. "Your friend there obviously knew something was up. She hated us on sight."

Nia shrugs, like it's no big deal and starts walking down the street, back to their house. "That's just Selene. She's always like that. Believe it or not, she's a lot better than she was before the Anger Management Counselor."

Tora widens her eyes and casts a quick glance at Astra. It's a little frightening to think that the future of the nine realms is dependent on an eighteen-year-old bitch of a Witch Goddess with a serious attitude problem and anger issues.

"She doesn't know she's a goddess, right?" Tora frowns and checks behind her.

"No." Brae interrupts.

"Actually, Selene found out a few days ago that she's a witch and a goddess, on her eighteenth birthday. She also just found out that she's adopted by a faery, a being she never thought existed, so cut her a bit of slack." Nia defends her friend.

Brae's ice-blue eyes flare in anger. "What?"

"Kiara had to tell her. Selene's powers are manifesting through the binding spell. It won't work on her anymore." Nia glances at Brae and quickly looks away. "It's fine. She's adjusting. Just give it time."

Screwing up her face, Tora drops back a few steps and tries to wrap her head around the fae logic. How is keeping the truth from an all-powerful being for eighteen years and dropping a truth bomb on her birthday a good idea? Especially when that powerful being appears to be emotionally unstable.

The world is so fucked. The realms are so fucked. They are all so fucking fucked.

CHAPTER TWENTY

Small blue wrens and hummingbirds dance in front of the bay window overlooking the front garden. The large arching branches of the beautiful fig tree in front of the guest bedroom swells with life, filled with butterflies, bees, and squirrels.

Tora can't remember the last time she saw a bird flying around Greenwich Village. They have birds, but most don't fly around anymore, too scared of what lies above and beyond the perimeter.

Retiring to the guest bedroom, Astra naps in the king-sized bed wrapped in a soft baby blue satin bedspread and sheets while Tora sits on the bay window seat, staring at the town below.

There must be something she's missing. Whatever is keeping the town safe should be visible to a Valkyrie, but there are no crystals or wards anywhere. Fae magic doesn't provide blanket protection. It doesn't work like that. Not that powerful anyway. It has to be something big. Something that surrounds the entire town. Something powerful. But there is literally nothing. Even on the edges of town, the destruction of the outside world is invisible.

Maybe the town is on top of some ancient fae burial ground? Not that fae burial grounds have power but what else could it be? She just hopes it's not because of the Witch Goddess. They're dead if it is.

Sighing, Tora smacks her head against the glass window and pinches her aching eyes closed, the stink of failure burning her nose. She can't return to Greenwich with nothing. Everyone will be dead within a week, Astra included. The warlock warned them. All hell is about to break loose if it hasn't already. The wolves were certainly new, as was the demon child. Who knows what's running loose around Greenwich now? As much as she hates the Valkyries, she's glad they are there.

"Tora?" Nia knocks on the door and pops her head inside. "Do you need anything?"

Astra stirs and rolls on her side.

Putting her finger to her lips, Tora joins Nia outside and closes the door behind her. "We're fine. Astra's just tired. I'll let her sleep for another hour if that's okay?"

"Of course." Nia smiles. "Dinner won't be for a while. Do you want to train with me and Brae?"

Tora raises her eyebrows. Training with the fae would be amazing. She could learn how they move, how they fight. It will give her a chance to get closer to Nia, try and get her to talk about the town's secret to keeping the portals out.

"Umm. I do, but…" Tora touches the closed door, reluctant to leave Astra unprotected.

"Astra will be safe," Nia reassures her. "Braxen will make sure of it."

Tora bites her lip, unsure what the satyr could do against the Valkyries should they find them, but an elf's house in the middle of Olivia is probably the last place they'd look for her.

"We'll only be in the backyard." Nia walks down the corridor and gestures for Tora to follow. "Come on. It'll do you good. Take your mind off things."

Following Nia out into the backyard, Tora gapes and slows her step. Thick large luscious trees surround the gigantic property brimming with all types of birds, insects, furry animals, and reptiles. Some look like they're from the human world but the small flying white fluffy fuzz balls must be from the Benevolent Fae Realm. So must the cute miniature hummingbirds flitting from tree to tree, the size of a bottle cap, the fur covered snakes, and the cat sized multi-colored dragons flying through hollow trunks and lighting the insides with shards of lightning breath, never once burning the bark.

They mix together with blue wrens, sparrows, ravens, crows, pythons, butterflies, and lizards, all living side by side in this impossible rainforest with a grassy clearing in the middle.

Tora finds herself drawn to the beautiful babbling brook somehow flowing through the base of arched hollow trees and the stunning aqua lagoon nestled amongst the pastel green and pure white ferns, just like in the Realm of Angels. In the corner, a small cliff waterfall feeds in freshwater, magically flowing out of an invisible portal.

The entire place reminds her of the Realm of Angels and stabs at her heart, cloaking her in a shadow of sorrow. With the coming war, the realms collapsing, and the Witch Goddess, she probably won't see her home again. The Realm of Angels will collapse with all the others, colliding into chaos, toxicity, and death.

"Ready?" Brae claps his hands to get her attention.

Jerking, Tora blinks away her spiraling thoughts and nearly chokes on her tongue as Brae draws a sword from the rack of glittery silver weapons stacked behind him, his bare chest and biceps rippling with lean muscles, his abs like a hard rock. Liquid silver crawls up his neck and shoulders in waves, constantly moving around his body. He wears a simple pair of loose black cotton pants.

"Let's see what the Valkyrie can do." Brae grins.

Chuckling, Tora ties her long black hair into a braid and joins him in the middle of the clearing. She's not sure what's more impressive; the elf's physique or their stash of weapons.

Nia sits on the ground with her legs crossed beneath her and claps. "She's going to kick your ass bro."

Brae rolls his eyes. "Thanks for the support sis."

"Just calling it how I see it." Nia broadens her smile.

Positioning her feet, Tora quietens the excitement in her blood, the blades strapped to her legs itching to let fly. There's no doubt in her mind that her mother would have wanted her to train with the fae, to get to know how they move. Her mother was a fierce fighter but she was also incredibly smart and strategic.

Without warning, Brae swings his sword and thrusts it at her stomach, the glittering metal singing like a bell. Tora gasps and arches her body to the side, her rapid heartbeat kick-starting her reflexes like an outboard motor, her mother's words echoing in her head. *Move Tora. Move! A fight doesn't start slow and neither should training.*

Grinning, Tora drops down low and sweeps her leg fast, trying to trip him but Brae flips over her head and lands behind her. She kicks her leg back like a horse and slams her boot into his thigh, missing his royal penis by inches.

Surprised, Brae stumbles back. He recovers quickly and swings and thrusts his sword over and over again in rapid succession, his response more frantic yet still precise.

Bobbing and weaving, Tora keeps her distance, her breathing laboring more out of aggravation than exertion. Valkyries are meant to be the ultimate warriors, so why the hell is a fae man able to kick her ass?

The fae she fought before didn't move like him. They could barely stand and were too drunk to fight. The ones who could fight were more feral and erratic, like a cornered animal, but Brae fights with precision and skill.

"Use your blades, Tora!" Nia yells out from the sideline.

Tora glances at Nia and feels the world shift beneath her. God, she's an idiot! Of course, the elf is kicking her ass. He has a weapon and she doesn't. Her stupid crush made her forget to use a fucking weapon! She could punch herself in the face.

Pulling a blade from her leg strap, she flips in the air as Brae lunges and sends it flying at his shoulder, realizing too late that fae may not heal as fast as Valkyries. For a split second, it looks like the blade will penetrate, but the liquid silver circling his body shifts and guards his chest.

"Shit. Sorry." Tora winces as the blade hits metal and falls to the ground, more than a little relieved it didn't harm him. "I shouldn't have tried to stab you."

"Stop holding back Tora. The armor protects him," Nia says. "It won't let any weapon penetrate his skin."

Tora raises her eyebrows. So, no matter what she throws at him, the armor will protect him. It would protect him from demons just like out in the Deadlands, it would protect him from weapons and burns... from anything.

"Can I get some?" Tora can't help but ask. Imagine the time she could save without having to heal before the next fight. She would never have to worry about Astra being hurt. She would be protected always, and it would come in more than handy in the coming war.

"No." Brae scoffs and lunges with his sword. "It's elven steel."

Tora dives out of the way and scrambles to her feet, turning to see Brae's sword directed straight at her stomach. She widens her eyes and releases her large white wings, their strength instantly pulling her back away from the sword and up into the air. Her wrist burns as her soul sword forms in her hand, glowing an unearthly purple.

"Oh. So that's how it is? Someone's got their own secret." Brae laughs, his voice loud and playful. "You've been a Valkyrie for what? A day? And you can already call on your sword and wings at will? Impressive. Most newbies can only do it out of fear."

Tora grins as an idea comes to mind, and it has nothing to do with pride. The elves might not want to tell her the town's secret, but maybe she can win it from them. "Speaking of secrets... how about we make things interesting?"

"Interesting how?" Brae tilts his head, the corner of his eyes crinkling in interest.

"If I win, you tell me how you keep the town safe," Tora bargains. "And if you win, I won't ask again."

"You can ask all you want." Brae's ice-blue eyes harden into a steely glare. "I won't reveal our secret against my mother's orders."

Tora jolts at his harsh tone. Shit! She pushed it too far, too soon. She should have waited and talked to Nia alone. Nia's the nice one, the one more likely to want to help them.

"What's the matter Brae?" Nia laughs. "Scared you'll lose?"

Brae whips his head around and glares daggers at his sister before returning his steely eyes back to Tora. "Fine. If you win, I will give you a hint as to what keeps the town safe. If I win, I get your sword."

It's a steep bet, one Brae thinks she'll decline, but she knows something he obviously doesn't. Her sword will disappear if he tries to take it.

"You can try and take it." Tora smirks.

Aiming her sword, she flies straight at him, using the strength of her wings to push her forward. Brae doesn't have time to move or react. He doesn't have time to do anything. One second, she's in the air, halfway across the clearing, the next, she's at his neck.

Nia gasps, but Tora pulls up short a split second before impaling her sword into his bare neck.

Brae widens his eyes, his face pale with shock.

"I win." Tora winks and taps the elven steal with the tip of her sword as it moves to protect his neck, a second too late.

Now that's the Valkyrie she's meant to be. Unbeatable and fast. Her mother would be proud. Greenwich is saved.

Brae shakes his head and snorts, unable to believe she was able to beat him. She half expects him to throw a tantrum or refuse to yield, but Brae bows his head in defeat and grins. "Double or nothing?"

Tora frowns. A black spot appears on the neck of Brae's glittering steel armor, seeping outwards as puffs of black smoke drift into the air. She's no expert but somehow, she doubts that's meant to happen. "Umm, Brae? Is your armor supposed to do that?"

"Do what?" Brae looks down but the armor stops smoking, leaving only a stain.

Tora points to his neck. "Your armor was…"

Nia suddenly screams and grabs her chest. She curls into the fetal position, the elven steel attached to her body quivering and spinning on and off her skin.

"Nia!" Brae rushes to her side followed closely by Tora. His hands hover close to her body, frightened to even touch her.

Cradling Nia's head. Tora frantically scans her body for injury as her wings and sword disappear. There's nothing. No blood, no wound, no nothing. She couldn't have been caught in the crossfire; they weren't throwing weapons.

"What happened?" Tora screws up her face, her voice tightening as concern knots her stomach. "Was she stung? Is she allergic to bees or something?"

"I don't know." Brae shakes his head in a panic; his ice-blue eyes wide with fear as Nia convulses on the ground.

"Nia!" Braxen the satyr runs out the back door and lifts Nia into his arms like she weighs nothing. He cradles her like a child and starts towards the house, his large hooves cutting chunks out of the grass.

"Hey!" Brae chases after him and levels his sword at the back of his head, his body shaking in anger and confusion. "What are you doing?"

Tora jumps to her feet, even though she knows the satyr wouldn't hurt Nia. He loves her. You'd have to be blind not to see it, and even then, you could feel it like a warm hug.

"I would never hurt her." Braxen stops, turns his head slightly and glares at Brae. A gigantic vein throbs out of the side of his neck. "Lower your sword."

Tightening his jaw, Brae drops his sword. His entire body sags in defeat, like his world is crumbling; like he failed to protect her.

It wasn't his fault. One minute she was watching them fight, the next, she's screaming in pain and convulsing on the ground. Even if one of their weapons hit her, it wouldn't cause a fit.

"Her soul has been damaged. I need to heal her." Braxen carries Nia inside the house.

Tora reels back. It's not possible. Souls can't be damaged. They can be trapped, recycled, and reprocessed, but you can't just damage your soul watching a sparring match.

Brae and Tora follow Braxen and watch uselessly as he lays Nia's lifeless body on the floor. He hurries around the room collecting white candles and lights them before putting them on the ground surrounding her. The liquid silver armor slithers over her body; quivering and disconnecting from her skin, flailing on the ground like dying fish.

Tora sits next to Brae just outside of the circle as he cradles his head in his hands, not daring to speak. Her throat tightens. It feels like it's her fault. Like she did something to hurt Nia. She can't even console him. It feels wrong somehow.

Leaning over Nia, Braxen chants melodically on his knees and gently caresses her face, the hum of his voice seeping into the walls, the furniture, and their skin, moving through their organs like a steady beating drum. The minutes tick into an hour as Braxen continues to chant and feed Nia a herbal drink with a crystal teaspoon.

Finally, Nia's eyes snap open. She gasps and sits up, almost headbutting Braxen in the process. The candle flame flickers.

Tora jumps and nearly cheers out loud. She doesn't know Nia that well but it would have broken her heart if she'd died. The elf girl is so pure, so full of love, warmth, and kindness; a light too bright to be stifled this early.

Brae releases a large breath and rubs his face, relief bringing tears to his eyes.

"Step away from my daughter!"

Tora whips her head around to see Queen Raina storming into the room, her face burning crimson red, the same color as her long flowing ball gown.

Scrambling to his feet, Braxen backs away and knocks over a candle, sending hot wax all over the floor. Fear blotches like a rash across his face.

"Stupid fool! Look what you've done!" Queen Raina snaps. Her ice-blue eyes flare almost white. "Clean that up! And for the last time, stay away from my daughter!"

Tora forces her tongue still. It must be a shock to find your daughter lying in the middle of the floor surrounded by candles, but seriously; what a fucking bitch! Braxen just saved her daughter's life and she treats him like absolute shit.

Pulling Nia to her feet, Queen Raina wraps her arm around her and drags her out of the room, Nia too weak to protest.

There's nothing any of them can do to stop it. Braxen stares after Nia, heartache and relief etched into his face. Brae burns bright, anger tightening his jaw. And Tora... Tora sits frozen watching the whole thing unfold.

"Fuck!" Brae gets to his feet and blows out the rest of the candles as Braxen immediately begins to clean up the mess.

Time ticks by slowly, dragging on as if in slow motion. Tora blinks and looks back and forth between Braxen and Brae. No one says a thing. Nia nearly died, then the Queen Bitch came in, blew up the guy who saved her, snatched her away, and no one has anything to say?

"What the hell just happened?" Tora throws her hands in the air and gets to her feet. Why didn't Brae stick up for Braxen? Why didn't anyone try to explain?

Braxen glances at her but says nothing as he continues to put away the candles and ease the soy wax from the floorboards, his movements slow as though he's in pain.

"Mother doesn't approve of Nia and Braxen socializing." Brae helps pack away the candles. "Satyrs are usually employed as domestic help, and as Nia is the Princess, the next in line for the throne... well, mother doesn't think it's appropriate."

"Employed?" Braxen scoffs, his forest green eyes hard and full of anger. "That's a nice way to say slave."

Tora flinches. Did he say slave? As in made to work for the bitch? What the hell? The so-called benevolent fae have slaves? No wonder satyrs are a myth back in the Realm of Angels. They were believed to live only until they turned eighteen, and Valkyries at least, believed they were extinct, but the asshole fae are keeping them hidden, keeping them as slaves.

"That's seriously messed up. And what happened to Nia?" Tora frowns. "Why did she scream? Why was her soul damaged?"

Brae shakes his head. "I have no idea."

"The steel." Braxen nods at Brae's liquid armor. "The steel must have been damaged somehow. It's the only explanation."

"Why would damage to the armor affect Nia?" Tora tilts her head. That makes absolutely no sense. Armor is supposed to protect you, not make you more vulnerable.

"They are connected. The soul of the steel and Nia," Braxen says. "Nia is its creator, but I don't understand how it was damaged. Nothing should be able to damage the steel."

Tora freezes in thought. The steel has a soul?

Oh shit. Her Valkyrie mark; her sword, her soul sword; it's used to collect warrior souls, create Valkyries, dispense demons...

Tora pales. Nia's soul is connected to the steel and her sword touched it.

"My sword," Tora whispers.

"What about it?" Brae shrugs.

Tora reluctantly looks into Brae's ice-blue eyes, afraid to tell him the truth, but knowing the benevolent fae need to know the weakness in their armor. "My sword is a soul sword. It's a part of me. It collects souls."

"Shit!" Braxen widens his eyes. "That must be it. Your sword must have drained part of the elven steel soul. Nia's soul."

"How the fuck does steel have a soul?" Tora's head spins. "And why is Nia connected to it?

"Nia created the elven steel by accident," Braxen says. "Five years ago, when visiting the armory, she felt a life force in the liquid steel and when she spoke, the steel responded."

"Nia somehow woke it up," Brae says, his eyes confused as he processes the fact that her sword damaged his sister. "No one knew until they tried to shape and cool it. It wouldn't harden. It wouldn't respond until Nia came back the next day."

"They tried everything to destroy the vat but the steel remained in liquid form. It wasn't until Nia objected that the steel rippled, hardened, and formed into bullions on its own. When she picked it up, the bullion liquified in her hand and spread over her body as armor," Braxen continues. "Others have tried, but the life force in the steel only responds to Nia's voice. An incantation by Nia allows others to use the steel as live armor, molding to each warrior, but Nia is the only one able to use it as a weapon."

Brae's eyes harden, his curious stare turning into a hate-filled glare.

Tora shrinks back, unsure how to apologize for stealing part of his sister's soul. It was an accident, she didn't know, but there's nothing she can say. She can tell from the look on his face. He hates her now, and there's nothing she can do to change that.

"I… I'm so sorry Brae." Tora lowers her head. "I didn't know."

Tightening his jaw, Brae storms out of the room. "Mother was right. We never should have let you stay."

Tora sighs, his words stabbing deep into her heart. So much for saving Greenwich Village. None of the fae will help them now. They're as good as dead.

CHAPTER TWENTY-ONE

Completely defeated, Tora goes back up to the guest bedroom to check on Astra, her muscles tense and aching with anxiety.

God, she can be so stupid. Why didn't she stay in the room with Astra? Why did she have to train with Brae? Why did she pull her soul sword?

If she had just waited and spoken to Nia about the town's secret alone instead of training with them, Greenwich wouldn't be doomed, and Nia wouldn't be near death.

But no. She had to train with her crush. She had to pull her soul sword to impress him and win some stupid bet. Brae was never going to tell her how to keep the town safe, and now Queen Raina will probably behead both her and Astra. They are so fucked and it's all her stupid fault.

"Star? I think we have to leave." Tora pushes open the large wooden door and finds the king-sized bed empty, the soft blue duvet and blanket half falling onto the floor.

"Star?" Tora frowns as a slither of concern grows in her stomach. She knows she nearly killed Nia, but they wouldn't have taken Astra because of that. Not this quickly anyway.

"Wha…" Astra chokes out from behind the closed bathroom door.

Tora lifts her eyebrows and eyes the door in suspicion as an odd sound, like a stalling water pump filters through the keyhole. Biting her lip, she pushes her ear up to the decorative wooden door and quickly recoils from the sound of someone heaving and throwing up into the toilet.

"Astra?" Tora starts to push open the door.

"No!" Astra slams the door shut, the wood shaking from the force. "I… ugh…. bler…"

Holding up her hands, Tora purses her lips together and backs away, her stomach rolling in sympathy. Ugh! Poor Astra. Hopefully it's not something she ate. So far, she feels fine, but they had the same burgers for lunch. "Umm yeah. Okay. I'll wait."

Sitting on the edge of the bed, Tora drops her head in her hands, wondering how everything got so messed up. Two days ago, she was fighting with her mother, hunting demons and fae, hanging out with the squad, and making out with Bo. Life was relatively simple, but now, everything's changed.

They're on the run from psycho Valkyries, her mother is dead, Teresa is dead, Victor is dead, she herself is technically dead, she nearly killed Nia, and she ruined her one chance of saving Greenwich Village.

Tora sighs. What is she meant to do now? They can't stay in Olivia. The Queen Bitch won't allow it, and if she takes Astra back to Greenwich, the Valkyries will kill her, or eventually a demon or fae will. It's inevitable. They're fucked no matter what they do.

"Oh god." Astra emerges from the bathroom covered in sweat, her face a light shade of green, her strawberry blonde hair sitting like a bird's nest on top of her head.

"Agh!" Tora jumps off the bed. "Oh… What… what happened to you?"

Astra flops down on the bed. "Morning sickness."

"But it's nighttime!" Tora argues and looks around the room. She doesn't know exactly what she's looking for but Astra looks like a zombie and a ghoul had a baby; On. Her. Face.

"It's just called that." Astra rolls her eyes and hugs a pillow. "It doesn't mean you only get it in the morning."

Backing up further, Tora sits on the bay window seat and stares at Astra in concern. She knows Astra is sick but they should stay somewhere else.

The house isn't safe anymore, not since some dumbass nearly killed Nia. The town has to have a hotel somewhere.

"It's not contagious you know?" Astra lifts her head off the pillow then drops it back down again, like it's too heavy for her body.

"Yeah, I know that." Tora snorts and rubs the back of her neck. "That's not it... It's a... I umm... I think we should stay somewhere else since I nearly killed Nia tonight."

"What?" Astra sits up fast causing her face to pale even further. Holding up her finger, she scrambles off the bed and runs into the bathroom, holding her hand over her mouth.

Tora cringes and stares out the window, trying to tune out the sound of Astra in the bathroom. If she was debating whether to have children or not, Astra's projectile vomiting would sway her towards a firm, hell no.

Town residents walk along the streets below, the cute cookie-cutter street lamps lighting their way as the glow of the shops and restaurants in the distance beckon them forward.

A sudden crack of thunder rocks the house as a dizzying display of lightning dances just off the coast and a torrent of rain blankets the ground.

The people of Olivia don't know how lucky they have it. If they were back in Greenwich Village, they would be in lockdown as soon as the sun set, or running for cover now the sudden storm has set in. Considering the portals open day and night now, she's not sure what kind of life the villagers have.

A minute later, Astra reemerges looking even greener with sweat dripping down her face. "Okay. Now tell me exactly what happened."

Sighing heavily, Tora explains, knowing they don't have much time left. Brae, Queen Raina, and her guards are probably getting ready to arrest her as they speak. She could just cry. She was so close to saving Greenwich, and now they're fucked. She failed miserably.

"Woah. That's... that's insane." Astra sits on the bed, her eyes wide. "Why would anyone tie their life force to armor? That's so dangerous."

"I don't think she did it on purpose," Tora says. "I think we should leave. Stay somewhere else tonight. We only need to get through tomorrow, and we're home free."

"Is anywhere in town safe though? And what about the protection for Greenwich?" Astra frowns.

"Like they're going to tell me now." Tora could kick herself. Why did she have to draw her sword? Why did she have to get cocky? If she had only used her blades, this might not have happened. "I'm lucky they didn't stick me in a dungeon. Maybe you're right. Maybe nowhere is safe."

Astra jumps as someone knocks on the door and stares at the knob, completely frozen in fear.

"Great." Tora groans and shakes her head, having no idea how she's going to escape this new shit show. "That's probably the royal guard now."

Poking her head around the door, Nia smiles and tentatively walks inside the room, her summer dress replaced with soft white linen pajamas and her long blonde hair held back loosely with a silver clip. Her cheeks are a little flushed, but otherwise, she looks completely healed.

"Is it okay I'm here?" Nia asks in a soft voice.

"Are you kidding?" Tora jumps to her feet, relieved to see her up and about, looking so well. "Oh my god Nia, I'm so glad you're okay. I'm so sorry. I didn't mean to hurt you. I didn't know."

"How could you have known." Nia brushes it off and joins Astra on the bed. "I didn't know. No one did. I'm kind of glad it happened though."

Confused, Tora sits on the floor at the base of the bed. "You're what?"

"I don't understand." Astra frowns. "Didn't you nearly die?"

Nia chuckles and tucks a loose strand of hair behind her ear. "Well, yes. I'm not glad about that, but as far as we knew, the elven steel had no weakness. Now we know it does."

"I'm so sorry Nia." Tora lowers her head, her cheeks burning in shame. They know it has a weakness because of her. They know because she had to show off. "I think it's best if we go. I doubt your mother wants me around anymore."

"Don't be silly. Mother doesn't like anyone around, and you're not going anywhere," Nia chides. "Come and join us for dinner. Mother's gone out anyway so we're having pizza in the family room."

Tora catches the pleading look on Astra's face and sighs. At least with the Queen Bitch gone, she can relax for a little while. Once they have dinner, she'll decide whether to leave or not. It's nice of Nia to forgive her so easily but there's no way Queen Raina will. Then again, Astra is probably right. Nowhere in Olivia would be safe from the Queen Bitch. "I umm… Yeah okay. I guess I could eat."

"Great. Let's go." Nia walks to the door. "I also made you some ginger tea Astra. It'll help with the morning… um… the nausea."

"What do you mean?" Astra sits up, her eyes wide. "I just ate something funny."

"Ah huh." Nia laughs. "Kiara knew you were pregnant the moment she saw you. Don't worry. It's only the two of us who know, and we won't say anything."

Tora grits her teeth as Astra's face pales.

Shit shit shit! If Kiara can tell, others probably can too. Fuck! They are so dead. What if the Valkyries figure it out? They will kill them, even after Astra's birthday, and Inga would do it with a smile. They would call it *'The will of the Gods'* rather than what it truly is… murder.

"Umm, thanks." Astra holds out her hand to Tora and gives her a meaningful look, telling her they'll deal with it later. "Come on Tor. Let's get something to eat."

Tora swallows hard and pinches her lips into a smile as she follows Astra and Nia into the family room. Rich heated tomato, garlic, herbs, cheese, and a mixture of meat wafts up her nose. She'll figure out a way to save Astra and the baby, even if she has to send her into the fae realm to do it.

"Tah Dah." Nia grins and holds out her arms, gesturing to the large rainbow picnic blanket covering the wooden floorboards with five large pizzas scattered around.

Casually dressed in black sweats, Brae and Braxen lift the dark wooden coffee table off the floor and leave it in front of one of the soft cream couches to give them room. A large television mounted to the wall plays soft music through the surround-sound speaker system.

If she wasn't so anxious about Astra, Tora would be impressed. It's the first time in months she's seen a television that hasn't been smashed to pieces. Only a few people in Greenwich keep televisions to watch old DVDs or play music, including the Odd Squad. They simply drain too much electricity.

"Peace offering?" Brae offers Tora a small apologetic smile and sits on the blanket.

Tora forces herself to smile and sits down, the fate of Greenwich and Astra heavy on her shoulders. She's not even mad about Brae's earlier reaction. She nearly killed his sister. If it were Astra, she would have lost her shit.

Despite her anxiety, Tora enjoys herself, relishing the rich woodfired dough and variety of flavors bursting on her tongue, laughing as Astra and Brae compete to eat the most. She just hopes Astra can keep it down.

"So how come you were able to heal Nia? Was that a spell of some kind?" Tora asks Braxen and locks her arms around the tops of her knees. Being able to heal a soul-related injury would come in handy given the Valkyries are after them.

"Satyrs have always been able to heal wounds, but Nia and I are twin flames so I was able to heal her soul." Braxen glances at Nia and smiles, the pure warmth in his gaze making her blush. "The song guides the soul, and the herbal brew kept her relaxed so it wouldn't hurt anymore."

"Music heals the soul?" Brae scoffs and rolls his eyes. "That is so corny."

"Not all solutions are complicated." Braxen shrugs and ties his dreadlocks in a knot at the back of his head.

"Are you two dating?" Astra blurts out and leans on her knees, her voice dreamy.

"Us?" Nia flinches. Her eyes dart around the room. "No. Why would you say that?"

"Mother would kill Braxen if he tried to date Nia." Brae gets to his feet and bundles the empty pizza boxes into his arms. "She caught them kissing a year ago and put him in the infirmary for a month."

Astra gasps as Brae leaves the room. "Oh my god!"

"Mother believes I should marry one of the elven warriors. I'm prohibited from dating anyone else, especially a slave." Nia swallows her tears as her voice breaks.

"My kind has been oppressed for centuries in the Benevolent Fae Realm; kept as slaves and prisoners." Braxen tightens his strong jaw. "Because of that, I am the last known satyr; the last of my kind."

"Why don't you just leave?" Astra frowns. "Runaway together."

"And go where? It's not like I can blend into a crowd with this ass." Braxen taps his backside. "And Raina would never stop looking for us, in any realm."

A tear rolls down Nia's cheek.

Tora lowers her gaze. It doesn't seem fair. It's obvious they're in love, but to see each other every day and not be able to be together must be killing them. It was hard enough resisting Bo, and they weren't even in love.

Returning to the room, Brae sits on the floor by Tora and briefly brushes her knee with his hand. Tora tries not to react as heat burns her cheeks and creeps down her neck, her nerves alive with energy. His clean rainforest scent clings to the air and draws her closer.

Shaking her head to clear it, Tora quickly turns away, hoping no one notices her ridiculous reaction to her crush. She's all too aware that her reaction to Brae has nothing to do with love like Nia and Braxen and everything to do with lust. She just needs to stop it. Brae's not interested, and the last thing she should be thinking of right now is hooking up with some elven guy.

"And the armor... you're still connected to it?" Tora asks, trying to distract herself and everyone else from her bright red face. "Doesn't that defeat the purpose of wearing armor?"

"We're working on that." Brae interrupts. "My warriors are searching for a way to disconnect them."

"You can't!" Nia pleads. "The steel and I are one. I can feel it. It's meant to be this way."

"And what happens when the war comes?" Brae snaps. "My warriors wear your armor. The entire army wears your armor. Our swords and weapons, the jewelry you make... all of it is connected to you. Fuck Nia! Most of the benevolent fae wear your designs in one way or another. Our architecture, furniture... everything has some form of elven steel in it."

"Wait, what?" Tora gapes, truly afraid for the sweet elven girl. "You're connected to all the steel?"

Who knows how many fae Nia is connected to through the steel? It's unbelievably dangerous. All she did was touch the armor with the tip of her sword and it damaged them both.

"But we're on the same side as the Valkyries, and only their soul sword can damage the armor," Nia argues.

"We don't know that. What happens if a Valkyrie sword touches an elven steel ring in the middle of a fight? Or taps our armor or architecture? Or what if the malevolent fae, demons, or Hades get their hands on a soul sword?" Brae pushes. "And demon blades work the same as Valkyrie swords. What if they do the same thing?"

"Umm... Sorry to interrupt." Tora holds up her hand. "But only a Valkyrie can hold a soul sword. The sword, like your elven steel is a part of me. No other being can take it. A demon tried on our way here and it just dissolved."

"See!" Nia gestures to Tora. "It's fine, and we already know that demon swords don't harm the armor. We've worn it for years in battle."

"It's not fine Nia." Brae sighs and suddenly looks at Tora, the full force of his ice-blue eyes making her flinch. "It was a loaded bet. Even if I'd won, I wouldn't have gotten your sword."

Tora widens her eyes. A nervous laugh bubbles from her lips. She opens her mouth to apologize but a familiar flash of glittering light catches her eye.

Frowning, she walks to the window and looks across the road at the park surrounded by large dark trees. An arch of weaving branches glows in the darkness, shining on the climbing castle. Aurora borealis lights spiral in the middle with shards of crystals lining the edge, just inside the branch arch, like a mirror.

Tora backs away from the window. Her heart thumps in her throat.

An elven warrior covered in armor steps through the spiraling lights, followed shortly by Queen Raina and another guard behind her.

"Mother's home." Brae glances over his shoulder, warning Braxen and Nia.

Without another word, Braxen kisses Nia's hand and disappears through the kitchen and out the back door.

"There's a portal in the park?" Astra gapes.

"There are portals everywhere, as long as you know where to look," Brae explains. "Think of them as our public transport. Like catching a bus. You've just got to have the right currency."

Tora helps Astra to her feet, wanting to get away before Queen Raina comes inside. "If there are portals everywhere, how do you stop the malevolent fae and demons using them?"

"Demons wouldn't try to cross into this pocket realm." Brae shakes his head. "And malevolent fae aren't as stupid as they look. They avoid us as much as we avoid them."

"But…" Tora starts to question him but Brae cuts her off by pointing to the hall.

"Mother's nearly at the door. I'd stay out of sight if I were you. Mother is not forgiving." Brae walks towards the front door and grins back at her. "Oh, and I want a rematch. I'm sure we can figure out something else you can bet."

Tora blinks. She's not entirely sure what the hell just happened, but she thinks Brae might have been flirting with her. Either that or she's completely delusional. Either way, she has no time to think about it. Astra links her arm and drags her away. The front door opens just as they close the door to the guest bedroom.

Sighing, Tora sits on the bay window seat and stares out into the darkness as Astra changes into a pair of soft cotton pajamas and crawls into bed. Within seconds, she's snoring softly and drooling on the pillow.

If they can just get through another twenty-seven hours, they can get the hell out of Olivia. Twenty-seven hours to find out what the secret is to keeping Greenwich safe. Twenty-seven hours until Astra is safe from the ritual.

Resting her head against the window, Tora watches as the weaving arch flashes with spiraling lights across the road, shining brightly on the sign that reads Makeshift Park, the vines and branches shifting around to shape an arched doorway, glowing in the dark night.

Brae said demons wouldn't cross into Olivia and the malevolent fae avoid them. There has to be some kind of meaning to his words. Some kind of clue. Why wouldn't demons or malevolent fae walk into Olivia? What makes Olivia so special? It's a simulated world. The perfect buffet.

Tora's eyes droop as the weight of Greenwich lays heavily on her shoulders. She sits by the window for hours, watching the street below, hoping for some kind of inspiration, but none comes.

Maybe it would be safer to leave Astra in Olivia. She would hate her for it, but at least she'd be protected. She's not going to be able to raise a baby in Greenwich if it's overrun with demons, fae, and Valkyries. As much as she hates to admit it, Astra would be safer in Olivia without her. She would even go and collect that douchebag Ethan so they can have the perfect little family Astra has always wanted.

Queen Raina wouldn't like it, but it's Tora she hates, not Astra.

Tora falls asleep, her mind made up. If she can't find the secret in twenty-seven hours, Astra stays in Olivia, and she'll bring Ethan back before the child is born.

CHAPTER TWENTY-TWO

Soft beams of sunlight filter through the bay window. Yawning, Tora wipes the sleep from her eyes and opens the window, peering down at the street below. A lone woman jogs down the road, veering onto the sidewalk in front of the elven house instead of jogging through Makeshift Park. The smell of baked bread and freshly brewed coffee wafts down from the town center.

It's morning, which means it's Astra's birthday. The day they've both been dreading and looking forward to for days. The Valkyries will be looking for them now, and if they haven't already, they will realize they're not in Greenwich Village. They'll be coming for them, but hopefully not in time to perform the ritual. The chances of them finding Olivia without knowing it exists are slim. If they can make it through the day and night without being found, Astra is safe.

"Tor?" Astra stirs and rolls onto her side. "What time is it?

Grinning, Tora leaps onto the bed and lands on her knees. "It's Birthday time!"

Chuckling, Astra sits up and pushes her hair out of her face. "Thanks. I can't wait for it to be over."

"Yeah well… Happy Birthday anyway." Tora laughs and digs around in her leg pocket. This will be the one and only birthday Astra has to fear. After today, there's nothing the Valkyries can do to make her a fully-fledged Valkyrie. At least that little problem will be over.

Finding the square box in her leg pocket, Tora triumphantly holds it up then hands it to Astra.

"What's this?" Astra blinks and tentatively touches the box.

"Open it and find out." Tora rolls her eyes. "I couldn't give you a party like you gave me, but I could get you a little gift."

Grinning like a child, Astra tears off the wrapping and lifts the lid on the box. She gasps and holds up the glittering silver chain with a crystal and silver pacifier pendant, the one Tora got from in town. "It's beautiful. I love it, but won't it make the Valkyries suspicious?"

"I promised the Valkyries I would join them, and I intend to when we return. I doubt they'll stay in Greenwich, and if they do, I can't imagine they'll notice your belly or necklace with demons running around and the impending war." Tora waves off her concern and lies through her teeth. Astra can't know her plans. Not yet. She needs to talk to Queen Raina first at least. "Now get ready. I want to be out of this house in thirty minutes."

Waiting until Astra is in the shower, Tora swallows her pride and seeks out Queen Raina. She's not exactly a difficult woman to locate with the four guards standing outside the door on the lower floor, towards the back of the house.

Tora approaches the guard and clears her throat, her heart beating hard against her ribs. "I wish to speak to Queen Raina."

If this doesn't go well, she's not sure what she's going to do. Not only will she have to get Astra and the baby back to Greenwich safely, she'll have to keep her hidden from the Valkyries and safe from the demons and fae that will or have already overrun the village. This has to work. Astra has to stay safe, even if she hates her for it.

The motionless elven guards stare her down, their ice-blue eyes hard and unwavering. Tora squirms under their gaze but stands her ground.

"Let the Valkyrie in." Queen Raina's venom-filled voice carries through the door.

The elven guards snap their legs together and turn sideways, allowing her access to the door. Tora swallows hard, the anxiety coiling in her stomach pushing acid up into her throat. It feels like she's walking the plank; like if she walks through those doors, she'll never walk out again.

Taking a second to steady her breath, Tora holds her head up high then opens the door. The entire room is surrounded by ceiling-to-floor bookshelves packed with thousands of old and new-looking books. A single mahogany desk sits in front of an arch-shaped window with a waterfall and lush forest as its view.

Seated at the desk, Queen Raina looks up from an ancient-looking book and closes the pages. Her ice-blue eyes narrow. "Shut the door."

Sighing, Tora kicks the door shut behind her, earning another glare from the Queen Bitch. One more day under the elven woman's roof and she'll never have to see her again. She hopes. All she has to do is be nice to her, apologize for nearly killing her daughter, and ask if Astra can stay somewhere in town. That's not so hard.

"You're here to apologize I assume?" Queen Raina rests her hands on the desk and raises her eyebrows.

"I am." Tora bows her head, searching for the right words. "You allowed us into your home, and in return, I nearly killed your daughter. Although accidental, it's unspeakable. I am truly sorry for any damage I caused Nia."

Queen Raina stares her down and sits like a statue. She doesn't blink, she doesn't move, she just stares at her for a full minute making Tora squirm even more.

"Fine," Queen Raina says simply and reopens her book. "You may go."

Tora reels back, surprised the bitch would forgive her so easily. It was way too easy. The woman hates her guts. She thought she'd make her grovel, or at least take a swing at her.

"Umm. Okay. Thanks." Tora looks down at her feet, not sure how to broach the subject of Astra. There's no way the Queen will let her stay. The woman hasn't got a compassionate bone in her body, but she has to try. She has to ask.

"Is there something else Valkyrie?" Queen Raina keeps her head down and glares at her from the top of her eyes.

"I..." Tora stutters. "Umm. I... I wanted to ask you about Astra."

Queen Raina leans on the desk and crosses her arms, her eyes burning a hole in Tora's head. "Learn to speak in full sentences, Valkyrie. It saves time, and maybe your life one day."

Tora flinches as though she was slapped but keeps her first response to herself. Now's not the time to antagonize the bitch, not when she wants something from her. "Can Astra remain in Olivia? It's not safe for her to return to our village, if there's a village to return to."

"You should have thought about that before thwarting the ritual," Queen Raina says with zero emotion on her bitch face.

"She would have been left catatonic," Tora argues, her face burning hot with anger.

"Better that than dead." Queen Raina returns to reading her book. "My answer is no. You both will leave at one past midnight tonight, or you will both suffer the consequences. Now get out."

"But…" Tora starts to argue but Queen Raina flies to her feet and slams her hands down on the desk.

Tora stumbles back, her eyes wide as the Queen struggles to contain her breathing and composure. Her heart beats like a double kick drum in her chest. The woman is crazy? What kind of queen loses her shit so easily? What kind of person denies the safety of another?

The guards rush into the room and stand at attention, awaiting her command.

"You nearly killed my daughter," Queen Raina says through clenched teeth. "Be grateful I am letting you stay until the end of the day. Death is not the worst thing that can happen to someone Tora Thurgood."

Clenching her jaw, Tora flares her nostrils and backs out of the room, never taking her eyes off the unstable queen. So much for playing nice. She should have known the Queen wouldn't care.

She storms down the hall, swearing under her breath. The end of the day cannot come fast enough. The sooner they're far away from Raina, the better. She'll find another way to protect Astra. She always has, and she always will. She doesn't need the bitch's help. Fuck her, and fuck the fae.

"Tora?" Nia chases after her and stops her outside the guest bedroom.

Tora whips her head over her shoulder and quickly wipes away her tears, not wanting Nia to know how upset she is. It's not because the bitch yelled at her, it's because of Astra. Maybe Queen Raina was right. Maybe she should have let the Valkyries perform the ritual. Astra would have a fighting chance at least. But then again, she'd probably be catatonic and the baby might not have survived. She doesn't know what's worse. Alive, mentally unstable, and losing the baby, or under constant threat on the run with a baby and that douchebag Ethan.

Both options suck!

"Are you okay?" Nia pinches her eyebrows together in concern. "I heard you in with my mother."

"I'm fine." Tora forces her lips into a grateful smile. "I just... I don't know. Don't tell Astra okay? I just want to keep her safe."

"I won't say a word. I promise," Nia says. "I didn't mean to eavesdrop. I only wanted to ask you and Astra out to lunch for her birthday, and saw you go into my mother's office."

"Oh, umm, sure." Tora shrugs. "We were just going to go out and take one last look around town this morning, so lunch sounds good."

"Great. We'll make it a late lunch, kind of like a farewell party." Nia grins and waves as she makes her way down the stairs. "Oh, and we're going to the Benevolent Fae Market for lunch. Don't worry. Mother won't be there. She'll be in the Benevolent Fae Realm."

Nia disappears before Tora can say anything. She's not sure whether she wants to go to the fae market, but it also doesn't look like they have a choice.

~

Hours later, after a large breakfast and a disappointing search around town for any clues as to what keeps the demons and malevolent fae at bay, Tora and Astra return to the elven home to pack for their return trip with extra boxes of protein, chocolate, and muesli bars they bought from the town store. That's one of the things they'll miss most about Olivia. How easy it is to get what you want. They have everything from before the war, but who knows how long that will last.

"Are you two ready?" Brae sticks his head inside the guest bedroom, dressed in a tight white v-neck shirt that molds to his generous muscles and black army pants.

"As we'll ever be." Tora blushes and gets to her feet. She didn't know Brae was going with them. She thought it was just the girls. Not that she cares if Brae goes with them. It's a free country; kind of.

Getting Astra to her feet, Tora follows Brae out the front door where they find Nia already waiting on the garden path.

"You're going to love the market." Nia beams, her soft white silk dress matching her vibrant mood.

Nervously glancing at each other, Tora and Astra tentatively follow Nia and Brae across the street into Makeshift Park. As far as fae go, Tora thinks she can trust Brae and Nia, but she can't help feeling uneasy. The benevolent fae are supposed to be more evolved than the malevolent fae and humans, but they're still fae. If they treat Braxen as badly as they do, how are they going to treat a Valkyrie and a pregnant fledgling?

Stopping in front of the portal arch Tora saw outside the window, Brae and Nia scan the area to make sure no humans are around.

"We're using a portal?" Tora widens her eyes and tries to push the excitement into the pit of her stomach. Sure, she's seen hundreds of demons and fae cross through the portals, but she's never been inside one herself. She's always wondered what it would be like.

"Watch." Brae stands in the center of four thick witch-hazel trees hidden from the path by a cluster of willows. He lifts his arms and commands the shaded space. "Latrop tneloveneb eaf tekram."

Light shimmers between the branches, casting dancing shadows on the grass. An arch appears, barely visible, blending and swaying with the trees.

Tora blinks as the arch wavers like a watery reflection. Vines, twisting roots, and flowers weave around the archway in elaborate knotted patterns. Neon lights whip manically within the shimmering surface. Beautiful amethyst crystals form around the edges, near the weaving vines, branches, and roots.

"Are you serious?" Astra chuckles. "You open the portals by speaking the location backward?"

"Huh?" Tora tilts her head. "What do you mean?"

"He just said portal Benevolent Fae Market, but he said it backward," Astra explains.

"Why is that so shocking?" Brae frowns. "Portals are doorways, windows, or mirrors into other realms. Hold a written word up to a mirror and it appears backwards. It's the same for the portal gates."

"Let me get this straight." Tora tries to wrap her head around the portal travel. "This portal is a constant doorway that opens to another constant portal. Is that right?"

"Basically, yes," Nia confirms. "The portals used by the demons and malevolent fae are tears in the fabrics of the realms. They aren't doorways which is why they open and close randomly, and why there is usually water and crystal gushing from the rip. The benevolent fae have been able to create structured doorways and arched portals to travel safely, otherwise god knows where you'd end up."

"So how did you jump out of the sky when you helped us?" Tora frowns.

"Ah. That was a tear, and a happy coincidence," Brae says. "We were discussing strategy with Tia at her bar, Flit Bitz, in the Malevolent Fae Realm when a large tear formed in her floor. We saw what was happening and jumped through to help."

"So malevolent fae aren't evil?" Astra screws up her face.

"No, they are." Brae scoffs. "No one knows Tia is helping us. They would kill her if they knew. And just so you know, Tia can be trusted, but she is still malevolent fae, so watch your back."

Tora looks at Astra and finds exactly the same confused look on her face. The bad guys need to wear a sign, like a big huge ass sign. It would just make life so much easier.

"Alright. Grab a partner and let's go." Brae grabs Nia's arm and jumps through the portal, disappearing into the aurora borealis lights.

There's no backing out now. The thought of being surrounded by fae, benevolent or otherwise is frightening, but by the sounds of it, if the realms clash together, they won't have much of a choice anyway. May as well get the introductions over with.

Gripping Astra's hand, Tora takes a deep breath, and together they step through the portal. Cool air gently caresses her face. The force within the portal massages against her skin as a watery image of a field and Brae and Nia urging them forward floats in front of her.

Together, they step forward, out into a field surrounded by large ancient trees. A cute medium-sized cottage sits in the distance with what looks like vegetable gardens out the front and a deck with a punching bag hanging from the rafters.

"Are you two seriously holding your breath right now?" An amused grin pulls at Brae's lips.

Feeling stupid, Tora discreetly releases her breath, her face blushing bright red. Astra suffers no such embarrassment. She releases her breath in a loud puff.

"It looked like water, and you didn't say what to do," Astra argues.

"Because you didn't need to do anything." Brae laughs and starts towards the trees.

Tora follows behind Nia and checks out the surroundings. She lifts her head and inhales the sea salt air as the sound of distant crashing waves echoes through the trees. Leaves dance and rustle in the high branches of the large willow and oak trees, brimming with hundreds of birds, butterflies, dragonflies, and small animals scurrying in and out of the trunks.

"It's beautiful here, isn't it?" Nia bumps Tora's arm.

"Stunning," Tora answers. It's so peaceful and far away from the village of Greenwich and the outside world where demons reign, but there doesn't appear to be a market unless it's in the trees. "But where are we going?"

"Here we are." Brae stops in the middle of the field. A shimmering veil of energy hovers behind him, the invisible fabric revealed only by golden rays of sunlight.

"The Benevolent Fae Market is under an invisible veil. Only the fae, some witches, and warlocks can see it. A few humans who have the sight can see it too from far away. It's connected both to the Realm of Man and the Benevolent Fae Realm." Nia steps into the shimmering fabric and disappears, Brae right behind her.

Glancing at each other, Tora and Astra shrug and follow. Brae and Nia haven't steered them wrong yet. Maybe there are some answers at the market. They sure as hell aren't getting any in town.

Soft water-like energy brushes against Tora's skin, the world outside muted in the cool air of the veil. Her boots pierce the tranquil bubble, unleashing an onslaught of noise, color, and movement.

Tora winces as a torrent of laughter, shouting, singing, and windchimes join in chorus with the loud rock music blaring through a PA system as a mixture of different fae mill together, moving from stall to stall.

Market stalls draped in white fabric come into sharp focus, no longer hidden by the fabric of the veil. Sunlight bounces off shiny stall trinkets. Cinnamon sugar, incense, and soy wax linger in the air.

"Welcome to the Benevolent Fae Market." Nia smiles over her shoulder.

Tora reels. It's more like a carnival than a market. They're never going to find anything in this place. That's it. She's done. There's no way to help Greenwich Village. They're all going to die, and there's not a fucking thing she can do to stop it.

CHAPTER TWENTY-THREE

Moving swiftly through the market, Tora grips Astra's hand, afraid to let go and lose her in this foreign realm. The last thing she wants is for either of them to end up stranded in a fae playground. They wouldn't last the day by themselves, benevolent fae or not.

Multiple-story sandstone structures housing inns and taverns separate the market, the property and land outside of the veil. Rows of stalls draped in white canvases line the edge of the forest, creating a semicircle bustling with activity, circling inwards to an area filled with picnic benches.

Curious eyes follow them around the field; bodies of translucent skin, pointy ears, wings, long inhumanly thin bodies, short-hairy bear-looking bodies, and abnormally long noses and fingers.

"So, can anyone just walk through here?" Tora pinches her lips into a polite smile as different types of fae stare and gawk at her. She had no idea there were so many species in the fae realm. She always assumed it was just the pixies, elves, and faeries, but from the looks of it, they're just the most dominant creatures.

"No, not at all," Nia says. "The veil protects the market from uninvited guests. Most turn back and don't remember what they saw, but every now and then, some curious human will try to cross, knowing they saw something shiny."

"When that happens..." Brae continues. "The veil pushes a shock wave of electricity through the body, plummeting sugar, and blood pressure levels dangerously low. It can be fatal."

Astra and Tora glance at each other, both thinking the same thing. Not only is that dangerous for humans, it might be dangerous for a pregnant fledgling Valkyrie and her baby.

"How did Astra walk through unharmed?" Tora frowns.

"We invited you." Brae gives her an odd look like she's an idiot and marches onward, his head held high and his shoulders back like he's in a parade. His eyes continuously scan the crowds as his shoulders tense. He nods at a couple of elven men as they pass, swirling glittery liquid silver rotating around their muscles.

Poking her tongue out behind his back, Tora rolls her eyes and shares an amused look with Nia. It was just a question. He doesn't have to be so testy about it. Back at the house, Brae was relatively relaxed, but at the market, it's like he's a completely different person.

"Brae's the Commander of the elven army," Nia whispers. "Those elves and the others you see roaming the field in pairs are his warriors."

A hot flash creeps up from Tora's chest, burning her cheeks and ears, drool practically dripping from her lips. There must be something seriously wrong with her. Valkyries are not meant to be attracted to fae men, and they're not supposed to get turned on by the fact that one is a Commander in an army. Her mother would be appalled.

"This is where Nia sells her jewelry." Brae bobs his head towards a stall dedicated to beautifully designed handmade jewelry. A crowd of at least fifty fae wait anxiously in line. "It's the only stall at the market that incorporates elven steel into the design. The other stalls are owned by witches who use silver, gold, and gemstones. You can find a few of Nia's designs around town too."

"You make jewelry and armor?" Astra glances at Nia. "And you go to school and have time to train and save our asses."

"I like to keep busy." Nia blushes and points to a triple-sized stall overrun with customers. "That's where I sell the elven steel bullions."

Tora looks over at the stall selling an array of differently designed armor; some pre-made, others custom fit. Only a handful of the older elven warriors wait at the counter, choosing to buy the pre-made suits while a hundred or more elven warriors wait for the attendants distributing the custom-fit liquid steel designs.

Transfixed, Tora watches as a black-haired elven woman in a white flowing gown presses a steel bullion onto the back of an elven man with a blonde buzz cut. The steel melts against his skin, moving like liquid, stretching down his muscular back before crawling over his shoulders, arms, and chest in elaborate knotted entwining designs.

Tora gawks and looks at Nia with a newfound respect. She thought she was the nice one, the one who could be manipulated into telling the secrets of Olivia, but she had her all wrong. The sweet young elf is a skilled businesswoman with many talents.

"Can only elves wear the steel?" Tora asks.

"I'm not sure." Nia frowns. "Everyone seems to be able to wear the jewelry and have no issues, so I assume they could wear the armor. No one's ever tried though."

Brae casts a concerned glance over his shoulder.

"I'm not going to wear it." Tora rolls her eyes. "I was just curious."

Satisfied, Brae turns back around but slows his pace as they reach a cluster of concerned-looking warriors.

"What an asshole!" An angry voice carries over the noise of the market.

The crowds hurry out of the way, parting like the dead sea, or scurrying away like rats as a blonde-haired girl storms through the market. The elven warriors take a step back, giving the girl a wide berth.

Tora's heart races at the sight of the girl only a few steps away. A stab of fear curdles her stomach. It's Selene, and she looks thunderous stalking through the market, her face contorted in rage.

Demons and malevolent fae don't scare her; Hades himself doesn't scare her, but this girl, this Witch Goddess... she makes her want to pee her pants. The realms literally depend on what mood she is in, and she always looks to be in a bad one.

"Good! Move!" Selene shouts at the scurrying fae and warriors, her shopping bags swinging all over the place, hitting a few of the fae on her way passed.

"We are so fucked." Tora groans. Valkyries may not be able to die by anything other than a Hell Blade or a Valkyrie sword, but something tells her the rules don't apply to this girl. If she wanted anyone or anything dead, nothing could stop her.

The girl has no filter. Her eyes spark with storm clouds and lightning. Her hair is streaked with silver fire, flying about her face. She is raw power, and it doesn't look like she can control it.

"Who's an asshole?" a little voice asks.

Selene's face instantly softens. The storm dissipates from her eyes as a small boy with dark black hair and deep brown eyes blinks up at her, dressed in black knee-length dress shorts and a midnight blue t-shirt. His bare feet and toes wiggle in the dirt.

Selene's entire demeanor changes. Her eyes return to their vibrant green; her hair soft and streaked blonde.

Tora squeezes Astra's hand and glances at her to see her face pale. The girl is a fucking nutcase. She just went from pure rage to warmth and love in a split second. It's like being stuck in a snow blizzard tornado hurricane then finding yourself in the eye of the storm. Deceitfully calm but you know you're going to die.

"Selene!" Nia waves her hand around, trying to get her attention.

Spotting them quickly, Selene waves back as the small boy drags her onto the dancefloor and points to the picnic tables, indicating she'll meet them there.

"Come on." Nia walks towards the stalls lining the edge of the entertainment quarter. "Let's get something to eat."

Shaking slightly, Tora keeps hold of Astra's hand and pulls her along. She would dead set pick a fight with a fire-breathing dragon over the Witch Goddess any day. It would be like swatting a fly in comparison.

"What do you want to eat?" Brae sidles up beside her.

"Huh?" Tora jolts and drags her eyes away from the dancefloor, the heat from Brae's body burning through her skin. Brightly colored fruits and vegetables hang from wooden frames holding up the white canvases. Herbs and spices mingle with cooked meats and sweet-smelling desserts.

"Oh. Umm." Tora looks at the many different food stalls and shakes her head. There's food from each part of the Realm of Man. She doesn't even know what half of it is, and truthfully, food is the last thing on her mind after witnessing the Witch Goddess's tantrum. "I'm not sure. Whatever I guess."

Brae grins. "Not a lot of choice in the Realm of Angels?"

"Not like this." Astra stares at the food longingly, her stomach growling loud enough for Tora to hear.

Tora can't help but laugh. There's a crazy Witch Goddess with a serious attitude problem about to join them for lunch, and Astra is thinking about food. The pregnancy is turning her into a garbage guts. By the time the kid comes along, she's going to be huge. "We'll just get whatever you guys get. Do they take human money here? I still have some left from the bowl."

"No need." Brae shakes his head. "Meals are free. Everyone's allowed up to three cooked meals a day at the market."

"So, who pays for it?" Tora frowns. They must have some sort of system in place. The food vendors can't all be volunteers.

"The fae council; sort of," Brae answers. "Fae who can't grow their own fruits and vegetables barter by volunteering their services in exchange for groceries. The rest of the stalls use fae currency."

"So, can I go up and get two plates? One for Astra and one for me so she doesn't have to fight the crowd?" Tora starts towards the stall.

"Yeah, that's fine, but I'll get it for you." Brae grabs her arm and pulls her back. "You stay with Astra. I'll just point you out to the vendor."

Winking, Brae leaves them on their own and lines up behind Nia.

"What was that?" Astra chuckles. "Did you just blush?"

"What? No!" Tora whips her head around and tries but fails to keep the smile off her face. It's probably all in her head. Brae hasn't shown her any romantic interest since they arrived in Olivia, why would he now? But she can't help the giddy jump in her stomach that he went to get their food. "You're crazy."

"Uh huh," Astra says and sings. "Tora's got a cru…ush"

Tora's cheeks redden further. Her skin burns. God, she hopes Brae can't hear them. He's going to think she's an immature idiot. "Shut up Star!"

Ignoring her, Astra continues to sing and dance in a circle, so Tora does the only thing she can do. She jumps on Astra's back and holds her hand over her mouth.

Snorting, Astra licks her hand, like she used to when they wrestled as kids.

"Eww!" Tora laughs harder and lets go. She wipes her hand on her pants. "That was so gross."

"You fight and kill demons covered in puss, slime, and blood, and that was gross?" Astra lifts her eyebrows in question.

By the time Brae and Nia return, Astra and Tora get their laughter under control and follow them to one of the wooden picnic tables surrounding the dancefloor where Kiara, the faery waits, and a four-piece rock band serenades the masses on a large metal stage.

After exchanging pleasantries, Tora and Astra dig into their lunches while Kiara, Brae, and Nia chat in hushed voices. With the others distracted, Tora uses the time to study the area for clues.

Besides the veil itself, there doesn't appear to be anything keeping the area safe from demons coming through the portal. She doesn't get it. There must be something tangible that keeps the town and the market safe. The Benevolent Fae Realm is safe from demons as well. Whatever they have in their realm, they must have transferred into this realm. It's right in front of their faces. She knows it. She just has to figure out what that is.

"Selene?" Kiara frowns. "What's wrong?"

Tora whips her head up, a stab of fear making her eye twitch. The girl looks like she's about to go on a killing spree, her face, skin, and eyes alive with electricity; like a firecracker about to explode, or a grenade, or nuclear bomb.

"Nothing!" Selene slams three lunch containers down on the table and flicks two to her mother as the elven warrior following close behind her gives a satisfied nod.

"What a magical little community you have here." Selene stabs her noodles.

Kiara turns to Brae and Nia and lifts her eyebrows in question.

"Nothing's on fire, her knuckles aren't bloodied or bruised, and she's not being hauled away by security." Brae lifts his eyebrows. "Count your blessings, Kiara."

Selene rolls her eyes.

"I'm going to take your brother his lunch." Kiara levels Selene with a stern look. "Behave while I'm gone. I'll be back in a minute."

"Haden's on the other side of the dancefloor with his friends." Selene shoves a large forkful of noodles into her mouth as her mother walks off. Her gaze settles on Tora and Astra as if she just noticed them sitting there. She narrows her eyes. "What are you two doing here?"

Tora flinches and struggles to breathe, unsure what to say under the Witch Goddess' penetrating glare.

"I invited them." Brae saves her. "They're checking to make sure the pandemic hasn't crossed into our world."

Scooping another mouthful of noodles into her mouth, Selene keeps her eyes trained on Astra and Tora, making them both squirm. The girl could dead set kill a demon with a look alone. It's like the air is being sucked out of her lungs, literally suffocating her.

"Oh my god." Nia laughs to lighten the mood and points to a group of young faeries and elves, their faces and bodies covered in red paint and feathers.

"They've obviously been to the fun hall." A man with wavy black hair down to his ears interjects and leans on the table, his eyes a deep royal blue. "Have you seen it? The new glass dome near the entrance? It's pretty cool. Most of the younger fae hang out there now they've stocked it with balloons full of paint, glitter, glue, and feathers."

Selene chokes on her noodles.

Tora jerks and drops her fork as Astra scoots a bit closer, her hands shaking under the table. Never in her life has she felt so on edge around anyone, and it's not just fear, it's like a static energy buzzing inside her bones that explodes every time the Witch Goddess moves.

"Watch it your highness." The man grins as he sits beside Selene and smacks her hard on the back to dislodge the food. "You don't want to choke."

Tora widens her eyes, wanting to kick the guy under the table. What the hell does he think he's doing? Why is he provoking her? It's as stupid as playing catch with a live grenade.

"And who are you?" Brae rests his elbows on the table, elven steel rippling around his arms and wrists.

"Name's Michael." He shakes Brae's hand, his muscles flexing as Brae strengthens his hold. "I run the cell phone stall at the back of the market where I just sold your friend here a cell."

"What the fuck?" Selene explodes. "What the hell do you want?"

Tora swallows hard. This guy has got to be the stupidest human alive baiting the Witch Goddess. Either that or he's got a death wish. He can't be that stupid though if he was the one who was able to set up a cell phone network during an apocalypse.

Astra hunches over the table and pretends to be preoccupied with the different types of marinated meats and salads on her plate.

If she had more time, she'd ask Brae and Nia about the cell phone reception to see if they could use the same sort of network in Greenwich, but just like their precious secret, she doubts they'd share the information anyway.

"I don't need anything thanks. I've already got my lunch." Michael holds up a sub-sandwich and innocently bats his eyelashes.

"Not what I meant dumbass." Selene narrows her eyes.

"Then what did you mean your highness?" Michael says around a mouthful of food.

"Stop calling me that!" Selene snaps. Sparks of silver and blue light flare off her fingers.

Eyes wide, Tora glances at Brae and Nia, hoping for some kind of direction, but Brae just shakes his head, telling her to ignore it.

"I can't help it. I don't know your na…" Michael coughs as his sandwich catches in his throat and red sauce drips on his black v-neck shirt and blue jeans. Laughing he clears his throat and wipes at his clothes. "Was that really called for?"

"Her name's Selene." Nia tilts her head innocently. "How do you not know that? It would have been on the form for the phone."

Selene gapes at Nia, and Tora can understand why. Selene clearly hates the guy, and didn't want him to know her name. She'd be pretty pissed off if Astra did that.

"You meet some crazy people here at the markets. This one girl ran into me twice so I'd notice her." Michael nudges Selene's arm, ignoring Nia's question. "The last time, she kicked me, then made me choke!"

"I did not!" Selene's head snaps up.

Brae and Nia chuckle. Tora stares at them, her hands clenching the bench. How can they be so casual about all this? The girl is a ticking time bomb. This Michael guy has to be the reason she came to the table in such a bad mood in the first place, and he's baiting her on purpose.

"Did too! I have the bruises to prove it." Michael lifts the leg of his blue denim jeans to expose a blooming bruise. He grins, two dimples denting his cheeks. "And how did I suddenly choke? Come on, admit it. It was a spell."

"Jam it up your ass Michael." Selene turns to watch the intermission performers take over from the band.

A shadow falls on the field, the market softening to a hum as a black-haired faery with oversized torn wings twirls a hula-hoop laced with fire around her hips, her face marked with nasty purple bruises.

Tora frowns as the crowd backs away from the dancefloor, from the faery with wide gothic-style silk wings bleeding with colors of purple and gray.

"Malevolent fae," Michael whispers to Selene. He nods towards two male faeries as they take to the stage, their gray and midnight blue wings torn and gothic like the female's; their heads shaved and covered in gashes and scars.

Tora reaches for the blade hidden in her boot, her wrist marking burning to the bone. Astra steadies her hand and nods towards Brae. He furrows his brow and shakes his head, telling her to stop.

Reluctantly, Tora removes her hand from her knife. Brae and Nia told her that malevolent fae wouldn't cross into this realm, and from what she knows of malevolent fae, they attack and feed off the fear and pain of others, including the benevolent fae. Why have them performing in the middle of the market? Why allow it? Is that the secret to keeping out the malevolent fae? Scheduled feeding?

Moving purposefully around the dancefloor, the female faery scowls. The flame-laced hula-hoop spins around her hips, pushing everyone off the dancefloor. Through the crowd, a short creature emerges, his ears pointed to tips, the hair covering his body bright red; his nose, long and thick. He whispers something in the female's ear and accidentally brushes her bare breast where her purple corset has slipped.

Revealing sharp fang-like teeth, the female faery snarls and fixes her corset. She drops the hoop and suffocates the flames, singeing the hem of her napkin short black skirt before making her way into the center of the dancefloor.

A buzz of excitement charges the air. The crowd inches forward and stands closer together. Using heavy weighted stands, the two male faeries secure a massive wooden board the size of a door to the dancefloor as haunting organ music drifts through the air, the notes moving like ink across their skin.

Selene shivers and Tora can't blame her. The air is thick with musk and perspiration. The malevolent fae are already feeding from the crowd. She can feel it, like someone slowly sucking the life force from your body.

Leaning her back against the boards, the purple-winged faery glares at the crowd, her inhumanly intense purple eyes flaring as the long-nosed creature holds up five sharp carving knives.

The silence grows thick. Tora tenses along with Selene and Astra. Brae and Nia are the only ones who seem unfazed and unaffected.

Blindfolding himself, the hair-covered man stands in front of the board, the tips of the five knives held between his fingers. The crowding fae cling to each other. Children hide behind their parent's legs.

The hair-covered man grins and simultaneously flings all five knives at the faery. The crowd gasps. The little ones scream. The faery lifts and catches all five knives, one in each hand, one with each set of toes, and one held firmly between her teeth, barely stopping it from lodging in her throat, but not before it slices the sides of her mouth.

Someone screams as the two male faeries fling an extra two blades each at the unsuspecting faery.

Selene gasps and sits on the edge of her seat, her eyes darting around the field until she locks eyes with a young faery boy across the dancefloor, his innocent blue eyes wide and full of fear. He stands by Kiara's side, his silk blue wings lined in a gray silver dust.

The female faery spins, creating a whirlwind of dust. The panels of her skirt lengthen to black blades and fling out around her to deflect the knives. They fall harmlessly to the ground.

"Your brother's fine Selene," Nia reassures her. "He's with your mother."

Tora raises her eyebrows, surprised to see the Witch Goddess looking like a scared teenage girl instead of the anger-filled destroyer she thought she was. The girl's first and only thought was to protect her little brother. Maybe they aren't so different after all. Maybe the Witch Goddess isn't as bad as she thought.

The crowd erupts into a chorus of cheers. Swaying on their feet, the group bow to the audience. The two male faeries grin manically while the female glares daggers at them, her lips pulled into a feral smile.

Selene blinks and claps her hands.

Tora frowns. The malevolent faery has blood dripping down her chin and the crowd is cheering them on. The crowd is literally feeding the malevolent fae and either no one realizes it, or they don't care. Besides Tora and Astra, Selene and Michael appear to be the only ones disturbed by the performance.

Greenwich is so fucked. The fae they've seen come through the portal are always drunk or intoxicated in some way or another, but these fae, they are calculating and cunning; much more dangerous. If they can't find the secret to keeping out the demons and fae, Greenwich Village won't survive.

CHAPTER TWENTY-FOUR

Unnerved by the performance, Tora, and Astra excuse themselves and start back towards the portal, wanting to put some distance between themselves, the Witch Goddess, and the fae.

"Krap tfihsekam," Nia calls after them.

Tora waves her thanks and links arms with Astra, not wanting to lose her for a second. Without Nia, she wouldn't have known how to say Makeshift Park backwards. They could have ended up anywhere when crossing through the portal back to the elven house.

"Did Nia just say Crap T Fear Sick Em?" Astra laughs.

Tora snorts. "Yeah, she kind of did."

They're not going to find answers at the market with Selene around, and they're wasting what little time they have left in Olivia. Maybe there's something back at the house that will tell them what the secret is. Without Nia or Brae there, and Queen Raina in the Benevolent Fae Realm, now's their chance to search. They just need to get rid of Braxen.

Pushing their way through the crowds, Tora and Astra head towards the market veil, the portal visible from the inside. After watching Selene's reaction to the malevolent fae, Tora kind of understands Brae and Nia's reluctance to hurt the girl. There is an aura of anger and bitterness about her, but she is also just a girl, a teenage girl with the same fears and hormones as any other teenage girl.

The first time they met, Selene was only trying to protect her friends and the town when she thought Tora and Astra were judging their pandemic practices. Her anger softened into aggressive suspicion when she saw them at the market, but despite the anger and bitterness radiating from her skin, the girl just wants to protect her family and friends, something Tora can relate to.

"Astra!" A familiar voice calls out behind them.

Tora freezes as ice spreads through her veins. That voice. It can't be. He can't be in Olivia or in the Fae Market. He's supposed to be back in Greenwich Village.

"Ethan?" Astra frowns and turns around.

Dark clouds roll across the sky, shrouding the market in shadow.

"Astra!" Ethan emerges from the crowd, running full pelt towards them.

Tora widens her eyes. The lying bastard is also supposed to be human.

"Oh my god, Ethan!" Astra squeals and jumps up and down as tears spring to her eyes.

Pure rage erupts in Tora's veins, her fast-beating heart pushing the venom of hatred through her entire body, her face burning red. She slams her fist into his face before he reaches Astra, the crunch of her knuckles breaking his nose sending waves of satisfaction through her bones.

Ethan falls to the ground and holds his face as blood splatters over his hands. Fuck that felt good. She's wanted to do that for so long. She knew there was something off about him. There's no way a human could travel across the Deadlands, stumble into Olivia, through the portal, and magically end up at the Benevolent Fae Market. Ethan is fae.

"Tora!" Astra pushes her out of the way and rushes to Ethan.

The Elven warriors circling the market break into a run. At first, Tora thinks they're coming for her, but they completely bypass them and head towards the dancefloor.

"Star! Get away from him." Tora grabs her arm and tries to drag her away. "He's not who you think he is."

"He's malevolent fae," Astra and Tora say in unison as Astra rips her arm free.

Nausea stabs deep into Tora's stomach. She blinks and shakes her head, the taste of betrayal bitter in her mouth.

"You knew?" Tora backs up a step, disgust erupting like acid reflux in her throat. "You knew and you still dated him? You lied to me?"

"Tor, just list..." Astra starts.

"No! You put everyone in danger! Victor, Teresa, my mother... they all died because of him!" Tora chokes back a sob and backs further away, her mouth dry.

How could Astra do this? Her best friend; her sister. She betrayed her, betrayed her mother, her friends... the squad. After everything they've been through.

"You can't blame Ethan for that!" Astra argues, her cheeks burning red. "He wasn't even there!"

"He knew the warlock Astra!" Tora explodes. Her hands shake violently. "That's how he knew where to find me! You know, the guy who tried to kill me! The guy who killed Victor! The guy who killed Teresa! The guy who got my mother killed! She wouldn't have been there if that fucker hadn't attacked me. The Valkyries wouldn't have found her vulnerable!"

A crack of thunder shakes the market. The crowd of fae scream and duck, like they expect an explosion or something. Astra gasps and grips Ethan's hand, fear aging her angelic face. Ethan looks at the sky and pales.

Frowning, Tora looks up. It was clear a few seconds ago but now the sky darkens with clouds laced in an ominous green glow.

"I came to warn you," Ethan pants. "The Valkyries know you left. They tracked you here. Flenn is here too, but he's not after you anymore Tora, he's after Astra. We need to leave now while he's distracted by the Witch Goddess. We only need to hide Astra for another ten hours."

"And why should I trust you?" Tora spits, drowning in her own hatred.

"I don't give a shit about you! I care about Astra. I love Astra. I need to get her out of here, and for whatever fucked up reason, she loves you, so I'm inviting you along." Ethan drops his glamor as his frustration grows.

The tips of his ears lengthen into points, the edges black and burned like charcoal. His eyes burn different shades of yellow, a stark contrast to the beautiful elven blue of Brae's. Burns and scars cover his face and neck, trailing under his shirt.

"You're a malevolent elf." Tora curls her lip, her eyes burning with hatred.

All this time Ethan has been malevolent fae, living in Greenwich Village, right under their noses. And Astra lied. She lied to Tora; lied to her mother;

lied to the squad, and for what? To keep some asshole who knocked her up safe?

"Ethan would never hurt me, Tor. We love each other." Astra pleads.

Lightning splits apart the sky as deep thunder rumbles. Gail force winds howl through the trees.

Tora jerks. The crowd gasps and recoils in fear.

"What's happening?" Tora yells over the chaotic winds and squints against the dirt and debris flying into her eyes. The stall tarps flap violently. Sparks of electricity flare from the direction of the dancefloor.

Ethan looks back over his shoulder and gets to his feet. "Flenn just pissed off the Witch Goddess."

"What? Why?" Tora gapes.

"Who cares! We need to go; now!" Ethan snaps and grabs Tora's arm.

Disgusted by his touch, Tora snatches her arm away and pushes him back.

"Just tell me one thing." Tora glares into his yellow eyes. "Did you tell Flenn where to find me the night he attacked? The night Victor, Teresa, and my mother died? And do not lie to me, or I swear to the gods, I will drive my soul sword straight through your chest."

Ethan sighs and bows his head.

"Ethan?" Astra shakes his arm, nothing but love and trust in her eyes. "Tell her you didn't do it. Tell her so we can go."

Ethan lowers his head, shame darkening his features. "Flenn knew I found the fledgling Valkyries. When he saw me with you and Astra at the market, he knew what you were from the way you attacked him. He wasn't sure about Astra, so I told him where to find you to distract him. I was hoping to escape with Astra to the Malevolent Fae Realm that night, but then you appeared at the apartment and the wolf demons attacked... I knew Astra would be safer with you. He doesn't want the Valkyries helping in the coming war. He's working for someone, but I don't know who."

Astra gasps and pinches her eyes closed.

A high-pitched ringing screams in Tora's ears. Frightened fae push passed her, running from the chaos of the Witch Goddess' temper but Tora just stands there, unable to move. Ethan is the reason Victor and Teresa died; the reason her mother died.

"But none of that matters." Ethan checks behind him. "You have to come with me to the Malevolent Fae Realm. It's the only way Astra will be safe."

Tora tightens her jaw, the markings on her wrist and forehead burning bright purple.

"Tora?" Astra trembles.

"None of that matters?" Tora says through clenched teeth, her heart beating like a bass drum in her ears. Her soul sword forms in her hand. Teresa. Victor. Her mother. Their deaths don't matter?

Ethan's eyes widen.

"None of that matters?" Tora yells and raises her sword, the marking on her forehead burning to the point of pain.

Ethan's pupils dilate as he cowers, but Tora doesn't care. Not anymore. She swings her sword.

"No!" Astra screams and jumps in front of him, raising her hand in front of her.

"Agh!" Tora stops an inch from hitting them and releases her soul sword. Her arms fall by her sides as she breathes heavily, inhaling in and out, her head aching with anger and loss.

Tears stream like a waterfall down Astra's cheeks. She chokes and sobs, desperately looking from Ethan to Tora. "Tor... Please? He didn't mean it. I love him. I'm having his baby."

Tora staggers back as a thousand tiny knives pierce her heart. She can't believe her ears. Astra is actually going to side with the guy who tried to kill her. The guy who basically killed her mother and friends.

She could forgive her for not telling her that he's malevolent fae, for lying to her for a year, but this... she can't forgive this. It's like she doesn't care what he's done. Like she doesn't care that Freya is dead, that Victor and Teresa are dead, and that he nearly succeeded in killing her.

Tears well in her eyes. Her shattered heart bleeds like liquid nitrogen through her veins. After all these years, after everything they've been through, Astra chose him.

"Fuck you Astra. Fuck you both," Tora spits and storms off through the veil. She breaks into a run and shouts, "Krap tfihsekam" as she jumps through the portal arch, Astra's desperate voice rising above the market chaos behind her, begging her not to leave.

Her jaw aches as she charges back through Makeshift Park to the elven home. Whether she finds the secret to protecting the town or not, she's going home to her squad, to her family, if there's a squad to go back to. Fuck the Valkyries for leaving Greenwich unprotected, fuck the fae, and fuck Astra.

She sacrificed the safety of Greenwich Village for her. She sacrificed the squad and her friends, and what does Astra do? She betrays her; chooses that fuckfaced limp dicked asshole over her. He is the reason her friends died, and the ultimate reason her mother died. Even knowing all that, she chose him.

How could she? They're family… like sisters, and she doesn't even care.

Tearing through the house, Tora wastes no time searching. First, she searches the guest room, then moves on to Nia's room, Brae's room, Queen Raina's room, the kitchen, the dining room, the living room, and the office.

She even searches Braxen's room and the foyer just to be thorough, but there's absolutely nothing.

It's so disgustingly pretty with its weaving wooden architecture tipped in silver, and so clean that nothing is even hidden in the drawers. And she means nothing. The house is practically empty, save for the kitchen cupboards and drawers filled with silver plates, cups, and cutlery. The armoires, entertainment units, shelves, and desks... there's not one scrap of paper; only clothes hanging in the closets and books filling the bookshelves. It's like a stage house. Like no one really lives there.

Standing in the hall, Tora slams her fist against the wooden wall, her frustration bubbling over into rage. Why is nothing ever easy? She may as well just give up, sit in the gutter, and wait for the Valkyries or a demon to kill her. She failed. She failed to protect Astra, she failed to protect Greenwich Village, and she failed to protect her friends and the squad. She's just a big fat failure. Everybody in Greenwich Village is going to die and there's nothing she can do about it.

Crumbling to the floor, Tora holds back frustrated tears and smacks her forehead repeatedly against the wood, hating herself for promising to keep the village safe. She misses her friends; she misses her squad; she misses Teresa and Victor... and she really misses her mother. She would know what to do. Hell, she would have tortured it out of the Queen already and killed Ethan on sight.

341

She sighs and tries to calm her anger and tears, listening to the steady tick of the antique grandfather clock. If she goes out in the Deadlands like this, a demon will eat her before she gets ten steps.

Concentrating, she closes her eyes and tries to get lost in the sound but a soft tapping beats in the opposite rhythm to the clock, like a vibration or a blind smacking against a window frame out of time.

"Agh!" Tora snaps and gets to her feet, determined to break whatever is creating that sound before she leaves. She follows the sound, pushing against the wooden wall palings until she finds one loose, tapping against the frame. Light sneaks under a crack at the bottom, casting muted shadows on the wooden floor.

Frowning, she pushes on the paling again and realizes it's a false wall, a secret door with the same spiraling architecture and antique fixtures as the rest of the house hidden behind it.

A rush of excitement sends goosebumps up Tora's arms. Butterflies jump around in her stomach. This could be it. This could be what she's been looking for. Taking a small blade from her boot, she jams it into the antique keyhole, twists, and lifts. Enough time has been wasted. She needs to find the secret and get the hell out of there.

The antique lock smashes under the force of her knife and hits the floor. Tora silently cheers. They'll know she broke into the room but she should be gone before they get back.

Tentatively she pushes open the door and pokes her head inside. A king-sized bed is neatly made in the middle of the room with a deep royal blue bedspread and matching pillowcases.

Tora widens her eyes and turns in a slow circle, gobsmacked by the framed photographs and paintings lining the walls. Brae and Nia's familiar faces smile out at her sandwiched between Queen Raina and a short plain-looking balding man with a big belly, bottle-thick glasses, and a kind face.

She can't believe it. Queen Raina is smiling like a love-sick schoolgirl in every single photo. Not only does she look happy, she looks nice, kind, and relaxed, staring at the unmistakable human man she loves with large doe eyes. She's like a completely different person. So, what the fuck happened to make her such a bitch?

"I knew better than to trust you." Queen Raina's voice booms off the walls.

Tora gasps and spins around. Her heart jumps, slamming into her throat. Queen Raina glares at her, her hateful ice-blue eyes penetrating deep into her soul, her clenched fists shaking by her sides. Three guards stand around her, their eyes hard and full of outrage, elven steel rippling around their necks and bodies.

"Guards. Show our guest to her new room." Queen Raina narrows her eyes and gestures to the door, her long blue velvet gown trailing on the floor.

Whipping her head from side to side, Tora jumps back and grips her blade, checking for exits as the three elven warriors surround her. Her stomach sinks like a doomed ship. There are two windows she might be able to jump through but not quick enough to escape three elven warriors, and if she pulls her soul sword, she will be risking Nia's life again. She can't trade her freedom for Nia's life.

Slumping her shoulders, Tora holds up her hands and lets her knife fall to the ground, the stench of failure stealing the last of her energy and hope. So much for saving Greenwich Village. Not only did she fail to find the secret to keeping out the demons and fae, she got caught. There's nothing left for her in this stinking realm. Her mother's gone, Astra left her, and her friends and family in Greenwich Village are probably already dead. Maybe the Queen Bitch could do her a favor and find a way to put her out of her misery.

Two of the elven warriors grab an arm each and drag her out of the room following Queen Raina down the hall into the kitchen, the other warrior close behind. Tora doesn't even fight them. What's the point? There's nothing left to fight for.

Queen Raina opens the pantry door and reveals a hidden flight of stairs leading down into a dark underground room. Tora scoffs, her thoughts about the benevolent fae justified. She was right. They do have a dungeon, and that's probably where the Queen will leave her to rot for the rest of her long life.

Forcing her down the stairs into a dark underground dungeon, the guards push her into a large empty cell. Drab dark gray stone walls surround her, the cell locked with metal bars, much like the human prisons before the War of the Gods. There are at least ten cells, all empty except hers and zero light, each with two neatly made beds and a toilet.

Tora flops down on the hard single bed and rolls onto her side, her heart numb. What's the point of fighting it? She's already lost everything. Let the Queen do her worst. It's nothing less than what she deserves after such an epic failure.

"Well, I must say..." Queen Raina stalks in front of the cell, her voice echoing off the walls. "I thought you'd put up more of a fight. No matter. When your friend returns, this will all be over. You can return with the Valkyries, and we can return to normal."

Tora laughs. So that's her plan. Give them to the Valkyries. It won't do them any good. Not without Astra. "You're too late bitch. Astra's gone. Good luck finding her."

Queen Raina's hard blue eyes flare as she grips the bars. "Do not mistake me for my daughter. I am not kind and I care nothing about you or the sanity of your friend. I will do whatever it takes to protect my people." She straightens her shoulders. "Your little friend won't make it far by herself outside of Olivia. The Valkyries will find her. They probably have already. And if they don't, my son will."

"Brae?" Tora scoffs and sits up. "Brae won't drag her back. He doesn't think Astra should be forced to be a Valkyrie any more than I do. He knows she could lose her mind. The Valkyries themselves think Astra is a risk."

Queen Raina laughs; a shrill sickening sound full of malice. Her eyes dance with the joy of a secret. "Who do you think summoned the Valkyries? My son is the Commander of the Elven Army. He understands the importance of the Valkyries and the role the seven of you will play in the coming war."

"N... no." Tora frowns and shakes her head, the Queen's words bouncing around in her head, planting their seed of doubt. Brae wouldn't betray them. He just wouldn't. "You're lying."

"Am I?" Queen Raina raises her eyebrows and steps away from the cell. "Was it my son who wanted to protect your friend, or did you assume he did because of my daughter's soft heart?"

"Go fuck..." Tora starts but someone rushes down the stairs, interrupting her.

"Mother?" Brae appears at the bottom of the stairs and looks back and forth between Tora and his mother. His eyes widen. "What are you doing?"

"Brae!" Tora grips the bars, the tension in her shoulders easing with his confusion. She knew he wouldn't betray her. The Queen Bitch is just trying to fuck with her head. "She's looking for Astra. The Valkyries are coming."

Brae just stares at her. He doesn't blink or smile, he doesn't twitch or move. It's like he's frozen and can't move.

"Brae?" Tora frowns.

Snapping out of it, Brae tightens his jaw and turns to his mother. "This wasn't the plan."

"Wait! What?" Tora lets go of the bars and takes a step back, her ears ringing with disappointment. Her heart squeezes, tightening her chest. It has to be a mistake. It can't be true. There has to be some other explanation. Brae wouldn't do this to them. He knows what it could do to Astra. Despite their fight, despite Astra choosing Ethan over her, she still loves her and doesn't want anything to happen to her, or her baby. "You called the Valkyries?"

Brae's fiery ice-blue eyes soften. His cheeks redden as he struggles to look at her. "I... it wasn't like that."

"Yes or no Brae!" Tora snaps, her throat burning with outrage. "Did you summon the Valkyries? Were you just stalling until they got here?"

Brae sighs. "Yes. For the good of the realms, yes."

Tears spring to Tora's eyes. She never should have trusted the fae. How could she be so stupid? Brae summoned the Valkyries. Offered them up without a second thought. It was all a lie. The entire time, he was just stalling until the Valkyries arrived. And to think she had a crush on him!

"Tora, you don't understand. One Valkyrie can restore thousands upon thousands of warriors to any army. We need as many Valkyries as we can get." Brae pleads with her to understand. "It could mean winning the war. When a warrior dies in battle, you can bring them back. Don't you get that? Don't you get how important one Valkyrie is?"

Queen Raina raises her chin, her face smug.

Curling her lip, Tora backs away from the bars. The importance of the Valkyries has never been the issue. The fact that Astra could become catatonic is. She and Astra may not be friends anymore thanks to that scum-sucker Ethan, but that doesn't mean she's going to hand her over. Becoming a fully-fledged Valkyrie should be a choice. It should not come at the risk of one's sanity.

"Just go away Brae." Tora turns her back and lays down on the bed, facing the wall. "Leave me alone."

"Tora... please..." Brae starts.

"Get out!" Tora snaps. They never should have left Greenwich Village. She didn't save Astra, and she didn't find out how to keep the village safe either. It was all for nothing. All she did was lose Astra to Ethan and get stabbed in the back. She may as well lay down and wait for the Valkyries to come and kill her. At least she won't have to look at Brae's lying face again.

Sighing, Brae leaves the dungeon with his smug bitch of a mother at his side. Like mother like son. It won't take long for the Valkyries to come. They may already be at the house, plotting how to torture Astra's location out of her. Ethan was right in the end. Astra wasn't safe with her, not anymore. He did the best thing he could have done taking her to the Malevolent Fae Realm. It might be the only reason she survives.

As much as she wants to hate Astra, she can't. She loves her and she'll do whatever she can to protect her. Bring on the torture. Bring on the Valkyries. There's a war brewing, and it's not just between the realms.

CHAPTER TWENTY-FIVE

"Huh!" A smug voice wakes Tora from her blissful sleep. She dreamt of nothing. Not of Astra; not of the Valkyries; not of the fae or the demons; not of a goddamned thing, and it was fucking fantastic.

"Traitors always get what they deserve in the end," the voice taunts.

Sighing, Tora sits up to stare her tormentor in the face. Inga; the biggest asshole Valkyrie in the history of the Valkyries. Her black and white hair is braided down both sides of her head, not a hair out of place. The white Valkyrie mark in the middle of her forehead glows brilliantly against her cinnamon skin.

"Fuck off Inga." Tora rests the back of her head against the wall. It looks like Inga's added some ink to her arm since the last time they saw each other, either that or it's some new marking she's never seen before. It spirals down the length of her right arm in delicate weaving vines entwined with white and gold feathers. "No one cares what you think."

"We've killed Valkyries for less than what you did Tora Thurgood." Inga crosses her arms over her chest and leans against the wall, a smug smirk on her bitch face. "Obstructing the ritual of another Valkyrie? Abandoning your post less than an hour after your own ritual? You should be proud. In the history of the Valkyries, no one has ever deserved death more."

"I'm aware that you kill your own kind, Inga." Tora glares at the murderous bitch, her hands shaking. "My mother's blood still stains your sword."

"Oh yeah!" Inga chuckles and moves towards the cell. "I forgot about that."

"Bitch!" Tora slams up against the bars, her Valkyrie mark burning as her soul sword shoots into her hand and she lunges, her teeth bared into a snarl.

"Fuck!" Inga curves her body away from the blade, her eyes wide.

"Inga!" Revna appears at the bottom of the stairs, her face a crimson red. Hundreds of tiny braids hold back her long lily-white hair. The same feathered tattoo-like marking as Inga spirals down her left arm, glowing against her dark skin, like feathered stars in the night. "Get upstairs now, and stop making things worse."

Shrinking back, Inga glares at Tora then storms upstairs, her purple eyes filled with raw hatred. Her angry scream carries down the stairs as she slams the heavy door behind her.

Tora releases her soul sword and grips the bars, her insides vibrating with anger. Even if the Valkyries kill her, she will come back from the dead and make Inga pay for murdering her mother. There is nothing in any of the realms that will be able to stop her.

Sighing, Revna pulls a chair up to the bars and slumps down, her purple eyes glowing in the dimly lit dungeon, her face drawn.

"Are you going to kill me now?" Tora sits on the bed, putting some distance between herself and Revna. She doesn't care if she dies anymore. Her mother is gone, Greenwich Village is probably gone, Astra betrayed her, and so did Brae. What's the point of fighting if she has no one and nothing to fight for? "Just get it over with. I'm over all this drama; over everything."

"No Tora. I'm not going to kill you." Revna rubs her face, her eyes rimmed in dark circles. "The gods are unaware of your transgressions, and it will stay that way. We cannot afford to lose anymore Valkyries, especially not naturally gifted ones like you. You take after your mother. She too was naturally gifted with Valkyrie abilities."

"Don't talk about my mother." Tora whips her head up and narrows her eyes. "You killed her. Inga killed her. The gods killed her. Your praise means nothing to me."

"That wasn't Inga's call Tora. It was mine." Revna looks her dead in the eyes, nothing but remorse swirling in her purple irises. "The gods ordered her death for abandoning them during the War of the Gods. If we didn't carry out their sentence, it would have been much more painful for your mother. The gods would have tortured her for centuries before granting her death. They are not forgiving."

No shit. Every single story or history lesson she has ever heard makes the gods sound like a pack of venomous assholes. She can't believe she ever wanted to be a fully-fledged Valkyrie and fight in the wars like her mother. The gods care nothing for them, just like her mother said.

"What do you want, Revna?" Tora pinches the bridge between her eyes, sick of her crappy life. "I'm not telling you where Astra is. I don't even know where she is exactly."

Revna leans her elbows on her knees. Dark circles surround her eyes like she hasn't slept in years. "Do you get what's coming? What part the Valkyries play?"

"Oh, just fuck off with that shit, will you?" Tora snaps. "You know I do, but it's not going to be at the expense of Astra. Stop trying to guilt me into telling you where she is. You know what will happen if she undergoes the ritual. You know she won't come out the other side intact."

"So, you just let her leave on her own?" Revna shakes her head in disbelief. "How long do you think she'll survive out there?"

"Who says she's alone?" Tora raises her eyebrows, her tone smug. There's no way they'll think to look for her in the Malevolent Fae Realm, at least not in the next few hours. If Ethan and Astra can hold out a little longer, Astra will survive, and they can play happy little family wherever the fuck they want.

"It doesn't matter who's with her." Revna sits back in her chair, her face drawn. "The best she can hope for out there is that a demon finds and eats her, because if the malevolent fae find her, they will torture and kill her slowly before midnight tonight. They've been looking for her for days."

Tora frowns. Her throat tightens. "Why would the malevolent fae care about a Valkyrie?"

"Because Valkyries can restore the souls of the dead," Revna says. "And an army of warriors who never truly die are difficult to defeat. They're biding their time. Waiting for the realms to collapse. Can you imagine the pain and chaos that will flood the realms when the veils completely collapse? It's going to be a smorgasbord."

Tora inhales sharply and gets to her feet, nausea attacking her in waves. Fuck. Astra. She just let her go off with Ethan. A lamb led to the slaughter by that evil fuckfaced jerk.

Fuck!

Shit!

F-augh-kkk!

"The warlock who tried to kill you? Flenn?" Revna continues. "He works with Hecate, Daughter of Hades, Keeper of the Crossroads, and Demon Goddess of Hell. Hecate has control of the Malevolent Fae Market and Council."

The hairs on Tora's arms and the back of her neck rise. Ice spreads through her veins. What has she done? Astra could already be dead. The baby could be dead. And she just handed them over without a fight. Ethan knew exactly what he was doing. He manipulated them so easily.

"Fuck!" Tora kicks the bed, smashing the wooden frame.

How stupid can she be? Astra is as good as dead. Ethan the scum-sucking fuckface set her up. How could she let her go to the Malevolent Fae Realm? She knew Ethan was a liar. She knew he couldn't be trusted. She's always known, and she still let Astra go with him. She let her emotions get the better of her; her pride. And now Astra, the only family she has left, is probably dead.

"Fuck!" Tora screams at the ceiling.

Revna flies to her feet, her eyes ablaze. "That's where she is; isn't it? The Malevolent Fae Realm?"

"Yes," Tora says begrudgingly, hating herself for being so stupid, for being so blinded by hatred.

"Brae!" Revna yells. "Get down here now!"

A few seconds later, Brae rushes down the stairs, the other Valkyries, Tove, Mist, and Liv close on his heels.

"You need to talk to your malevolent fae contact; Tia or whatever her name is. Do it now. Astra is in their realm with..." Revna clicks her fingers at Tora, expecting her to answer.

"Ethan." Tora sighs. "She's with her boyfriend Ethan. He was with us in Greenwich Village. I only found out at the market today that he's malevolent fae; an elf."

"And you let him take her?" Brae widens his eyes.

"I didn't have a choice!" Tora spits. "She wanted to go with him. They were running from the Valkyries and Flenn. He claims to love her, and the idiot that she is, she believes him."

"Brae! Now!" Revna snaps her fingers.

Flinching, Brae gives Tora one last look and shakes his head before sprinting up the stairs.

Tora smacks her head against the bars, any anger she had towards Astra disappearing at the prospect of her death. At this point, she doesn't care if they're never friends' again, as long as Astra is alive, as long as she is safe.

"This is bad." Tove paces the floor, her lily-white skin almost translucent. She runs her hand over her long black braid and plays with the end. "This is so bad."

"He must have been keeping tabs on you. No wonder Flenn knew where to find you the night of your birthday." Revna tenses her jaw. "I should have done more research. I should have intervened earlier, but I didn't want your mother to take you on the run."

"There's no point to this conversation," Mist says, her voice firm.

Tora glances at her but says nothing.

"Mist is right. Can't change the past." Liv says, her pale skin smudged with dirt. Three tight braids hold her golden locks away from her face. "Let's go get ourselves a Valkyrie."

"Hold on." Revna rolls her eyes. "We don't even know where she is. The Malevolent Fae Realm is exactly the same as every other realm. Impossible to scour in an hour, and they could be anywhere."

Tora widens her eyes. She had no idea it was so late. It's only Astra's birthday for another hour. She almost made it.

Brae rushes down the stairs and jams his cell phone in his pocket. "They're at the Malevolent Fae Market. Ethan was stupid enough to try and hide her in his tent. The fae smelt her fear. She ran but it's only a matter of minutes before they find her."

Fuck! Astra must be freaking out. At least she's still alive, and if Tora has anything to say about it, she's going to stay that way.

"Let me out of here now." Tora growls.

Brae glances at Revna and lifts his eyebrows in question.

"Unlock it. We're going to need the six of us for this." Revna waves her hand in approval.

"You mean seven. I'm coming too," Brae says as he unlocks the cell door.

"No. Definitely not." Revna shakes her head. "The fae will smell you a mile away and kill her instantly."

"And they won't smell you?" Brae scoffs and falls back into the bars as Tora barges him hard in the shoulder on her way out of the cell.

"No. They won't." Mist confirms. "Fully-fledged Valkyries don't experience fear, not like fae, not like humans, angels, or gods."

"That's bullshit!" Brae snaps. "Everything feels fear."

"Not the same as a Valkyrie who has undergone the ritual. Our fear is much like your excitement," Revna explains.

"Umm, that can't be true," Tora interrupts. "I've been scared plenty of times since leaving Greenwich."

"You're new. It would have faded into nothing by now," Mist says.

"But I experienced definite fear at the market today," Tora argues. She doesn't know why she's arguing. She doesn't want the traitorous bastard Brae to go either.

Revna frowns. "What do you mean?"

All eyes turn to Tora. She squirms and looks at her feet, like she's done something wrong. "I experienced fear around the Witch Goddess Selene."

Revna bites her lip in thought, her gaze troubled. "You're sure?"

"Yeah." Tora nods. "Why would I lie?"

"What does it mean?" Liv looks to Revna for guidance, her eyes unsure.

"Who cares." Mist dismisses their worries. "We'll deal with that later. We aren't taking the Witch Goddess with us."

"Okay. It's settled then. I'll get Inga from time out and then we go." Liv bounces up the stairs like a child on her way to a birthday party, her unease forgotten.

Tora follows the others up the stairs. If there is even a tiny chance of getting Astra away from the fae and the Valkyries, she has to try. And she'll put her sword through Ethan's chest on the way just for the fuck of it. Fuck the consequences.

CHAPTER TWENTY-SIX

A crisp breeze blows through the trees as Brae, Tora, and the Valkyries rush across the road to the portal. Leaves rustle high in the branches. An owl stares down at them with disapproving eyes, hooting viciously, and flapping its wings. The moon beams down on the grass and play equipment of Makeshift Park, casting an eerie glow on the lagoon.

Standing in the center of four thick witch hazel trees hidden from the path by the willows, Brae checks their surroundings, making sure no curious eyes are following them. Tora and the rest of the Valkyries stand behind him.

"Latrop Teram Eaf Tnelovelam," Brae commands the portal and stabs at the middle of the arch with a small blade.

Vibrant lights spiral to life within the arch, quickly turning to hues of gray and black. Red splotches bleed like a stab wound through the once shimmering surface. Garnets crust the outer edges of the portal, lining the wooden arch.

"It's done." Brae clenches his jaw and takes a step back, clearly unhappy about having to stay behind. Ten elven warriors emerge from the trees and join him by the portal.

"What is this?" Revna levels Brae with a suspicious glare. "You cannot come."

"Calm down." Brae rolls his eyes. "There are no permanent portals in the Malevolent Fae Realm, and we don't want to make one. The fabric's been torn to allow you through, but it needs to stay open if you want to return. You'll arrive just outside of the market. My warriors and I need to guard the gate to make sure nothing else comes through the portal uninvited."

Tora frowns. If that's true, then how did Ethan get to the Benevolent Fae Market? How did he return with Astra? Did they piggyback the performers?

"We have forty-five minutes to find the girl and perform the ritual. No fighting, bickering, or bullshit between any of you. Okay?" Revna warns. "I won't kill you, but I will personally torture the crap out of you."

Inga bristles under Revna's gaze, knowing the speech is directed at her. Satisfied, Revna steps through the portal, followed closely by Inga, Mist, Tove, and Liv.

As Tora moves to step through the portal, Brae grabs her arm and lowers his head. "Tora? I'm sorry if you feel I betrayed you. It was not my intention to hurt you."

Tora scoffs and pulls away. "You knew exactly what you were doing. And I didn't feel like you betrayed me. You did betray me. Astra too. At least own your actions, you coward."

Brae flinches, his face burning hot with shame. The surrounding warriors avert their eyes.

Without another word, Tora steps through the portal. Fuck Brae. She doesn't have time for his shit. If it wasn't for him, the Valkyries would still be searching for them, and Ethan wouldn't have been able to convince Astra to go to the Malevolent Fae Realm.

If Astra dies because of him, she's going to drive a blade straight through his pretty little head. There are plenty of other weapons she can use besides a soul sword that won't affect Nia. It's not her fault her brother is a dick.

Shadows fly around the portal like a kite caught in the wind, brushing past Tora's skin as she's sucked through the realms, each touch stinging like an ant bite. Nausea curdles her stomach. Her ears pop and ache. A foul odor fills her nose and contaminates her lungs, the heavy scent of sulfur lingering in the air.

A sudden blast of water slams into Tora's face and surrounds her body. She holds her breath, her eyes wide as an endless ocean of water engulfs her; lava, rock, and crystal forming a huge flaming circle around her.

A force pushes her left and right, up and down, like an extreme washing machine. Her throat and lungs ache, demanding fresh air. She briefly wonders whether Valkyries can drown, but a force slams into her back, pushing out the last of her breath as she's evicted from the portal. The flaming ball of water, lava, rock, and crystal smashes to pieces as she slams into the ground.

Gasping, Tora crawls in the dirt, drenched to the bone. Dark brown trunks with purple and red leaves fill the surrounding forest, the smell of musk and lavender overwhelming, like a heavily perfumed field. The ferns are dark purple instead of green, the flowers deep colors of red, black, gray, and brown.

Traveling through a rip is nothing like traveling through a portal gate. It's painful and nauseating. It's probably also the reason Greenwich hasn't been overrun by demons or fae.

The warlock said things are changing, that demons and fae will attack in Greenwich Village all the time now. If she's right, it means the demons and the malevolent fae have been able to create a portal gate, like the one in Makeshift Park. It has to be. It's the only plausible explanation.

There may be a way to save the village without the stupid elven secret after-all. If they find the portal gate, they can destroy it.

"Ugh." Tora groans and struggles to not throw up, every muscle, organ, and bone in her body aching. Everything looks toxic and dangerous in the forest, like if you brushed up against one of the leaves, you'd lose an arm.

"Shh!" Revna appears through the deep purple ferns, wet but still perfectly put together, and motions for Tora to follow. "Rips are harder to travel through than gates, especially for angelic beings."

No shit! It would have been nice if someone told her that she might drown inside the stupid portal. She still would have jumped through, but she would have been better prepared.

Crab walking through the dense forest, Revna takes her to the other Valkyries waiting ahead, peeking over the side of a crater. She crouches beside Liv and follows their line of sight, her already tender stomach squeezing at the sight of an archway of warped trees, wrapped in barbed wire, purple glow bugs impaled on each spike.

A double-kick bass drum begins slowly and softly, growing in speed and volume with every hit. The air is thick with barbecued burnt meat.

In the distance, an army of tents litter the field. Large warped bending trees create a dome over the market, arching over the fae below. All types of intoxicated filth-covered fae stumble around the clearing; fighting, arguing, and drinking. It's like feeding time in the tiger's den.

Following Revna's direction, Tora creeps silently into the market, keeping to the outer circle, hiding in the shadows, and trying not to throw up as the smell of dirt, raw meat, sweat, sewerage, rotting corpses, and nauseating sulfur hits her square in the face.

Majority of the malevolent fae appear to be alcoholics, drowning their sorrows and pain. Female fae stumble around in short dresses, clutching bottles of spirits, threatening anyone who gets close to them, the dress fabric much like the performers at the Benevolent Fae Market, unassuming but deadly. Others line up outside the outer fighting ring, sneering at the bloodied and bruised males on the sidelines.

The faeries' enormous two-toned, tattered, and torn gothic-style wings jut out of their backs and bleed through blacks and grays with deep colors of purple, fuchsia, red, and blue.

Tora gasps as a male faery with black, gray, and blue tattered and torn ombre wings is thrown from a makeshift ring and lands by her feet. He grips his neck and screams in pain, his blood soaking into the dirt.

The Valkyries freeze and stare at the fae, waiting to see what they'll do; if they'll notice what they are, but the fae are too intoxicated to care.

Oblivious, a pixie covered in more black spirals than red skin laughs manically in the ring and beats his chest like a gorilla, his mouth and teeth dripping with the faery's blood. He squeals like a pig and dives on top of the faery, tearing into his flesh with its teeth.

The Valkyries exhale and continue forward as a group, searching for Astra, with Tora a few steps behind. Smoldering buildings circle the market, the wood black and charred to a crisp. Rows of stalls line the field, selling knives, swords, axes, bows, throwing stars, and god knows what else, each stall competing for the most damage-inflicting device.

Fire breathers, knife eaters, and daring high-flying acts, all fight for the attention of the crowd, like some morbid gruesome circus. The fae only cheer when they fall, when they stab themselves, or in a few cases, impale themselves on iron spikes hurled at them by the crowd.

The nastier fae throw rotten food, spears, and rocks at the performers to knock them off balance while one group fights for the chance to throw machete knives at someone or something tied to a thin wooden pole.

Tora widens her eyes but doesn't slow her pace as she realizes what is tied to the pole. The Unlucky. Humans who have been taken by the malevolent fae or lured under false pretenses. And there's more than one.

A man clothed in rags stumbles after an elven man, the leash around his neck drawing blood. A barely clothed blonde-haired woman leans on her hands and knees; wooden mugs and a steaming plate of chicken resting on her bare back, burning her skin.

Tora knew this was their fate, but seeing it is completely different to hearing about it. This can't be the fate of those in Greenwich Village. She has to save them somehow. She won't leave her squad and friends to this fate, not while she can still fight.

An elaborate steel stage warps and molds around horns reaching toward the sky, forming a protective barrier around the band. Frantic notes scream through the sound system as two beaten-down pixies, a dirt-covered faery, and an elven drummer attempt to entertain the crowd.

The pixie guitarist locks eyes with the pixie organ player, fear easily read on their faces as the drummer's veins protrude out of his forearm, the double kick drum and snare losing their ferocity.

"Keep playing!" the faery bass player screams, his black and blue wings flexing as his fingers move frantically up and down the fretboard. Shouts erupt from the mosh pit as the fae throw glass bottles at the band, echoed by threats and feral growls.

Through the stage smoke and fire, a beautiful deadly-looking faery in white jeans and a black see-through top appears. Her intricately designed steel metal bodice shines through the chiffon. She grips the microphone and releases a heartbreaking haunting voice.

The crowd cheers as the singer whips her head around in circles, dancing to the heavy metal music, her white locks shimmering with streaks of blue, red, purple, and black, matching her multi-colored tattered wings.

They're feeding from her. The crowd is feeding on the singer's emotional pain, the other members of the band too. It's not just the humans and benevolent fae they feed on, it's their own kind.

"This is where they'll bring her. They'll make a spectacle out of the killing," Revna whispers and pulls the Valkyries back into the tree line.

"So, what's the plan?" Tora asks. Everyone seems to know the plan for saving Astra except her. She looks from Revna to Tove, to Mist, and to Liv, but no one says a word. "And where the fuck is Inga?"

"Shh!" Mist cautions. "Inga is disguised in the crowd."

Tora frowns. "Why?"

"To brand her as they carry her through the market of course." Liv screws up her face, like it's the most obvious thing in the world.

Tora pales. Brand her? They're going to carry out the ritual? Right here… at the market. Under the noses of the fae. They're still going ahead with the ritual?

"We need to get up into the trees; into the branches above the stage. Once Inga brands her, we can perform the ritual there and drop down at the last second to penetrate the pineal gland." Revna eyes the trees. "Mist, Tora, and Liv; fan out. Circle the market to the other side and climb the trees. They'll be bringing her out of one of the tents in a minute. They'll want to torture her a bit more first. Inga will come back to me and climb one of the trees here. It's the best circle we can create under the circumstances. It will still work."

Dazed, Tora blinks at the ground as she follows Mist and Liv around the outskirts to the other side of the market, her stomach curdling. The Valkyries don't care that Astra is being tortured. They don't care about anything except for completing their stupid ritual. She doesn't know when the Valkyries turned into cold hearted bitches, but she can't just allow them to steal Astra's sanity, to destroy the girl who has always been like a sister to her. She needs to find Inga and make sure she doesn't succeed. That's if she's not too late.

Waiting until the Valkyries are in position, Tora jumps from branch to branch, back down the tree as quietly as possible. The others don't seem to notice, their focus solely on the fae festivities below.

Creeping into the market, she steals a cloak from an unconscious elven man and moves unnoticed through the fae, her short stature working in her favor for a change. There's no way in hell she's just going to sit back and wait for Astra to either die or be made into a Valkyrie. She has to at least try to save her.

Shoulder barging fae out of the way, she storms through the market, towards the tents, kicking and tripping as many of the asshole fae as she can on her way. The crowd cheers on the performers as the music changes, the beat more tribal and frantic.

"Astra!" A croaky voice groans, just barely audible.

Tora stops dead in her tracks. The hairs on the back of her neck stand up. She knows that voice. It's a voice she has hated for nearly a year now; Ethan. And where there's Ethan, there's Astra.

Gripping the hilt of the blade strapped to her hip, Tora slowly turns. Ethan lays tied to some sort of stretching device with rope; his face and body bloodied and bruised, metal spikes sticking out of his limbs.

"Ethan." Tora curls her lip and bumps one of the metal spikes as she gets closer.

Ethan screams and spits at her feet as he drops his head forward. Blood drips from his nose and mouth. He struggles to open his right eye, the left one swollen completely shut. "I hope you burn in flames! I hope she tears you apart."

"Where is she Ethan?" Tora snarls and pushes her blade against his throat, the smell of sweat and blood thick in the air. "Where is Astra?"

"Tora?" Ethan jerks in his restraints as he recognizes her voice. He tries to turn his head but the rope around his throat cuts deep and keeps it in place. "Oh, thank fuck. You have to save her. Please, save her."

"Shut up!" Tora snaps and whips her head around, making sure no one heard. "Where is she? Where do they have her?"

Ethan struggles against the ropes, the fabric cutting deep into his wrists as he tries to lift his arm and point. Blood and dirt cover his body and clothes, the deep lacerations in his skin cut near to the bone.

Tora swallows hard, the smell of rotting flesh and blood making her eyes water. It looks like he was put through a meat grinder and fashioned into a sausage. As much as she hates him and wants him to suffer, she can't just leave him like this. She needs his help to find Astra.

Gritting her teeth, Tora cuts the ropes binding his arms and tries to pull out a metal spike impaled into his wrist.

"No! Don't!" Ethan screams.

Fuck! Tora scans the crowd but no one pays them any attention, too distracted by their own feeding frenzy and the now near-naked spectacle on the stage. If she pulls out the spikes, Ethan will bleed out in seconds. She doesn't know what to do. Astra would want her to save him, but she's not sure she can, not without killing him in the process.

"Where Ethan?" Tora stands out of his way so he can see. "I need to know which tent?"

Wincing, Ethan struggles to lift his arm as the crowd cheers loudly and jumps up and down, reveling in the chaos of the market. His entire body convulses but he manages to point into the distance with his middle finger, the only finger he has left on his right hand.

"Are you serious?" Tora shakes her head in disbelief at the large double-spaced tent with Christmas lights hanging around the edges. If he wasn't so stupid, she might feel sorry for him. "You dumb fuck! Christmas lights? You thought Christmas lights were a good idea in a place that feeds on pain? You may as well have painted a bullseye on the side of your tent!"

"I wanted to make it pretty for her. A place to call home." Ethan chokes out. His arm drops.

Idiot! The fae didn't just sniff out Astra's fear, they were drawn to her by Ethan's stupidity. There's nothing pretty in this realm. Everything looks dead, even the trees, bugs, and the grass looks dead. She could kill Ethan for being the dumbest fucktard alive.

"Are we ready for the main event?" An amplified female voice booms across the market.

Goosebumps spread across Tora's skin as a warm seductive voice slithers around her neck. The crowd of intoxicated filth-covered fae cheer, scream, howl, and fight each other in excitement. Blood, alcohol, and urine sink into the dirt as some of the fae literally pee themselves in excitement at the sound of the woman's voice.

Tora slowly turns, the tension in the air thick against her skin. A tall pale-skinned woman graces the stage, her hip-length black hair cascading in waves down her back. Her eyes burn an unearthly green, taking in the crowd. A shiny black ink-like substance moves across her body like a second skin, forming a bodice to cover her generous breasts, torso, and legs. Her toes remain bare except for the deep purple nail polish on her toenails.

Tora's eyes water, like she's staring at the sun. Her throat tightens. This is not one of the fae. Fae don't look like this woman. Humans don't look like this woman. Not even angelic beings look like this woman. The woman exudes pure power and lust. This… is a god. And if Tora had to guess, she would say this is Hecate; Daughter of Hades; Keeper of the Crossroads, the Demon Goddess of Hell.

But even the Demon Goddess in all her glory can't distract Tora from the girl in a soft floral summer dress being passed over the heads of the fae, crowd surfing towards the stage. The girl is barely conscious, with bites, bruises, and slashes covering her arms and legs.

Gasping, Tora heaves and hunches over as a wave of grief sucker punches her in the stomach. She stares at the girl, tears stinging her eyes. She gasps for air, her chest tightening and burning up to her throat. The world swims in colors.

"You're too late." Ethan drops his head back down, tears mixing with his blood as it drips from his face.

The girl. It's Astra. Her sweet sweet Astra. She's barely hanging on, only seconds away from death.

Tora glares at Ethan, wanting to hate him, wanting to beat him until he can't breathe but she can't. She can see it on his face. Ethan didn't double-cross Astra. He was honestly trying to save her; to hide her. He loves her. His only crime is being an idiot. "It's not too late."

Astra's shrill pain-filled scream rips through the market. Tora whips her head around and plunges into the crowd, pushing her way through the disgusting fae covered in blood, urine, and filth.

Most of the fae are distracted by the Demon Goddess and are feeding from Astra's pain, but a few grab at her arms, shoulders, and hair, trying to catch her.

With no time, Tora pulls out her blade and stabs blindly, slicing through their flesh and adding to the fae's feeding frenzy. The wounded are quickly dragged to the ground and devoured, the cannibalistic pixies showing no mercy.

The crowd surges forward and forces her back as the fae jump and climb over each other to get closer to the stage. Pixies, elves, faeries, and sprites scratch and bite at Astra's arms and legs, and lick the blood from her skin.

Astra screams.

"Stop!" Tora yells but no one hears her, not above the swarms of malevolent fae, and even if they could hear her, no one cares.

It's hopeless. No matter what she does, no matter how hard she charges at the crowd, or how many of the fae she stabs, the pure number of bodies completely overwhelms her. It's like swimming in quicksand.

"Fuuuuck!" Tora screams and stabs a red-skinned pixie in the middle of the forehead as he charges her, taking out her frustration on the fae. She breathes heavily, sweat dripping down the sides of her face, searching for any path through the swarm of fae, any path that will lead her to Astra.

Then she sees it. A six-foot hooded figure pops up amongst the revelers, right next to Astra's side, as though she had been sitting there patiently on a chair and simply rose when Astra neared.

"No!" Tora yells, her heart screaming in her chest, but it's no use.

With stealthy speed, Inga pushes a disc to Astra's wrist, branding and burning her skin. Astra cries out in pain, but no one notices or cares. The fae moan and laugh in ecstasy, drunk on Astra's fear and pain.

"Tonight; we kill the Valkyrie!" Hecate shouts into the microphone. "And since they're so fond of rituals, we're going to perform one of our own. One she won't wake up from!"

The crowd cheers and gnashes their teeth, passing Astra forward. The band members lift her onto the stage and tie her to a long flat gray stone table at the back.

Tora gasps. She's going to kill Inga and the goddamned fae. From the looks of the pulley system surrounding the stone, it will fold forward and lift Astra into the air like a floating sacrifice. This can't be happening. She can't let this happen.

Whipping her head back and forth, she desperately searches for a way to the stage and spots a break in the masses. A slither of hope blooms in her chest. Using her full strength, she rams through the intoxicated fae like an enraged bull, trampling some beneath her boots.

It has to be close to midnight. She's running out of time and running out of options. Her only hope is to sneak Astra off stage somehow. She's short enough that the horns and spikes surrounding the stage will partially hide her from view, and she can duck down behind the stone table once on stage.

It's her only hope. Her only shot at saving Astra. The fae are distracted, drunk on fear and pain. They shouldn't notice her, not at first anyway, and if they do, they will hopefully think she's helping set up the ritual. She just hopes her plan works.

If it doesn't, Astra is dead, and when the Valkyries get hold of her, so is she.

CHAPTER TWENTY-SEVEN

Climbing the horns at the back of the stage, Tora keeps low and scrambles to the stone table while the band plays one last song, her heartbeat matching the heavy metal bass drum. The Demon Goddess faces the crowd, dancing like a slithering snake and laughing as the fae below tear into each other in the mosh pit.

The stars above shine brightly as the moon beams down on the market, highlighting the blood and sweat spraying onto the stage, covering the band and the goddess.

Tora's throat tightens as she nears Astra and sees the damage the fae have caused. Her hands shake. Tears threaten to burst free from her eyes. Chunks of Astra's luscious strawberry blonde hair have been torn out by the roots. Blood drips down from a large gash on her forehead, and her beautiful light purple eyes are heavily bruised and swollen. Her right leg looks like it's turned sideways and her wrist is bitten and bruised while the other has the branding burn of the Valkyries.

"Hold on Star," Tora whispers behind Astra's head. "I'm going to get you out of here."

Fresh tears fall down Astra's cheeks as sobs rattle her chest. She jerks against her restraints, knowing the sound of Tora's voice instantly.

Tora takes her knife and glares up at the five sets of angry purple eyes staring daggers down at her from the overarching trees above. She cuts the rope around Astra's neck and arms first then leans down close to her ear. "Don't move unless you see the Valkyries above you move. The fae can't know you're free yet."

Glancing up at the Valkyries one last time, Tora sticks up her middle finger and kisses the back of it, the gesture directed towards Revna. The dumbass bitches should have known she wouldn't let them sentence Astra to a life of insanity. Astra will flinch away if the Valkyries move, and they know it. They won't get another chance to perform the ritual now. Astra is safe from the Valkyries at least.

Ignoring the angry bitches, Tora creeps around the side of the stone, keeping her eye on the Demon Goddess Hecate who dances in the moonlight, oblivious to Tora behind her. The band nears the end of their song, continuing to distract the crowd as they feed from their pain.

Tora takes one last steadying breath and scowls at the five Valkyries waving frantically from the branches, telling her to stop, but nothing will stop her from saving her friend, especially five asshole Valkyries who just want to use her, fuck the consequences.

Darting to the front of the stone, Tora slices through the rope binding one of Astra's ankles, and moves to cut the next, knowing she only has seconds to escape.

"Hello there little Valkyrie," a silky voice coos.

Tora freezes and swallows hard, her throat suddenly hot and dry. Slowly she looks up and flinches back, her eyes stinging deep into the nerve. The Demon Goddess stands over her, a huge pair of leather bat-like wings spread out behind her. Her emerald green eyes blaze with specs of fire as her luscious red pouty lips curve into a menacing smile.

Sharp pain explodes across Tora's cheek as the goddess backhanders her hard across the face, sending her sprawling on the stage. Her blade flies out of her hand and slides off the edge of the stage.

Intense pain explodes in her skull, spreading like a tsunami down her neck and back. Tremors rack her body as blood drips from her eyes, nose, and mouth onto the stage, pooling beneath her face, the world fading in and out of a kaleidoscope of colors.

The members of the band stop playing and turn to look down at her, all grinning except for the female faery singer. Tora jolts as understanding hits her square in the jaw. They knew. They knew all along that she was there. That's what the Valkyries were trying to tell her when they were waving their arms around. The Demon Goddess knew she was there. The Valkyries were trying to help her.

The band members put down their instruments and exit the stage, grateful they're no longer the main attraction or the main feeding source of the crowd. Tora looks up through blood-soaked eyes and blinks as the faery singer passes her, her hair streaked in a rainbow of pastel colors. Tora frowns. She knows the faery's face. She's seen her before.

For a second, she dares to hope it's Tia about to help her, but she's not that lucky. It's the faery Tia called Britney. The one who popped her head through the portal in the tunnel, and from the fear easily read on the faery's face, Tora knows she's on her own. No one is coming to their rescue. Not now. Not ever. She failed. The Demon Goddess damaged her nerves with one hit, and now Astra is going to die, and so will she.

"Agh!" Astra suddenly roars and springs up from the stone. She grabs the Demon Goddess's long black hair and reefs it back with all her might, one ankle still bound to the stone.

A flood of hope brings a smile to Tora's lips as Hecate stumbles backward but the warlock Flenn appears out of the darkness and slams Astra's head back against the stone, knocking her out cold.

"Star!" Tora yells and tries to push herself up but she collapses under her own weight, her body bruised and aching as though she were hit by a truck, her vision wavering in and out of darkness. Blood drips from her nose and mouth. The hope she felt turns to acidy rage, burning a hole in her stomach.

"Stupid little girl." Hecate laughs and smooths out her long black hair, the malice of her words conflicting with the melodic siren quality of her voice.

"We may not be able to smell your fear Valkyrie." Hecate runs her fingers over Flenn's lips. "But we smelt your friend's hope the moment she saw you. We don't get a lot of that around here."

Tora frowns. Fae, demons, and hellbeings should only be able to smell and taste pain and fear. They feed from the darker emotions, the ones that corrupt the soul like greed, bitterness, and hate. They shouldn't be able to smell hope or even love.

"Oh, you didn't know? Hellbeings feed on all emotions. It fuels our power." Hecate paces around her as the black inky liquid substance covering her body slithers around her ankles and glides over her feet to form spiked heels.

Tora swallows hard. If the realms collapse, no human, fae, god, or angel would be safe. Hell, nothing would be safe. Almost everything feels some sort of emotion. Hellbeings would completely devour all the realms, leaving nothing.

"I must say though, pain is the most decadent." Hecate smirks and slams a heeled boot down onto Tora's right hand and wrist.

Tora screams as her bones shatter, sending red-hot pain up her arm into her neck. Sweat pours down her face, the intense pain burning her from the inside out. The crowd of devilish fae cheer and celebrate, turning their faces to the sky and sticking out their forked tongues to taste her pain in the air.

Shaking violently, Tora holds her shattered wrist to her chest, tears streaming down her face. She can't even pull her soul sword. The Demon Goddess made sure of that when she targeted her right wrist. She failed. Astra is going to die, and she can't do anything about it.

Desperately, she pats her legs and hips for a weapon. If she's going to die, she's at least going to hurt the bitch and die with a weapon in her hand.

A slither of hope splashes like cold water on her burning body as her hand touches something cold, hard, and metal in her pocket, like the hilt of a blade. She forces herself to stand and pulls out her weapon, holding it in front of her like a lifeline while the other arm is locked close to her body.

Hecate throws back her head and laughs, as does the crowd of fae.

Blinking through the blood, Tora looks down at her weapon and drops her shoulders in defeat. Fresh tears spring to her eyes, her chest aching for Astra and her baby, for Teresa, for Victor and her mother. It's not a blade at all. It's a silver rattle, the one she bought for Astra's baby.

"We are the Choosers of the Slain, the Shield Maidens of Myth. Join us now sister, come forthwith."

Through the chaos of laughter and boisterous fae, Tora hears a familiar melodic chanting floating through the market. The Valkyries Song. The ritual is beginning. As much as she hates it, the ritual is her only hope of saving Astra now. Catatonic or not, pregnant or not, it's the only way Astra lives.

"Not all Valkyries are as stupid as me." Tora glares at the Demon Goddess and spits blood at her feet as Revna jumps from a branch and descends with her soul sword pointing down at Astra's forehead.

"Yes, they are little Valkyrie." Hecate grins and throws up one hand, freezing Revna in midair, her sword held tight in her hand, struggling against an invisible force holding her in place.

Tora widens her eyes. Her mouth drops open in surprise. It's impossible. No beings are able to freeze a Valkyrie in place. Not fae, not demons, not even gods. Valkyries are effectively souls.

"I am Hecate. Demon Goddess of Hell, Daughter of Hades. Keeper of the Crossroad. The Keeper of Death." Hecate laughs. "I control the souls in between realms, in between life and death. That includes you little Valkyrie."

Tora gasps. How did they miss that? Valkyries are effectively dead. In between realms. Their powers are useless on this Demon Goddess.

With one simple hand gesture, Hecate sends the Valkyries flying out of the trees, through the air, back out of the market. Revna's angry desperate scream is the last thing she hears before they disappear through the trees.

"Now you get to watch me kill your friend." Hecate winks and turns towards Astra, her emerald green eyes twinkling.

"No!" Tora struggles against the restraints holding her feet in place. Desperately she tries to pull her soul sword but the sword refuses to form, the pain in her arm causing her to scream. The only weapon she holds is a baby's rattle.

Flenn grins his smug creepy lop-sided grin and turns to watch the goddess. The crowd of malevolent fae sway on their feet, drunk on her pain, and dance in the moonlight, reveling in the chaos.

"Oh, don't worry." Hecate glances back over her shoulder, her eyes burning like green fire. "You get to die too, but she got here first. It's only fair."

Chuckling, Hecate pulls a Hell Blade from the triple crescent moon symbol on her wrist, three interlocking crescent moons, the same as Tora would her soul sword. In the distance, Ethan screams for Astra to get up and run, but she remains unconscious on the altar.

Tora continues to struggle, straining her muscles against the restraints to free herself, to save her friend, the Valkyries, and the realms.

Defeat burns through her veins as failure falls heavy on her shoulders. She never should have tried to save Astra. The Realms will fall to Hades without the Valkyries to bring back the souls. She ruined everything. All her friends will die, and there is absolutely nothing she can do about it.

This is it. This is death. It was all for nothing. The last year; Teresa's death, Victor's death, her mother's death... It was all for nothing.

"Bitch!" Tora roars and pegs the baby rattle at Hecate's head, her entire body shaking with anger.

At the last second, Hecate turns and strikes out with her sword, stabbing Tora in the arm, right near her bicep. Tora screams as fire ignites in her blood, the pain burning down to the bone. The rattle smacks Hecate in the middle of the forehead and hits the ground, powerless.

Stunned, Hecate laughs. "You threw a rattle at me?"

Sneering, Tora holds her arm and grits her teeth against the waves of pain spreading down to her fingertips. Pins and needles bubble under the surface of her skin, climbing up her neck to her face.

The fae stare up at the stage silently, their eyes suddenly wide with ravenous hunger. Hecate's laughter quickly dies as a silver bruise burns into her forehead. She touches her long-nailed fingers to her head and frowns at the liquid silver substance staining her hand.

"Elven steel!" Hecate screams as the liquid metal burns like acid, eating away at her skin, scorching her trademark symbol of three crescent moons into her forehead and blackening her fingertips. She drops her sword and falls to the ground with her hands held close to her face. "My face!"

A roaring cheer erupts from the market. The fae laugh, dance, and stumble around the grounds, feeding on the goddess's pain. Their eyes roll back in their heads in ecstasy.

Tora widens her eyes and looks back and forth between Hecate and the rattle. God, she's stupid. Elven Steel! That's what protects Olivia. It's been in front of her face the whole time. It has to be it. It's everywhere. That's the benevolent fae's secret. The rattle is made of it.

Free to move, Tora scrambles across the ground and grabs the elven steel rattle as Flenn rushes to Hecate's side. One side of the rattle is partially melted from where it connected with the Demon Goddess's head, the steel still alive and burning the goddess.

An angry scream echoes through the forest, pushing the ravens and blackbirds from the trees. Tora whips her head over her shoulder. It's Revna. The spell on the Valkyries must have broken, the goddess no longer has control of them.

"What's happening?" Flenn yells over the chaos and tries to pull the goddess to her feet.

"Don't touch me!" Hecate snaps and pushes him away. "I'll be fine in a second."

That's all the time and distraction Tora needs. She rushes over to Astra and cuts the last remaining rope around her ankle with a piece of a broken bottle.

"Stop her!" Hecate screams and throws out her hand, trying to use her power.

Tora gasps, ready for the attack, but nothing happens. Relief floods her veins, turning into laughter. The elven steel must have messed with her abilities. "Fuck you bitch!"

Smirking, Tora wraps her arm around Astra and uses her wings to try and lift her but it's too awkward with one arm.

Hecate laughs manically. "Having trouble little Valkyrie?"

"Shut up!" Tora shakes Astra's shoulders, trying to wake her. She slaps her hard in the face but still, she refuses to wake. "Astra! Wake up!"

"Take her." Hecate waves her hand, commanding Flenn. "I'll take them both to Hell with me."

"We are the Choosers of the Slain, the Shield Maidens of Myth, join us now sister, come forthwith." The chant echoes around the market in a circle as the Valkyries near.

Flenn charges Tora, a dirty knife held in his hand, his lips pulled into a lop-sided grin.

Silent tears fall down Tora's cheeks. Her stomach rolls. Death or Insanity. Those are Astra's choices. She can either die in Hell or live as a fully-fledged Valkyrie with the risk of losing her mind.

Tora clenches her jaw and pinches her eyes closed as she calls on her soul sword, the shattered bones, damaged ligaments, and nerves burning deep into her shattered hand and wrist. At least as a fully-fledged Valkyrie, Astra has a chance.

A scream rips free from Tora's mouth as the Valkyrie mark on her wrist flares brightly and the hilt of her soul sword glides down into her shattered palm. She struggles to remain conscious as pain surges through her arm like a serrated knife tearing through her veins.

In the distance she sees Revna fly through the trees into the clearing as Brae charges through the trunks with a small army of elven warriors.

"No!" Hecate screams. Flenn dives towards her. But they're too late.

"I love you Star." Tora uses the last of her strength to lift her sword over Astra's head and wraps her left hand over her shattered right. With the Valkyries chant echoing in her ears, she cries and closes her eyes. "Forgive me."

"We are the Choosers of the Slain, the Shield Maidens of Myth, join us now sister, come forthwith." Tora drives her blade through Astra's forehead, forever sealing their fate as Flenn slams into her side.

Tora hits the ground hard. The world goes black.

CHAPTER TWENTY-EIGHT

Gasping, Tora snaps open her eyes and blinks rapidly to clear the spinning kaleidoscope of colors flashing in front of her face. Her head throbs mercilessly as she frantically looks from side to side, trying to figure out what the hell happened and where the fuck she is.

Familiar elegant spiraling architecture weaves around the room, the furniture and walls lined in glittering white silver. The soft baby blue bedspread covering her body is ruined with specs of mud and dirt. Leaves and blades of grass litter the matching pillowcase by her head.

"You're back!" Nia's smiling face looks down at her. "God, you had us all worried."

Tora jolts up.

"Agh! Fuck!" She grips her shoulder, trying to contain the shock waves of pain shooting through her right arm, shoulder, and neck as memories spew out of her like a volcano; the market, the Valkyries, Flenn, Hecate, and Astra. "Where's Astra? Is she okay? Is she… is she Astra?"

Gently, Nia pushes her back down on the bed and wipes the dirt from her forehead. "Astra's resting. She hasn't woken from the ritual yet but Mist said some fledglings take longer for the change to bring them back."

Sighing, Tora sinks into the soft pillows and winces as pain, sharp and fierce shoots down the right side of her body. Astra's okay. She's going to be okay. She may be a fully-fledged Valkyrie now, but she's alive; Astra is alive.

"I can't believe you were stabbed with a Hell Blade," Nia says, her voice breaking as her eyes fill with tears. "Lucky Revna and Brae were able to save you guys before the Demon Goddess could take you."

Cradling her right arm, Tora flexes her fingers and wrist, pleased to see they're nearly healed. Another day and she should be able to pull her soul sword. The rusty stab wound Flenn's last ditch effort to subdue her is barely a memory. She peels back the dressing wrapped around her bicep and cringes. The wound bubbles with blood and white foam, sizzling through the gauze, the muscle blackened and tinged in green.

"It's not healing?" She swallows the bile rising in her throat and suppresses a wave of nausea, the sight of her rancid-looking arm making her want to puke. Black tendrils leach out under the surface of the skin, looking a lot like blood poisoning.

Nia shakes her head and wipes at her eyes. "A Hell Blade wound continues to umm… to umm…"

"It's going to eat away at your arm." Inga shoves open the door and sits on the window sill. She breaks apart a croissant and hoovers half into her mouth. "Give it a year and it'll basically be a rotten corpse arm. You'll be lucky if you can still pull your sword in a month. Too bad Astra underwent the ritual. She was meant to be a healer, wasn't she? Probably could've healed you."

Tora curls her lip and puts the dressing back in place. She's too tired for this shit. Inga can just fuck off. She's going to lose her arm. She's going to lose her sword, maybe even her life if the toxins eat into the rest of her body.

In the end, she will only be a Valkyrie for a year anyway. Her mother saving her from the gods was for nothing. Her mother's death was for nothing. She may as well have undergone the ritual and died with honor a year ago.

"Leave her alone, Inga." Brae stands in the doorway and waves his hand down the hall. "Your girlfriend wants you downstairs. And seriously, close your mouth when you eat."

Clenching her jaw, Inga glares at Brae as she crosses the room and casts one last look at Tora before storming into the hall, her royal purple eyes betraying a flicker of concern.

Tora snorts. She must be hallucinating. Inga would never show her any concern. The girl hates her. She probably would have celebrated if she had died at the market. "Who the hell would date Inga?"

"Revna." Brae scoffs. "The only one who can stand her."

Tora raises her eyebrows. It's not so surprising now that she thinks about it. Revna is the only one Inga listens to, and she's constantly stealing glances at her. If Inga wasn't such a murderous bitch, she'd be happy for them. Valkyries rarely find love. There are none she knows of.

"Ah, Nia?" Brae sits on the end of the bed and nods towards the door. "Mother's looking for you."

"Great." Nia slumps her shoulders like all the energy has been sucked from her limbs. She pinches her lips into a smile and kisses Tora on top of the head before leaving her alone with Brae.

Brae leans over her legs and exhales loudly. "Can we talk?"

"Do we have to?" Tora rolls her eyes and sinks further down under the covers. Great. This is all she needs; a deep and meaningful with Brae, the traitorous bastard. "Look I'm grateful you helped save us at the market, but I'm not in the mood right now."

"I'm so sorry Tora," Brae pushes the conversation. "I know I betrayed you, but I didn't have a choice. I had to tell the Valkyries. The nine realms were at stake. You would have done the same thing in my place."

Tora tightens her jaw. It's true; she would have done the same thing if it didn't involve Astra. The Valkyries could mean winning the war, and saving the realms, but that doesn't make it hurt any less. Because of him, she nearly lost her best friend; her sister. If he had kept his mouth shut, Astra wouldn't have left Olivia; she wouldn't have been tortured, she wouldn't have undergone the ritual, and she wouldn't have been stabbed with a hell blade. She's going to lose her arm for fucks sake. It's not something she can easily forgive, especially when all she really wants to do is punch him in the face. "I'll get over it, Brae. Just not right now."

Hanging his head, Brae gets to his feet and leaves the room, his shoulders hunched with guilt. There's nothing he can say to change the way she feels. He's an asshole; full stop, end of story. She'll probably forgive him one day, but she could never trust him again. She can't believe someone as sweet as Nia is related to someone as cold as him or came out of their bitch of a mother.

If it wasn't for Nia, she'd be dead right now, so would Astra. The elven steel saved her life. It's the key to everything. It's the key to saving Greenwich Village, maybe even the realms.

"Shit!" Tora springs up off the pillow and blinks at the vanity mirror across from the bed. Her reflection stares back, her face black and bruised, her black hair matted with bits of forest debris and dirt. Her light purple eyes burn with guilt, judging her as she judged Brae.

If she wants to save the realms, the Valkyries, and Greenwich Village, she has to betray Nia, just like Brae betrayed her and Astra.

"Fuck!" Tora grunts and throws her legs over the side of the bed. She has to tell the Valkyries what the elven steel can do, that it keeps the malevolent fae, demons, and hellbeings away. The elven steel could protect the Valkyries from Hecate's control. Greenwich would be safe. The Realm of Man would have a chance. All the realms would. But it means putting Nia at risk.

Now who's the asshole?

Ping-ponging off the walls, Tora stumbles out of the room and down the hall, her stomach rolling with guilt. She's just as bad as Brae, if not worse, but there's no way around it. Without the steel, they're all as good as dead, including Nia. Brae was right. To save the realms, the lives of a few mean nothing, even Nia and Astra's lives.

Raised voices lead Tora into the sitting room where the Valkyries talk animatedly with Queen Raina, Brae, and Nia. Tora chuckles as both Queen Raina and Inga welcome her with curled lips and narrowed eyes. It's nice to know she can at least bring an end to their argument with their united hatred for her.

"Tora! You're okay!" Liv rushes over and barrels into her, hugging her tight.

Surprised, Tora stumbles back and winces as a fresh wave of pain shoots down her side. She wasn't aware they were at the hugging stage of their relationship but she's got nothing against Liv. Inga's the only one she wants to kill.

"I know it was hard for you Tora Thurgood." Revna sits on the edge of the armchair with Inga standing close behind her, her arms crossed over her chest. "But you saved her. You understand that right?"

Letting Liv guide her to the couch, Tora nods once and sits down next to Tove. If she had to choose again between catatonic Valkyrie, or a dead Valkyrie, she would still choose the same way. Astra is alive. That's what matters. They just won't know what that means for Astra or the baby until she wakes.

"How did you defeat the Demon Goddess?" Mist sits on the floor with her legs crossed beneath her and leans on her knees. "How did you break her power over us?"

"Mist!" Tove rolls her eyes. "She just woke up."

"I'm fine." Tora waves off her concern and forces her eyes to stay focused on Revna, resisting the urge to look at Brae or Nia. "Elven steel. That's how I broke her spell. It repels demons and burns hellbeings."

Revna cocks her head in interest.

"I bought something in town made of elven steel and threw it at Hecate when I had nothing left." Tora keeps her head low as her cheeks redden, betrayal pumping hard and fast into her heart. "It basically melted Hecate's face. That's how they keep the demons and malevolent fae out of Olivia."

A heavy blanket of anger and betrayal spreads throughout the room as Revna turns her intense purple eyes on Queen Raina. "And you hid this from us? Why?"

Glaring at Tora, Queen Raina arches one eyebrow and refuses to speak. Elven steel ripples around Brae's neck and shoulders, moving down his arms and under his shirt as his ice-blue eyes flare brightly then dim, like a flickering candle in the breeze.

"She was protecting me." Nia stands and wipes imaginary dirt from her tanned vest and pleated pants. Elven steel glides across her skin, moving in circles around her body, unsure whether she's in danger or not.

"Nia!" Brae jumps to his feet and grabs her arm, his face red with irritation. "Stop."

"No Brae." Nia pulls her arm away and shakes her head. "They need to know."

Clenching his jaw, Brae sits back down beside his mother and glares daggers at Tora, his entire body tense. Tora squirms under his hateful gaze, the pure rage and hatred radiating from his eyes burning a hole in the side of her face.

"I am the creator of the elven steel. My soul is connected to it," Nia says. "Until recently, we thought it was indestructible but Tora's soul sword touched Brae's armor when they were sparring, and it sucked part of the soul out of the steel, and me."

Revna and Inga glance at each other, but say nothing. Liv gasps.

"How could you?" Brae snarls at Tora, his eyes darkening with murderous intent while Queen Raina smirks beside him, clearly pleased by his reaction.

"The elven steel could save all the realms and you know it," Tora argues. "You were willing to risk Astra's life for exactly the same thing."

Brae flinches. "So, this is revenge?"

"What? No." Tora's face reddens. "I…"

"Tora's right Brae." Nia interrupts and offers her a warm smile, not a shred of anger on her angelic face. "The realms are more important."

Tora smiles in gratitude, relieved Nia at least understands. She's not proposing they gear up in elven steel and hit the hellbeings. The Valkyries need to know so they can come up with a plan; find a way to use the steel safely.

"Can't you just disconnect the Princess from the steel?" Mist frowns.

"Or find a way to protect her soul from our swords?" Trove offers.

Queen Raina scoffs.

"No; we tried," Brae growls low in his throat. The elven steel covering his biceps quivers and glides around his back. "It doesn't work like that."

"We don't know that yet." Nia meets Brae's angry glare, her eyes pleading with him to understand. "Our people are still working on it."

"Then figure it out." Revna exhales loudly and stands. "Hecate will heal quickly and if she can control the Valkyries, the realms are fucked. Until then, we stay here in Olivia, where it's already protected by your elven steel and the Demon Goddess can't reach us."

"No!" Queena Raina and Tora both object at the same time.

"You cannot." Queen Raina glares at Tora and raises her chin. "The prophesized Witch Goddess is here. We still have a chance to stop the prophecy, but we cannot do it with outsiders around. You must leave."

Revna flares her nostrils. Her eyes burn with anger and frustration as Brae stands by his mother's side, the muscles in his neck flexed.

"And what's your problem short stuff?" Inga mocks. "Is it too far from your little boyfriend? Bo, is it?"

Brae flinches and glances at Tora out of the corner of his eye.

"Fuck off Inga." Tora rolls her eyes. "If the benevolent fae can prevent the coming war, fine, great, but I want to go home to Greenwich. I need to protect my village; my squad, and I need elven steel to do that. There are good people there. Good fighters. I don't know what stopped our village from being overrun by demons in the past, but from what the warlock said, it's not going to last. I think they've been able to open a permanent portal; maybe more than one."

"What are you proposing?" Revna frowns. "If we leave, Hecate will come after us and we've already established we can't wear the elven steel until the Princess has been disconnected from it."

"I get that," Tora explains. "But it's not the armor that protects this town; it's the architecture; the glittering silver linings on all the buildings and structures; the forcefield around Olivia. I think it's already on the crystals on the perimeter of Greenwich and the gargoyles. That's what I'm asking for. Help to fortify the village then we can stay there protected from the Demon Goddess."

Revna raises her eyebrows then looks to each of the Valkyries for their vote. Tove, Mist, and Liv nod once while Inga sneers.

"Well? Revna looks at Queen Raina.

Nia grins and winks at Tora, giving her the reassurance she needs. If they use the same protection as Olivia in Greenwich Village, it will stop the portals; it will stop Hecate. It will keep her friends and her squad safe.

Taking her time, Queen Raina slowly stands and finally nods. "Agreed. We will help fortify this Greenwich Village. But no one outside of this room finds out about the steel's newfound weakness."

"Done." Revna nods in agreement.

Tora could cry. She did it. She really did it. She found a way to keep Greenwich Village safe; her friends, her squad, her home. And Astra... Astra is still alive.

"Once Astra wakes, we can g..." Revna starts but a loud crash down the hall cuts her off.

The Valkyries spring to their feet and pull their soul swords as Brae and the elven warriors draw their elven steel swords. All eyes point towards the hall.

"What was that?" Tora jumps up and cradles her arm, feeling like a child now she is unarmed and too injured to pull her soul sword.

"Astra!" Nia gasps and widens her eyes. "She's in my room."

Tora blinks and tries not to panic. It could be anything. Astra could have fallen when she woke up. It could be something innocent, but in the deep pit of her stomach, she can feel something is wrong.

Not waiting for the others, Tora tears down the hall and pushes open the door. She whips her head back and forth looking for any threats, but she only finds Astra standing calmly by the large wooden queen bed with intricate embedded silver designs, the silver butterfly duvet discarded carelessly on the floor, and the pillows strewn across the room.

Astra faces the large window overlooking the back garden, her head hung low, her torn summer dress replaced with a simple pair of black cotton pants and a black vest, like she's wearing a casual version of what the rest of the Valkyries wear. Flecks of gold and amber glisten in her hair, the warm sunlight casting a glow around her head, like a halo.

"Star?" Tora chokes back tears as they threaten to spill down her cheeks.

The last time she saw Astra, she was unconscious, covered in bruises, gashes, and bites, and she was driving a sword into the middle of her forehead. But here she is. Astra is alive. It worked. Astra is a Valkyrie. She survived. She's okay.

"Oh my god Star!" Tora starts towards her but Brae runs into the room and grabs her arm, holding her back. The others pile in behind him.

"What the hell!" Tora struggles to free herself, her muscles and wounds protesting with any movement.

"Look properly," Brae says through clenched teeth and shakes her arm.

The Valkyries gasp. Queen Raina backs out of the room.

Frowning, Tora looks at Astra and takes in the scene around her. At first, she doesn't know what he's talking about. The room looks like it did before, like a staged bedroom in a display room with beautiful wooden furniture carved in weaving spirals and silver tips; the armoire, the vanity, the bed, the soft silver and blue rug, all perfectly positioned around the room.

That's when she sees it. The reason Brae tried to keep her back. Tora inhales sharply. Her throat tightens to the point of choking.

"No!" Nia screams and drops to the ground. She crawls on her hands and knees to the still body lying unconscious on the floor, a pool of blood surrounding him.

"Braxen," Tora whispers and covers her mouth. Her hands shake as Astra slowly turns. Her once beautiful pastel purple eyes burn deep amber with flecks of blood swimming in her irises. Her once smiling face is contorted in a feral snarl.

"Star?" Tora widens her eyes and looks to Revna for answers. Is this what it means to be catatonic? Did the ritual fail? Is Astra going to die? Is she even Astra anymore? "Revna? Is she... is she catatonic?"

Tightening her grip on her sword, Revna shakes her head and glances back at Inga. "No Tora. This is something else."

"I don't understand." Mist frowns. "We performed the ritual. We took her life. There was no life! The ritual should have worked."

The words bounce around in Tora's skull. There was no life. No life... Valkyries undergo the ritual to break the ties to one realm, to become a spirit maiden. But Astra... Astra was pregnant; bound with life.

"She was... is pregnant," Tora whispers as the air is stolen from her lungs.

"What?" Revna whips her head around, her voice sharp and panicked. "Why didn't you tell us?"

"Oh no." Liv gasps and holds her hand over her mouth. "The malevolent fae... the elf."

"I didn't know it would affect the ritual!" Tora says, instantly on the defensive. "Haven't Valkyries ever been pregnant during the ritual?"

"No; you idiot!" Inga scoffs. "You can't perform the ritual if the Valkyrie is pregnant!"

Tora runs her fingers through her hair and holds it at the back of her head. The world spins in front of her eyes. They didn't need to run from the Valkyries at all. All they needed to do was tell them that Astra was pregnant. She put Astra in danger for no reason. It's her fault Astra is damaged. It's her fault the baby might have died. This is all her fault.

Astra grins, her blackened lips curling at the sides. Her bright orange eyes zone in on Tora, the blood-red specs expanding and shrinking spontaneously.

"Star?" Tora takes a tentative step towards her. "Can you hear me?"

Astra flinches and throws out her arms, commanding a pair of black swan-like wings to spring free from her back, the feathers thick and jet black, her eyes burning with rage.

Gasping, Tora jumps back, surprised by the black wings hanging from Astra's back. The Valkyries and Elves hold their swords in position, waiting for an attack.

"This isn't good Rev," Inga mutters and moves closer to Revna's side, tightening her grip on her sword. "Black wings? We're going to have to put her down."

"No!" Tora yells, her voice breaking and quivering.

Fuck! They're going to kill Astra if she can't get through to her. It can't end like this. After everything they've been through, after how far they've come, Astra cannot die at the hands of Inga, not the same as her mother did. She has to get through to her somehow; there has to be a way.

"Astra?" Tora searches her face, looking for any sign that her friend is still in there. "Please Star. Talk to me. Give me a sign."

Astra widens her bright orange eyes. She looks around the room as her bottom lip quivers and her hands begin to shake. If not for the color of her eyes, lips, and wings, Astra would look like a scared little angel.

"Oh, thank god." Tora slumps her shoulders and starts towards her, relieved to see the friend she has always known and not just the frightening being standing in front of her. Inga can't kill Astra now, not when she's showing signs of being herself.

"Stop!" Brae pulls her back, practically ripping her arm out of the socket.

"Fuck Brae!" Tora yanks her arm away but jerks as Astra suddenly snaps her teeth and juts out her head like a feral animal, trying to take a bite out of her arm.

Tora freezes and stares at Astra, unable to believe her childhood friend just tried to bite her. Astra really just tried to bite her. Silence settles in her ears as her chest tightens and squeezes the air from her lungs. She blinks and fights back tears, finally seeing what everyone else is seeing. A new fully-fledged Valkyrie filled with malevolence and darkness.

Astra's not there anymore. It's just a shell of what she used to be. The friend she has always known is gone. Astra is gone. Her family is gone.

Snarling angrily, Astra darts towards the window, her amber eyes blazing crimson. Before anyone has a chance to move, she smashes through the glass and takes off into the sky, a shower of black feathers trailing behind her.

"No!" Tora rushes to the window and releases her wings to follow, but Mist tackles her to the ground. She kicks and screams, trying to get free but it's useless. Mist is too strong, Tora is too weak, and Astra is gone. That is not Astra. Not anymore. The Astra she knew is dead.

"Great!" Inga kicks the wall. "Now the other side has a Valkyrie too. Nice going Tora."

"Fuck you." Tora pushes Mist away and charges at Inga with tears in her eyes. Mist grabs her once again and pulls her back.

"Stop it!" Revna holds Inga back as she too lunges. "None of this is her fault."

Tora pulls away and cradles her aching arm. It doesn't matter that it's not her fault. It doesn't change anything. It doesn't bring back Teresa or Victor, it doesn't bring back her mother, and it doesn't bring back Astra.

Everything's gone to shit. She lost. She failed. It's over.

CHAPTER TWENTY-NINE

"Just get out!" Tora snaps and starts pushing people out of the room, tears streaming down her face as her grief threatens to overwhelm her. "Leave me alone!"

Revna doesn't fight her. Neither does Inga. They usher the others away as Nia and Brae carry an unconscious Braxen from the room, leaving Tora alone. She crumbles to the ground and sits with her knees close to her chest, sobbing unapologetically as she cradles her head, letting out her grief and pain; the pain of losing her mother, the pain of losing her own life, the pain of losing Teresa and Victor, and the pain of losing Astra.

Nothing will be the same anymore. The realms will collapse, and when the war comes, she and Astra will be on opposite sides. She doesn't even know how to comprehend that. For her entire life, she's tried to protect

Astra, and now thanks to a nasty twist of fate, she may end up fighting against her.

Tears soak through her clothes; her sobs catch in her throat, hiccupping until there are no tears left. She hugs herself for what seems like hours, rocking on the ground, disbelief and denial comforting her broken soul.

"Tora? It's time to go." Mist tentatively walks into the room and helps her to her feet.

Tora doesn't resist. In a daze, she follows the Valkyries across the street into Makeshift Park where Brae, Nia, Queen Raina, and at least ten elven warriors wait around the portal arch.

Tora stares blindly at the swirling colors dancing in the portal. A cold bitter numbness ices her heart, like all the love she has ever felt flew out the window when Astra left.

"The village survivors will be told that their architecture is undergoing structural repair to make the area safe from collapse," Revna says and eyes each of the Valkyries, including Tora. "Do not deviate from the story."

In the back of her mind, Tora knows she should care. She should be happy the village will be safe, but a cavern of emptiness carves into her chest. Nothing matters, not without Astra.

"Are you ready Tora?" Brae nods towards her, his ice-blue eyes lit with concern.

Tora lifts her head and blinks, her lips numb. His words echo in her ears. Is she ready? Ready for a life without her mother? Without Astra? Is she ready to go back to Greenwich Village and fight to save the realms?

No! She's not fucking ready! Her mother is dead. Astra is gone. What the fuck is she fighting for? She lost the only two people she truly loves; so no! She's not fucking ready! She'll never be fucking ready!

"Do you want me to go through the portal with you?" Nia moves to stand beside her and holds out her hand.

"Oh, for fucks sake!" Inga snaps. "Stop babying her! She's a Valkyrie. She should act like it!"

Without warning, Inga shoves Tora hard in the back and pushes her into the portal. Stumbling, she plunges face first into the spiraling lights, layers of lava, rock, water, and crystal spinning in a vortex around her.

"Agh!" Tora screams in anger and chokes on a wave of water as it slams into her face, the cold bitterness seeping into her heart, overtaking her grief. Sharp pain shoots down her arm and up into her neck, the hell blade wound reminding her she will never be healed.

Fucking Inga. She's going to kill the evil bitch if it's the last thing she does, and she's going to make it hurt. All she's done since they met is make her life miserable. The bitch deserves to die screaming.

The vortex pulls her left and right, up and down, and spins her in circles like a washing machine as wave after wave of water slams into her body. She grits her teeth against the intense pain erupting down her arm and neck and shields her eyes from the spouts of steam and rock shooting out of the vortex. Bright shining crystals form in clusters on top of her skin, sticking to her like frosted ice.

Tora screams as a force of suction suddenly latches onto her body and drags her out of the portal, tearing at the wound on her bicep and spitting her out onto a concrete path.

Landing on her hands and knees, Tora coughs violently, spitting up water while Nia and Brae step elegantly out of the portal, the hell blade wound stinging like a fresh burn. She remains on the ground coughing and spluttering until the Valkyries and the last of the elven warriors emerge, each of the fae wearing glamors to hide their true appearance. The portal slams shut behind them.

"Oh, gods. She can't even go through a portal without having a breakdown." Inga steps over her and looks down in disgust. "Fuck Tora. Get your shit together."

"Leave her alone." Nia pushes Inga away and helps Tora to her feet. "You're the one who pushed her, and you'd be sick too if you were poisoned by a hell blade."

Ignoring the stinging pain spreading further from her bicep to her jaw, Tora pinches her lips into a grateful smile. She didn't notice it before, but Nia reminds her of Astra, the way she used to be. Protective, loyal, and unbelievably forgiving. Tora still hasn't forgiven Brae for betraying her and Astra, yet Nia forgave her betrayal instantly; something even Astra couldn't have done.

"I never asked about Braxen." Tora lowers her voice, shame burning bright on her cheeks. All she's been able to think about is her loss, her pain. They found Braxen in a pool of blood and she hasn't even asked if he's alive. "Is he... is he okay."

"He's healing." Nia glances back over her shoulder, making sure the elven warriors aren't listening. "Astra only knocked him out. I don't know where the blood came from."

Tora frowns. How is that possible? Braxen was surrounded by a pool of blood, and if it didn't come from him, then where the hell did it come from? She widens her eyes.

"Astra." Tora pinches her eyes closed. The blood had to have come from Astra. "She must have lost the baby."

"Oh no. I... I'm so sorry Tora." Nia covers her mouth in horror. "I... I don't know what to say."

No wonder Astra lost her shit. Not only did she die and wake up a fully-fledged Valkyrie, she lost her baby. That's enough to turn anyone into a crazy evil bitch.

"Yeah. Me too." Tora rubs her face, her mind a mess. She doesn't know what that means for Astra. Does it mean there's still hope? That once she comes to terms with the miscarriage, she could come back? Or does it change nothing?

"Tora?" A voice echoes across the street.

Tora freezes at the sound of the voice, a voice she knows well. She slowly turns and looks across the street, hardly able to believe her ears.

The afternoon sun bounces off the roundabout carousel, the playground area covered in new burn marks and deep red and black stains. Pier 51; the very place Tora and Bo took down the child demon less than a week ago.

Could it be? Could he be alive?

It feels like a lifetime ago since she faced the demons of Greenwich Village. So much has changed since that night, including Tora herself, and not just because she's a fully-fledged Valkyrie. She doesn't know how her mother did it. How she went for centuries losing friends in battle and kept going on day by day. It's no wonder she blocked off her emotions. It's the only way to get through; the only way to survive the losses.

A tall man dressed in black pants and a black shirt stands across the street, a brilliant smile on his face. New scars line the side of his neck and face like he shaved with a cheese grater. "Tora!"

"Bo?" A flush of warmth spreads through Tora's chest as her lips slowly creep into a smile.

Bo!" Tora breaks into a sprint and charges straight into Bo's strong open arms, ignoring the pain in her shoulder. Her throat tightens as he lifts her into the air and turns her around in circles laughing and crying at the same time.

From around the corner, the remainder of the squad emerge. First Phil, then Maree, Shannon, Mandy, and Cheryl. Behind them, Dr Arnold, and Mrs Arnold carrying a new crying baby peek around the corner. They all look like they've taken a beating, but they're alive. They're all alive.

The Odd Squad stop and stare for a minute, not daring to believe their own eyes while Dr and Mrs Arnold bolt towards her with their newborn child in their arms.

Fresh tears spill down Tora's face as the squad and her friends rush around her, taking turns hugging her and asking a million questions about the newcomers, Montauk, and the Deadlands. Even Cheryl hugs her, her anger from the abandonment disappearing with Tora's reappearance.

Everyone is too scared to ask about Astra, and for that, Tora is grateful. She knows the questions will come eventually, and when she's ready, she'll tell them what happened, but right now, she just wants to enjoy this moment and be happy that her squad and friends are still alive. She doesn't care what the other Valkyries think, she doesn't care what Brae or the warriors think; she doesn't even care about the god's retribution. She's home; finally home, and she's not alone. The Odd Squad and her friends are her family, and she will do whatever it takes to protect them.

The war is coming, and she won't let the demons of Hell, the malevolent fae, the gods, or their new malevolent Valkyrie take any more than they already have, even if she has to torch the realms to do it.

Game on bitches.

-THE END-

ABOUT THE AUTHOR

TRL Boyd is an Australian author with dreams of one day breaking into the fae realm and causing havoc. She loves exploring the possibility of new worlds and looks for fae traps on the many forest walks she and her beautiful little black English Staffy Kiwi go on.

TRL Boyd lives on the South Coast of New South Wales Australia, the perfect combination of forest, sand, surf, and sun.

www.ingramcontent.com/pod-product-compliance
Lightning Source LLC
Chambersburg PA
CBHW060816120726
47909CB00006B/1945